P9-DVG-122

503
4

9

Selected Works of Djuna Barnes

SELECTED WORKS O

Djuna Barnes

Spillway / The Antiphon / Nightwood

Farrar, Straus and Cudahy, New York

Special contents of this volume
Copyright © 1962 by Djuna Barnes
Library of Congress catalog card number: 62–7185
First Printing, 1962
Manufactured in the United States of America
by H. Wolff, New York

Contents

SPILLWAY

    Aller et Retour 3
    Cassation 12
    The Grande Malade 21
    A Night among the Horses 29
    The Valet 36
    The Rabbit 44
    The Doctors 54
    Spillway 61
    The Passion 71

THE ANTIPHON

    Act One 81
    Act Two 115
    Act Three 190

NIGHTWOOD

Introduction 227
    Bow Down 233
    La Somnambule 255
    Night Watch 272
    "The Squatter" 284
    Watchman, What of the Night? **294**
    Where the Tree Falls 316
    Go Down, Matthew 330
    The Possessed 363

Spillway

TO MOTHER

These stories first appeared in somewhat different form in *A Book*, copyright © 1923 by Boni & Liveright, Inc. and were reissued as *A Night among the Horses*, copyright © 1929 by Horace Liveright, Inc., with material removed and two stories added from Ford Madox Ford's Transatlantic Review. "The Grande Malade" appeared in the later volume under the title "The Little Girl Continues"; it was also published in Transition and in the anthology *Americans Abroad*, Sevire Press, The Hague, Holland.

Aller et Retour

The train travelling from Marseilles to Nice had on board a woman of great strength.

She was well past forty and a little top-heavy. Her bosom was tightly cross-laced, the busk bending with every breath, and as she breathed and moved she sounded with many chains in coarse gold links, the ring of large heavily set jewels marking off her lighter gestures. From time to time she raised a long-handled lorgnette to her often winking brown eyes, surveying the countryside blurred in smoke from the train.

At Toulon, she pushed down the window, leaning out, calling for beer, the buff of her hip-fitting skirt rising in a peak above tan boots laced high on shapely legs, and above that the pink of woollen stockings. She settled back, drinking her beer with pleasure, controlling the jarring of her body with the firm pressure of her small plump feet against the rubber matting.

She was a Russian, a widow. Her name was Erling von Bartmann. She lived in Paris

In leaving Marseilles she had purchased a copy of *Madame Bovary*, and now she held it in her hands, elbows slightly raised and out.

She read a few sentences with difficulty, then laid the book on her lap, looking at the passing hills.

Once in Marseilles, she traversed the dirty streets slowly, holding the buff skirt well above her boots, in a manner at once careful and absent. The thin skin of her nose quivered as she drew in the foul odours of the smaller passages, but she looked neither pleased nor displeased.

She went up the steep narrow littered streets abutting on the port, staring right and left, noting every object.

A gross woman with wide set legs sprawled in the doorway to a single room, gorged with a high-posted rusting iron bed. The woman was holding a robin loosely in one huge plucking hand. The air was full of floating feathers, falling and rising about girls with bare shoulders, blinking under coarse dark bangs. Madame von Bartmann picked her way carefully.

At a ship-chandler's she stopped, smelling the tang of tarred rope. She took down several coloured post cards showing women in the act of bathing; of happy mariners leaning above full-busted sirens with sly cogged eyes. Madame von Bartmann touched the satins of vulgar, highly coloured bedspreads, laid out for sale in a side alley. A window, fly-specked, dusty and cracked, displayed, terrace upon terrace, white and magenta funeral wreaths, wired in beads, flanked by images of the Bleeding Heart, embossed in tin, with edgings of beaten flame, the whole beached on a surf of lace.

She returned to her hotel room and stood, unpinning her hat and veil before the mirror in the tall closet door. She sat, to unlace her boots, in one of eight chairs, arranged in perfect precision along the two walls. The thick boxed velvet curtains blocked out the court where pigeons were sold. Madame von Bartmann washed her hands with a large oval of coarse red soap, drying them, trying to think.

In the morning, seated on the stout linen sheets between the mahogany of the head and foot boards, she planned the rest of her journey. She was two or three hours too early for her train. She dressed and went out. Finding a church, she entered and drew her gloves off slowly. It was dark and cold and she was alone. Two small oil lamps burned on either side of the figures of St. Anthony and St. Francis. She put her leather bag on a form and went into a corner, kneeling down. She turned the stones of her rings out and put her hands together, the light shining between the little fingers; raising them she prayed, with all her vigorous understanding, to God, for a common redemption.

She got up, peering about her, angry that there were no candles burning to the *Magnifique*—feeling the stuff of the altar-cloth.

At Nice she took an omnibus, riding second class, reaching the outskirts about four. With a large iron key she opened the high rusty iron gate to a private park, and closed it behind her.

The lane of flowering trees with their perfumed cups, the moss that leaded the broken paving stones, the hot musky air, the incessant rustling wings of unseen birds—all ran together in a tangle of singing textures, light and dark.

The avenue was long and without turning until it curved between two massive jars, heavy with the metal spirals of cacti, and just behind these, the house of plaster and stone.

There were no shutters open on the avenue because of insects, and Madame von Bartmann went slowly, still holding her skirts, around to the side of the house, where a long haired cat lay softly in the sun. Madame von Bartmann looked up at the windows, half shuttered, paused, thought better of it, and struck off into the wood beyond.

The deep pervading drone of ground insects ceased about her chosen steps and she turned her head, looking up into the occasional touches of sky.

She still held the key to the gate in her gloved hand, and the seventeen year old girl who came up from a bush took hold of it, walking beside her.

The child was still in short dresses, and the pink of her knees was dulled by the dust of the underbrush. Her squirrel coloured hair rose in two ridges of light along her head, descending to the lobes of her long ears, where it was caught into a faded green ribbon.

"Richter!" Madame von Bartmann said (her husband had wanted a boy).

The child put her hands behind her back before answering.

"I've been out there, in the field."

Madame von Bartmann, walking on, made no answer.

"Did you stop in Marseilles, mother?"

She nodded.

"Long?"

"Two days and a half."

"Why a half?"

"The trains."

"Is it a big city?"

"Not very, but dirty."

"Is there anything nice there?"

Madame von Bartmann smiled: "The Bleeding Heart—sailors—"

Presently they came out into the open field, and Madame von Bartmann, turning her skirt back, sat down on a knoll, warm with tempered grass.

The child, with slight springiness of limb, due to youth, sat beside her.

"Shall you stay home now?"

"For quite a while."

"Was Paris nice?"

"Paris was Paris."

The child was checked. She began pulling at the grass. Madame von Bartmann drew off one of her tan gloves, split at the turn of the thumb, and stopped for a moment before she said: "Well, now that your father is dead—"

The child's eyes filled with tears; she lowered her head.

"I come flying back," Madame von Bartmann continued good naturedly, "to look at my own. Let me see you," she continued, turning the child's chin up in the palm of her hand. "Ten, when I last saw you, and now you are a woman." With this she dropped the child's chin and put on her glove.

"Come," she said, rising, "I haven't seen the house in years." As they went down the dark avenue, she talked.

"Is the black marble Venus still in the hall?"

"Yes."

"Are the chairs with the carved legs still in existence?"

"Only two. Last year Erna broke one, and the year before—"

"Well?"

"I broke one."

"Growing up," Madame von Bartmann commented. "Well, well. Is the great picture still there, over the bed?"

The child, beneath her breath, said: "That's my room."

Madame von Bartmann took her gloves off again, unfastening her lorgnette from its hook on her bosom, put it to her eyes and regarded the child.

"You are very thin."

"I'm growing."

"I grew, but like a pigeon. Well, one generation can't be exactly like another. You have your father's red hair. That," she said abruptly, "was a queer, mad fellow, that Herr von Bartmann. I never could see what we were doing with each other. As for you," she added, shutting her glasses, drawing on her gloves, "I'll have to see what he has made of you."

In the evening, in the heavy house with its heavy furniture, Richter watched her mother, still in hat and spotted veil, playing on the sprawling lanky grand, high up behind the terrace window. It was a waltz. Madame von Bartmann played fast, with effervescence, the sparkles of her jewelled fingers bubbled over the keys.

In the dark of the garden, Richter listened to Schubert streaming down the light from the open casement. The child was cold

now, and she shivered in the long coat that touched the chill
of her knees.

Still swiftly, with a *finale* somewhat in the grand opera manner,
Madame von Bartmann closed the piano, stood a moment on the
balcony inhaling the air, fingering the coarse links of her chain,
the insects darting vertically across her vision.

Presently she came out and sat down on a stone bench, breath-
ing warmth.

Richter stood a few steps away and did not approach or speak.
Madame von Bartmann began, though she could not see the child
without turning:

"You have been here always, Richter?"

"Yes," the child answered.

"In this park, in this house, with Herr von Bartmann, the tutors
and the dogs?"

"Yes."

"Do you speak German?"

"A little."

"Let me hear."

"Müde bin Ich, geh' zu Ruh."

"French?"

"O nuit désastreuse! O nuit effroyable!"

"Russian?"

The child did not answer.

"Ach!" said Madame von Bartmann. Then: "Have you been to
Nice?"

"Oh, yes, often."

"What did you see there?"

"Everything."

Madame von Bartmann laughed. She leaned forward, her elbow
on her knee, her face in her palm. The earrings in her ears stood
still, the drone of the insects was clear and soft; pain lay fallow.

"Once," she said, "I was a child like you. Fatter, better health—
nevertheless like you. I loved nice things. But," she added, "a dif-
ferent kind, I imagine. Things that were positive. I liked to go

out in the evening, not because it was sweet and voluptuous—but to frighten myself, because I'd known it such a little while, and after me it would exist so long. But that—" she interrupted herself, "is beside the point. Tell me how you feel."

The child moved in the shadow. "I can't."

Madame von Bartmann laughed again, but stopped abruptly.

"Life," she said, "is filthy; it is also frightful. There is everything in it: murder, pain, beauty, disease—death. Do you know this?"

The child answered, "Yes."

"How do you know?"

The child answered again, "I don't know."

"You see!" Madame von Bartmann went on, "you know nothing. You must know *everything*, and *then* begin. You must have a great understanding, or accomplish a fall. Horses hurry you away from danger; trains bring you back. Paintings give the heart a mortal pang—they hung over a man you loved and perhaps murdered in his bed. Flowers hearse up the heart because a child was buried in them. Music incites to the terror of repetition. The cross-roads are where lovers vow, and taverns are for thieves. Contemplation leads to prejudice; and beds are fields where babies fight a losing battle. Do you know all this?"

There was no answer from the dark.

"Man is rotten from the start," Madame von Bartmann continued. "Rotten with virtue and with vice. He is strangled by the two and made nothing; and God is the light the mortal insect kindled, to turn to, and to die by. That is very wise, but it must not be misunderstood. I do not want you to turn your nose up at any whore in any street; pray and wallow and cease, but without prejudice. A murderer may have less prejudice than a saint; sometimes it is better to be a saint. Do not be vain about your indifference, should you be possessed of indifference; and don't," she said, "misconceive the value of your passions; it is only seasoning to the whole horror. I wish—" She did not finish, but quietly took her pocket handkerchief and silently dried her eyes.

"What?" the child asked from the darkness.

Madame von Bartmann shivered. "Are you thinking?" she said.

"No," the child answered.

"Then *think*," Madame von Bartmann said loudly, turning to the child. "Think everything, good, bad, indifferent; everything, and *do* everything, *everything*! Try to know what you are before you die. And," she said, putting her head back and swallowing with shut eyes, "come back to me a good woman."

She got up then and went away, down the long aisle of trees.

That night, at bed time, Madame von Bartmann, rolled up in a bed with a canopy of linen roses, frilled and smelling of lavender, called through the curtains:

"Richter, do you play?"

"Yes," answered Richter.

"Play me something."

Richter heard her mother turn heavily, breathing comfort.

With frail legs pointed to the pedals, Richter, with a thin technique and a light touch, played something from Beethoven.

"*Brava!*" her mother called, and she played again, and this time there was silence from the canopied bed. The child closed the piano, pulling the velvet over the mahogany, put the light out and went, still shivering in her coat, out onto the balcony.

A few days later, having avoided her mother, looking shy, frightened and offended, Richter came into her mother's room. She spoke directly and sparingly:

"Mother, with your consent, I should like to announce my engagement to Gerald Teal." Her manner was stilted. "Father approved of him. He knew him for years: if you permit—"

"Good heavens!" exclaimed Madame von Bartmann, and swung clear around on her chair. "Who is he? What is he like?"

"He is a clerk in government employ; he is young—"

"Has he money?"

"I don't know: father saw to that."

There was a look of pain and relief on Madame von Bartmann's face.

"Very well," she said, "I shall have dinner for you two at eight-thirty sharp."

At eight-thirty sharp they were dining. Madame von Bartmann, seated at the head of the table, listened to Mr. Teal speaking.

"I shall do my best to make your daughter happy. I am a man of staid habits, no longer too young," he smiled. "I have a house on the outskirts of Nice. My income is assured—a little left me by my mother. My sister is my housekeeper, she is a maiden lady, but very cheerful and very good." He paused, holding a glass of wine to the light. "We hope to have children—Richter will be occupied. As she is delicate we shall travel, to Vichy, once a year. I have two very fine horses and a carriage with sound springs. She will drive in the afternoons, when she is indisposed—though I hope she will find her greatest happiness at home."

Richter, sitting at her mother's right hand, did not look up.

Within two months, Madame von Bartmann was once again in her travelling clothes, hatted and veiled, strapping her umbrella as she stood on the platform, waiting for the train to Paris. She shook hands with her son-in-law, kissed the cheek of her daughter, and climbed into a second-class smoker.

Once the train was in motion, Madame Erling von Bartmann slowly drew her gloves through her hand, from fingers to cuff, stretching them firmly across her knee.

"Ah, how unnecessary."

Cassation

"Do you know Germany, Madame, Germany in the spring? It is charming then, do you not think so? Wide and clean, the Spree winding thin and dark—and the roses! the yellow roses in the windows; and bright talkative Americans passing through groups of heavy German men staring over their steins at their light and laughing women.

"It was such a spring, three years ago, that I came into Berlin from Russia. I was just sixteen, and my heart was a dancer's heart. It is that way sometimes; one's heart is all one thing for months, then—altogether another thing, *nicht wahr*? I used to sit in the café at the end of the Zelten, eating eggs and drinking coffee, watching the sudden rain of sparrows. Their feet struck the table all together, and all together they cleared the crumbs, and all together they flew into the sky, so that the café was as suddenly without birds as it had been suddenly full of birds.

"Sometimes a woman came here, at about the same hour as myself, around four in the afternoon; once she came with a little man, quite dreamy and uncertain. But I must explain how she looked: *temperementvoll* and tall, *kraftvoll* and thin. She must have been forty then, dressed richly and carelessly. It seemed as though she could hardly keep her clothes on; her shoulders were always coming out, her skirt would be hanging on a hook, her pocket book would be mislaid, but all the time she was savage with jewels, and something purposeful and dramatic came in with her, as if she were the center of a whirlpool, and her clothes a temporary débris.

"Sometimes she clucked the sparrows, and sometimes she talked to the *weinschenk*, clasping her fingers together until the rings stood out and you could see through them, she was so vital and so wasted. As for her dainty little man, she would talk to him in English, so that I did not know where they came from.

"Then one week I stayed away from the café because I was trying out for the *Schauspielhaus*, I heard they wanted a ballet dancer, and I was very anxious to get the part, so of course I thought of nothing else. I would wander, all by myself, through the *Tiergarten*, or I would stroll down the *Sieges-Allee* where all the great German emperors' statues are, looking like widows. Then suddenly I thought of the *Zelten*, and of the birds, and of that tall odd woman, and so I went back there, and there she was, sitting in the garden sipping beer and chuck-chucking the sparrows.

"When I came in, she got up at once and came over to me and said: 'Why, how do you do. I have missed you. Why did you not tell me that you were going away? I should have seen what I could do about it.'

"She talked like that; a voice that touched the heart because it was so unbroken and clear. 'I have a house,' she said, 'just on the Spree. You could have stayed with me. It is a big, wide house, and you could have the room just off my room. It is difficult to live in, but it is lovely—Italian you know, like the interiors you see in Venetian paintings, where young girls lie dreaming of the Virgin. You would find that you could sleep there, because you have dedication.'

"Somehow it did not seem at all out of the way that she should come to me and speak to me. I said I would meet her again some day in the garden, and we could go 'home' together, and she seemed pleased, but did not show surprise.

"Then one evening we came into the garden at the same moment. It was late and the fiddles were already playing. We sat together without speaking, just listening to the music, and admiring the playing of the only woman member of the orchestra. She was very intent on the movement of her fingers, and seemed to be leaning over her chin to watch. Then suddenly the lady got up, leaving a small rain of coin, and I followed her until we came to a big house and she let herself in with a key. She turned to the left and went into a dark room and switched on the lights and sat down and said: 'This is where we sleep; this is how it is.'

"Everything was disorderly, and expensive and melancholy. Everything was massive and tall, or broad and wide. A chest of drawers rose above my head. The china stove was enormous and white, enamelled in blue flowers. The bed was so high that you could only think of it as something that might be overcome. The walls were all bookshelves, and all the books were bound in red morocco, on the back of each, in gold, was stamped a coat of arms, intricate and oppressive. She rang for tea, and began taking off her hat.

"A great war painting hung over the bed; the painting and the bed ran together in encounter, the huge rumps of the stallions reined into the pillows. The generals, with foreign helmets and dripping swords, raging through rolling smoke and the bleeding ranks of the dying, seemed to be charging the bed, so large, so rumpled, so devastated. The sheets were trailing, the counterpane hung torn, and the feathers shivered along the floor, trembling in the slight wind from the open window. The lady was smiling in a sad grave way, but she said nothing, and it was not until some moments later that I saw a child, not more than three years old, a small child, lying in the center of the pillows, making a thin noise, like the buzzing of a fly, and I thought it was a fly.

"She did not talk to the child, indeed she paid no attention to it, as if it were in her bed and she did not know it. When the tea was brought in she poured it, but she took none, instead she drank small glasses of Rhine wine.

" 'You have seen Ludwig,' she said in her faint and grieving voice. 'We were married a long time ago, he was just a boy then. I? Me? I am an Italian, but I studied English and German because I was with a travelling company. You,' she said abruptly, 'you must give up the ballet—the theatre—acting.' Somehow I did not think it odd that she should know of my ambition, though I had not mentioned it. 'And,' she went on, 'you are not for the stage; you are for something quieter, more withdrawn. See here, I like Germany very much, I have lived here a good many years. You will stay and you will see. You have seen Ludwig, you have noticed that he is not strong; he is always declining, you must have noticed it yourself; he must not be distressed, he can't bear anything. He has his room to himself.' She seemed suddenly tired, and she got up and threw herself across the bed, at the foot, and fell asleep, almost instantly, her hair all about her. I went away then, but I came back that night and tapped at the window. She came to the window and signed to me, and presently appeared at another window to the right of the bedroom, and beckoned with her hand, and I came up and climbed in, and did not mind that she had not opened the door for me. The room was dark except for the moon, and two thin candles burning before the Virgin.

"It was a beautiful room, Madame, '*traurig*' as she said. Everything was important and old and gloomy. The curtains about the bed were red velvet, Italian you know, and fringed in gold bullion. The bed cover was a deep red velvet with the same gold fringe: on the floor, beside the bed, a stand on which was a tasselled red cushion, on the cushion a Bible in Italian, lying open.

"She gave me a long nightgown, it came below my feet and came back up again almost to my knees. She loosened my hair, it was long then, and yellow. She plaited it in two plaits; she put me down at her side and said a prayer in German, then in Italian, and ended, 'God bless you.' and I got into bed. I loved her very much because there was nothing between us but this strange preparation for sleep. She went away then. In the night I heard the child crying, but I was tired.

"I stayed a year. The thought of the stage had gone out of my heart. I had become a *religieuse*; a gentle religion that began with the prayer I had said after her the first night, and the way I had gone to sleep, though we never repeated the ceremony. It grew with the furniture and the air of the whole room, and with the Bible lying open at a page that I could not read; a religion, Madame, that was empty of need, therefore it was not holy perhaps, and not as it should have been in its manner. It was that I was happy, and I lived there for one year. I almost never saw Ludwig, and almost never Valentine, for that was her child's name, a little girl.

"But at the end of that year I knew there was trouble in other parts of the house. I heard her walking in the night, sometimes Ludwig would be with her, I could hear him crying and talking, but I could not hear what was said. It sounded like a sort of lesson, a lesson for a child to repeat, but if so, there would have been no answer, for the child never uttered a sound, except that buzzing cry.

"Sometimes it is wonderful in Germany, Madame, *nicht wahr?* There is nothing like a German winter. She and I used to walk about the Imperial Palace, and she stroked the cannon, and said they were splendid. We talked about philosophy, for she was troubled with too much thinking, but she always came to the same conclusion, that one must be, or try to be, like every one else. She explained that to be like every one, all at once, in your own person, was to be holy. She said that people did not understand what was meant by 'Love thy neighbour as thyself.' It meant, she said, that one should be like all people *and* oneself, then she said, one was both ruined and powerful.

"Sometimes it seemed that she was managing it, that she was all Germany, at least in her Italian heart. She seemed so irreparably collected and yet distressed, that I was afraid of her, and not afraid.

"That is the way it was, Madame, she seemed to wish it to be that way, though at night she was most scattered and distraught, I could hear her pacing in her room.

"Then she came in one night and woke me and said that I must come into her room. It was in a most terrible disorder. There was a small cot bed that had not been there before. She pointed to it and said that it was for me.

"The child was lying in the great bed against a large lace pillow. Now it was four years old and yet it did not walk, and I never heard it say a thing, or make a sound, except that buzzing cry. It was beautiful in the corrupt way of idiot children; a sacred beast without a taker, tainted with innocence and waste time; honey-haired and failing, like those dwarf angels on holy prints and valentines, if you understand me, Madame, something saved for a special day that would not arrive, not for life at all, and my lady was talking quietly, but I did not recognize any of her former state.

" 'You must sleep here now,' she said, 'I brought you here for this if I should need you, and I need you. You must stay, you must stay forever.' Then she said, 'Will you?' And I said no, I could not do that.

"She took up the candle and put it on the floor beside me, and knelt beside it, and put her arms about my knees. 'Are you a traitor?' she said, 'have you come into my house, his house, the house of my child, to betray us?' and I said no, I had not come to betray. 'Then,' she said, 'you will do as I tell you. I will teach you slowly, slowly; it will not be too much for you, but you must begin to forget, you must forget *everything*. You must forget all the things people have told you. You must forget arguments and philosophy. I was wrong in talking of such things; I thought it would teach you how to lag with her mind, to undo time for her as it passes, to climb into her bereavement and her dispossession. I brought you up badly; I was vain. You will do better. Forgive

me.' She put the palms of her hands on the floor, her face to my
face. 'You must never see any other room than this room. It was
a great vanity that I took you out walking. Now you will stay here
safely, and you will see. You will like it, you will learn to like it
the very best of all. I will bring you breakfast, and luncheon, and
supper. I will bring it to you both, myself. I will hold you on my
lap, I will feed you like the birds. I will rock you to sleep. You
must not argue with me—above all we must have no arguments,
no talk about man and his destiny—man has no destiny—that is
my secret—I have been keeping it from you until to-day, this very
hour. Why not before? Perhaps I was jealous of the knowledge,
yes, that must be it, but now I give it to you, I share it with you.
I am an old woman,' she said, still holding me by the knees. 'When
Valentine was born, Ludwig was only a boy.' She got up and stood
behind me. 'He is not strong, he does not understand that the
weak are the strongest things in the world, because he is one of
them. He can not help her, they are adamant together. I need
you, it must be you.' Suddenly she began talking to me as she
talked with the child, and I did not know which of us she was
talking to. 'Do not repeat anything after me. Why should children
repeat what people say? The whole world is nothing but a noise,
as hot as the inside of a tiger's mouth. They call it civilization—
that is a lie! but someday you may have to go out, someone will
try to take you out, and you will not understand them or what
they are saying, unless you understand nothing, absolutely noth-
ing, then you will manage.' She moved around so that she faced
us, her back against the wall. 'Look,' she said. 'It is all over, it has
gone away, you do not need to be afraid; there is only you. The
stars are out, and the snow is falling down and covering the world,
the hedges, the houses and the lamps. No, no!' she said to her-
self, 'wait. I will put you on your feet, and tie you up in ribbons,
and we will go out together, out into the garden where the swans
are, and the flowers and the bees and small beasts. And the students
will come, because it will be summer, and they will read in their
books—' She broke off, then took her wild speech up again, this

time as though she were really speaking to or of me, 'Katya will go with you. She will instruct you, she will tell you there are no swans, no flowers, no beasts, no boys—*nothing*, nothing at all, just as you like it. No mind, no thought, nothing whatsoever else. No bells will ring, no people will talk, no birds will fly, no boys will move, there'll be no birth and no death; no sorrow, no laughing, no kissing, no crying, no terror, no joy; no eating, no drinking, no games, no dancing; no father, no mother, no sisters, no brothers—only you, only you!'

"I stopped her and I said, 'Gaya, why is it that you suffer so, and what am I to do?' I tried to put my arms around her, but she struck them down crying 'Silence!' Then she said, bringing her face close to my face, 'She has no claws to hang by. She has no hunting foot; she has no mouth for the meat—*vacancy*!'

"Then Madame, I got up. It was very cold in the room. I went to the window and pulled the curtain, it was a bright and starry night, and I stood leaning my head against the frame, saying nothing. When I turned around, she was regarding me, her hands held apart, and I knew that I had to go away and leave her. So I came up to her and said, 'Good-bye my Lady.' And I went and put on my street clothes, and when I came back she was leaning against the battle picture, her hands hanging. I said to her, without approaching her, 'Good-bye my love,' and went away.

"Sometimes it is beautiful in Berlin, Madame, *nicht wahr?* There was something new in my heart, a passion to see Paris, so it was natural that I said *lebe wohl* to Berlin.

"I went for the last time to the café in the Zelten, ate my eggs, drank my coffee and watched the birds coming and going just as they used to come and go—altogether here, then altogether gone. I was happy in my spirit, for that is the way it is with my spirit, Madame, when I am going away.

"But I went back to her house just once. I went in quite easily by the door, for all the doors and windows were open—perhaps they were sweeping that day. I came to the bedroom door and knocked, but there was no answer. I pushed, and there she was, sitting up in the bed with the child, and she and the child were making that buzzing cry, and no human sound between them, and as usual, everything was in disorder. I came up to her, but she did not seem to know me. I said, 'I am going away; I am going to Paris. There is a longing in me to be in Paris. So I have come to say farewell.'

"She got down off the bed and came to the door with me. She said, 'Forgive me—I trusted you—I was mistaken. I did not know that I could do it myself, but you see, I can do it myself.' Then she got back onto the bed and said, 'Go away,' and I went.

"Things are like that, when one travels, *nicht wahr*, Madame?"

The Grande Malade

"And there we were, my sister Moydia and I, Madame. Moydia was fifteen and I was seventeen and we were young all over. Moydia has a thin thin skin, so that I sit and look at her and wonder how she has opinions. She is all white except the cheekbones, then rosy red; her teeth are milk-teeth and she has a small figure, very pretty and droll. She wanted to become '*tragique*' and '*triste*' and 'tremendous' all at once, like the great period Frenchwomen, only fiercer and perhaps less *pure*, and yet to die and give up the heart like a virgin. It was a noble, an impossible ambition, *n'est-ce pas*, Madame? But that was the way it was with Moydia. We used to sit in the sun when we were in Norway and read Goethe and did not agree with him at all. 'The man is *pompeux* and too *assuré*,' she would say, shutting her teeth, 'and very much too *facile*.' But then, people say we do not know.

"We are Russian, Moydia and I, and but for an accident, the most terrifying of our life up to then, we would not have known that our grandmother was a Jew—why? because she was *allowed*

THE SELECTED WORKS OF DJUNA BARNES 22

to drink champagne on her death-bed, and Jews are forbidden champagne you know. So, being 'damned' as it were (both in her dying *and* the 'permission'), she forced mother to drink champagne too, that she might be damned in living as the dying in extremity. So we are Jew and not Jew. We are *where* we are. We are Polish when we are in Poland, and when in Holland we are Dutch, and now in France we are French, and one day we will go to America and be American; you will see, Madame.

"Now I have forgotten all the Polish I knew and all the Russian I knew and all the Dutch, except, that is, a poem. Ah, that poem, that small piece of a poem! a very touching thing, heavy sweet— part of a language. It makes you feel pity in your whole body, because it is complete but mutilated, like a Greek statue, yet whole, like a life, Madame.

"Now I have come to Paris and I respect Paris. First I respected it in a great hat. I am short and a great hat would not, you see, become me, but I wore it for respect. It was all a jumble of flowers and one limber feather; it stood out so that my face was in the middle of a garden. Now I do not wear it any more. I have had to go back in my knowledge, right back to the remembrance, which is the place where I regard my father, and how he looked when in from the new snow. I did not really see him then. Now I see he was truly beautiful all the time that I was thinking nothing about him at all—his astrakhan cap, his frogged coat, with all those silver buttons, and the tall shining boots that caught him just under the knee. Then I think of the window I looked down from and saw the crown of that hat—a wonderful, a mysterious red felt. So now, out of respect for that man, I wear my hats small. Someday, when I have money, my shoes will be higher and come under my knee. This is my way, Madame, but it is not the way it is with Moydia. She has a *great memory in the present,* and it all turns about a cape, therefore now she wears a cape, until something yet more austere drives the cape away. But I must explain.

"First, we are very young as I said, so because of that one becomes *tragique* very quickly, if one is brave, is it not so? So Moydia, though she is two years younger than I, became exhausted almost at once.

"You know how it is in Paris in the autumn, when the summer is just giving up the leaf. I had been here with Moydia two autumns; the first was sad and light on the heart, the way it is when all one's lovers live in spite of the cold. We walked in the Tuileries, I in my small cap and Moydia in a woolly coat, for that was the kind of coat she wore then, and we bought pink and blue candies outside the Punch and Judy show and laughed when the puppets beat each other, Moydia's face tight beneath her skin with the lemon flavour, and tears coming down from her eyes as we thought how perfect everything was, the dolls at their fight and the trees bare, the ground all shuffled in with their foliage—then the pond. We stopped at the pond. The water was full to the edge with water-lily pads and Moydia said it was a shame that women threw themselves in the Seine, only to become a part of its sorrow, instead of casting themselves into a just-right pond like this, where the water would become a part of them. We felt a great despair that people do not live or die beautifully, nor plan anything at all; and then and there we said we would do better.

"After that I noticed, almost at once, that Moydia had become a little too florid. She sprinkled her sugar in her tea from too great a height, and she talked very fast. That was how it was with my sister Moydia in that autumn.

"And of course sophistication came upon us suddenly. We hung two long lace curtains over our beds and we talked of lovers and we smoked. And me? I went about in satin trousers for respect to China, which is a very great country and has *majesté* because you can not know it. It is like a big book which you can read but not understand. So I talked of China to Moydia; and we kept three birds that did not sing, as a symbol of the Chinese heart; and Moydia lay on her bed and became more and more restless, like a story that has no beginning and no end, only a passion like flash lightning.

"She was always kicking her feet in the air and tearing lace handkerchiefs and crying in her pillow, but when I asked her why she was doing all this, she sat straight up, wailing, 'Because I want *everything*, and to be consumed in my youth!'

"So one day she knew everything. Though I am two years older than Moydia, it is different with me. I live more slowly, only women listen to me, but men adore Moydia. To her they do not listen, they look. They look at her when she sits down and when she walks. All at once she began to walk and to sit down quite differently. All her movements were a sort of *malheureuse* tempest. She had her lover and she laughed and cried, lying face down, and whimpering, 'Isn't it *wonderful!*' And perhaps it was indeed wonderful, Madame. From all her admirers she had chosen the most famous, none other than Monsieur X. His great notoriety had thinned him. He dressed very *soigneusement*, white gloves, you know, and spats and a cape, a very handsome affair with a military collar; and he was *grave* and *rare* and stared at you with one eye not at all, but the other looked out from a monocle, like the lidless eye of a fish that keeps deep water. He was the *protégé* of a Baron. The Baron liked him very much and called him his 'Poupon prodigieux,' and they played farces together for the amusement of the Faubourg. That was the way it was with Monsieur X, at least in his season when he was, shall we say, the *belle-d'un-jour* and was occupied in writing fables on mice and men, but he always ended the stories with paragraphs *très acre* against women.

"Moydia began to cultivate a throaty voice. She became an *habitué* of the opera; fierce and fluttering, she danced about Monsieur X during the entr'acte, pulling her flowers to pieces and scattering them as she went, humming, '*Je suis éternellement!*' The audience looked on with displeasure, but the Baron was enchanted.

"Because I and my sister have always been much together, we were much together now. Sometimes I visited the Baron with her and had many hours of dignity just watching them. When the Baron was entertaining, he was very gay and had great control of a sort of aged immaturity, and Moydia would play the kitten or the great lady, as the occasion demanded. If he seemed to forget

her for an instant, she became a *gamine*, sticking her tongue out
at his turned back, hissing '*Ah, tu est belle!*' at which he would
turn about and laugh, she falling into his lap, all in one piece,
stiff and *enragé*. And he would have a long time stroking her and
asking her, in his light worn feminine voice, what was the matter.
And once she would not open her eyes, but screamed and made
him hold her heart, saying, 'Does not the creature beat dread-
fully?' and he entreated her, 'Because? Because?'

Then clapping her hands she would burst into tears and cry: 'I
give you too many destinies with by body. I am Marie on the way
to the *guillotine*. I am Bloody Mary but I have not seen blood. I
am Desdemona, but Othello—where is he? I am Hecuba and
Helen. I am Graetal and Brunhilda, I am Nana and Camille. But
I'm not as bored as they are! When shall I become *properly*
bored?'

"He was bored, and he put her off his knee. She flew at him then
and pulled his clothes about and ripped his gloves, and said with
absolute quiet: 'It amazes me how I do not love you.'

"But when we got home, I had to put her to bed. She was shiver-
ing and laughing and she seemed to be running a fever.

" 'Did you see his face? He is a monster! A product of *malaise*.
He *wants* me to be his sacristan. He'd like me to bury him. I am
positive of it. Katya, are you not positive of it? He is an old soul.
He has come to his mortal end. He is beastly with *finis*. But Death
has given him leave. Oh!' she cried, 'I adore him! I adore him!
I adore him! Oh, I do adore him!' And she refused to see him
until he went quite out of his head and called for himself. She
went running ahead of him all down the hall. I could hear the
sharp report of her heels, and her lisping voice quoting: '*La héron
au long bec emmanché d'un long cou,*' in a sing-song as she
jumped the last step into the day, exclaiming '*C'est la Fontaine,
la Fontaine magnifique!*' And you could hear his cane tapping
after her.

"Then this last autumn, before this last winter set in (you were
not here then, Madame), Moydia had gone to Germany to visit

papa, and all the night before we had sat up together, the three of
us, Moydia, her lover and I. We drank a great deal too much. I sang
my Dutch song and talked a long time, rambling on about father
and his cap and boots, and that splendid coat of his. It pleased
Moydia and it pleased me, but to Monsieur X, probably we seemed
like beggars recalling remembered gold. So I danced a Tartar dance
and raged that my boots did not reach to my knees, and all the
time Moydia was lying on her lover's shoulder, both welded as if
they were an emblem. But when I stopped whirling, he called me
over, and he whispered that I should have a pair of great boots
some day, which gave me great joy. But Moydia sprang up. 'I do
not love this man, Cookoo, do I?' She always called him Cookoo
when she was most fond, as though she were talking about some-
one else. 'I only love Cookoo when I am drunk. So now I do not
love him at all, because I am not drunk at all. Oh, we Russian
women drink a great deal, but it is to become sober—this is some-
thing the other peoples do not take into account! Is it not so,
Katya? It's because we are so extravagant that we do not reach
justice . . . we reach poetry. You adore me, you see,' she said to
him, 'and I *let* you, but that is the way it is with Polish women.'

" 'Russian,' he corrected, and sat staring through the boss of his
monocle straight at the wall.

"Well then, Moydia went away to Germany to visit papa, who is
a travelling man now and buys and sells diamonds. He will not
send us money unless he sees us at least once a year. He's that
way. He says he will not have his girls grow up into something he
does not like paying for. Sometimes he sends money from Russia,
sometimes from Poland, sometimes from Belgium, sometimes from
England. He has said that some day he will come to Paris but he
does not come. It is very confusing to get so many kinds of moneys,
we never know what we will have to spend, we have to be very
careful; perhaps that is the whole idea. But at this point Moydia
had lost all caution. She bought herself a new dress to please
Monsieur X, and to go away in, and not to alarm father—all at
the same time. So it was a cunning dress, very deft and touching.

It was all dotted *suisse*, with a very tight bodice, and into this bodice, just between the breasts, was embroidered, in very fine twist, a slain lamb. It might, you see, mean everything and it might mean nothing, and it might bring pleasure to both father and lover.

"After she had gone, I sat in the café every afternoon and waited for her return. She was not to be gone longer than two weeks. That was the autumn that I felt great sadness, Madame, I read a great deal and I walked about all by myself. I was in need of solitude. I walked in the Tuileries and visited the pond again, and went under the trees where the air was cool and there were numbers of people who did not seem to be gay. The autumn had come differently this year; it was already oppressive in September—it was as though there were a catafalque coming into Paris from a long way and everyone knew it; men buttoned their coats tight and the women tipped their sunshades down, as if for rain.

"So ten days passed, and the season hung heavy in a mist that blotted almost everything out. You could scarcely see the Seine when you went walking on the bridges, the statues in the parks were altogether withdrawn, the sentries looked like dolls in boxes, the ground was always damp, the café *brasiers* were going full heat. Then I knew, suddenly I knew—Moydia's lover was dying! And indeed that night he died. He had caught a chill the evening that Moydia left, and it had grown worse and worse. It was reported the Baron was always with him, and when the Baron saw that Monsieur X was truly going to die, he made him drink. They drank together all night and into the morning. The Baron wanted it that way: 'For that,' he said, 'he might die as he was born, without knowing.'

"So I went straight to the Baron's house, and right up to the door, and rapped—but he would not let me in. He said through the door that Moydia's lover had been buried that very morning, and I said, 'Give me something for Moydia,' and he said, 'What shall I give you?' and he added, 'He left nothing but a deathless name!' And I said, 'Give me his cape.' And he gave me his cape, through the leeway of the chain on the door, but he did not look out at me, and I went away.

"That night Moydia arrived back from Germany. She had a terrible fever and she talked very fast, like a child. She wanted to go directly to Monsieur's house; I had great difficulty in keeping her in. I put her to bed and made her tea, but I could not keep still, so I brought her the cape and I said, 'Cookoo is dead and this is his cape and it is for you.' She said, 'How did he die?' and 'Why?'

"I said, 'He was taken ill the night you left, and it became a fever that would not leave him, so the Baron sat with him and they drank all night that he might die as he was born, without knowing.'

"Moydia began beating on the bed then with both hands and saying, 'Let us drink, and pray God I shall die the same death!' We sat up all night drinking and talking together without much sense. Toward morning she said, 'Now I have a great life!' and she wept and went to sleep, and by noon she was quite well.

"Now Madame, she wears it always. The cape. Men admire her in it, indeed she looks very well in it, do you not think so? She has grown faster than I; you would take her for the elder, would you not? She is gay, spoiled, *tragique*. She sugars her tea from far too great a height. And that's all. There's nothing else to tell, except— in the *débâcle* my boots were quite forgotten. The next day all the papers carried pages and pages about Monsieur X, and in all of them he was wearing a cape. We, Moydia and I, read them together. They may even have printed something about him in America? Truly, we speak a little French, now we must be moving on."

A Night among the Horses

Toward dusk, in the summer of the year, a man in evening dress, carrying a top hat and a cane, crept on hands and knees through the underbrush bordering the pastures of the Buckler estate. His wrists hurt him from holding his weight and he sat down. Sticky ground-vines all about him; they climbed the trees, the posts of the fence, they were everywhere. He peered through the thickly tangled branches and saw, standing against the darkness, a grove of white birch shimmering like teeth in a skull.

He could hear the gate grating on its hinge as the wind clapped. His heart moved with the movement of the earth. A frog puffed forth its croaking unmemoried cry; the man struggled for breath, the air was heavy and hot, as though he were nested in a pit of astonishment.

He wanted to drowse off; instead he placed his hat and cane beside him, straightening his coat-tails beneath him, lying out on his back, waiting. Something quick was moving the ground. It began to shake with sudden warning and he wondered if it was his heart.

A lamp in the far away window winked as the boughs swung against the wind; the odour of crushed grasses, mingling with the faint reassuring smell of the stable, fanned up and drawled off to the north; he opened his mouth, drawing in the ends of his moustache.

The tremour lengthened, it ran beneath his body and tumbled away into the earth.

He sat upright. Putting on his hat, he braced his cane against the ground between his out-thrust legs. Now he not only felt the trembling of the earth but caught the muffled horny sound of hooves smacking the turf, as a friend strikes the back of a friend, hard, but without malice. They were on the near side now as they took the curve of the Willow Road. He pressed his forehead against the bars of the fence.

The soft menacing sound deepened as heat deepens; the horses, head-on, roared by him, their legs rising and falling like savage needles taking purposeless stitches.

He saw their bellies pitching from side to side, racking the bars of the fence as they swung past. On his side of the barrier he rose up running, gasping. His foot caught in the trailing pine and he pitched forward, striking his head on a stump as he went down. Blood trickled from his scalp. Like a red mane it ran into his eyes, and he stroked it back with the knuckles of his hand, as he put on his hat. In this position the pounding hoofs shook him like a child on a knee.

Presently he searched for his cane and found it snared in the fern. A wax Patrick-pipe brushed against his cheek as he leaned down. He ran his tongue over it, snapping it in two. Move as he would, the grass was always under him, crackling with twigs and cones. An acorn fell out of the soft dropping powders of the wood. He took it up, and as he held it between finger and thumb, his mind raced over the scene back there with the mistress of the house, for what else could one call Freda Buckler but 'the mistress of the house,' that small fiery woman with a battery for a heart and the body of a toy, who ran everything, who purred, saturated with impudence, with a mechanical buzz that ticked away her humanity.

He blew down his moustache. Freda, with that aggravating float-ing yellow veil! He told her it was 'aggravating,' he told her that it was 'shameless,' and stood for nothing but temptation. He puffed out his cheeks, blowing at her as she passed. She laughed, stroking his arm, throwing her head back, her nostrils scarlet to the pit. They had ended by riding out together, a boot's length apart, she no bigger than a bee on a bonnet. In complete misery he had dug down on his spurs, and she: "Gently, John, gently!" showing her wide distilling mouth. "You can't be ostler *all* your life. Horses!" she snorted, "I like horses, but—" He had lowered his crop. "There are other things. You simply can't go on being a groom forever, not with grace like that, and you know it. I'll make a gentleman out of you. I'll step you up from being a 'thing.' You will see, you will enjoy it."

He had leaned over and lashed at her boot with his whip. It caught her at the knee, the foot flew up in its stirrup, as though she were dancing.

And the little beast was delighted! They trotted on a way, and they trotted back. He helped her to dismount, and she sailed off, trailing the yellow veil, crying back:

"You'll *love* it!"

Before they had gone on like this for more than a month (bowl-ing each other over in the spirit, wringing each other this way and that, hunter and hunted) it had become a game without any pleasure; debased lady, debased ostler, on the wings of vertigo.

What was she getting him into? He shouted, bawled, cracked whip—what did she figure she wanted? The kind of woman who can't tell the truth; truth ran out and away from her as though her veins were pipettes stuck in by the devil; and drinking, he swelled, and pride had him, it floated him off. He saw her standing behind him in every mirror, she followed him from show-piece to show-piece, she fell in beside him, walked him, hand under elbow.

"You will rise to governour-general—well, to inspector—"

"Inspector!"

"As you like, say master of the regiment—say cavalry officer. Horses, too, leather, whips—"

"O my God!"

She almost whinnied as she circled on her heels:

"With a broad, flat, noble chest," she said, "you'll become a pavement of honours. . . . Mass yourself. You will leave affliction—"

"Stop it!" he shouted. "I *like* being common."

"With a quick waist like that, the horns will miss you."

"What horns?"

"The dilemma."

"I *could* stop you, all over, if I wanted to."

She was amused. "Man in a corner?" she said.

She tormented him, she knew it. She tormented him with her objects of 'culture.' One knee on an ottoman, she would hold up and out the most delicate miniature, an ivory cupped in her palm, tilting it from the sun, saying: "But look, look!"

He put his hands behind his back. She aborted that. She asked him to hold ancient missals, volumes of fairy tales, all with handsome tooling, all bound in corded russet. She spread maps, and with a long hat-pin dragging across mountains and ditches, pointed to 'just where she had been.' Like a dry snail the point wandered the coast, when abruptly, sticking the steel in, she cried *"Borgia!"* and stood there, jangling a circle of ancient keys.

His anxiety increased with curiosity. *If* he married her—after he *had* married her, what then? Where would he be after he had satisfied her crazy whim? What would she make of him in the end; in short, what would she leave of him? Nothing, absolutely nothing, not even his horses. Here'd be a damned fool for you. He wouldn't fit in anywhere after Freda, he'd be neither what he was nor what he had been; he'd be a *thing*, half standing, half crouching, like those figures under the roofs of historic buildings, the halt position of the damned.

He had looked at her often without seeing her; after a while he began to look at her with great attention. Well, well! really a small mousy woman, with fair pretty hair that fell like an insect's feelers into the nape of her neck, moving when the wind moved. She darted and bobbled about too much, and always with the mindless intensity of a mechanical toy kicking and raking about the floor.

And she was always a step or two ahead of him, or stroking his arm at arm's length, or she came at him in a gust, leaning her sharp little chin on his shoulder, floating away slowly—only to be stumbled over when he turned. On this particular day he had caught her by the wrist, slewing her around. This once, he thought to himself, this once I'll ask her straight out for truth; a direct shot might dislodge her.

"Miss Freda, just a moment. You know I haven't a friend in the world. You know positively that I haven't a person to whom I can go and get an answer to any question of any sort. So then, just what *do* you want me for?"

She blushed to the roots of her hair. "Girlish! are you going to be girlish?" She looked as if she were going to scream, her whole frame buzzed, but she controlled herself and drawled with lavish calm:

"Don't be nervous. Be patient. You will get used to everything. You'll even like it. There's nothing so enjoyable as climbing."

"And then?"

"Then everything will slide away, stable and all." She caught the wings of her nose in the pinching folds of a lace handkerchief. "Isn't that a destination?"

The worst of all had been the last night, the evening of the masked ball. She had insisted on his presence. "Come," she said, "just as you are, and be our whipper-in." That was the final blow, the unpardonable insult. He had obeyed, except that he did not come 'just as he was.' He made an elaborate toilet; he dressed for evening, like any ordinary gentleman; he was the only person present therefore who was not 'in dress,' that is, in the accepted sense.

On arrival he found most of the guests tipsy. Before long he himself was more than a little drunk, and horrified to find that he was dancing a minuet, stately, slow, with a great soft puff-paste of a woman, showered with sequins, grunting in cascades of plaited tulle. Out of this embrace he extricated himself, slipping on the bare spots of the rosin-powdered floor, to find Freda coming at him with a tiny glass of cordial which she poured into his open mouth; at that point he was aware that he had been gasping for air.

He came to a sudden stop. He took in the whole room with his frantic glance. There in the corner sat Freda's mother with her cats. She always sat in corners and she always sat with cats. And there was the rest of the cast—cousins, nephews, uncles, aunts. The next moment, the *galliard*. Freda, arms up, hands, palm out, elbows buckled in at the breast, a praying mantis, was all but tooth to tooth with him. Wait! He stepped free, and with the knob end of his cane drew a circle in the rosin clear around her, then went backward through the French windows.

He knew nothing after that until he found himself in the shrubbery, sighing, his face close to the fence, peering in. He was with his horses again; he was where he belonged again. He could hear them tearing up the sod, galloping about as though in their own ball-room, and oddest of all, at this dark time of the night.

He began drawing himself under the lowest bar, throwing his hat and cane in before him, panting as he crawled. The black stallion was now in the lead. The horses were taking the curve in the Willow Road that ran into the further pasture, and through the dust they looked faint and enormous.

On the top of the hill, four had drawn apart and were standing, testing the weather. He would catch one, mount one, he would escape! He was no longer afraid. He stood up, waving his hat and cane and shouting.

They did not seem to know him, and they swerved past him and away. He stared after them, almost crying. He did not think of his dress, the white shirt front, the top hat, the waving stick, his abrupt rising out of the dark, their excitement. Surely they must know him—in just a moment.

Wheeling, manes up, nostrils flaring, blasting out steam as they came on, they passed him in a whinnying flood, and he damned them in horror, but what he shouted was "Bitch!", and found himself swallowing fire from his heart, lying on his face, sobbing, "I *can* do it, damn everything, I can get on with it; I can make my mark!"

The upraised hooves of the first horse missed him, the second did not.

Presently the horses drew apart, nibbling and swishing their tails, avoiding a patch of tall grass.

The Valet

The fields about Louis-Georges' house grew green in very early spring, leaving the surrounding countryside to its melancholy gray, for Louis-Georges was the only farmer who sowed his fields to rye.

Louis-Georges was a small man with a dark oval face that burned like a Goya and supported a long raking nose in which an hoar-frost of hair bristled. His arms swung their stroke ahead of his legs; his whole person knew who he was—that sort.

He had fierce pride in everything he did, even when not too well executed, not too well comprehended; he himself was so involved in it, tied in it.

Sometimes standing in the yard, breathing the rich air, nose up, he enjoyed his lands utterly, rubbing the fingers of one hand with the fingers of the other, or waving the hands above the horns of his cattle where, in buzzing loops, flies hung, or slapping the haunches of his racers, saying to the trainer: "There's more breeding in the rump of one of these, than any butt in the stalls of Westminster!"—pretending that he understood all points from muzzle to hoof—in short, a man who all but had a 'hand in being.'

Sometimes he and Vera Sovna would play hide-and-seek about the grain bins and through the mounds of hay, she in her long flounces and high heels, screaming and leaping among the rakes and flails.

Once Louis-Georges caught a rat, bare hand, and with such skill that it could not use its teeth. He disguised his elation, showing her how it was done, pretending it a cunning he had learned in order to protect the winter grain.

Vera Sovna was a tall creature with thin shoulders which she shrugged as if the blades were too heavy. She usually dressed in black, and she laughed a good part of the time in a rather high key.

She had been the great friend of Louis-Georges' mother, but since the mother's death she had, by her continued intimacy, fallen into disrepute. It was whispered that she was 'something' to Louis-Georges. When the landholders saw her enter his house, they could not contain themselves until they saw her leave it; if she came out holding her skirts carefully above her ankles, they found the roofs of their mouths with disapproving tongues; if she walked slowly, dragging her dress, they would say: "What a dust she brings up in the driveway!"

If she knew anything of their feelings she did not show it. Driving through the town, turning neither to right nor left, she passed right through the market square looking at nobody but obviously delighted with the rosy bunches of flowers, the bright tumble of yellow squash and green cucumbers, the fruits piled in orderly heaps on the stands. But on the rare occasions when Louis-Georges accompanied her, she would cross her legs at the knee, or lean forward, or shake a finger at him, or turn her head from side to side, or lean back laughing.

Sometimes she visited the maids' quarters to play with Leah's child, a little creature with bandy legs and frail neck, who thrust out his stomach for her to pat.

The maids, Berthe and Leah, were well-built complacent women with serene blue eyes, fine teeth and round firm busts that flourished like pippins. They went about their duties chewing stalks of rye and salad leaves, reefing with their tongues.

In her youth Leah had evidently done something for which she now prayed at intervals, usually before a wooden Christ hanging from a beam in the barn, which was so familiar that she did not notice Him until, sitting down to milk, she raised her eyes; then, putting her forehead against the cow's belly, she prayed, the milk splashing over her big knuckles and wasting into the ground, until Berthe came to help her carry the pails, when she would remark: "We are going to have rain."

Vera Sovna spent hours in the garden, the child crawling after her, leaving the marks of his small hands, wet with saliva, on the dusty leaves; digging up young vegetable roots with such sudden ease that he would fall on his back, blinking up at the sun.

The two maids, the valet Vanka, and Louis-Georges were the household, except when augmented by the occasional visits of Louis-Georges' aunts, Myra and Ella.

Vanka was Russian. He bit his nails. He wore his clothes badly, as though he had no time for more than the master's neatness. His rich yellow hair was dishevelled though pomaded, his eyebrows shaggy and white. His eyes, when he raised their heavy lids, were gentle and intelligent. He was absolutely devoted.

Louis-Georges would say to him, "Now Vanka, tell me again what was that they did to you when you were a boy."

"They shot my brother," Vanka would answer, pulling at his forelock. "They shot him for a 'red.' They threw him into prison with my father. Then one day my sister, who took them their food in two pails, heard a noise; it sounded like a shot and that day father returned only one pail, and they say he returned it like a person looking over his shoulder." Vanka told that story often, sometimes adding with a sigh, "My sister, who had been a hand-some woman (the students used to visit her just to hear her talk) —became bald—over night."

After such confidences, Louis-Georges would shut himself up

in his study where, in a large scrawling hand, he wrote to his aunts. Sometimes he would put in a phrase or two about Vanka.

Sometimes Vera Sovna would come in to watch, lifting her ruffles, raising her brows. If Vanka was present she would return his stare. In both there was the cold precision of steel.

She would stand with her back to the fireplace, her heels apart, tapping the stretched silk of her skirt, saying:

"Come, come, that is enough!" adding, "Vanka, take his pen away."

Vanka remained immobile. Louis-Georges went on, smiling and grunting, but never lifting his hand from his written page. As for Vanka, he simply stood there, catching the pages as they were finished.

Finally with a loud scrape and a great shove, Louis-Georges would push back the chair and standing up would say, "Now, let us have tea."

In the end he fell into a slow illness. It attacked his limbs; he was forced to walk with a cane. He complained of his heart, but he persisted in going out to look at the horses, and to amuse Vera Sovna he would slash at the flies with his stick, enjoying the odour of milk and dung.

He had plans for the haying, for getting in the crops, but he had to give over to the farm hands who, left to themselves, wandered off at any odd hour, to their own acres, to their own broken fences.

Six months later Louis-Georges took to his bed.

The aunts came, testing the rate of decay in the beams of sunlight, as they portioned out paregoric like women in charge of a baby, remarking to each other with surprise, "He never *used* to be like this," easing the velvet straps that bit into their shoulder flesh, peering at each other from either side of his bed.

They were afraid of meeting Vera Sovna. Their position was difficult. Having been on friendly terms with her while Louis-Georges' mother was alive, they felt that once the old lady was dead, they had to increase in dignity and reserve. Then, too, the townsfolk seemed to have turned against Vera. Still, the aunts did not wish to be too harsh, so they left Louis-Georges' bedside for an hour every evening that Vera Sovna might come to see him, and Vera Sovna came, creeping softly and saying, "Oh, my *dear!*" She would tell him stories, told before, all about her own life, as if that life, not yet spent, might be of help. She told him of her week in London, of a visit to The Hague; of adventures with hotel-keepers in impossible inns, and sometimes, leaning close to him, he thought he heard her weeping.

But in spite of this—the illness and the tension in the air—Vera Sovna seemed strangely gay.

During the foundering of Louis-Georges, Leah and Berthe served as nurses, changing his sheets, turning him over to rub him with oil and alcohol, crossing themselves and giving him the spoon.

The valet stood at the foot of the bed, trying not to cough or sigh or annoy his master in any way. But sometimes he would fall asleep holding to the bedpost, and wake to dreams of the "revolution," dreams which faded as he caught himself into waking.

Vera Sovna had taken to dining with the girls in the kitchen, a long bare room that pleased her. From the window one could see the orchard and the pump and the long easy slope of the meadow. From the beams braided onions and smoked meats dangled over the long table, strewn with a thin snow of flour, and hot loaves of new bread.

The girls accepted Vera Sovna's company cheerfully. When she went away, they cleared the board, talking of other things, sharpening knives, forgetting.

The matters of the estate went on as usual. Nothing suffered because of the master's infirmity. Crops ripened, the haying season passed; the orchard sounded with the thud of falling fruit. Louis-Georges ripened into death, detached, as if he had never been. About Vera Sovna there was a quiet brilliance. She tended the medicine bottles as though they were musical intervals; she arranged him bouquets as though they were tributes. And Vanka?

There was the one who took on utter anguish, he bent under the shortening shadow of his master, as one at last permitted the use of grief for himself.

Myra and Ella in shock, shook crumbs from their laps, sending each other in to visit Louis-Georges, and pretending each to the other he much was improved. It was not that they were afraid he might die, they were afraid they were not prepared.

When the doctor arrived they shifted their uncertainty. They rushed about getting subscriptions filled, spoons polished; they closed their eyes, sitting on either side of his bed, picturing him already shriven and translated, in order to find pleasure in opening their eyes to find him just as usual.

When they knew that he was dying indeed, the aunts could not keep from touching him. They tried to cover him up in those parts that too plainly exposed the rate of his depletion, the thin arms, the damp pulsing spot in the neck, the fallen pit of his stomach. They fondled his knuckles, and generally drove the doctor and the new nurse frantic. At last, in desperation, Myra, eluding everyone, knelt by Louis-Georges and stroked his face. Death did not seem to be anywhere; that is, it did not seem to stay in one place, but with her caresses seemed to move from quarter to quarter. At this point she was locked out with her sister. They wandered up and down the hall, afraid to speak, unable to cry, passing each other, bracing their palms against the walls.

Then when Louis-Georges did die, there was the problem of Vera Sovna. However, they soon forgot her, trying to follow the instructions left by the dead man. Louis-Georges had seen to it that everything should go on as usual; he would not interrupt the seasons, he had "planned" next year.

The hens praised their eggs as usual, as usual the stables resounded with good spirits. The fields shed their very life upon the earth, and Vanka folded and put away the dead man's clothes.

When the undertaker arrived, Vanka would not let him touch the body. He washed and dressed it himself. It was he who laid Louis-Georges in the shining coffin that smelled like violin rosin; it was he who banked the flowers, and he who finally left the scene on the whole flat of his suddenly clumsy feet. He went to his room and shut the door.

He paced. It seemed to him that he had left something undone. He loved service and order; he loved Louis-Georges who had made service necessary and order desirable. This made him rub his palms together, holding them close to his sighing mouth, as if the sound might teach him some secret of silence. Of course Leah had made a scene, hardly to be wondered at, considering. She had brought her baby in, dropping him beside the body, giving her first order: "You can play together, now, for a minute."

Vanka had not interfered. The child had been too frightened to disturb the arranged excellence of Louis-Georges' leavetaking, and both the child and mother soon left the room in stolid calm. Vanka could hear them descend to the lower parts of the house, the deliberate thump of Leah, the quick clatter of the child.

Walking his room, Vanka could hear the trees beating the wind; an owl called from the barn, a mare whinnied, stomped and dropped her head back into her bin. Vanka opened the window. He thought he caught the sound of feet on the pebbled border that rounded the hydrangea bushes; a faint perfume, such as arose from the dancing flounces of Vera Sovna's dress, seemed to hang in the air. Irritated, he turned away; then he heard her calling.

"Vanka," she said, "come, my foot is caught in the vine."

Her face with its open mouth came up above the sill, and the next moment she jumped into the room. And there they stood, looking at each other. They had never been alone before. He did not know what to do.

She was a little dishevelled; twigs clung to the flounces of her skirts. She raised both shoulders and sighed; she reached out her hand and said his name.

"Vanka."

He moved away from her, staring.

"Vanka," she repeated, and came close to him, leaning on his arm. With great simplicity she said, "You must tell me everything."

"I'll tell you," he answered automatically.

"Look, your hands!" Suddenly she dropped her head into his palms. He shivered; he drew his hands away.

"Oh look, you fortunate man!" she cried. "Most fortunate man, most elected Vanka! He let you touch him, close, close, near the skin, near the heart. You knew how he looked, how he stood, how the ankle went into the foot!—" he had ceased to hear her, he was so astonished—"his shoulders, how they set. You dressed and undressed him. You knew him, all of him, for years. Tell me—tell me, what was he like?"

He turned. "I will tell you," he said, "if you are still, if you will sit down, if you are quiet."

She sat down: she watched him with great joy.

"His arms were too long," he said, "but you know that, you could see that, but beautiful; and his back, his spine, tapering, slender, full of breeding—"

The Rabbit

The road had been covered with leaves on the day that the little
tailor had left his own land. He said good day and good bye in
the one breath, with his broad teeth apart as if he had been hauled
out of deep water. He did not leave Armenia because he wanted to,
he left because he had to. There wasn't a thing about Armenia
that he did not want to stay with forever; it was necessity, he was
being pushed out. In short, he had been left a property in New
York City.

Leavetaking did not tear him to pieces, he wept no tears, the
falling leaves sent no pang through him, he treated the whole
business as a simple and resigned man should. He let Armenia
slip through his fingers.

His life had been a sturdy, steady, slow, pleasant sort of thing.
He ploughed and tended his crops. Hands folded over the haft of
his scythe, he watched his cow grazing. He groomed the feathers
and beaks of his ducks to see that the feathers lay straight, the bills
unbroken and shining. He liked to pass his hands over the creatures

of his small land, they were exactly as pleasing as plants; in fact he could not see much difference, when you came right down to it.

Now it was otherwise. His people advised him (as he was a single man) to accept the inheritance, a small tailoring business his uncle had left him. With a helper, they said, it might be the very best thing for him. It might 'educate' him, make him into an 'executive,' a 'boss,' a man of the world.

He protested, but not with any great force; he was a timid man, a gentle man. He cleaned the spade, sharpened the saws, shook the shavings out of the plane, oiled his auger and bit, rubbed fat into the harness, and pulling his last calf from the drenched and murmuring cow, wondered what to do.

The day he was to leave he went first into the forest where he had brought boughs down, tying them, to make a hut against the sun. His jug of molasses and cinnamon water was still there by his sitting log. The woods spilled over into the road; the shadows, torn through with bright holes of sunlight, danced in patches of bloom. Mosquitoes from the swamp sang about his head. They got into the long hairs of his beard below his chin, and clung, whining in the mesh, wheeled against his cheek, flying up above his clashing hands, and as he slapped his face he thought of himself sitting in quiet misfortune, sewing, up on a table, as though he had died and had to work it out.

So one day, to the lower part of Manhattan (to the street of the shop of Amietiev the tailor) came a stranger, the latest Amietiev, with a broom. The passers-by saw him swinging it over the boards of his inheritance, a room not much more than twelve by twenty-four, the back third curtained off to hide the small bed and the commode beside it. He tested the air, as he had tested the air of his country, he sneezed; he held the room up in his eye by the scruff of its neck, as you might say, and shook it in the face of his lost acres.

He had learned the tailors' trade when he was a young boy, when this now dead uncle had been his guardian, but his fingers

were clumsy and he broke the needle. He worked slowly and pain-
fully, holding his breath too long, puffing it out in loud sighs.
He toiled far into the night, the goose between his knees. People
on the way home peered in at him as he sat on his long table, half
hidden by the signs in his windows, the fly-specked fashion book
open at the swaggering gentlemen in topcoats; out-of-date an-
nouncements of religious meetings, and bills for the local bur-
lesque. Loiterers, noting how pale he was, remarked to each other,
"That one will die of the consumption, see if he doesn't!"

Across the way, laid out on a butcher's slab (vying with
Amietiev's remnants of silk linings, shepherd checks and woollen
stuffs), were bright quarters of beef, calves' heads and knuckle
bones; remnants of animals, pink and yellow in layers of fat. There
were muscle meats and kidneys, with their webbings of suet; great
carcasses slashed down the center, showing the keyboard of the
spine, and hanging on hooks, ducks dripping head-down into
basins.

When the little tailor looked up, it made him horribly sad; the
colours were a very harvest of death. He remembered too easily
the swinging meadows of his own country, with the cows in the
lanes and the fruits overhead, and he turned away and went on
stitching.

Behind the curtain was a small gas-ring on which he warmed his
breakfast; sometimes a sausage, always coffee, bread, cheese. In
the summer it was too hot, in the winter the shop was deadly with
heavy air; he could not risk opening the door; he was flooded with
chill whenever a customer came in (no one ever seemed to think
he might feel the wind), so he sat in the foul air, made infinitely
worse by the gas stove, and day by day his eyes grew further back
in his head, the dark brows more and more prominent. The chil-
dren of the neighbourhood called him "coal eye."

In the second summer business picked up, he worked more
quickly, did excellent patchwork, charged very little and never
gave himself any time for his own life at all; he stitched, turned,
pressed, altered, as though the world were a huge barricade of old

clothes. At about this time he had become attached to a small, ill, slender Italian girl, who had first appeared carrying her father's coat. She smelled tart, as of lemons.

Her straight black hair, parted in the middle, was as black as her eyes; under a dipping nose blazed her mouth, firm, shut. Almost anything bright caught at him. He thought of all the calendars with all the madonnas that he had seen, and he made the mistake of shuffling this girl in with them. The sharp, avaricious cruelty of her face pleased him; he confused the quick darting head with brightness. He himself was not a good looking man; this did not trouble him, he was as good looking as anyone in his family and that was that. He was quite unconscious that for the size of his head, his body was rather small; the fact that he had coarse hair made matters worse.

This girl, Addie, mentioned all these things. It hurt him because he was beginning to like her. He noticed that when he showed it, by the trembling of his needle, she looked starved. He was puzzled. "Why," he asked, "when you say such things about me, do you look so pretty?"

This being the very worst thing he could say, it encouraged her, it flattered her. She throve on whetting, and he was always putting an edge on her: after all, she was neither as nice as he thought, nor as young. Finally, after much debate with himself, with slow tortuous convulsions of mind, he asked her if she had thought of love and marriage. Of course she had; here was a business right there before her for the taking, it was promising and seemed to be going to "flourish" as you might put it, and wasn't she already used to him? In a quiet, canny, measured way (that he was much too much of an idiot to notice) she had made her plans. She was pleased to admit the attachment, but what she said was, "You are a poor sort of man!" She said it roughly (as if blaming him for something). She said it bridling, pulling her pleated skirt between two fingers in a straight line. He felt that she was very stout; himself, very nothing.

"What do you want that I shall do?"

She shrugged, flipped her hair back, opened her entire mouth, exposing the full length of the crouching tongue.

"I mean, if I must do something, what is it? If, as you say, I am only—"

"You'll never *be* anything," she said, then she added, "You'll never be anything *else*."

"True, not something else, but perhaps more?"

"Now there's a likely." She had a way of clipping her meanings short, it was her form of scorn.

"What do you mean by 'a *likely*'?"

"You are not the sort, for instance . . ."

"For?" He turned his body, looking at her closely.

"You are hardly a *hero!*" She laughed in a series of short snapping sounds, like a dog.

"Are heroes the style?" he asked with such utter guile and with such a troubled face that she tittered.

"Not in your family, I take it."

He nodded. "That is true, yes, that is quite true. We were quiet people. You do not like quiet people?"

"Foo!" she said, "they are women!"

He pondered this a long time. Slowly he got off his table; he took her by both shoulders, shaking her softly from side to side.

"That is not true and you know it; they are something else."

She began shouting, "*So*, now I'm a liar. This is what it has come to! I'm abominable, unnatural, unnatural!" She had managed to get herself into the highest sort of pretended indignation, pulling her hair, swinging it like a whip from side to side. In so laying hold on herself, in disarranging her usually composed, almost casual ease, the sly baggage had him in as great a state of distress, as if he had had to witness the shaking of an holy image.

"No, no!" he cried, clapping his hands together. "Don't do it, leave yourself alone! I'll do something, I'll make everything as it should be." He came to her, drawing her hair out of her fist. "For you I will do *anything*. Yes, surely, I will do it, I will, I will!"

"You will do *what*, Amietiev?" she asked with such sudden calm that his anxiety almost stumbled over her. "What is it that you will do?"

"I shall be less like a woman. You called me a woman; a terrible thing to say to a man, especially if he is small, and I am small."

She came forward, her elbows tight to her sides, her palms out, walking sideways: "You'll do anything for me? What? Something daring, something really *big*, something grand just for me?"

"Just for you." He looked at her in sorrow. The cruel passing twist of the mouth—(everything about her was fleeting), the perishing thin arms, the small cage of the ribs, the too long hair, the hands turning on the wrists, the sliding narrow feet, and the faint mournful sharp odour of lemons that puffed from her swinging skirt, moved him away from her; grief in all his being snuffed him out. She came up behind him, caught both his hands, pulling them backward, and leaning against him, kissed him on the back of the neck. He tried to turn around, but she held him, so they stood for a moment, then she broke away and ran out into the street.

He set to work again, sitting cross-legged on the table, he wondered what he was supposed to do. Nothing like this had happened before; in fact he had always told her how he longed for a country life, with her beside him in the fields, or sitting among the plants and vegetables. Now here he was faced with himself as a hero . . . what was a hero? What was the difference between himself and that sort of man? He tried to think if he had ever known one. He remembered tales told him by the gypsies, a great time ago, when he was in his own land; they had certainly told him of a lad who was a tremendous fighter, who wrestled with his adversary like a demon, but at the end, not being able to kill anything, had thrown himself off a mountain. But for himself, a tailor, such a thing would be impossible . . . he would only die and that would not get him anywhere. He thought of all the great people he had read of, or heard of, or might have brushed against. There was Jean the blacksmith who had lost an eye saving his child from a horse; but if he, Amietiev, lost an eye, Addie would not like him at all. How about Napoleon? There was a well-known man; he had done everything, all by himself, more or less, so much so that he even crowned himself Emperor without any help at all, and people so admired him they hung his picture all over the world, because of course he had been such a master at killing. He thought about this a long time, and finally came to the inevitable conclusion: all heroes were men who killed or got killed.

Well, that was impossible; if he were killed he might as well have stayed in the country and never laid eyes on Addie—therefore he must kill—but what?

He might of course save someone or something, but there would have to be danger of one kind or another, and there might not be any for days and days, and he was tired and afraid of waiting.

He laid his work aside, slid off the table, lowered the light, and lying face down on his cot tried to think the whole thing out.

He sat up, rubbing both hands on the sides of his face; it was damp under the beard, he could feel it. He tried to make a picture for his mind, a picture of what killing was like. He sat on the edge of the cot, staring at the small piece of carpet with its Persian design, his mind twisted in it.

He thought of trees, the brook where he went fishing, the green fields, the cows who breathed a long band of hot air from their nostrils when he came close; he thought of the geese, he thought of thin ice on the ponds with bushes bristling out of it . . . he thought of Addie, and Addie was entwined with the idea of killing. He tried to think of himself as of someone destroying someone. He clapped his palms together, lacing the fingers in a lock. No, no, no! That wouldn't press out the life of a thrush. He held his hands apart, looking at the thumbs. He rubbed them down the sides of his legs. What a terrible thing murder was! He stood up, shaking his body from side to side, as if it hurt him. He went into the shop, pulling up the shade as high as it would go.

Exactly opposite, two bright lights burned in the butcher's window. He could see sides of beef hanging from their hooks, the chilled lakes of blood in the platters, the closed eyes of the calves' heads in ranks on their slabs, looking like peeled women, and swaying in the wind of the open door, game, with legs knocked down.

He came out of his shop carefully, stepping into the street on the tips of his toes, as though someone might see or hear him. He crossed, and butting his forehead against the butcher's plate-glass front, stared at all the hooded eyes of the squabs, the withered collapsed webs of the ducks' feet, the choked scrap-barrel, spilling out its lungs and guts. His stomach gave way, he was sick. He put his hand on the pit of his belly and pressed. He pulled at his beard, rolling the russet hairs that came away between his fingers.

He knew the butcher well; he also knew when he stepped out for a short beer at the saloon. He knew his habit of keeping the back door on the latch, he knew exactly what was stored in the back room. He expected no hindrance and got none. He pushed the back door in easily enough. For a moment the dimness left him blind, the next instant he emerged carrying a box. Now furtive, hurried, stumbling, he crossed back to his own door, opened it with his foot, and all but fell in.

The reflection of the ruby glass of the butcher's lamps ran red over his fashion-plates and strutting cardboard gentlemen. The little tailor put the box down in the farthest corner. His heart was beating high up in his neck. He groped about in his mind for something to stop at, some place to steady himself. He must make himself resolute. He clenched his chattering teeth, but it only made him cry. To stop that, he clasped both hands behind his neck, bending his neck down, and at the same time he sank to his knees beside the box and lowered his hands and forehead to the floor. He must do it! He must do it! He must do it *now*! His mind began its wandering again. He thought himself into his own country, in another season. Sunlight on the forest floor. He remembered the mosquitoes. He leaned back upon his heels, his arms hanging. The

bright and sudden summer! Ploughing, seeding, the harvesting—
what a pity it was. He paused, what was a pity? he only noticed
it now!

Something moved in the box, breathing and kicking away from
him; he uttered a cry, more grunt than cry, and the something in
the box struck back with hard drumming fright.

The tailor bent forward, hands out, then he shoved them in be-
tween the slats of the box opening, shutting them tight! tight!
tighter! The terrible, the really terrible thing, the creature did not
squeal, wail, cry: it panted, as if the wind were blunt; it thrashed its
life, the frightful scuffling of the overwhelmed, in the last trifling
enormity.

The tailor got to his feet, backing away from what he had done;
he backed into the water pail, and turning, plunged his hands in.
He beat the water, casting the waves up into his face with the
heels of his hands. Then he went straight for the door and opened
it. Addie fell face in, she had been standing straight up against the
panel, her hands behind her back.

She righted herself without excuse or apology; she could tell by
his face that he had done something enormous for the first time
in his life, and without any doubt, for her. She came close to him,
as she had to the door, her arms behind her. "What have you
done?" she said.

"I—I have killed—I think I have killed—"

"Where? What?" She moved away from him, looking into the
corner at the box. "That!" She began to laugh, harsh, back-bend-
ing laughter.

"Take it or leave it!" he shouted, and she stopped, her mouth
open. She stooped and lifted up the small grey rabbit. She placed
it on the table; then she came to Amietiev and wound her arms
around him. "Come," she said. "Comb your hair."

She was afraid of him, there was something strange about his
mouth swinging slightly sidewise. She was afraid of his walk, loud
and flat. She pushed him toward the door. He placed one foot after

the other, with a precision that brought the heel down first, the toe following. . . .

"Where are you going?"

He did not seem to know where he was, he had forgotten her. He was shaking, his head straight up, his heart wringing wet.

The Doctors

"We have fashioned ourselves against the Day of Judgement."
This remark was made by Dr. Katrina Silverstaff at the oddest
moments, seeming without relevance to anything at all, as one
might sigh "Be still." Often she said it to herself. She thought
it when on her way home, walking along the east wall of the river,
dangling from her finger the loop of string about the box of seed-
cakes she always brought home for tea; but she always stopped to
lean over the wall to watch the river barges, heavy with bright
brick, moving off to the Islands.

Dr. Katrina and her husband Dr. Otto, had been students in the
same *gymnasium* at Freiburg-im-Breisgau. Both had started out
for a doctorate in gynecology. Otto Silverstaff made it, as they
say, but Katrina lost her way somewhere in vivisection, behaving
as though she were aware of an impudence. Otto waited to see
what she would do. She dropped out of class and was seen sitting
in the park, bent forward, holding Otto's cane before her, its
golden knob in both hands, her elbows braced on her legs, slowly

poking the fallen leaves. She never recovered her gaiety. She
married Otto but did not seem to know *when*; she knew why—
she loved him—but he evaded her, by being in the stream of time;
by being absolutely *daily*.

They came to America in the early twenties and were instantly
enjoyed by the citizens of Second Avenue. The people liked them,
they were trustworthy, they were durable; Doctor Katrina was
useful to animal and birds, and Doctor Otto was, in his whole
dedicated round little body, a man of fervour, who moved about
any emergency with no dangling parts, aside from the rubber reins
of his stethoscope. When he rapped his knuckles on a proffered
back, he came around the shoulder with bulging eyes and tense
mouth, pronouncing verdict in heavy gusts of hope, licorice and
carbolic acid.

The doctors' name-plates stood side by side in the small tiled
entry, and side by side (like people in a Dutch painting) the doctors
sat at their table facing the window. The first day was the day she
first remarked, "We have fashioned ourselves against the Day of
Judgement." A globe of the world was between them and at his
side a weighing machine. He had been idly pushing the balancing
arm on its rusting teeth when she began speaking, and when she
finished abruptly he stopped, regarding her with a mild expression.
He was inordinately pleased with her; she was "sea water" and
"impersonal fortitude," neither asking for nor needing attention.
She was compact of dedicated merit, engaged in a mapped territory
of abstraction, an excellently arranged encounter with estrange-
ment; in short she was to Otto incomprehensible, like a decision
in chess, she could move to anything but whatever move, it ap-
peared to the doctor, would be by the rules of that ancient game.

The doctors had been in office hardly more than a year when
their first child was born, a girl, and in the year following a boy;
then no more children.

Now as Doctor Otto had always considered himself a liberal
in the earlier saner sense of the word (as he would explain later,
sitting with his neighbors in the Hungarian grill, his wife beside

him), he found nothing strange in his wife's abstraction, her withdrawal, her silence, particularly if there was a xylophone, and a girl dancing on her boot's pivot, in the pungent air of the turning spit. Katrina had always been careful of music, note for note she could be said to have "attended." She collected books on comparative religions, too, and began learning Hebrew. He said to everybody, "So? are we not citizens of *anything*?"

Thus their life went into its tenth year. The girl had taken up dancing lessons, and the boy (wearing spectacles) was engrossed in insects. Then something happened that was quite extraordinary.

One day Doctor Katrina had opened the door to the ring of a travelling peddlar of books. As a rule she had no patience with such fellows, and with a sharp "No thank you!" would dismiss them. But this time she paused, the doorknob in her hand, and looked at a man who gave his name as Rodkin. He said that he was going all through that part of the city. He said that he had just missed it last year when he was selling Carlyle's *French Revolution*; this time however he was selling the Bible. Standing aside, Doctor Katrina let him pass. Evidently surprised, he did pass and stood in the hall.

"We will go into the waiting room," she said. "My husband is in consultation and must not be disturbed." He said, "Yes, of course, I see." Though he did not see anything.

The waiting room was empty, dark and damp, like an acre risen from the sea. Doctor Katrina reached up and turned on a solitary light, which poured down its swinging arc upon the faded carpet.

The peddlar, a slight pale man with an uncurling flaxen beard, more like the beard of an animal than of a man, and with a shock of the same, almost white hair, hanging straight down from his crown, was—light eyes and all—hardly menacing; he was so colourless as to seem ghostly.

Doctor Katrina said, "We must talk about religion."

He was startled and asked why.

"Because," she said, "no one remembers it."

He did not answer until she told him to sit down, and he sat down, crossing his knees; then he said, "So?"

She sat opposite, her head slightly turned, apparently deliberating. Then she said, "I must have religion become out of the reach of the *few*; I mean out of reach *for* a few; something impossible again; to find again."

"*Become?*" he repeated, "that's a queer word."

"It is the only possible word," she said with irritation, "because, at the moment, religion is claimed by too many."

He ran a small hand through his beard. "Well, yes," he answered, "I see."

"No, you don't!" she rapped out sharply. "Let us come to the point. For me everything is too arranged. I'm not saying this because I need your help. I shall never need your help." She stared straight at him. "Understand that from the beginning."

"Beginning," he repeated in a loud voice.

"From the beginning, right from the start. Not help, *hindrance*."

"Accomplish what, Madame?" He took his hand away from his beard and lowered his left arm, dropping his books.

"That is my affair," she said, "it has nothing to do with you; you are only the means."

"So, so," he said. "The means."

A tremour ran off into her cheek, like a grimace of pain. "You can do nothing, not as a person." She stood up. "I must do it all. No!" she said, raising both hands, catching the ends of her shoulder scarf in a gesture of anger and pride, though he had not moved, "I shall be your mistress." She let her hands fall into the scarf's folds. "But," she added, "do not intrude. Tomorrow you will come to see me, that is enough; that is all." And with this "all" the little peddlar felt fear quite foreign to him.

However he came the next day, fumbling, bowing, stumbling. She would not see him. She sent word by the maid that she did not need him, and he went away abashed. He came again the day following, only to be told that Doctor Katrina Silverstaff was not in. The following Sunday she was.

She was quiet, almost gentle, as if she was preparing him for a disappointment, and he listened. "I have deliberately removed remorse from the forbidden; I hope you understand."

He said "Yes" and understood nothing.

She continued inexorably: "There will be no thorns for you. You will miss the thorns but do not presume to show it in my presence." Seeing his terror, she added: "And I do not permit you to suffer while I am in the room." Slowly and precisely she began unfastening her brooch. "I dislike all spiritual decay."

"Oh, oh!" he said under his breath.

"It is the will," she said, "that must attain complete estrangement."

Without expecting to, he barked out, "I expect so."

She was silent, thinking, and he could not help himself, he heard his voice saying, "I want to suffer!"

She whirled around. "Not in my house."

"I will follow you through the world."

"I shall not miss you."

He said, "What will you do?"

"Does one destroy oneself when one is utterly disinterested?"

"I don't know."

Presently she said: "I love my husband. I want you to know that. It has nothing to do with this, still I want you to know it. I am *pleased* with him, and very proud."

"Yes, yes," Rodkin said, and began shaking again; his hand on the bed post set the brasses ringing.

"There is something in me that is mournful because it is being."

He did not answer; he was crying.

"There's another thing," she said with harshness, "that I insist on—that you will not insult me by your attention while you are in the room."

He tried to stop his tears, and he tried to comprehend what was happening.

"You see," she continued, "some people drink poison, some take the knife, others drown. I take you."

In the dawn, sitting up, she asked him if he would smoke, and lit him a cigarette. After that she withdrew into herself, sitting on the edge of the mahogany board, her hands in her lap.

Unfortunately there was now ease in Rodkin. He turned in bed, drawing his feet under his haunches, crossed, smoking slowly, carefully.

"Does one regret?"

Doctor Katrina did not answer, she did not move, she did not seem to have heard him.

"You frightened me last night," he said, pushing his heels out and lying on his back. "Last night I almost became somebody."

There was still silence.

He began quoting from his Bible: "Shall the beasts of the field, the birds of the air forsake thee?" He added, "Shall any man forsake thee?"

Katrina Silverstaff remained as she was, but something under her cheek quivered.

The dawn broke, the street lamps went out, a milk cart rattled across the cobbles and into the dark of a side street.

"One. One out of many . . . *the* one."

Still she said nothing and he put his cigarette out, breathing with difficulty. He was beginning to shiver; he rolled over and up, drawing on his clothes.

"When shall I see you again?" A cold sweat broke out over him, his hands shook. "Tomorrow?" He tried to come toward her, but he found himself at the door. "I'm nothing, nobody—" he turned toward her, bent slightly, as though he wished to kiss her, but no move helped him. "You are taking everything away. I can't feel— I don't suffer, nothing you know—I can't—" He tried to look at her. After a long time he succeeded.

He saw that she did not know he was in the room.

Then something like terror entered him, and with soft and cunning grasp, he turned the handle of the door and was gone.

A few days later, at dusk, his heart the heart of a dog, he came into the street of the doctors and looked at the house.

A single length of crêpe, bowed, hung at the door.

From that day he began to drink heavily. He became quite a nuisance in the cafés of the quarter, and once, when he saw Doctor Otto Silverstaff sitting alone in a corner with his two children, he laughed a loud laugh and burst into tears.

Spillway

Behind two spanking horses, in the heat of noon, rode Julie Anspacher. The air was full of the sound of windlasses and well water, and full too of the perfumed spindrift of flowers, and Julie stared as the road turned into the remembered distance.

The driver, an old Scandinavian and a friend of the family, who knew exactly two folk tales, one having to do with a partridge, the other with a woman, sat stiffly on his box, holding the reins slack over the sleek-rumped mares; he was whistling the score of the story about the partridge, rocking slowly on his sturdy base, and drifting back with the tune came the strong herb-like odour of hide, smarting under straining leather.

The horses began ascending the hill, moving their ears, racking down their necks. Reaching the ridge, they bounded forward in a whirl of sparks and dust. The driver, still rigid, still whistling, taking in rein in a last flourish, raised the whipstock high in the air, setting it smartly into its socket. In a deep pitched voice he said, "It's some time since we have seen you, Mrs. Anspacher."

Julie raised her long face from her collar and nodded.

"Yes," she said shortly, and frowned.

"Your husband has gathered in the corn already, and the orchards are hanging heavy."

"Are they?" She tried to recall how many trees were of apple and pear.

The driver changed hands of the reins, turned around: "It's good to see you again, Mrs. Anspacher." He said it so simply, with such hearty pleasure, that Julie laughed outright.

"Is it," she answered, then checked herself, fixing her angry eyes straight ahead.

The child sitting at her side, loose limbed from excessive youth, lifted her face up, on which a small aquiline nose perched with comic boldness. She half held, half dropped an old fashioned ermine muff, the tails of which stuck out in all directions. She looked excited.

"You remember Mrs. Berling?" the driver went on. "She married again."

"Did she?"

"Yes, Ma'am, she did."

He began to tell her of a vacancy in the office for outgoing mails, taken by her husband's nephew.

"Corruption!" she snorted.

The child started, then looked quickly away as children do when they expect something and do not understand what. The driver brought the whip down on the horses, left and right; a line of heavy froth appeared along the edges of the trappings.

"You were saying, Mrs. Anspacher?"

"I was saying nothing. I said, all is lost from the beginning, if we only knew it—always."

The child looked up at her, then down into her muff.

"Ann," said Julie Anspacher suddenly, lifting the muff away from the child. "Did you ever see such big horses before?"

The child turned her head with brightness and bending down tried to see between the driver's arms. She smiled.

"Are they yours?" she whispered.

"You don't have to whisper," Julie said. She took a deep breath, stretching the silk of her shirtwaist across her breasts. "And no, they are not mine, but we have two—bigger—blacker—"

"Can I see them?"

"Of course you will see them—don't be ridiculous!"

The child shrank into herself, clutching nervously at her muff. Julie Anspacher returned to her reflections.

It was almost five years since Mrs. Anspacher had been home. Five years before, in just such an autumn, the doctors had given her six months to live . . . one lung gone, the other going. They sometimes call it the 'white death,' sometimes the 'love disease.' She coughed a little, remembering, and the child at her side coughed too, as if in echo, and the driver, puckering his forehead, reflected that Mrs. Anspacher was not cured.

She was thirty-nine; she should have died at thirty-four. In those five years of grace her husband Paytor had seen her five times, coming in over fourteen hours of rail, at Christmas tide. He cursed the doctors, called them fools, and each time asked her when she was coming home.

The house appeared, dull white against locust trees. Smoke, the lazy smoke that rises in the autumn in a straight column, rose up into an empty sky as the driver pulled the horses in, their foaming jaws gagging at the bit. Julie Anspacher jumped the side of the carriage at a bound, the short modish tails of her jacket dancing. She turned around, thrusting her black gloved hands under the child, lifting her to the path. A dog barked somewhere as they turned in at the gate.

A maid in a dust cap put her head out of a window, clucked, drew it in and slammed the sash, and Paytor with slow deliberate steps moved toward his wife and child across the gravel.

He was a man of middle height with a close cropped beard that ended in a gray wedge on his chin. He was sturdy, pompous, and walked with his knees out, giving him a rocking, dependable gait;

he had grave eyes and a firm mouth. He was slightly surprised. He raised the apricot coloured veil that hid Julie's face, and leaning, kissed her on both cheeks.

"And where does the child come from?" he inquired, touching the little girl's chin.

"Come along, don't be ridiculous," Julie said impatiently, and swept on toward the house.

He hurried after her. "I am so glad to see you," he said, trying to keep up with her long swinging stride that all but lifted the child off her feet in a trotting stumble.

"Tell me what the doctors said—cured?"

There was happiness in his voice as he went on: "Not that I really care *what* they think—I always predicted a ripe old age for you, didn't I? What were the doctors' methods in regard to Marie Baskirtseff, I ask you? They locked her up in a dark room with all the windows shut—and so of course she died—that was the method then; now it's Koch's tuberculin—and that's all nonsense too. It's good fresh air does the trick."

"It has worked for some people," she said, going ahead of him into the living room. "There was one boy there—well, of that— later. Will you have someone put Ann to bed—the trip was hard for her—see how sleepy she is. Run along, Ann," she added, pushing her slightly but gently toward the maid. When they disappeared she stood looking about her, taking off her hat.

"I'm glad you took down the crystals—I always hated crystals—" She moved to the window.

"I didn't, the roof fell in—just after my last visit to you in December. You're looking splendid, Julie." He coloured. "I'm so pleased, glad you know, awfully glad. I was beginning to think— well, not that doctors *know* anything—but it has been so long—" He tried to laugh, thought better of it, and stammered into "It's a drop here of about fifteen hundred feet—but your heart—that is good—it always was."

"What do you know about my heart?" Julie said angrily. "You don't know what you are talking about. Now the child—"

"Yes, well?"

"Her name is Ann," she finished sulkily.

"A sweet name—it was your mother's. Whose is she?"

"Oh, good heavens!" Julie cried, moving around the room on the far side of the furniture. "Mine, mine, mine of course! whose would she be if not mine?"

He looked at her. "Yours? why Julie, how absurd!" All the colour had drained from his face.

"I know—we've got to talk it over—it's all got to be arranged, it's terrible; but she is nice, a bright child, a good child."

"What in the world is all this about?" he demanded, stopping in front of her. "What are you in this mood for—what have I done?"

"Good heavens, what have *you* done! What a ridiculous man you are. Nothing of course, absolutely nothing!" She waved her arm. "That's not it; why do you bring yourself in? I'm not blaming you, I'm not asking to be forgiven. I've been on my knees, I've beaten my head against the ground, I've abased myself, but—" she added in a terrible voice, "it's not low enough, the ground is not low enough; to bend down is not enough, to beg forgiveness is not enough, to receive?—it would not be enough. There just isn't the right kind of misery in the world for me to suffer, nor the right kind of pity for you to feel; there isn't a word in the world to heal me; penance cannot undo me—it is a thing beyond the end of everything—it's suffering without a consummation, it's like insufficient sleep; it's like anything that is without proportion. I am not asking for anything at all, because there is nothing that can be given or got—how primitive to be able to receive—"

"But Julie—"

"No, no, it's not that," she said roughly, tears swimming in her eyes, "of course I love you. But think of this: me, a danger to everyone—excepting those like myself—in the same sickness, and expecting to die: fearful, completely involved in a problem affecting a handful of humanity—filled with fever and lust—not a self-willed lust at all, a matter of heat. And frightened, frightened! and nothing coming after, no matter what you do, nothing at all, nothing at all but death—and one goes on—it goes on—then the child—and life, hers, probably, for a time—"

"So."

"So I couldn't tell you. I thought, I'll die next month, no one will ever see anything of any of us in no time now. Still, all in all, and say what I like, I didn't want to go—and I *did*—well, you know what I mean. Then her father died—they say her lungs are weak—death perpetuating itself—queer, isn't it—and the doctors—" She swung around: "You're right, they lied to me, and I lived through—all the way."

He had turned away from her.

"The real, the proper idea is," she said in a pained voice, "—is design, a thing should make a design; torment should have some meaning. I did not want to go beyond you, or to have anything beyond you—that was not the idea, not the idea at all. I thought there was to be no more me. I wanted to leave nothing behind but you, only you. You must believe this or I can't bear it . . . and still," she continued, walking around the room impatiently, "there was a sort of hysterical joy in it too. I thought, if Paytor has perception, that strange other 'something,' that must be at the center of everything (or there wouldn't be such a sensuous desire for it), that something secret that is so near us all at times, that it is all but obscene—well, I thought, if Paytor has this (and mind you, I knew all the time that you didn't have it), this 'grace,' I thought, well, then he will understand. Then at such times I would say to myself, after you had been gone a long time, *now* he has the answer, at this very moment, at precisely ten-thirty of the clock, if I could be with him *now* he would say to me, 'I see.' But as soon as I had the timetable in my hand, to look up the train you would be on, I knew there was no such feeling in your heart—nothing at all."

"Don't you feel horror?" he asked in a loud voice.

"No, I don't feel horror—horror must include conflict, and I have none; I am alien to life, I am lost in still water."

"Have you a religion, Julie?" he asked her, still in the same loud voice, as if he were addressing some one a long way off.

"I don't know, I think so, but I am not sure. I've tried to believe in something external and enveloping, to carry me away, beyond—that's what we demand of our faiths, isn't it? It won't do, I lose it; I come back again to the idea that there is something more fitting than release."

He put his head in his hands. "You know," he said, "I've always thought that a woman, because she *can* have children, ought to know everything. The very fact that a woman can do so preposterous a thing as have a child ought to give her prophecy."

She coughed, her handkerchief before her face; she laughed with sharp brightness. "One learns to be careful about death, but never, never about—" She didn't finish but stared straight before her.

"Why did you bring the child here, why did you return at all then, after so long a time?—it's so dreadfully mixed up."

"I don't know. Perhaps because there is a right and a wrong, a good and an evil, and I had to find out. If there is such a thing as 'everlasting mercy' I wanted to find out about that. There's such an unfamiliar taste to Christian mercy, an alien sort of intimacy—" She had a way of lifting the side of her face, closing her eyes. "I thought, Paytor may know—"

"Know what?"

"Division. I thought, he will be able to divide me against myself. Personally I don't feel divided; I seem to be a sane and balanced whole, but hopelessly mixed. So I said to myself, Paytor will see where the design divides and departs, though all the time I was making no bargain, I wasn't thinking of any system—well, in other words, I wanted to be set *wrong*. Do you understand?"

"No," he said in the same loud voice, "and what's more, you yourself must know what you have done to me. You have turned everything upside down. Oh, I won't say betrayed me—it's much less than that, and more, it's what most of us do, we betray circumstances, we don't hold on. Well," he said sharply, "I can't do anything for you, I can't do anything at all; I'm sorry, I'm very sorry, but there it is." He was grimacing and twitching his shoulders.

"The child has it too," Julie Anspacher said, looking up at him. "I shall die soon. It's ridiculous," she added, the tears streaming down her face. "You are strong, you always were, and so was your family before you—not one of them in their graves before ninety— it's all wrong—it's quite ridiculous!"

"I don't know, perhaps it's not ridiculous; one must be careful not to come too hastily to a conclusion." He began searching for his pipe. "Only you must know yourself, Julie, how I torment my-self, if it's a big enough thing, for days, years. Why? Because I come to conclusions instantly, and then have to fight to destroy them!" He seemed a little pompous now. "You see," he added, "I'm human, but frugal. Perhaps I'll be able to tell you something later—give you a beginning at least. Later." He turned, holding his pipe in the cup of his hand, and left the room, closing the door behind him. She heard him climbing the stairs, the hard oak steps that went up into the shooting loft, where he practiced aim on the concentric circles of his targets.

Darkness was closing in, it was eating away the bushes and the barn, and it rolled in the odours of the orchard. Julie leaned on her hand by the casement edge and listened. She could hear far off the faint sound of dogs, the brook running down the moun-tain, and she thought, water in the hand has no voice, but it really roars coming over the falls. It sings over small stones in brooks, but it only tastes of water when it's caught, struggling and running away in the hands. A sense of tears came into her eyes, but they did not fall. Sentimental memories of child-hood, she said to herself, which had sometimes been fearful and had strong connections with fishing and skating and the day they had made her kiss the cheek of their dead priest—*Qui habitare facit sterilem—matrem filiorum laetantem*—then *Gloria Patri*— that had made her cry with a strange backward grief that was swallowed, because in touching his cheek she kissed aggressive passivity, entire and cold.

She wondered and wandered in her mind. She could hear Paytor walking on the thin boards above, she could smell the smoke of his tobacco, she could hear him slashing the cocks of his guns.

Mechanically she went over to the chest in the corner; it was decorated with snow scenes. She lifted the lid. She turned over the upper layer of old laces and shawls until she came to a shirt-waist of striped taffeta . . . the one she had worn years ago, it had been her mother's. She stopped. The child? Paytor didn't seem to like the child. "Ridiculous!" she said out loud. "She is quiet, good, gentle. What more does he want?" but no, that wasn't enough now. She removed her gloves—why hadn't she done that at once? Perhaps she had made a mistake in coming back. Paytor was strong, all his family had been strong like that before him, and she was ill and coughing. And Ann, she herself? She had made a mistake in coming back. She went toward the stairs to call Paytor and tell him about it, pinning up her veil as she went. Time drew out. But no, that wasn't the answer, that wasn't the right idea.

The pendulum of the wooden clock on the mantel above the fireplace pulled time back and forth with heavy ease, and Julie now at the window nodded without sleep—long grotesque dreams came up to her, held themselves against her, dispersed and rolled in again. Somewhere Ann coughed in her sleep; Julie Anspacher coughed also, holding her handkerchief to her face. She could hear feet walking back and forth, back and forth, and the smell of tobacco growing less faint.

What could she do, for God's sake, what was there that she could do? If only she had not this habit of fighting death. She shook her head. Death was past knowing and one must be certain of something else first. "If only I had the power to feel what I should feel, but I've stood so much so long, there is not too long, that's the tragedy . . . the interminable discipline of learn-ing to stand everything." She thought, "If only Paytor will give me time, I'll get around to it." Then it seemed that something must happen. "If only I could think of the right word before it happens," she said to herself. She said it over. "Because I am cold I can't think. I'll think soon. I'll take my jacket off, put on my coat . . ."

She got up, running her hand along the wall. Where was it? Had she left it on the chair? "I can't think of the word," she said, to keep her mind on something.

She turned around. All his family . . . long lives . . . "and me too, me too," she murmured. She became dizzy. "It's because I must get on my knees. But it isn't low enough," she contradicted herself, "but if I put my head down, way down—down, down, down, down . . ." She heard a shot. "He has quick warm blood—"

Her forehead had not quite touched the boards, now it touched them, but she got up immediately, stumbling over her dress.

The Passion

Every afternoon at four thirty, excepting Thursday, a smart carriage moved with measured excellence through the Bois, drawn by two bays in shining patent leather blinkers embellished with silver R's, the docked tails rising proudly above well-stitched immaculate cruppers.

In this carriage, with its half closed curtains, sat the princess Frederica Rholinghausen erect, in the dead center of a lace medallioned cushion, with unmoving head. Behind the tight drawn veiling that webbed the flaring crown of a Leghorn hat, burdened with ribbons and roses, the imperturbable face was no longer rouged to heighten the contours but to limn a noble emaciation. The tall figure with its high shoulders, like delicate flying buttresses, was encased in gray moiré, the thin knees dropping the stiff excess in two sharp points, like the corners of a candy box. No pearl in the dog-collar shook between the dipping blue of the veins, nor did the light radiance on the long nails deviate from their custom by any personal movement, nor the buckles on the shoes, nor the piercing eyes. The whole glitter and attention was turned by the turning of the coach, as the horses, passing the lake, startled the swans who shook their clattering complaint across the waters. The strollers under the trees (when the carriage brought the eye upon them) seemed tiny and trapped, for the great branchless boles of the trees made straight barred shadows. Thus this scented case moved through the day.

The coachman, sitting up on the box with his son, was breaking in the young man for a life of driving, in which the old man would have no part. On every Thursday when the princess was at home, the empty carriage was driven at a smart rocking pace, and every Thursday the Allée de Longchamp rang with the old man's shouts of *"Eh, doucement, doucement!"*

The family retainers, now only five, worked with as little effort as was compatible with a slowing routine. Every morning the books in the library, with their white kid bindings and faded coat-of-arms, were dusted, and every afternoon, when the sun wasn't too blazing, the curtains in the conservatoire were drawn, but as the princess moved from room to room less every year, one chamber was closed for good every twelvemonth.

In the kitchen, regular as the clock, the cook whipped up the whites of three eggs with rum and sugar for the evening soufflé, and just as regularly the gardener watered the plants at nightfall, as though promoted, for in the still splendour of the chateau gardens he drank the dark cumbersome majesty, as of a Versailles.

The lap-dog, long since too old to get up from her basket of ruffled chintz, slept heavily, a mass of white fur, unmarked of limb or feature, save for the line of dark hair that placed the eyelids, and the moist down-drooping point below the chin.

On her Thursdays the princess arose at three, dressing herself before a long oak stand, shining with faceted bottles. She had been nearly six feet tall; now she had waned but little under it. There were cut flowers where she went, but she did not tend them. The scenes of the chase, hanging on the wall between the tall oak

chairs (she had painted them when she was young) were feathered
with dust and out of mind. The spinet in the corner, covered with
a yellow satin throw, embroidered by her own hand, was crum-
bling along the bevel of the lid, signifying silence of half a century.
The scores, lying one above the other, were for soprano. One was
open at *Liebes-lied*. The only object to have seen recent service
was the candelabrum, the candles half burnt upon their spikes,
for the princess read into the night.

There were only two portraits, they were in the dining hall;
one, her father, in uniform, standing beside a table, his plumed hat
in his hand, his hand on the hilt of a sword, his spurred heels lost
in the deep pile of a rug. The other, her mother, seated on a
garden bench dressed in hunter-green, a little mannish hat tilted to
one side. In one fist she held a cascade of ruffles above high riding
boots. A baroque case held miniatures of brothers and cousins;
rosy cheeked, moon haired, sexless children smiling among the
bric-a-brac; fans, coins, seals, porcelain platters (fired with eagles),
and, incongruously, a statuette of a lady looking down through the
film of her night-shift at her colourless breasts.

Sometimes it rained, splashing drops on the long French win-
dows, the reflection stormed in the mirrors. Sometimes the sun
struck a crystal, which in turn flung a cold wing of fire upon the
ceiling.

In short, the princess was very old. Now it is said that the old
cannot approach the grave without fearful apprehension or re-
ligious rite. The princess did. She was in the hand of an high
decay: she was *sèche*, but living on the last suppuration of her will.

Sometimes, not often, but sometimes she laughed with the sharp-
ness of something remembered inappropriately, and laughter in an
ancient is troubling because inclement and isolated. At times,
raising her eyeglasses at the uncompromising moment, she had sur-
prisingly the air of a *gallant*, a *bon-vivant*—but there was a wash
of blue in her flesh that spoke of the acceptance of mortality. She
never spoke of the spirit.

Now and again two rusty female aunts called, accompanied by

tottering companions, equally palsied and broken, who neverthe-
less managed to retrieve fallen objects, mislaid spectacles, and
crumbled cake—patiently bending and unbending, their breast
watches swinging from silver hooks.

Sometimes an only nephew, a "scamp," not too childish in his
accomplishments, impudent and self-absolved, strolled in—after
stabling his horse—walking with legs well apart, slapping his
puttees with the loop of his crop, swaggering the length of the
room, promising "deathless devotion," holding out, at arm's length,
a sturdy zinnia. Then collapsing into a chair with the indifference
handed on to him in courtly femur and fibula, in unhampered
bone and unearned increment, he sipped at the frail tea cup and,
biting wide crescents in the thin buttered bread, stared out into
the fields with a cold and calculating eye; and when the princess
left the room, he really didn't notice it.

Kurt Anders, a Polish officer, of some vaguely remembered regi-
ment, who almost never appeared in uniform, was the chiefest
among her callers. Once a month, on the second Thursday, for
some thirty years, he had presented himself, drinking delicately
from the same china as though he were not a giant, well trussed
and top heavy. Two long folds spread away from the long dipping
nose under which his mouth, too small and flat for the wide teeth,
pursued the cup. He spoke with a marked accent.

He was a widower. He collected plate and early editions, firearms
and stamps. He was also devoted to the seventeenth century. He
wore puce gloves which, when he rolled them down in one true
stroke, sent a faint odour of violet into the room. He had the
bearing of one who had abetted license; he looked as though he
had eaten everything: but though elegant in his person, there was
something about not far from the stool.

Sometimes calling a little early, he would go off to the stables
where the two bays, now the only horses, stamped and were curried,
and where a pleasing brawl of bitches, weighed down with the
season's puppies, fawned and snapped. Anders would stoop to

stroke their muzzles, pulling at their leather collars, pausing long enough to balance their tails.

This man, whose history was said to have been both *éblouissant* and dark, and who, the gossips said, had most certainly disappointed his family in youth, was without doubt a figure of *scandale*. He had been much too fond of the *demimonde*. He enjoyed any great man's "favourite". He had a taste for all who would have to be "forgiven." He had been much in the company of a "darling" of the academy, scion of the house of Valois, the one they called "L'Infidèle"—or so he said—who, though passionately "modern" could not keep away from museum or wax-work, particularly the roped-off sections housing royal equipages, or the now historically safe beds of lost kings.

The truth? Anders enjoyed the manoeuvre, the perfected "leap," the trick pulled off, and the general sane weather. Imposing, high stomached, spatted, gloved, he strolled the Luxembourg, watching the leaves falling on the statues of dead queens, the toy boats on the pond, the bows bobbing on the backsides of little girls, the people sitting and saying nothing. If one is someday to enjoy paradise? Then the one irreparable loss is any park in Paris that one can no longer visit.

Later, coming into the music room, stripping off his gloves, he would speak of the dogs, of the races, of the autumn, of the air in relation to the autumn and the air of other countries; he would speak in praise of this or that cathedral, this or that drama. Sometimes he set up before the princess a rare etching that he hoped she would like, or he would walk up and down before her until she noticed the pockets of his coat into which he had stuck small flowers. Sometimes he forgot horses and dogs, etchings and autumns, and would concentrate on the use and the decline of the rapier and of the merit of the high-boot for the actor. The princess would quote Schiller. Then Anders would plunge into the uses of the fool in Shakespeare, turning and turning a thin gold band on his little finger (winking with a ruby as tender as water) weighing a point the princess had made regarding the impracticability of maintaining tradition now that every man was his own fool. They might get off onto literature in general and she would ask if he were well versed in the poetry of Britain. He would answer that Chaucer caught him and was a devil of a fellow to shake off. She would smile, inquire gravely, "Why shake?" and then drift off to a discussion of painting and how it had left the home *genre* when the Dutch gave way to the English. They would argue for and against indoor and outdoor subjects for oils; and now and then the whole argument would turn off to a suggested outing, to view a fine piece of Spanish furniture. Sometimes he left the etching.

Of course everyone assumed the princess the one true passion of his life. It was taken for granted that, but for a rupture suffered in the Franco-Prussian war, he would have claimed her for bride. Others were just as certain that the princess was far too niggardly to share the half of her bed. The rest insisted that they had been lovers in youth and were now as good as husband and wife. All of this was nonsense. They were pages in an old volume, brought together by the closing of the book.

On the last call but one there had been something of a strain. He had mentioned Gesualdo and the sorrows of the assassin; and from the assassin to the passion of Monteverdi 'at the tomb of the beloved.'

"The 'walking straight up to dreadfulness,'" he said, "that is love."

He stopped directly in front of her as he spoke, leaning toward her to see how she did, and she, bent back and peering, said, "The last attendant on an old woman is always an 'incurable'." She set her tea cup down with a slight trembling of the hand, then added with mordant acerbity, "But—if a little light man with a beard had said 'I love you,' I should have believed in God."

He called only once after that, and only once was the princess seen riding in the Bois, a mist behind a tight drawn veil. Shortly after, she did not live.

The Antiphon

TO THE MEMORY OF EDWIN MUIR

Cautionary Note

As a misreading of *The Antiphon* is not impossible, it might be
well to keep in mind that this play is more than merely literal; that
(through Act I) Jack is breezy, not raffish; that Augusta is in person
stark and spare, and in spirit harsh and timid by turns. Miranda,
though inured to ordeal, can rise to impassioned fury. But between
the two there is no whining; their familiarity is their estrangement,
their duel is in hiatus, their weapons tempered.

D.B.

PERSONS

The widow AUGUSTA BURLEY HOBBS
JONATHAN BURLEY, her brother
MIRANDA, her daughter
DUDLEY ⎫
⎬ her sons
ELISHA ⎭
'JACK BLOW', 'coachman'
Several travellers, on the way to port.

Time: During the war of 1939
Place: England, Burley Hall, in the township of Beewick, formerly a college of chantry priests, in the Burley family since the late seventeenth century.

Act One

To right and left, wide shallow steps leading to the gallery. Over the balustrade hang flags, gonfalons, bonnets, ribbons and all manner of stage costumes. Directly under the gallery, an arched doorway without a door. In the hall proper, a long table with a single settle facing front, at either end of which is set the half of a gryphon, once a car in a roundabout.

The table is laid in formal order, dominated by heavy candlesticks, a large china tureen, a brass curfew bell, and a battered gilt mardi-gras crown.

To the left, standing before a paneless Gothic window, a dressmaker's dummy, in regimentals, surrounded by music stands, horns, fiddles, guncases, bandboxes, masks, toys and broken statues, man and beast.

To the right, through the tumbled wall, country can be seen, and part of a ruined colonnade. In the aperture, back view, a grey baize donkey, sitting.

MIRANDA, *a tall woman in her late fifties, enters from the cloister. She has a distinguished but failing air, wearing an elegant but rusty costume, obviously of the theatre, a long cloak, buckled shoes and a dashing tricorne blowing with coq feathers. She favours her left side on a heavy headed cane.*

She is followed, at a respectful distance, by JACK BLOW, *a bearded fellow, of about the same age, wearing a patch. He is in high boots and long coachman's coat and carries a whip and creel. At his entrance he is holding his billycock straight up over his head, as though he expected applause from the gallery. His manner during this act is racy, mordant, clowning.*

MIRANDA

Here's a rip in nature; here's gross quiet,
Here's cloistered waste;
Here's rudeness once was home.

JACK

There's no circulation in the theme,
The very fad of being's stopped.

MIRANDA

The wall is chapped where once the altar stood,
The basin dry, the music-stands in dust.
Horn and fiddle . . .

JACK

Muted as *Missae pro Defunctis*.
What prank of caution brought you back again?
Can no man imp this one life out,
Becalmed in havoc, like a flag,
Dismissed but present?

MIRANDA

This field, this stay, this haunt of time, this mound,
This starting-post from which my mother ran . . .

JACK

It smells of hunting, like a widow's breath.

MIRANDA

Check well, Jack Blow, we leave it in the morning:
Then farewell this Benedictine shoe
That shod my mother's foot, and her dismay.

JACK

Truly. But where's your uncle Jonathan?
You said you came to kiss him fond farewell.
The scene is set but seems the actor gone.
No tither, weeper, wait or *cicerone*;
No beadle, bailiff, barrister, no clerk;
In short no audience at all.
My hands will have to be your clamour, lady.

MIRANDA

Not so fast. It's true the webbed commune
Trawls up a wrack one term was absolute;
Yet corruption in its deft deploy
Unbolts the caution, and the vesper mole
Trots down the wintry pavement of the prophet's head.
In the proud flesh of the vanished eye
Vainglory, like a standing pool,
Rejects the thirsty trades of paradise.
The world is cracked—and in the breach
My fathers mew.

JACK

Now that's a nip in zero that undoes me!
Who springs a trap, and it be not molested?

MIRANDA

When called his other name, whom heels the dog?
To what depths does one arise on hearing 'Love'?
This dated stumble, this running gig of days,
This dust that curries man and commons him—
This lichen bridled face of time . . .

JACK

Had Beewick not been on the way to port;
Had you not told me travellers afoot
Use Burley Hall these days for shelter,
I'd have said avoid it.

MIRANDA
Would you?

JACK
[*Rolling his bowler down from his crook'd elbow to his palm*]
Well, there perhaps you have me;
This being, after all, your darling England.

MIRANDA

This ruined address was once my mother's cot.
Here Augusta, that good woman, piped.
And if tradition and long tenancy,
In case however small be called the scale,
Keep and castle of the mind's dominion,
Say here upon a shield was diapered.
Tombs were her primers, cautions, sums;
Beewick her town, and Burley Hall her school.
Her spirit nested with the Tudor bat,
That sphincter rose that barnacled the groin
Of her hatched purpose; the very hub and rate
That kept the term of her diameter,
The very orbit of her inclination.

JACK
[*Rolling his hat back up his arm*]
Well!
Aspired to aristocracy and glory?

MIRANDA
She so leaned on royalty and legend
She replaced herself as adversary,
Till she faulted to oblivion,
And like a compass whirling without seat
Fell victim to a dial without hours—
Marriage to my father, and his folly.

JACK
I always said, there's not a pedestal
Won't shift its hero's bottom at some blow.
I myself, in my own boots, am fugitive.
There's nothing like destruction for an aim.
And here's its very pip.

MIRANDA
If that be so, good man, screw on this ruin:
As the jeweler his prying loupe debates,
Mark you the pomp and practice of the ant;
Do all the conflating burdens of the wind
Disperse her apt and current hurry?

JACK
                         No.

MIRANDA
If, say, this afternoon the earth should quake
Sending a thousand flaggings stark upright,
Would not the canted beetle stick his mark?

JACK

Would he?

MIRANDA

And on the dial's dislocated time
Wind up his purpose?

JACK
  Why, I think so.

MIRANDA

Yet here Augusta, my poor mother, tipped
The comely balance of her country state
To the staggered compass of barbarian—
My father, Titus Higby Hobbs of Salem—

JACK

She who once hung swinging on a gate . . .

MIRANDA

Boating the hedges with her open hand,
Peering down the lanes for visitors;
Striking back at springtime, like a kid
Hopping and skipping to the summer's day;
Bawling and baaing out her natural glee
With such an host of ignorant visions fed
She peeped about with gladness, just to hark
'Sleeper awake!' and ran on katydids.

JACK

An insect not indigenous—

MIRANDA

With that mistake you have the tragedy.
Harnessed to spring, and lisping on the bit,

A long wind playing out her cast of hair,
Hopping and singing went she, when in one
Scant scything instant was gaffed down,
Lying still as water in a stick
That carpenters do level with:
All backward in a flail of locks went to,
With cobalt eye in passion's clabber drowned,—
Holding a single flower upright.

JACK

God's mercy!

MIRANDA

Thus, puddled public as the stable-fly
Performing the tragic ballet on her back,
She swarmed the impacted seasons with offence,
And of that marriage pupped truncated grief,
As women must who mother discontent,
And any dream come short.

JACK

And you the arms and legs of it!

MIRANDA

Of that sprawl, three sons she leaned to fairly:
On me she cast the privy look of dogs
Who turn to quiz their droppings.
Yet in her hour, her either end being terror,
The one head on the other stared, and wept.

JACK
[*With a long whistle*]
What a ferocious travel is your mind!
How then do you find *this* term of silence?

MIRANDA

Most moved. It is not well to be so moved
In lost familiarity—
                    And I fear merchants.

JACK

Look—
Don't turn me roundabout, but tell me squarely
How did your father get here anyway?

MIRANDA

Grandmother brought him in, from Middletown,
And set him on her perch in Grosvenor Square.

JACK

[*With mock astonishment*]
Trotting up on culture, brief in hand,
His horse shot under him at forty-five degrees!
O the dreadful moves of vanity!

MIRANDA

Say less, Jack Blow, for knowing nothing of it.

JACK

I'd say more, for the very same default.
For who is wiser than the total stranger?
Have I not the picture of the man?
In every quarter of his disposition
Complete perfection sat!

MIRANDA

You talk too much, too much leave out.

JACK

In my mind's gallery he sits entire;
In tip-top belly-leather, watch-swag swinging

At his bulk, like ferry chains on docks;
Stickler for the freedom of the sexes.
Ranged behind his easy seated bum,
Fearfully detained, and standing up,
(You've told me he believed in Brigham Young)
His pack of 'wives' in Concord cameos,
Flushed out in tabby, chatelaines and bugles—
Their bustles riding them as close as jockeys—
Flanked by warming-pans, bassoons and bastards.

MIRANDA

One would almost say you knew the man.

JACK

I wander where men walk; remember, lady?
I found you, a pilgrim, in the way.

MIRANDA

I thank you for it, let that be enough:
Therefore, lock down the windows, shut the doors.

JACK

Pull up the walls, saw down the wind, scoop up the sea!
Strut back the bridge, lock up the stars and sky!
Lady, be not such a party to yourself;
Do not abuse your present expectation
With such an haggard look.
If you propose, by bolting up the air,
To manacle perdition—
    [*Humming*]
                        Hey then, 'Who
Passes by this road so late,'
Always gay?

MIRANDA

I've told you—I fear merchants.

JACK

Merchants, merchants, merchants!
Ten forty times you've muttered merchants!
What merchants? Moslems? traders
     [*Pulling at his chin*]
Stroking their abominable amber,
Greedy landlord to outchambered flies?
Or would it be
A Lama, swaddled up in buzzard grey,
Seeding a stopped watch of its hours?
Or something nearer home?

MIRANDA

Enough—enough.

JACK

     [*Finger to the side of his nose*]
Brothers? with their ticker tapes and totals?
Or worser yet perhaps, your widowed mother
Checking up on what is not her business?

MIRANDA

     [*Turning straight around upon him*]
Starve your tongue, Jack Blow, be still—
I fear brothers.

JACK

     [*Swinging his whip*]
But not your mother, what?
O meridian of ague, how you wane,
Your finger ring is tumbled to the joint.
Slow scampering time has picked the locks,
And of your credit thrown the key away!
Still you fare forward, hapless voyager.
I think you've told me something short.

MIRANDA

Assume the mischief.

JACK

Mischief Madame! I expect to be,
In this knock-about of general war,
Up to my neck in steeples; starting stoats,
Hens in hats, and sailing ships in lanes.
And by the edging off of custom, get me bit
By grounded gargoyles that once staled the sky
With rash Orion's water. Mischief lady?
I expect to see myopic conquerors
With pebbled monocles and rowel'd heels,
In a damned and horrid clutch of gluttony
Dredging the Seine of our inheritance.
Or dragging from the Tiber and the Thames
Cruppers, bridles, bits and casket handles,
Rocking-horses, sabres from the fair.
Trawling the Hellespont for log and legend
And all things whatsoever out of grasp.
But, to get us back to *terra firma*—

MIRANDA

Who *are* you, Jack Blow?

JACK

At the moment I've not the faintest notion.
As I was saying—

MIRANDA

[*Listening*] Psst! I hear something!

JACK

They say a snail from Caesar's grave
Crawled into Napoleon's snuff-box.

MIRANDA

Where are we, indeed, that we are only here?

JACK

Let us say that presently we haunt.
Would oiling thrushes get them through a sieve?
Nay, rigour does it. Who has a right to rigour?

MIRANDA

Miranda has.

JACK

Then go brace it, girl.

MIRANDA

I'll go to the back, and see what I may see.
Let no one in.

[*Exit*]

JACK

Let no one in? The very air is out!
Now there's one who's heavy with escape!
[*He goes up to inspect the table. He lifts the cover of the
tureen, sticking his finger in.*]
Bouillabaisse? That tussle of the sea?
Aii! Steep, and empty as the upper lip of Finnegan!
[*He replaces the cover nervously, sensing he is not alone*]
Ah, well, being October, and my shilling lean,
I'll thrive in vacancy—but yet—
[*The brothers appear,* DUDLEY *at the window,* ELISHA *on the
gallery, unseen, but sensed by* JACK]
I do not like a feast where dogs lie still.
[JACK *moves around to the head of the table and stands before
the winged half of the gryphon*]

I've seen a judge
Sitting in the credit of his chair,
So abandon justice that his ears
Stood, in abdication, on his head.
Yet did the astounded air gag up the verdict?
It did not.

[*Pretending a nonchalance he does not feel, sings, under his
breath*]

'Who passes by this road so late—'
They say soliloquy is out of fashion,
It being a kind of talking to your betters.

[*He climbs into the chair*]

But then what motion but betrays oneself?
Esau's heel trips every man his running.
But Jack—not running—disinherited?
Do I move under, like the pilot-fish?
Am I a cow-bird, shill, or Judas goat,
Gaited to walk on other people's pools
As the skating-fly who skips on sleeping water?
Or do I, by some private irritation
Set about to step on my own rope?
Do I unplot my head by plucking hairs?
Or throw my lines away between my teeth?
Or do I so entirely slip from custom
That I sprawl in any place a king?
Why then, so be it.
If crouching on a throne's called sitting
I'll sit this out.

[*He stiffens, hearing a noise in the gallery, but does not turn*]

Do I hear the world approaching at my back?
Then though the world be present, I'll be proctor—

[*With increasing bravado, calling, like a barker*]

Hurry! Hurry! This way for the toymen:
This way, strutters, for the bearded lady;
The human skeleton, the fussy dwarf,

The fat girl with a planet in her lap;
The swallower of swords whose hidden lunge
Has not brought up his adversary yet!

[JONATHAN BURLEY, *an old man, and slight, enters from a door
under the gallery.* DUDLEY *and* ELISHA *dodge out of sight*]

BURLEY

Good evening.

JACK

The devil!

BURLEY

At your service.

JACK

Bless me, I thought I had advantage here.

BURLEY

A not uncommon misapprehension, sir.

JACK

Who was that woman?

BURLEY

What woman?

JACK

You must have seen her.
She went out as you came in.

BURLEY

My dear sir, many come and go.
Since the war, this hall has been a refuge
For every sort of person out of keys.

[*With hint of irony*]
In other words, a kind of Hampton Court
For gentle folk—afoot.

JACK

Is this not that sometime Burley seat
Since the early something seventeen,
That I hear referred to as 'The Abbey'?

BURLEY

Metaphorically.

JACK

College of chantry priests, more properly?

BURLEY

Benedictine.

JACK

Well then, good fellow, be not sly with me.
This being open house, be open also.
Was that not Miranda, late of Burley?

BURLEY

Late? She visits often. As you see,
She leaves her bonnets, flags and boxes.
She's fond of carnivals and all processions.
Might I ask you, did you come by horse?

JACK

Horse it was, and carriage. I hear Hobbs
(The Lady's father, whom you may recall)
Once rode horseback, through this very lobby;
Up one bank of steps and down the other,
Like a bloody Gascon. Did he?

BURLEY

He did indeed.

JACK

Well, I'm lesser—I tied mine to a tree.

BURLEY

Come, I'll give you a hand.

JACK

Hand? What for?

BURLEY

Surely you have luggage?

JACK

Why, yes, to a shaving—

BURLEY

Then come with me.

JACK

Wait a minute. Are you steward here?

BURLEY

In a way of speaking.

JACK

Long?

BURLEY

Very. All my life.

JACK

Then I'll tell you, this luggage that you mention,
Could it be, good sir, or could it not,

A beast-box, say, a doll's house, or an Ark?
 [*Aside*]
Now am I a well made fool!
 [*Aloud*]
An unholy covenant, a pact,
Sealed by the jaw-bone of an ass?

####### BURLEY

I do not follow you.

####### JACK
 [*Preparing to go with* BURLEY]
I follow *you*, but not now for the box.
I would my horse be foddered out of hand.
Starving, sir, as all the world is.

     [*Exeunt* BURLEY *and* JACK]

[DUDLEY *steps in through the window,* ELISHA *through the door.*
DUDLEY *is the elder of the two, very much the executive,
heavily set, chewing on a cigar, still wearing his hat and carry-
ing his umbrella, open. In his left hand he holds a large gold
watch, chain dangling. He meets* ELISHA *in the middle of the
hall,* ELISHA *diligently strewing almond shells as he comes.*
ELISHA *is younger and on the smarter side.*]

####### ELISHA
What do you make of it?

####### DUDLEY
 [*Turning slowly, in one piece*]
Not very much.
A beastly brawl in nature; broken Greeks;
An orchestra, decamped, and petticoats.
A blasted donkey, and a baby's ball.

[*He kicks it*]
In short, when I don't understand a thing—
I kick it!

ELISHA

[*Following the example, kicking a fallen statue*]
When I see a thing I cannot rate,
I rate it.
Why did mother speak Beewick so high?

DUDLEY

The strangers, who are they? The old one
And the younger hanky-panky fellow?
Somehow I failed to count on company,
Except sightseers, every other Friday.

ELISHA

Every other day, and not this day?

DUDLEY

Fox-earth, for sure.

ELISHA

And not a sign of brother Jeremy.
And just as well—he'd fits of clemency.

DUDLEY

Who is man that he should stand down wind?

ELISHA

That's not the point, the point is flying sister;
Somehow I had not counted on Miranda.
And that *was* Miranda, by her back, or was it?
Everything's a little out of context.

DUDLEY

Our deadly beloved vixen, in the flesh.
What more could two good brothers want?

ELISHA

Less of her self-possession—less of vagrancy
That in a wink she makes nine points of law.
There's nothing to be gained befriending that one:
So I say, let's have no sentiment.

DUDLEY

You've lost the stirrup—who said sentiment?
Could that old man be bribed?

ELISHA

[*Cracking a nut*]

                    I doubt it.
A saying has it, each man in the other's eye
Rides game, and hunting up-side-down
Grapples his spectre to his ghost;
You won't tear that commitment from itself.

DUDLEY

The old retainer all tied up in custom!
You know, sometimes it seems both Mother and Miranda
Are so entirely breezed up by the Mighty
That if they saw me backward in a mirror,
I'm not so sure what sort of beast they'd see.

ELISHA

Turn them to the wall, your mirror's blank.
What else, dear boy?

DUDLEY

What else? I often wonder.
Here am I, watchmaker to the world,

Master of a more than thousand souls,
Yet what of me does that leave when I whistle?

ELISHA

One thousand mice.

DUDLEY

Precisely. So I'll tell you what I wish:
I wish I'd built a mouse-trap big as God,
And caught myself—Master and Man.

ELISHA

Is it possible we're father's blasphemy?

DUDLEY

By my Jove—I wonder.

ELISHA

What, dear boy?

DUDLEY

Do all old women have a savage death?

ELISHA

Well, I always say that dog eats dog.
Why are you holding up that tell-tale watch?
Remember, we are marvellous clever fellows.

DUDLEY

Timing.

ELISHA

Timing? What time have you?

DUDLEY

Borrowed.
Mother will come in at any moment—
She can't sleep forever in the car—
And Miranda?

ELISHA

Plainly out of patron and of money.

DUDLEY

We'll never have so good a chance again;
Never, never such a barren spot,
Nor the lucky anonymity of war.
All old people die of death, remember?
We're strangers here; they people that estrangement.
Good, here's innocence, let's taste it.
Landscapes alter everything. The sea
Will wash us. Tomorrow we are men:
Swing in my stability, Elisha.
The ground they stand on, let's uncover it,
Let's pull their shadows out from under them;
Let's get them over!

ELISHA

But Jeremy, who's favoured by their love
And can be kind, where's Jeremy? Where's he?
    [*Hearing the approach of* BURLEY *and* JACK, DUDLEY *and*
    ELISHA *dodge out of sight.*]

JACK

Now dinner!

BURLEY

First, sir, I must ask you for credentials.

JACK

What, in a bare-faced open forum?
This is nothing short of black suspicion!

BURLEY

Perhaps. But yet I ask where from?

JACK

O underwriter!
Would you that I spell it?

BURLEY

                 I would.

JACK

Can I say, that from an unseen perch,
A feather's fallen and that I have caught it?

BURLEY

                 No.

JACK

No?
But to tell you, fret by fret, would wear you.
Therefore call me Tom-O-Bedlam, Lantern Jack;
We are the waifs of Paris—
Orphans of the war.

BURLEY

Less skipping, if you please.

JACK

Suspect *her* as a member of the Odeon;
A dresser to the opera—and say,
She swept the Comédie Française for tragedy.

Me—plain Jack—who followed close behind,
The whipper-in, the prudent ferryman.

BURLEY

Courtesy requires that when you speak,
You make it more than silence.

JACK

Now there's a comely but demanding argument:
We're sailing in the morning.

BURLEY

Are you Miranda's friend?

JACK
                        Friend?

BURLEY

Where did you meet her, sir?

JACK

I said I followed—but let us now to dinner!

BURLEY

Perhaps it's best I tell you who I am.
I am, sir, Jonathan of Burley, steward;
Miranda's uncle.

JACK

Bless us! Studied for the ministry,
That one, and didn't make it?

BURLEY

That one.

JACK

She told me of you, all the way from Dover;
A truly soaring high opinion, too.

BURLEY

You met my niece in *Dover*?

JACK

Wait. Say I fell in, a time ago in Paris.
I, with the single, she, the compound eye
Met back to back—a kind of paradox.
Descending the terraces of Sacré Cœur
I saw her stand before the city literal,
Tall, withdrawn, intent and nothing cunning;
Incorporate with the air, and more than still,
Her hands dropped and thoroughly performed—
The tension lost, as in tragediennes
Who've left the tragic gesture to the stage,
And so go forth alone to meet disaster–
At this said I to me,
'Lord, excellence and fierce vulgarity
So overlap this last hour of the world,
She's forsaking covert for some prowl,
As the leopard in a land made desolate.'

BURLEY

Shall we get on with it?

JACK

                    It can't be halted, as I'm well aware.
My ash-plant, on its own, began to beat
Like a rod possessed, and barking into bloom
Went tapping in her footsteps, one on one.
Now I am he who knows that Lucifer
Not only fell, but came down bunged in stars.

BURLEY

You do?

JACK

I do.
I said she hears trapped silence, or I much mistake
The thunder on the anvil of the ear.
Say we met in parting—on the drum's first rouse.

BURLEY

But your rig in Dover?

JACK

Say I have a horse in every port—and say
I saw a pilgrim, wandering and walking.

BURLEY

And half-way hard on Beewick—caught her?

JACK

Half-way home I caught her, if you say so.
From the Sacré Cœur down to the lower city.
Strict headed horses of the *Garde Republicaine,*
In dark rank flew prancing all before us,
Drilling a reek of cobbles, as an iron
Plunging in a quarry reeks out stone.
Tails that once had flown the buttocks' fosse
Now flew the helmets of the haughty riders,
Rushing past the hospice yard, where little men
Beneath stone effigies, weighed down in birds
Smoked black cigars, while on the balconies
The patients, clock-wise, practised their recovery.

BURLEY

I see—or do I?

JACK

You've made it in one. Thus we went down together,
Down to the markets of the Avénue du Maine.

BURLEY

Why?

JACK

Why?
Trade being over, and the pushcarts gone,
One can map the public privacy
Of wretched destitution. Note each soul
Without the what to live on, eat to die,
Dragging its acre and its bedroom on a string,
Dressed in a gown that in another age
Will come to style again without its notice.
Its head, bearded to the chin with shaking bows,
(Though solicited of absolutely nothing)
With every palsied nod, bobs its rejection,
Its every taken breath drawn as emetic.

BURLEY

Why all this?

JACK

O literal of mind! O earth-bound checker!
You'd snap a rubber band around an eagle!
Miranda was going *backward* through her target,
Her face set grim for Beewick:
This was her company, a portion—

BURLEY

[*To himself*]

Fantastick—Scapin!

[*To* JACK]
You should have been an actor.

JACK

I was, I am, the company unseen;
I think they call it 'carrying the spear'.

BURLEY

So Miranda leaned against the Gate of Punishment
And looked?

JACK

Not yet, not then; she had stops to make—
        [*Hearing a noise*]
Someone about?

BURLEY

The wind. A traveller—

JACK

                Traveller? Not tonight, I hope.

BURLEY

One or two perhaps, before the morning.

JACK

        [*with nervous animation*]
There being more things on earth than we have dreamt of?
Good. So, raising up my billycock in air
I cried—extempore—'This must be the day!'
And was about to leap into its breach
With, 'Lady, Dame confounded, Madame, hey!'
Being vertical is one of her positions,
And toppling where she lies one of her stations—
When she was off, and such a look she had,
I can assure you, froze me to the heel.
Then ping! We're in the middle of a party
All hung around with fireflies and with lanterns,

A *bahnhof*, Waterloo, Grand Central Station,
A terminal for tea, and no trains running;
A ministry of protocol, a Rumpelmayer,
The very top *haut ton* of everything.
And bowling through, old beasties bobbed and bibbed.
Some hidden by a hedge of paper roses;
Some with their chips down, like the mighty blind
Playing patience on an higher level, found it,
Tapping the long tooth with a leather fan.
Others, in rehearsal of climacteric
Held back the fading crescent of eclipse,
Turning the eye-ball to the bitter dark:
But for my soul, I could not date the day.

BURLEY

It would seem to me Miranda's private hour.
Were you welcome?

JACK

Welcome? Bless you, sir, I'm well past welcome:
Of man's despairs we've had the deal and dole.
This was Miranda's public, her herd in hobble;
Her once-upon-a-time; her court, her people;
Her bleak-of-spirit, and her consternation.
For she is one who knows that man is prouder
Of his fame than of the way he made it;
Knowing nothing now is wrought by hand
To give into the hand particular,
Nor pride of execution.

BURLEY

Then came the footmen, with the cakes and ices?

JACK

Then came the flunkies with the tea and tarts.
I never saw so many famished O's

Gulping as their gape depended on it.
Pasties there were, in every form and fancy.
(Woman's last love always ends in batter
In the semblance of some local 'nob',
Or some monstrous windy senator.)
So there they were, kickshaws *au miel, montée,*
Laced down with *menthe,* with *aquavit* and rum,
Strolled about with sorgum and with treacle;
Almonds, salted, chestnuts, glazed, and jellies—
Compotes, marchpane, apricots and figs—
And every mould an image to the life,
Of whatsoever party fame was killing.

BURLEY
[*Nervously striking one closed hand into the other*]
Then you made your move?

JACK
No. Too near the famish. Those who realized
That present speed was making obsolete
Their very memory, or any term to tell it—
Tried to get into the act, by panting.
Holinight! What a powdered smoke of sugar 'rose
Making sweets of dowagers and dandies!
When, zut! Miranda and the old *Belle Laide* of d'Oc—
The one who'd roiled the bowels of the bank
To such effect, at ninety-one she stood
Stiff as a hitching-post, and neighing diamonds—
Met face to face.

BURLEY
Did you say of Langue d'Oc?

JACK
                    I said it.

BURLEY

Bless my soul! That must have been Elvira,
The only sister got herself to France.
Did she sit it out?

JACK

In a slashing zone of taffeta, she did.
Her head, gabled in a cone of voile, was caught
In a mesh that wove the face away,
Curbing the waspish bodkin of her eyes,
Spurring the fornication of the mint.

BURLEY

Now you made your move.

JACK

Tut! Tut! both hands were numb
From thumbing down the runaway of ages.
This nag of night, all rigging and dead heat
Made carbon of her gems, and oxides of her metals.
Yet on the changing of the spirit's guards,
Spoke in tones stentorian, a smother
Like Field-Marshal, head-down in a cistern:
All in all, I'd say, a grand *savate*—

BURLEY

Come, come, good man, I know as well as any
The lily, onion and confessional
Have many layers. Pare on, acquaint me.
This life is not the first encounter, sir.

JACK

Would you have me tell of dedication
Dead-pan, tight-lipped, minced, and orthodox?
Or will you have this forthright?

BURLEY

Forthright.

JACK

[*In a stage whisper*]

I'm not too sure what's brewing hereabouts.

BURLEY

[*Starting*]

Eh?

JACK

No. But 'fore God, abet me,

That I not default. Now, then, where was I?

BURLEY

Just up to Elvira—

JACK

So I was. Her hip well stapled back, the thigh

In its cup full quartered, lay and couched

Where she sat checking on her gap in time—

In one hand she held her bracelets up,

Loose on the bone.

BURLEY [*nodding*]

Weighing the rate of her departure.

JACK

Exactly.

Posting finger high, I cried out 'Olé!

At the apex, lady, do not scream.'

BURLEY

To whom?

JACK [*increasing in bravado*]
Miranda. 'The *croupier* is raking in,' said I,
'Ignore it.
We're all at profile in this session, girl—
    [DUDLEY *and* ELISHA *begin to close in, moving sideways as*
    children in a game of tag, unseen by JACK, *seen by* BURLEY]
And orphaned on both sides, it's in the plot.
But you, or I mistake my cyclone-lamp,
Are headed for nobility of one.
An advantage, some there are who say
Of thirty years, providing you are royal.
Failing that, why *lento, lento,* lady;
You must learn to buckle to extremity;
Fall face down upon a field Tiepolo—
Even though it is upon the ceiling.
Whip up your splendours and your consternations,
Stand to the trumpets and the terrors;
Give tongue for tongue,
All the tapestries have thrown their spears!'

BURLEY

All that?

JACK

Entire.
I did believe that day all boisterous hell
Was loosed. I tell you that you be informed—
I take it that you are her last of Burley?
That day I made such haste I met myself;
I knew I looked on launched catastrophe.
So, cracking in the middle of my flurry
I cried, 'Mass, mass, piano and piano!'
What else can one, who sees perform its absence
So stark a soul, at such a rate, but keep

One hand above the other gasping, 'Presto!'
What do you make of it?

BURLEY

Nothing.

JACK

And that's precisely why Jack Blow came running,
Swallowing himself and muttering:
'Will Miranda reach the weir upright?'
And will she, being such an upland play?
I tell you who have not seen her many years,
That you may be the wiser.

BURLEY

Of late I've seen her often.
        [*Inadvertently the* BROTHERS *make a noise.*]

JACK

Halt! What's that?

BURLEY
[*His eyes fixed on the* BROTHERS]
Nothing. Travellers—

JACK

Or something worse. I wondered
Will she recover from the stroke that felled her
At her people's gate, a life ago?
So I watched as for a while she stood,
The seven choice bones of her neck down-turned,
The tall plumed turret of her hat becalmed.
Thus the aquiline regard of two worlds met:
'Someone owes a cock to Aesculapius,' she said.
That moment I became her man—
Out of the high fear.

BURLEY

Then you will betray her.

JACK

It won't be necessary; she is her own collision.
She walks like majesty, but is a bumpkin.
She has rash fortitude; she will undo herself,
Meeting herself but totally unarmed.
Therefore, let us begin it.

[*At the same moment that* MIRANDA *appears on the gallery,*
DUDLEY *and* ELISHA, *without further caution, move forward.*
ELISHA *leans, still cracking almonds, against the dressmaker's
dummy, while* DUDLEY, *hat still on, umbrella up, sits in the
chair at the head of the table, his feet braced against its top.*]

[*Without too much surprise*]
What have we here?

MIRANDA

[*On the balcony, softly striking the heel of her hand upon the
balustrade, speaking under her breath as she hears the faint
tapping of a ferule on the flagging*]
No, no, no, no, no, no!

CURTAIN

Act Two

[*The widow* AUGUSTA BURLEY HOBBS, *gaunt, determined, dressed in the severity of long black, gown and overcoat; collared and cuffed in spotless linen, wearing a flat crowned, straight brimmed felt hat, comes on from the colonnade, tapping the paving with the ferule of her umbrella, more for emphasis than caution.*]

AUGUSTA
Why was I left to drowse my coming home?
So then, I'm in my father's house again!
Who said I must be present? He did
Jeremy my son—where is he?

DUDLEY
Hi there mother!

BURLEY

Welcome.

AUGUSTA

[*Peering about*]
My plan is subtler than to mourn
The horrid wrack of Burley standing down;
I'm my own habit yet, and take to sitting—
Shall I know him when I see him?
[*Noticing her daughter on the balcony*]
Ah, how are you old, Miranda?

MIRANDA

Being apt.

AUGUSTA

Now that we're here, all but the one, a chair!

BURLEY

[*Hurriedly turning the prow end of the gryphon*]
At once! Immediately!

AUGUSTA

[*Seating herself*]
Thank you, I hold no brief for standing.
As I came up the terraces of Beewick,
Looking about to see how Beewick stands,
I saw the gables raining down their rooks
In such a belching squall, I cried 'God's mercy,
I do believe they're throwing birds away!'
Or could it be there's funeral in air?

BURLEY

Have you transacted birds?

AUGUSTA

Certainly not!

BURLEY

They hang upon the finger like a gage,
Thrown down of an unseen adversary;
Suddenly you're prisoner of space,
And like St. Francis' fist, hemmed up in flight.

AUGUSTA

[*Attentively*]
It's terrible to come on high ghostly things
When one is old and ravelled to the ground.
I pushed four children from my list and yet
One stayed in the web to pull it down—
But enough of that. I see no hen,
Nor happy squire standing on his turf.
What wild suppers must the squirrels eat
Who find their harvest such a scattered game.

BURLEY

This Jeremy?

AUGUSTA

Though he put me out to pasture, that same son
Has called me back to Beewick and to England.
He should be here, considering he left me.

DUDLEY

Half a lifetime since, to be correct.

AUGUSTA

[*Searching her pocket*]
I have his letter here—now where is it? Don't tell me
I have lost—mislaid my son—I had it.
    [*Noticing the chair she is sitting on*]

Isn't this the beast I sat upon
Staring at his father—that dead man?

BURLEY

Rest.

AUGUSTA

Rest, you say? Where now I sit that man
Rotted out a plan was to have been
A fortress to us all.
    [*Seeing the curfew-bell*]
Ah, the curfew-bell of cousin Pegamont!
He used to ring it over barley broth
To call his needy pensioners—a charity
He watered at the pump.

BURLEY

Come, come, he was a gentle fellow;
Though even as a child so Attic salt
The nurse refused to change him, without gloves.

AUGUSTA

Then you knew my cousin Pegamont?
    [*To her sons*]
He locked the turnkey up, with his own iron.
Best carpenter in Burley. What a craftsman!
Set up his own roof-tree. I say no man
Has a home, who has not smelled his scaffold.

BURLEY

Precisely.

AUGUSTA

What shall they inherit now?
I've told them all the silver spoons are swallowed.

ELISHA

Hardly cricket, what?

AUGUSTA

Don't behave as though you'd never travelled—
Though it's true, you haven't.
    [*To* JACK]
Who are you, boy?

JACK

Plain Jack—juggler.

AUGUSTA

    [*Turning to* BURLEY]
A good scant face. Do I know it?

BURLEY

Your brother Jonathan.

AUGUSTA

    [*With a slight scream*]
Jonathan! My very altered brother—
How glad I am to see you!
I came the long way out to find my home,
My brother, and my son, the wanderer.
Have you seen Jeremy?

BURLEY

I don't think so.

AUGUSTA

I find my cradle, unlike the rocking-stone
That recovers quickly when it's pushed,
Rocked out of date. I find my brother's hairs
Fallen to their valance; my dear son?
I find him not at all.

BURLEY

Give him time.

AUGUSTA

It's strange that he has sent for me all on a sudden,
Who have not seen him twenty years.
And by those twenty years twice twenty stranger;
I dread my sons, and love them bitterly.
    [Recollecting herself]
But what am I about, not made you known—
Jonathan—I see you know my daughter—
This is Dudley, manufacturer of clocks—

DUDLEY

                    Watches.

JACK

'The king was in his counting house—'

ELISHA

    [Spitting out shells]
Touché!

AUGUSTA

Both of them, as you observe, successful—
    [To ELISHA*]*
And stop bleating!
Jonathan, Elisha, Dudley's publicist.

ELISHA

Hi!

AUGUSTA

They say, in short, it's why they came this way—
I could have managed all alone for Jeremy.
And what does Jeremy?—

ELISHA

[*Spitefully*]
He goes off, to improve his taste
For everything, including muscatel—Moldavian

AUGUSTA

[*Ignoring this with contemptuous pity*]
Children, my brother Jonathan.

BURLEY

Welcome, gentlemen, and prosper you.

MIRANDA

Be each other's creatures cautiously.

AUGUSTA

Knowing my daughter, what do you think of her?

BURLEY

I think her as I know her.

JACK

How does she stand?

BURLEY

Complete.

AUGUSTA

[*Appraising Jack*]
My good man, who did you say you are?

JACK

A friend.

AUGUSTA

Friend?

JACK

In trust.

AUGUSTA

Jonathan was my favourite brother—

BURLEY
[*With troubled modesty*]

No, no.

AUGUSTA

Studied for the ministry—

BURLEY

Glad to settle for the stewardship of Burley.

AUGUSTA

Truly, a master of the organ—

BURLEY

Ah, that's a long, long time ago.

AUGUSTA

How are our people, Jonathan?

BURLEY

Alas, my dear Augusta.

AUGUSTA

I feared it. As I came up to Burley
I saw no faces that I saw—
    [*To* ELISHA]
Elisha, stop it! Stop cracking nuts!
    [*To* DUDLEY]
Put the umbrella down, you're not that out of doors!

BURLEY

There are aunts somewhere, and uncles doubtlessly—

AUGUSTA

Nephews and nieces? Do you live in the house?

BURLEY

No, for the present in the village.

AUGUSTA

Who brings you tea?

BURLEY

[*Dense in regard to the suggestion*]
Sometimes my boy brings me a pot of ale;
Sometimes, in the butler's pantry, tea—
The pantry's still intact.

AUGUSTA

[*Sweeping the formal arrangement of the table with pleased
eye*]
The table—just as it used to be.

BURLEY

For custom's sake.

AUGUSTA

My husband, Titus, sitting at that end
Gobbled like a turkey.

BURLEY

Like usurper.

AUGUSTA

I such a prudent, such a country girl!

BURLEY

But?

AUGUSTA

I thought to be the mother of Aristocrats
And got me ruffians. Three boys in trades, and one—

DUDLEY

Gosling, on the loose.
[*There is a noise off-stage of people passing*]

AUGUSTA

Heavens, what is that?

BURLEY

Nothing, strangers, passing—a ship leaves in the morning.

AUGUSTA

[*Still somewhat apprehensive*]
Do you presume it possible his wenches
Still roam the countryside? I almost wish
They walked again, I'd have a fourth at bridge—
But I was coming to Miranda—

DUDLEY

Behold Miranda! In the zodiac
She stands for Virgo—just for laughs in heaven.

BURLEY

Don't you like your sister?

DUDLEY (*sarcastically*)
Dear uncle, we adore her, in the highest—

ELISHA

But to know her is extravagance—so British!

AUGUSTA

Pay no attention to my boys, they ape their father,
Who looked down on the British with the utmost envy.
I'd hoped my children would have shone in manners,
And Miranda come in terrible with honours.

BURLEY

And did she?

DUDLEY

Mother thought to knock a queen down with her broom—
She, with the peerage in her pocket,
Father, with Josh Billings in his boot!

ELISHA

I hear Miranda's all get-out in France,
And apparently a scribbler in England.

BURLEY

She is praised here and across the channel,
She's particularly welcome here in Beewick.

DUDLEY

Beewick's a little place—no credit in New York.

AUGUSTA

Jonathan, forgive my sons their malice,
It comes of being the first time over-water—
They're out of custom; let us then to fortunes.
Now where are my cards?

JACK

Cards in Carthage!

AUGUSTA

                    Why not in Carthage? No? Then chess.

DUDLEY

Chess? A strategy
To keep two solemn dead men sitting up.

AUGUSTA

[*A spool of twist falls from her pocket as she searches for her*
cards]
Ah my bones and bobbins!
    [*The spool rolls out of sight*]
I used to make me laces, Jonathan,
To keep from sulking over worser matters.
    [*Sighs*]
For lace? No journey it adapts to;
People? No journey brings them home.
    [*The spool rolls back into the hall*]
Gracious, someone *is* about!

BURLEY

Children—pilgrims—on the way to port—
I regret I've nothing here to lift the spirit.

AUGUSTA

                              You know I never touch a thing!

BURLEY

My dear Augusta, I know nothing.

AUGUSTA

                              But I starve!

BURLEY

    [*Hastily*]
Let's see what we can do for that.

AUGUSTA

[*Anxiously*]
No, no, don't move.

ELISHA

[*Clapping the carnival crown upon his head*]
'The Queen was playing cards, with the Bishop of Limoges—'

DUDLEY

But she found 'the cupboard bare—'

AUGUSTA

They always play the fool; pay no attention—
Eh, there's the wind again, someone *is* prowling.
I've said I sometimes wish my husband's hussies
Walked again; in time the mind forgets
What they were used for.

BURLEY

[*Startled*]
What did you say?

AUGUSTA

Nothing. The story ended as you said it would,
In a rowdy pack of bitches.

BURLEY

My dear!

AUGUSTA

No sooner 'opinioned' out of Beewick
Consequence of all his proclamations—

JACK

Free-love—

DUDLEY

Free lunch—

ELISHA

Free everything.

JACK

And naturally the 'Quality' estranged—

AUGUSTA

When, naturally, we all took ship at Plymouth.
Arriving at New York, in late December—

DUDLEY

To a cabin, cocked in Pendry Cove—

ELISHA

From Pendry Cove, slap, to Spuyten Duyvil—

AUGUSTA

To a house he liked to call 'Hobbs Ark'.

DUDLEY

A farm he never farmed—

ELISHA

A house he couldn't keep—

AUGUSTA

But to his credit, built the thing himself.

JACK

And not a year standing, when his beasts,
The girls—

AUGUSTA

They do not matter now. No more contingent
Than granite figures up on foreign roofs;
As temperless as tuning-forks unbuzzed.

JACK

[*With a sudden cry*]
Ai-i-i-i-i-i! How they buzzed!

AUGUSTA

[*Sharply*] Who is that fellow?

BURLEY

Why, it was he who found Miranda walking
Down from Dover.

JACK

[*Recovering his composure*]
No, from Sacré Cœur.

AUGUSTA

Found her walking. Gave her a lift? Well, frankly
I'm not so sure what kind of kindness that was.
What did you say your name sir?

JACK

Jack Blow, madame.

AUGUSTA

Jack Blow? What sort of name is that?
Come into the light; you wear a patch?

JACK

The better to see you with, madame.

AUGUSTA

Levity depraves some part of man—
Mend, boy.

JACK

I mend, madame.

AUGUSTA

Miranda?—Did you say walking?

ELISHA

She's lame.

DUDLEY

[*Sarcastically*]
Turned her ankle, coming down from church.

AUGUSTA

In some sort of mischief, I've no doubt.

JACK

No, madame, war.

AUGUSTA

What!
Dressed as though there were no God—
All those feathers blowing from her hat;
And such a drag of velvet!

DUDLEY

Stand-in for a final curtain!

AUGUSTA

I didn't know Miranda would be here.

JACK

In the shutting down of Paris, we took off
In whatsoever part we had been playing.

ELISHA

Herself, the Duchess!

DUDLEY

Queen of the Night!

ELISHA

Wherein she bit the Devil's thumb.

AUGUSTA

Do not affront her; she's that part of me
I can't afford.

ELISHA

You know that we admire her, stubbornly,—
With prudence!

AUGUSTA

Do I?

BURLEY

[*Changing the subject*]
Did Jeremy have word that you were coming?

AUGUSTA

He said 'Come home to Beewick'; gave no address.
Where then would he be, but here at Burley?
To tell the truth, he's my astonishment.
I wonder, shall I know him when I meet him?
They say he looks like me [*to* BURLEY] I'd say our father.
Guileless, not girlish, disengaged, but taken.

DUDLEY

Think you're going to smell him out?

AUGUSTA

[*Annoyed*]
Your grandfather smelled like hemlock, but he leaned,
Like the hollow weed, close by the wall,
For hearts-ease, and so might Jeremy.

DUDLEY

[*With off-hand impudence*]
'She loved her husband dear-i-lie,
But another man twic't as well.'

AUGUSTA

Jeremy can do no wrong, if I don't say it.

ELISHA

'When Eve delved, and Adam span—'

AUGUSTA

Forgive them, Jonathan, they're unrecorded.

DUDLEY

He's the image of Papa, in congress gaiters—
Regency Rake.

AUGUSTA

Jeremy is Jeremy.

ELISHA

Which put Jeremy to such fright, he bolted,
Twenty years ago.

DUDLEY

She'll have him back—and climbing up her string,
Like tin monkeys forty years ago.

AUGUSTA

[*To* BURLEY]
I haven't told you how it was with Jeremy,
That is, after reformed from excellence.
He left me, howling in an alien room,
And I can't know why.
Left me stranded on an high bad bed,
With legs too short to tap upon the floor;
Shedding the airy tears of age, and rocking
My one and happy memory, the hour
We went hunting, all alone together,
In the Catskill mountains.

JACK

Hunter, hunting hunter,
Turns the tiger to a rabbit's skin
To wrap his mama Bunting in.

BURLEY

[*Sadly*]
Foxes their holes, birds their nests—but man—

AUGUSTA

The more I see of man, the more bereaved.
When I am gone, Miranda, put me in a tree.
Remember, you who have the habit of recalling.

DUDLEY

Hoi, the Queen is dead, long live the Queen!

ELISHA

She's dying tall, she's English!

DUDLEY

When Jeremy was home, it's true we rocked
In his gusts of generosity—
For policy—
But Jeremy once gone, Miranda's nothing,
Brother, are we free-beaters!

JACK

[*Sarcastically*]

Cent-per-cent?

DUDLEY

Look here, I say stand on your own two feet.
Down with sentiment, and up, by God, with trade!

JACK

The rich enjoyment of cupidity?

AUGUSTA

Oh, be quiet, all of you, or go away!
As I was coming up the terraces of Burley
What should I see? A perishing diameter,
Where once a bandstand stood, and *Kapellmeister* Stack—
Remember Stack?—upon it, like a seal
Pawing the air with consecrated hand
In which, like a twig in snow, his baton
Thawed out a trumpet voluntary.

ELISHA

Ooom-pa-pa, umm-pa-pa—I'll bet a go at taps!
[*He snatches up a horn, blowing a passage from Purcell*]

BURLEY

I give you 'I love, and I must.'

[DUDLEY *beats a drum*]

AUGUSTA

[*Holding her ears*]
I told you they were talented, or did I?

BURLEY

And once instructed.

AUGUSTA

I was coming to my major-general—

ELISHA

Your major-general? Miranda's first cadet.

AUGUSTA

[*Ignoring the impudence*]
A very autumn cone he was, all scaled in medals;
Braced in knocking points; ribboned, buckled—
I do love a man who jangles!

ELISHA

[*Wandering about and drawling*]
A-A-a-a-a! 'Froggie would a wooing-go.'

AUGUSTA

Vulgarity!
Jonathan, how do you understand it,
No son of mine has been so favoured
That he died in war?

JACK

In spite of progress, and free-enterprise?

AUGUSTA

In spite of everything.

DUDLEY

She mourns as one who could be comforted.

JACK

[*To* AUGUSTA, *in a loud whisper*]
Not so much the bravery is welcome,
As the fortunate removal of the body?

AUGUSTA

[*Startled*]
I trust men till they whisper!

BURLEY

Do I remember the major-general?

AUGUSTA

Of course you remember the major-general.
Except for the one bold bend that seated him,
Complete upright.

JACK

Cancelled out with great fine sanguine sashes,
Crossing up his guts from hip to hame,
Like a comfit box, *experto crede.*
For epaulettes? A swab of Furies.

ELISHA

[*Turning in from the garden*]
I doubt the whole damned thing—
Conductor Stack *and* the palace medals.

BURLEY

[*Drowsily*]
One two, one two—
Compounded motion, like slow strutting honey,

Polling Thomas Tallis on his hook,
And getting Monteverdi put about.

AUGUSTA

And Couperin.
See how defaulted I am Jonathan.

DUDLEY

See how Miranda's staring at you.

AUGUSTA

O, ho, my foot Miranda!
I think I've hurt my foot.

[MIRANDA *begins to move out.*]

DUDLEY

Why call on Miranda? She's afraid of life.

AUGUSTA

You're a proper fool. She's afraid of nothing.

MIRANDA

Not afraid of life, but your opinion of it.

ELISHA

The Ruffian Queen! Miranda's coming out!

AUGUSTA

[*As* MIRANDA *comes toward her*]
My foot, Miranda, I have hurt my foot!

MIRANDA

[*Stooping to her*]

Woman, remember you.

AUGUSTA

Why?

ELISHA

'Chicken today, feathers tomorrow.'

AUGUSTA

Farewell, daughter.

MIRANDA

Hail, Mother.

AUGUSTA

Recall me to them all, Miranda.

DUDLEY

'Make her a child again, just for tonight.'

MIRANDA

The flank-plume of the greater bird of paradise
Racked not more pride, than did the dancing lappet
Prowling at your hip that summer day
When you walked off the world.

AUGUSTA

[*Pensively*]
Your father said: 'Don't wag your bottom!'

BURLEY

That sad, tender and hilarious
Portion of the anatomy—the bottom.

AUGUSTA

Jonathan!

ELISHA

But to your mother–though you were Solomon–
Is always bare!

BURLEY

You always tease your family?

ELISHA

Sure. I gouge my chin into the shoulder bone,
And whiz my thumb into the buttock joint.

BURLEY

                              You do?

ELISHA

I love a leaper.

BURLEY

                    The pecking ranks—the jackdaw trick—

DUDLEY

The what?

BURLEY

                    He walks behind his love, to kick her down.

AUGUSTA

   [*To* BURLEY]
I've bungled my escape.
   [*Aloud*]
My sons boisterous, my daughter? Sudden quiet.
When she's quiet—and indeed she's quiet,
As dragging silk upon some unseen chain—
I think it lying—she who is forthright.

DUDLEY

I heard you call her vixen at fifteen.

AUGUSTA

She's so ambiguous, that mourning dogs
Follow her off graves, with weeping tongues.
But when she rouses to the mark, I think
She's one of awful virtue, and the Devil.

BURLEY

Am I to assume you happier in sons?

AUGUSTA

Of course, men are a pleasure. What's a woman?

DUDLEY

A cow, sitting on a crumpled grin.

AUGUSTA

Jonathan, pretend they are not here:
You I welcome back to Beewick.

MIRANDA

                              He never left it.

BURLEY

Staying in one place is man's address—
Mind, I did not say instruction.

AUGUSTA

[*With commendable pride*]
His the hand that shored up Burley Hall:
Nor would he pull the stops on *vox humana*
As Titus would, no matter how he trembled.

MIRANDA

And Titus trembled, good God, how he trembled!

AUGUSTA

[*Noticing* MIRANDA'*s rings*]
What pretty rings. You never gave me rings.

MIRANDA

[*Giving* AUGUSTA *her rings*]
                              You never remember any rings I gave you.

ELISHA

[*Stepping up to* AUGUSTA, *and tapping her with his closed
hand*]
Who killed Cock Robbin?

DUDLEY

It's true, Miranda gave the world away
And no one seemed to pay the least attention.
Her acts kill themselves, as does the sting the bee.

ELISHA

And what a goad she's got!

AUGUSTA

[*To* MIRANDA]
I'll remember that you held my foot
When I am in my grave.
What do I owe you?

BURLEY

                              Oh, unkind!

ELISHA

There's only one kind inch on any woman—
Between her tot and tail—
There's kindness!

AUGUSTA

[*With shocked and frightened laughter*]
My sons are wonderfully ignoble, Jonathan,
Equality has only made them vulgar;
Forgive them. As for Miranda, brother, tell them
How I was handsomer than she.

BURLEY

I remember you as handsome as my niece,
And both of you as handsome as each other.
You in the winter of your starch
As proud as spring—

AUGUSTA

[*Bridling*]

Wasn't I?

BURLEY

A very accordion of pleated linen—

AUGUSTA

Underset in laces, bodkin inched,
Binding a rosy satin 'round the knee.

JACK

Hated the house, and all the housework in it?

AUGUSTA

Impudent!
Miranda, tell them how I must have been
When I was thrown up for the gun.

DUDLEY

Out of nothing I can paint that picture:
Smart ramshackle, as any stable queen.
That stark, strict impeccable askew—

JACK

One associates with rectified disaster—

ELISHA

That standing up, as promised, that full stop—

JACK

That variety instructed.

ELISHA

Bodkins?
Papa used 'em, and a cork, swan-upping
Of his drabs, to prove himself promoted
Monarch of the clutch.

AUGUSTA

Don't name his creatures when you speak of me!

ELISHA

Why not? You also did exactly what he told you,
And let him get away with anything.

DUDLEY

[*With anger*]
Uh, even as a baby in your arms
You let him lash me with his carriage whip.

BURLEY

Is this the thing you hold against your father?

DUDLEY

I have against my father that he whipped me
Before I knew him.

MIRANDA

That puzzles children—

ELISHA

And that mother, dutiful and balking
Lived cheek-by-jowl with all his brats and brides;
Slaved, without undue astonishment,
The while the ladies lapped up cakes and ale.

DUDLEY

Come down! The biddies drank their coffee black.
All in the selfsame sty, warbling and crying,
Except of course, Augusta.
Down on her knees, with holy-stone and soap
Scrubbing 'round grandmother, missionary,
Knitting 'little things' for the Swahili.

ELISHA

Oh, come again.

DUDLEY

Father, marking in the book of Genesis:
'Give me my wives and children, for whom I have served thee, and
let me go.'
Egoist and Emperor. Sufficient
To a thousand geese, like Abraham.

AUGUSTA

[*Starting from her chair, which sends her sons* **backing away**]
O, madness to know anyone!
He was an eager, timorous, faulty man.

ELISHA

[*Ducking, but continuing the banter*]
All the while that mule, Brigid-Matilda
His first paramour (popped out at placket)
Stitched on her hoop of bloody twist,
Crying in a loud voice, to her needle:
'We'll sew us out of bondage yet!'

BURLEY

Did she?

AUGUSTA

[*Sitting down again*]
That I should be reminded now and here
Of all the gaudy that has gone before.
[*To* BURLEY]
She was *not* the one who got away.
Where do we sleep tonight?

BURLEY

It is arranged.

AUGUSTA

Good. Then let us speak of Beewick as our country.

DUDLEY

Don't mind us. We're only poor provincials.

AUGUSTA

Off with you! I'm talking to my brother
Of the time when you were not at all.
Jonathan was Norman, I not tame—

ELISHA

[*Braying*]

Hee-haw, hee-haw!

AUGUSTA

With hems that haunted everywhere I walked,
My brindled tweed full gallooned to the foot,
While about my head a leghorn reeled,
Bridling in the wind.

DUDLEY

[*Pretending admiration*]

No!

ELISHA

[*Taking him up*]

Yes.
A daring act of caution, cut to size.
Hips as chaste as slate to tailor to—

AUGUSTA

Play the fool, patronize yourself.

DUDLEY

The coif seized upward on a murd'rous pin
Till the bare bone, under shaking mull
Reared up an ear, like to a crescent fluke
To stay the browsing fall—

AUGUSTA

                       Whose browse?

ELISHA

Why father's—what else?

DUDLEY

                       Old Baron Ox!

ELISHA

The whole thing sounds, I'd say, more like Miranda.

AUGUSTA

Let it be Miranda.
She's all Augusta laid up in Miranda;
Born again to be my new account—

And all my candidature.
Daughter, when I die, I charge you, lay me in a tree,
I'll hop to heaven.

DUDLEY

Back in trees again!

ELISHA

When the bough bends?

DUDLEY (*to his mother*)
What is Miranda that she profits your estate?

ELISHA

What profit anyone who trips the foreign scene?

DUDLEY

And prefers her bloodshed in an alien tongue
And writes her savage comedies in French?
As far as I am concerned, expatriate's
The same as traitor.

BURLEY

Then my son, you are in darkness,

DUDLEY

[*Hypocritically*]
Don't misunderstand, we loved the lamb—
Till she turned mutton.

AUGUSTA

If one child was meant to be a gifted child
It should have been a boy, and that boy Jeremy.
But Titus overwhelmed all but Miranda.
You do remember my dead husband, Jonathan?

BURLEY

Alas my dear, and all that way from London.

AUGUSTA

Hearing you a master of the organ—

JACK

Came to learn, stayed to instruct?

BURLEY

And with him his mother.

AUGUSTA

If there's to be description of Victoria
I'll give her.

JACK

Middletown Récamier no doubt.

AUGUSTA

The rage of London!
All the grandees of her day pulled at her door,
Like cranes at feeding time. And then the artists!
The most eccentric and the most renowned:
And just for catnip (and but late of Hang-town),
Lotta Crabtree sang upon her lap,
As it had been a last command performance!

JACK

Making England safe for London?

DUDLEY

[*Snappishly*]
What do you know about it!

MIRANDA

Free-soiler, free-thinker, nonconformist, mystic—
Abolitionist, Hyde Park orator—

AUGUSTA

But kept her cordials in the caddy!

JACK

Titus, with broad parochial stare
Of a Sankey and a Moody ranter.
Ravished by the knocking sisters Fox,
By prophets, martyrs, and by levitations
Wheeled to the East. . . .

ELISHA

And ended up a silly spry old fool
High hat and all!

DUDLEY

Old ladies do adore a frisky party!

AUGUSTA

[*Again rising, in indignation*]
If there's one thing less pleasing than another,
It's a brisk and nimble antic man,
Who, to prove himself both young and able,
Leaps over hedge and ditch, clashing his castors.
I am a grave and proper woman.

DUDLEY

Proper!
You've pissed like a cat to hear of lechery!

AUGUSTA

[*In consternation, sitting down again*]
O!

ELISHA

[*Aside to* DUDLEY]
That's torn it!

DUDLEY

[*Aside to* ELISHA]

Patience. Keep it funny.

AUGUSTA

I wonder who we are, we still have time for it.
I who loved all things fastidious
Get me lewd men.

DUDLEY

What else? We're timely.

AUGUSTA

And without innocence;
Nor have you the special dispensation of Daguerre,
Whose any touch was new baptism laid.
Beneath his stroke your father was a child.
His love-locks then did fret his cheeks as youth
Had found new courtesy.

JACK

But his chin, un-saw'd like mine?

AUGUSTA

Who are you, young man, to know
How a widow's dead man looks?

JACK

Checkmate!

AUGUSTA

On his cheek-bones' plush, bees buzzed and hung
As he had been a park.

MIRANDA

I thought you said you never liked the man.

AUGUSTA

Except his teeth. His teeth were my delight.

MIRANDA

Defend a better point; four children hang upon it.

AUGUSTA

None of you were anywhere when I first saw him.

BURLEY

A man who crept around his own circumference,
As he were looking for the exit.
    [*To the sons*]
How do you see your father?

JACK

    [*Off guard*]
That old Ram! Cock-pit Bully Boy!

AUGUSTA

Our coachman is an orator!

JACK

[*Bowing*] At your service, madame.

ELISHA

Fe-fo-fi-fum—I smell the blood of an Englishman!

AUGUSTA

[*Paying no attention*]
He was of the self-appointed race, American.

BURLEY

In our hey-day many came to Burley,
Your father was but one among the hurly.
Apologists and special pleaders came,
Peers, encyclopaedists, architects—
They said they came to chart our bull-nosed beams—
And not one but somehow lost his balance
And all but toppled headlong for his brougham
Ogling my shy and cunning sisters—
The little peeking brigantines!

AUGUSTA

Barristers and watchful judges came
Balancing their verdict on their knee—
That second outward ponder of the head—
The curled, full-bottomed wig of jurisprudence.

BURLEY

Gentle folk, who proved to be unkind;
Chaplains, jobbers, and processions came;
Once, and only once, with frantic eye
The Dean.

MIRANDA

And Victoria?

AUGUSTA

I said if it's to be Victoria, I'll give her.
There was one who thought herself of Royal Jelly,
And had, she said, the touch was once the King's.

Was I, a country girl, to disbelieve her?
May I be forgiven, I believed her utterly;
She was so tender and perfidious;
A faulty scholar, but a witty one:
And such a pair of transcendental eyes!

BURLEY

Late out of Bangkok, for the press.

AUGUSTA

When having run her ways, backed into dock,
(Her more than Oriental rooms in Grosvenor Square)
An awesome hull in feral brilliants paved,
Wearing on her head a turban's bale,
A coil twice as cunning as her mind;
Her draw-glove among the Lions pitched,
(The choicest of her guests rolled in the swell!)
Followed by a Blackamoor and spaniel
The spaniel followed by her second husband,
All ivory tush, and fearful waxed moustaches,
A Spaniard of the utmost rich vulgarity
Whom, for too much love, she'd married with two rings—
(He left her later for a Cheapside Strumpet)
Well, be that as it may—*Enter Victoria!*

JACK

In such bight and squall of twinklings shod,
Her tasselled, taped and parried abdomen,
Banded like the skin-trussed boxer-hornet,
Hummed and shook beneath the midnight lamps:
And at its middle swung the drowsy stone
Named for the moon.

DUDLEY
    [*Crowing in mock admiration*]
Cock-a-doodle-do!

AUGUSTA

Though not proper that you marry twice,
And certainly improper to have lovers,
(In her mind all love was truth and honour—
She was mourned indeed by fifty silk umbrellas—
It always rains straight down on prodigies).
She could cluck in anyone for daughter.
She whistled, and the girls, like thieves, came running.
A ready and a milking tongue could stroke
One out of store as quick as any ant
As keeps a cow.

ELISHA

'Mademoiselle was new at court, and nervous!'

DUDLEY

'And had but a penny a day'—

AUGUSTA

She had my purse, my person, and my trust
In one scant hour.
Even stones wear down beneath the lick of flattery
And I but rock-salt to her stallion son,
Before whose rough unbridled head I dwined
At his fast leisure.

BURLEY

Poor, wretched and unhappy child!

AUGUSTA

So sure was he of his sufficience,
Composed his own libretti; stuck his pigs,
Sawed the gryphon up, the what-not down;
Voiced the whooping clocks to keep his hours;
Wrote his credo, helped the cows to calve;

Then maul-stick *en garde,* and palette at careen,
Painted little men, on river banks.

JACK

But, to slake a thirst more raging than Narcissus
Leaning at the brink, the cod fell in.

DUDLEY

He had a way of rising on rebuke.

ELISHA

And vain! A child's block underneath his heel
And he was up and crowing like a cock.

AUGUSTA

What a tandem that was!
I've had it on the best authority
Vesta Victoria sang in Leicester Square
'Behold the ears of my heart are set before thee,'
Just to please Victoria, that darling!

DUDLEY

Rake, God knows, footpad and Regent bawd;
As mad a peddler's kingdom as conceivable.

MIRANDA

But in the dead of winter, rode a Gothic sleigh
To fetch the bacon home.

AUGUSTA

Scavenger!

MIRANDA

[*Controlling her anger*]
Do not frequent her absence. There was one

Knew how to be a scavenger.
Her rip-tide bore us up and rocked our cradle.
Ship-chandler she, to any wreck off coast.
A creeping shrine, keel barnacled, and listing
Under the children's votive offerings,
Marbles, ribbons, pebbles, broken dolls
And all such things that frightened children leave
In tigers' dens. A staggered sanctuary
With a circus and a juggler on its back:
She knew how to perish totally.
Peddler, puddler, foot-pad, lean-to, grot;
But, as St. Peter shut the door, her heel
Stayed by, to let the children through.

                      AUGUSTA
You always took her side.

                      MIRANDA
                              Did I?

                      AUGUSTA
But I, poking finger in my counterpane
Felt what? A woman caterpillar to my touch,
And knew her son Bull Titus had commenced
The monstrous practice of polygamy.

                      DUDLEY
In short—beast one.

                      AUGUSTA
                              Exactly.

I called my child—
My second child—
A grief—

BURLEY

My dear sister, why were you surprised?
Titus began his practice here in Beewick.
How far he went, no one this age can say:
He flushed one siren, certainly,
Wrangling on a zither.

JACK

Miss Mephistopheles!

BURLEY

[*Faintly amused*]
Wolfed in fire even to galoshes:
All in scarlet, like a Cardinal,
A cherry ribbon 'round her neck, as murdered.
Once on the stairs, she mounted like a lizard
Crying 'Are you intense?'

DUDLEY

[*Who has got himself up in the gallery*]
Was that Louise, with butt librarian;
You know—looking for a good book, on low shelf?

ELISHA

It was not. It was the trollop bawled
'Sic 'em!' to the visions in her mind—
The one that dad hooked off a barge in Erie.

AUGUSTA

No, no. You're mixing that one with Belinda.
Belinda was, thank God, before your time.
You refer to Juliette of Camberwell.

DUDLEY

Did we have fun!
I was thinking of Kitty Partingale,

The one grandmother hauled in out of Blackpool,
Or was it Brighton? Anyway a harper
Harping on her harp in cockle time.

JACK

Plucking its high-hipped shrouds, with insect teasings;
She got no further than 'The Little Nipper'
When she was catched.

AUGUSTA

[*Tartly*]
She was playing Mozart, and it was Covent Garden.

DUDLEY

Whichever lay it was, knocked down for tone.

AUGUSTA

[*In a loud whisper to* BURLEY, *who is nodding*]
Don't move, and do not go to sleep!
[*Aloud*]
Kitty was the silliest of them all.

MIRANDA

A lost clairvoyant, that is all, poor creature.
Said she saw Lord Kitchener in a cloud
Chasing Oom Paul Kreuger over Africa,
Waving the Doomsday Book before him as he ran.

AUGUSTA

[*Suddenly snapping her fingers*]
Trudy Frisch from Bruges!
There was an estimable vixen cleared his bed;
One Fleming who, in pride of grease
Kept it for her countrymen.

JACK

'In tender grass sat Phyllis' fighting
Tooled in beauty anyway she turned.

MIRANDA

No matter how she rolled, the raging sun
Fleeced her verge with bright and shining mane;
And where the wrestle lashed among the rushes
Up came Jeremy, that bullish baby, clapping
His left hind thumb-wing in his father's face,
Lisping 'Seducer!'

BURLEY

Out of the frying-pan, into the fire.

DUDLEY

You said it.
When the law caught up with us, behind the wall—
Which he'd built up high for fear of tongues—
He burned his credo, chucked up his account.
And having utterly betrayed betrayal,
Turned us out like bastards, being none:
Hauled off on a stone-boat from the Cove
That he might make at least one hussy legal.

BURLEY

And then he died?

AUGUSTA

He dawdled more than died.

BURLEY

I never really understood how you condoned it.

AUGUSTA

Don't come at me too! I was a victim:
I've done my duty to the state—in children.

ELISHA

>Oh, not *that* again.

AUGUSTA

He claimed himself a Saint of such day
Would sweep the world of whores; I but believed him.

BURLEY

>My dear girl!

AUGUSTA

In my day we did not leave our husbands.

JACK

Particularly when he put on side
Pretending to the Earldom of old Pendry?

ELISHA

O heavens, and the Baron of Castaigne!
For sheer impudence and foreign tone
Went scratching in the barnyard straw
Searching his escutcheon.

DUDLEY

Spitting prunes among the Philistines;
A Puritan too close to his apostasy,
A moralist!
And of such tender sensibility
Burned mother's feather boa, but killed the cocks.

BURLEY

I was afraid of it. But you Augusta,
Though balancing a kingdom in your mind,
How did you lose the purpose of your life?
Our squires of Burley

Had no need of prophets in the midst
To ask them on 'which side' it was they dressed,
They bred their state upon them as they went;
Dressed fitly, as the velvet to the horn.
In fortitude they were all over Burley;
In whatsoever key they tolled, they belled
Forthright, even to the cannon. So I find
It more than strange that you wore Titus.

                    AUGUSTA
He said he was the stud to breed a kingdom.

                    JACK
    [*Humming*]
'Who passes by this road so late?'—
Look: a pedigree's not got by rubbing, lady,
Two nights together.

                    BURLEY
    [*Rising in haste*]
I'll fetch the lamps.

              DUDLEY AND ELISHA
Take Jack with you.

                    AUGUSTA
    [*Holding* BURLEY]
Don't move.
    [*Aloud*]
Of course, there's always snaffle in opinion.
Say I was sitting on an ottoman
Swallowing, at a gulp, the Trinity—
Father, son and most unholy cause.

                    JACK
That was the day the sky fell down on chicken—

AUGUSTA

That was the day that story-book Augusta
Feather-headed, fairy-tale Augusta
In her mind's wild latitude laid out
And armed such battlefield, tilt patch and list
As out-geared Mars!
I hung the bright shields up, I spun the drill,
Clubbed the spears and standards, axe and mace.
I teased the olive, and all budding things
Into the hoop that wheels a victor's head
And for his blood their own bright berries drop.
I snared the empty target of the heart—
That builds its nest in metal chains and rings—
With the colours of a ghosted mother:
Planted the visored helmet, shark-side up
And to its yawn I threw my gauntlet in.
Then, then I waited for the clash of arms!
And what did my sons? Did rise and prime
Along the march, like Birnam Wood?
No. Lay by, and fiddled!
Moles could have trooped it!

BURLEY

                    Miranda did.

AUGUSTA

Who's Miranda?
She gives her weapons to the enemy.
Look how in magnificence defeated!
In short, I can't afford her
She's only me.

BURLEY

Only more offended.

AUGUSTA
        Well, well, enough of that; I'm starving.

BURLEY
Then here's where Jack comes in. He tells me
He has a creel of secret Burley scandal
Should strip the town of bread.
Jump Jack! Go fetch my sister supper.

JACK
    [*Starting off*]
Count me gone no longer than your blessing.

                                                [*Exit*]

AUGUSTA
            A wild and saucy air.

BURLEY
A wild and saucy fellow. I would say
Fond of Miranda, for her style;
And puzzled.

AUGUSTA
If you ask me—and no one ever asks me—
I'd say Miranda's in the ink-fish fog
Thrown off by her father, when recanting
Now many years ago. She has the air,
Ruthless as the damned in heaven:
Yet in abandon of variety
She's lost the journey of her life
As does the owl the journey of his head.

BURLEY
In short, you are mistaken.

AUGUSTA

In short you seem to think so; still it's known
She's in and out of wills, like dogs through hoops.
Somehow, some way, my children *must* be marvellous.

ELISHA

[*Cracking nuts*]
Why?
Who are you to rate a marvellous child?
As for Miranda, she was always wrapped
In such confounded condescending clemency
I wouldn't trust her, even were she slapped.

DUDLEY

Mother liked her when her head was hanging.

AUGUSTA

When a little girl, the look was charming—
I liked her most when she looked wanted.

DUDLEY

You had her so convinced she was the devil,
At seven, she was cutting down the hedges,
To furnish brier to beat her to your favour;
All time since, been hunting for her crime.

ELISHA

[*To his mother*]
That reminds me of the contra-bitch, the dog
That with both hands, at father's wish, you held
Cowering on the selvage of the night,
While with gun, fed fat on your love letters,
He cored the beast, just as the moon arose!

BURLEY

A wicked thing a child should see the moon
Rise in the belly of a dog.
Did *no* one get away?

AUGUSTA

Flora, the nameless one.
He laid that girl housekeeping in the earth.
Greenland got her, doubled down, a cozy
To his brat.

MIRANDA

I sometimes wonder what it is a woman
Sweats between her palms when she is merciful.

AUGUSTA

Don't look at me! Your father was to blame
For everything.

MIRANDA

Yet was he not the man
Lay thrashing on the floor, one kill night through?
Death's first deposit, his dead bastard child,
Face shut, foreclosed, and in its golden burr,
Riding the saddle of his pounding heart,
Where he struck foot, as running up the air
To fail her exit, clapping hands and shouting
'Halt!' There was a cry.

ELISHA

Still mother wept the strings, and craked
'Cuckoo'.

MIRANDA

And still dung-beetle Atlas carried on.

BURLEY

Still I do believe Elvire started it—
A girl who stroked the very heart but breathing.
But to name her as the world would name her—lurcher—
(It was her foot tripped our Lord Dearly down!)
Yet, of such phlegm, she let him palm her off
To a chap in busby.

AUGUSTA

A busby that he groomed just like a cat.

BURLEY

The very backsides of his buttons whistled!

AUGUSTA

[*Stubbornly*]
It was Victoria.

BURLEY

Titus?

AUGUSTA

The two between them could so gild a mischief,
Though it festered to high heaven, smelled most sweet.

DUDLEY

Posh! Tossed his biddies headlong in the ring,
Upon whose fighting heels, may it be noted,
According who the pullet for the day,
Slashed his wicked spurs.

AUGUSTA

I still hear the distant whining of his gulls
Down the furthest reaches of my ear:
Procuress, procured, and bastard!

MIRANDA

Et cetera, et cetera, et cetera!
If you, who were once docile, ardent, credent
Can say that to us now, then I say, madame,
You are in husband, child and every act
A most abominable cheat.

AUGUSTA

I say sluts!
Pander, beast, and prostitutes!

MIRANDA

Hear me:
And if you hear, when you hear
The infinitely distant, pining voice
Of any creature punished in the web,
Or spinning sorrows trap-door in your ear;
Or, broken on the wheel of bitter vision
Some phantom shatter on the glacier of your eye,
Some spirit buzz the shutter of your heart:
If the unleashed hand of Cicero, your hand
Spreads to his creeping octave, on your wall,
And having writ '*non nobis*' in your script
Moves on, then under the listing of the veil
Either other head, empalmed, incline.
Find her, if you find her, turn her:
Stroke out misfortune's fortune.

AUGUSTA

Oh my God!
To everybody I'm the other person!

BURLEY

[*Quickly, to* MIRANDA]
Come, niece, help me with the lamps.

[*Exeunt* BURLEY *and* MIRANDA]

AUGUSTA

[*Nervous on finding herself alone with her sons*]
I wonder what it is Miranda's dressed for.
Though compounded of a thousand ills,
Embroidered, and embossed for some high scandal,
She is, all in all, magnanimous—

ELISHA

So? The whole fool's present in Miranda.

DUDLEY

If rigged for anything it's trouble.
A strolling player indeed! Without Protector,
Husband, son or bank-account? Phizz, phizz!
She'd better been a strolling salesman,
With all that *tutti* and *continuo*;
And walking 'round creation once a day,
And been no menace to our purse.

AUGUSTA

Don't falsify. She never whined your purse.
What I find strange is that she is not famous.
I really thought she'd get into the papers.
She's met everyone of any consequence.
Would she make a note of their addresses?
She would not.

ELISHA

Still you swept the strings, and still she cried,
'My mother, oh my mother!'

AUGUSTA

I've observed the more my daughter lives
Up to the general precepts of her scruples,
The more she is abandoned.

ELISHA

She's resented according how she rates:
Those who can't afford her, push her.

AUGUSTA

Who pushed her?

DUDLEY

                                    You pushed her.

ELISHA

When you, grass-widow, were set out to pasture,
Finding it a time of locusts and of famine—
Thinking only of your sons—and rightly so—
Pushed her, into the dark, as sole provider,
And she as green as any simpleton—

AUGUSTA

[*Trembling*]
Don't you dare that speech before my brother!
Miranda didn't need a push, she went.
Are you so derelict of common custom
You bait your mother to her consternation?
Then I do not hear you.

DUDLEY

[*Grinning*]
Deaf, sure; but break wind in a muff
Then do you startle.

ELISHA

And when she startles with her carving knife—
Three boy mice, see how they run!

AUGUSTA

[*In a level, scornful voice*]
You'd not lose so much as one *castrato*
His dear weight to bruit my case in alt;
Nor you never bought *me* anything to flaunt!

DUDLEY

[*As always, when she is sharp, more pleased than offended*]
Gad! Spirit—what!

[*At this moment* JACK *enters with a well whittled mutton
bone and a mug. He presents them to* AUGUSTA *with a flourish.
She accepts with a child's thoughtless gusto.*]

JACK

Allow me, madame, as good Sir Thomas said:
'All flesh that we behold'—you know—'in at the mouth'—
Remember it.
[*Making for the door*]
If you'll excuse me, I'm knocking up high-tea,
In the pantry.

AUGUSTA

[*Her mouth full*]
Hear anything of Jeremy?

JACK

Jeremy? Not a word of Jeremy.
[BURLEY *and* MIRANDA *enter, with lamps.*]

AUGUSTA

[*Regarding the mutton bone*]
Truly, a monstrous munching earth. But stand upon it
And you find you stand on appetite.
Age? A tenant fool—all fork and pot,
And unpremeditated sleep.

DUDLEY

I say reign, for God's sake, or get off the pot!

BURLEY

[*Setting his lamp under the shadow of the balcony*]
No light may show.

MIRANDA

[*Setting her lamp by the dressmaker's dummy*]
Starlight would have seen us through.

JACK

Bless you, *and* darkness, I'm off.

[*Exit*]

AUGUSTA

[*Noticing for the first time the vines that have encroached on
    the hall*]
See how the bind-weed hauls against the ground
And on the winch of autumn puts out hooks,
To clamber greatness down. How like the vine,
The female-vetch, that low perfidious crawl,
That winding thief with estuary mouth
That nibbles at the root, and topples boys,
And thinks by climbing to the privet of the head
To be the glory that she fattens on.

ELISHA

[*Whistling*]

Couldn't be anyone we know?

DUDLEY

Nor anybody standing in this hall?

AUGUSTA

Why not, dear Dudley?

ELISHA

Because, damn it, we're neither crowned nor credited—
Which is, I will admit, a monstrous blunder.

DUDLEY

Though handsomely well-heeled, I'm sure my wife
Married me for money, lovely money.

AUGUSTA

Exactly.
Glory used to be the aim—now it's possessions.
My heart's as heavy as the emery
I stick my needles in to say it.
But I know women, son. Before I'm cold
They'll have me off the sheets, as I were cork,
And thrown up in the air to my new office.
Before you can say 'Knife!' take pot and pan;
Snatch my very pediment; and from my poke,
(With finger-tips like greedy Florentines
Compounding mischief with the hurricane)
Take all, clasping my hand, for sorrow's seal,
Though in truth but cunning's gyve, to grapple
The finger-rings from hungry *rigor mortis*.
Then will they ease.

DUDLEY

[*Leaning forward, hands on knees*]
Son-of-a-sea-cook, is she tender!

MIRANDA

                    And correct.

AUGUSTA

I've seen the creatures when they thought
My third eyelid was down.

ELISHA

How is it some women have no breasts
Till they have buried children?

AUGUSTA

[*Starting straight up, then sitting down again*]
Oh, unnatural, brutish boy, you nursed me standing!
The suckle-canker yet hangs on your lip!
[DUDLEY *claps his hands.*]

BURLEY

If I might put in a word—

AUGUSTA

Words, words! I would that I'd been shrew,
I'd have pegged my bosom to a thorn:
Or that I'd been the convoy-fish whose maw
Is swamp and cradle to its spawn—
I'd have rocked my children up!

MIRANDA

[*Hotly, to her brothers*]
Base, base!
The fearful purpose of the tiger's prowl,
Consulted in that inch the paw debates,
Was not more still than mine,
When from our mother's stalk I cut you down
And held you like a turtle on my hand—
Saint and turtle are the same upon their back—
And wondered, then, which of the two I'd caught.

ELISHA

[*Making the sound of shivering*]
Brrrrr! The climate of the hand was cold.

MIRANDA

The climate of the hand was terror. Taking purpose
For ferocity is how you lose me.

AUGUSTA

You all seem to know much more than I do.
I, like the poor man-handled mendicant
Sit down alone, to banquet in a dream:
Say I mothered children in a vision.

BURLEY

[*Sadly*]
Has any here, against a worser day
Laid by one kinsman in his sentry-box
To patrol the after time? Not one?
Nothing for the winter of estrangement?

DUDLEY

[*With derision*]

Sure, Miranda.

BURLEY

Though I met Miranda much too late
I've found her, in most part, full excellent.

DUDLEY

But there's depopulation in her yaw.

BURLEY

Augusta, how do you find?

AUGUSTA

In this last, worst hour of my astonishment
I find that I'm a fool.

I've walked me in the Strand and Piccadilly;
I've stroked the lions in Trafalgar Square.
I learned everything in Pendry Cove, yet still
I don't improve, because I won't ask questions.
I won't ask questions because I find I sweat me
In three several horrid generations,
And would know nothing.

JACK

[*Entering*]
The damned, who won't capitulate!
[*To* BURLEY, *who is nodding*]
Hi, warden! Wake up! We're off.

BURLEY

[*Starting*] Eh? What?

JACK

Give me a hand. I've got a thing in boot
Is timely.
[*Exeunt* BURLEY *and* JACK. *They are no sooner gone than silently
and swiftly the two sons—*DUDLEY *donning a pig's mask,* ELISHA
*an ass's, as if the playthings would make them anonymous—
rush the two women.* ELISHA *knocks* MIRANDA's *cane away, seiz-
ing her and pinning her arms behind her.* DUDLEY *pushing* AU-
GUSTA *about in an attempt to make her dance.*]

DUDLEY

I'll huff, and I'll puff, and I'll blow your house down!

AUGUSTA

[*Thinking they are really playing*]
A game! A game!

DUDLEY

[*Dropping her, dancing about in a crouching position, striking out in light rapid taps, as of a boxer sparring*]
Want to play with baby? Going to play with baby?
Who's afraid?
He'll let you off at Windsor!

ELISHA

[*Pushing* MIRANDA *from behind with his knee, still holding her arms*]
Now then, my somewhat well-used spinster,
Now that your precious uncle Jonathan
Has for the moment turned down his metronome
And bushel'd off, what shan't we do with you?
You'd never listen to your brothers, would you, Toots?
Tick-bird, riding out the Grand Conception,
Which father's lack of guts, left in your corner.
      [*Raising his knee*]
Let's see, if by your scumber, you are fox!

DUDLEY

[*Over his mother's shoulder, to* ELISHA]
Slap her rump, and stand her on four feet!
That's her best position!

ELISHA

The damned and dedicated 'victim'. Just another
Self-appointed increment! I never knew
Such an earnest stinker!
Couldn't you have lived up to your brothers?

AUGUSTA

[*Out of breath*]
O praise her! Praise her!
      [*Recovering*]

You never would—you know you never would
Listen to your brothers.

MIRANDA
[*Suddenly freeing herself*]
Hands off, you too near thing!
[*To* AUGUSTA]
Would you that I leap into myself
There dismiss me of my occupation
To set me in the slum of their regard?
Would have me clapped between the palms of their approval?
Get me rated
In the general horror of the common mouth;
And to the verdict of the vulgar, stand me down
Crying 'I'm a fool!' to ease a fool?

DUDLEY
Crack her crown with thimbles, wring her nose!
Look out, boys, the holy dam has bust!

MIRANDA
There is a kind of ticking in a little man
Announces him.

ELISHA
[*Kicking* MIRANDA'S *skirt*]
That amulet you wore upon your leg—
Not rusted yet?
[*Loud laughter.* DUDLEY, *now in possession of* JACK'S *whip,
makes darting motions with it at* AUGUSTA. *His and* ELISHA'S
*remarks follow so closely they are spoken in a sort of free-for-
all.*]

DUDLEY
[*To* AUGUSTA]
Hi! I love to see a sway-back on the run;

It's game to haul a bang-tail by the scut;
It's rare to watch a crab stuck on a skewer
When the parasite is sidling in for keeps,
Hog-backed and dousing for a grave!

ELISHA

[*To* MIRANDA]

Ho! continental shoat—eh? Got the staggers?
Made the run from gate-post to the gate?
Got best rating from the bloody intellectuals?
Aristocrat, pauper, artist, beggar!

[*Snapping his fingers over her head, as in show*]

Trim, trim, up, up! Quarter—quarter!
Who's going to run again, wayfarer stalking
In the earth? Not you, not ever you.
Rakehell, toss-pot, salamander, punk!
You'll be crawling in my gutters yet
If I don't watch it—with your starving puss
Like some abominable slug of vengeance, risen
Waist-high, pointing your shaking finger at me,
And who can stand a beggar who can point,
Even in her most 'distinguished' drunkenness?
Get yourself an occupation—souser!

MIRANDA

If drink for drink, mine, business guile, as yours:
If for my brother Brutus I belched dollars,
I'd find he wore me to the elbow.
Merchant—away with you!

ELISHA

Away, says she!
Do you think, by your rank continence to stay
The generations?

[*Seizing her*]

Manless, childless, safeless document—
I'll staff you!

[*He is weeping as he mauls her.*]

MIRANDA
[*Quietly pushing him away*]
Do not think to climb me, brother.
See how it is with man who has no history
To make him innocent. See how deaf the face is.
How the crouching tongue turns in the mouth
To sting me down; look how pricks up his ear!
You'll rump it to the judgement seat, poor trader,
Dragging the lumber of your tail.

ELISHA
[*Standing back*]
Damnation and the devil!
[*He trips her*]

                                           Sanded, am I?

Then go be my wag!

DUDLEY
Look, the mendicant bell-wether's down.
Who's sanded now!

AUGUSTA
                                           Let her go.
Should she drop the flag of her surrender,
Do not pick it up: it charges in the cambric!

ELISHA
[*Giving* MIRANDA *a violent shove towards* AUGUSTA]
She's your dog, do as you like with her.

AUGUSTA

[*Considering the recommendation*]
Even dogs are not abandoned in a ruin, Elisha.

ELISHA

Oh yes, they are. It's practice keeps them still,
And what other practice has she but her ruin?
If we take her home and loose her on our ledgers,
She'll blot us up.

AUGUSTA

Fie, fie! I've seen my daughter die before, and make it.

DUDLEY

[*Swinging* JACK's *whip before him*]
The sun being in the lower ward, you plead her?
    [*He turns the whip, handle down, making imaginary squares
    on the ground, as children do in street games*]
'Step upon a crack, you break your mother's back—'
Jump, old woman, jump! jump off the world!
Be dead, be done, be modest dead, be quick!
A snipe can smell his meat ten inches underground;
On scent, old crow, downward to the feast!
    [*He attempts to make her dance,* AUGUSTA *tries to obey, her
    mouth open as one who screams*]
Dance! Dance! Dance!

AUGUSTA

                    Eighty's a cold mouse!

DUDLEY

[*Whirling her about*]
Who's eighty yet?

MIRANDA
[*Coming between them*]
Stop it!
[*To* AUGUSTA]
Unclench the cramp in Dudley's hand, poor woman.
As some rudiment of forgotten nature squalls
In the horned-toad's eye, that it spills blood
Who is too hideous to mourn, so your son's palm
Might spill lost innocence in kind,
The baby fleece he cropped up, journeying his crib.
There is he mapped—if he be mapped at all—
Yet I think, that of himself, he's washed his either hand.

[BURLEY *and* JACK *enter, carrying a covered object. Placing it
in the centre of the table,* JACK *pulls the cover off, exposing a
doll's house.* DUDLEY *and* ELISHA *hurriedly unmask, holding the
masks under arm.*]

JACK
[*Quietly*]
I give you Hobb's Ark, beast-box, doll's house—
That little alchemy unhems a man.
Madame, your contagion.

ELISHA
The House That Jack Built:
Feed her to the toy!

[*He lifts* AUGUSTA *to the table, unprotesting. Cross-legged she
sits before the toy, picking up the first thing to catch her at-
tention—a stick hung with dolls.*]

AUGUSTA
Tumblers! Seven straightened mistresses!
[*She pushes the lock on the roof of the doll's house, and up
pops a doll*]

Why, it's your father, Titus, tamed! An imp,
A midge, a tick, a peg, a bob, a gnat,
A syllable all buttoned up in cypress!
A chip, a doll, a toy, a pawn,
A little man soon cooled. A nothing!
Now he has struck a size that suits him!
Was this the stick that leapt me, gentlemen?
Where now the stallion yard lay beating on the turf
Its whistling vent? So proud of it he was
He asked to be but laid beside it in the grave.

JACK
                                Tall burial?

ELISHA
Watch her go!

AUGUSTA
This size I could have jumped him, and have been
Happily unacquainted with you all.
    [*Scanning the puppet*]
A thieving magpie's borne his beard away!

MIRANDA
To build a nest on Babylon.

JACK
Evoe! You have an husband in the hand,
A slave, a fit of pine to do your bidding.
Was this the inch that set you out at hack?
Then 'tis a kissing splinter for a catch,
And you can game again!

MIRANDA
    [*Sharply*]
On what errand was the knife that whittled this?

JACK
                    Wood-offering.

AUGUSTA
Whose malice was it hacked him down?

JACK
                    Mine.

AUGUSTA
I said, who are you that you should know
How a widow's dead man looks?

JACK
                    Nobody, madame.

AUGUSTA
Miranda has been talking.

JACK
                    Possibly.

AUGUSTA
Not any theme at all will make this strut again.

MIRANDA
Now has the mountain fallen on Mohammed.

AUGUSTA
How do we thaw from history. How many
To this splinter have, like porcupines,
Made careful love? What apes our eyes were
Saw him great because he said so.
So, lay him down.

MIRANDA

If death's a green unruly thumb, I'd say
Do not lay down that breeding inch;
It was the cause.

JACK

[*Tapping on the attic window of the doll's house*]
Put your wink against this window pane,
What do you see?

AUGUSTA

[*Putting her eye to the small window*]
A bedroom, no bigger than my hand.

MIRANDA

Do you remember what that cock-loft saw;
For that window is become your eye.
What do you see?

AUGUSTA

[*Recoiling*]
I don't care what you've done, I forgive me.

MIRANDA

                        Do you?

AUGUSTA

[*With great agitation*]
Stop them, Miranda. I'm a stranger here.

JACK

                        Stranger, or accomplice?

AUGUSTA

I do not understand you.

JACK
No? Look to.

AUGUSTA
[*Her chin on the window ledge*]
As in a glass darkly, a frost of fury spent;
As ghosts of hot-house plants in summer shed
A static flight impaled upon the pane:
As in a profaned monstrance, see conspire
The fighting shadow of the Devil and the Daughter.

MIRANDA
Miranda damned, with instep up-side-down,
Dragging rape-blood behind her, like the snail—

JACK
Beneath her, in a lower room, her father
Rubbed down his hands.

BURLEY
There towered an infant on her face!

JACK
And thereafter, all the sad forlorn.

AUGUSTA
Who are you that you know anything?

JACK
The crystal, like a pregnant girl, has hour
When it delivers up its oracle,
Leaving the chamber to the adversary.
The eye-baby now you're pregnant with
You'll carry in your iris to the grave.
You made yourself a *madam* by submission
With, no doubt, your apron over head,

Strewing salt all up and down the stairs
Trying to catch an heel on its last mile—
A girl who'd barely walked away sixteen—
Tipped to a travelling cockney thrice that age,
Indeed Brigid-Matilda's brother. Why?
Titus had him handy—

AUGUSTA

Stop it!

JACK

Though Miranda cried first, like the ewe,
'Do not let him—but if it will atone—'
Offering up her silly throat for slashing,
The jolted tongue
Blowing off the hacking caw—

AUGUSTA

[*In great agitation*]
I did not see it! I did not hear it!

JACK

[*Relentlessly*]
—So I say, between you both, you made
Of that slaughter house a babe's *Bordel*.

AUGUSTA

[*Looking wildly about, and seeing stray travellers who have
climbed up the back way into the gallery, staring down, she
throws herself over the doll house, beating at it with both
hands*]
No, no! Stop it! Enough! Away!
Wolves! Mountebanks! Historians!
Whatever trapper hunts me overhead,
Whistle off your prophets and your doves,
Who fouled this house, lest one proclaim

What this fearful haunt has seen!

> [*All the heads disappear from the balcony.* MIRANDA *helps her
> mother down from the table, putting her own cloak about
> her.*]

MIRANDA
Come, come to supper.

AUGUSTA
How have my reflections gone from out
The pools of Burley. How I've fumbled my escape!

> [*As all go towards the pantry,* ELISHA *gives* MIRANDA *the ass's
> head.*]

ELISHA
Miranda, I give you our weapons, Jack, to you
My compliments. You pulled a trick unseats us all.

BURLEY
> [*Taking* AUGUSTA'S *arm*]

                          My arm, Augusta.

MIRANDA
> [*Allowing all to pass in, detains* BURLEY, *who gives* AUGUSTA'S
> *arm to* DUDLEY]

A moment, uncle:
For the rest I do absolve you of the company.
You have a conduct in yourself so admirable,
So delicate in passion, in judgement sweet;
In succour tidy, and in anything of self,
So mild and just,
That your address is pardon in itself.

But here's a rate too special for your years.
You've seen us shaken in diminutives
And brought down low, like Hector, by the heel—

BURLEY

Dear niece, Hector is always dead.

MIRANDA

I ask you be not present, be prevented.
As the ballerina on perfected toe
Spins to the axis of a fortitude
That is the sum of all her yesterdays,
To this loadstone of passions I must turn.
In your spare fastidious alarm
I think you think to sit this session out.
Abjure it. You sit between two beasts in chancery
Who fight, head down, between them for a grave
That neither of them has a conduct for.

BURLEY

Dear Miranda—

MIRANDA

Dear uncle, you have a climate in yourself
So amenable to destiny, I love you for it.
But here is something more than monstrous wicked;
The spirit being chameleon to the mind
And that mind vulgar, I tell you be not present.
As a victim in the wash of crime—
Like a bell-buoy in the running tide—
Rocks but to the leeway of the roll,
So my spirit voyages at tether:
For I do swear, dear uncle, I have loved
Three sons, and one woman to the heart.

BURLEY

Sons?

MIRANDA

What else, if I am she, and she Miranda?

BURLEY

'A poet is a light and winged thing, and holy',
As Plato said. You're in the wash of such;
The which your people know; it is their cruel pleasure.

MIRANDA

[*With affection*]
If all the martyrs in the catacombs
Should take it in their heads to move away,
You'd compute the dissolution augury,
And just on chance you'd keep the dove-cote swept.
I think you must have heard the dead unpack
Their wings before, for here's a clapping air.
But no, not yet. This is a clocked encounter
To which I would not have you sacristan.
You are unfit for stumble in conformity—
And wonderfully is man made counterfeit.
Therefore, when you have supped, return
And help me make of this divided beast
An undivided bed.

[*Exit* BURLEY]

CURTAIN

Act Three

The gryphon has been brought together. The tented lace cur-
tains clubbed in the carnival crown. On this car MIRANDA *lies*
sleeping.

[AUGUSTA *enters, followed by* BURLEY, *carrying a lamp.*]

AUGUSTA

See, she has a sleep. I gave it her.
My hoard of me, remission, recompense.
See how she darkens; how compounds me.
But does she not breathe short of ransom?

BURLEY

[*To himself*]

In circus Vaticanus fallen.

AUGUSTA

It's terrible to walk behind old children, Jonathan,
Who once tipped back their heads to drink.

BURLEY

I think it time you saw her as Miranda.

AUGUSTA

I think it's time I saw me as Augusta.
There's the curfew-bell, and it's o'clock, and bedlam.
Shall I ring and wake her?

BURLEY

Do not wake her. There's a ligature in sleep
Binds us to waking; lease her.
Good night, Augusta.

AUGUSTA

                                        Where are the boys?

BURLEY

Above you, resting in the gallery.

AUGUSTA

Good night, Jonathan.
And Jack?

BURLEY

                                        For safety, with his horse.

MIRANDA

    [*Waking*]
Is that you, Uncle?

BURLEY

                                        Good night, my dear.

MIRANDA

Good night, Uncle.

[*Exit* BURLEY]

AUGUSTA

Good night.
        [*Inspecting the gryphon*]
A solid beast, an excellent stage, fit for a play.

MIRANDA

To bed, to bed.

AUGUSTA

I think I have forgotten Beewick and the beast.

MIRANDA

I think it.

AUGUSTA

Will you stay?

MIRANDA

That depends.

AUGUSTA

On what?

MIRANDA

On many things.

AUGUSTA

You have it very pleasant here.

MIRANDA

So travellers say—of other people's stations.

AUGUSTA

So, let us play. The epilogue is over,
The boys asleep, and we are girls again
Nor need not think of them this part of night.
When you were young and out of company
I made you sitting donkeys, one like that
But only smaller. I made you ducks and drakes
Of butter-coloured flannel.
        [*She mounts the bed, facing* MIRANDA]
My amends—for every kind of thing.
Now the animals are put up in their box,
Let's be young again and tell us of our lives.
Recount to me, Miranda, who have been
Too much slain in public, how it is.
What news of me?

MIRANDA

Looking down the barrel of your eye,
I see the body of a bloody Cinderella
Come whirling up.

AUGUSTA

My last of worlds, my trick of tricks,
My store, my ace in hole,
Come flying up with me!
Come, play me daughter.

MIRANDA

Hold, woman!
There was a time when we were not related.
When I first loved thee— I say 'thee' as if
It were to use a lost endearment
That in the loss has lost the losing world—
When I first loved thee, thou wert grazing:
Carrion Eve, in the green stool, wading,

In the coarse lilies and the sombre wood;
Before the tree was in the cross, the cradle, and the coffin,
The tragic head-board, and the victim door,
The weeper's banister, the cunning panel.
When yet the salt unspilt, the bread unbroken,
The milk unquested, unwept for, and unsprung,
You came braying for a victim lover.
The cock crew, the spur struck, and Titus Adam
Had at you with his raping-hook
And you reared back, a belly full of thumbs.

AUGUSTA

By my heaven, that was my greenest sickness!
I was slumming when I let you wear by belly.

MIRANDA

Have it so. Then began the trick—
The balking embryo, that mischief's parcel,
That legless flight, that gizzard brain,
That sitting hummock crouching in the head,
Computing its slow minting inch—that orphan,
Purblind, faceless, jellied in its course,
Rolling in a palm-full of the belly's Thames,
A dockless hawser 'round about its neck,
Praying without hands—lolled on its thumb,
And time commenced.

AUGUSTA

[*Frightened—but without gesture*]
Shssssh!

MIRANDA

The salt spilled, the bread broke. Unmuzzled bone
Drew on the hood of flesh, entombing laughter:
Tongues came forth, and forth the hissing milk

Its lashing noose, and snared the gaping mouth.
A door slammed on Eden, and the Second Gate,
And I walked down your leg.

AUGUSTA

> Alas, your father!

MIRANDA

Alas, my mother!
I would his groin had been as shadowless
As Origen's, ere I had rustled in his lap.

AUGUSTA

> What's here!

MIRANDA

What's not here!

AUGUSTA

To think I have a daughter for Inquisitor!

MIRANDA

To think I had a mother should betray me!
Tax me guilty both of audit and default;
Tot me up, as idiots their droppings,
And as indifferently, tick off the count.

AUGUSTA

What has wrought you to this sudden fury?

MIRANDA

What? Thinking on the shoddy lamentation
Rung about so desolate a journey.
Only yesterday, the heaped up chronicle—
Where you crossed your palms upon your gown

To guard the secret of the belly's botany—
Was grappled by my father's bloodhound hand
And I ripped public for the scapegoat run.

AUGUSTA

[*Knuckle to eye*]
Love is death, Miranda. I am tame
As I'm forgotten.

MIRANDA

Even the frightened die.

AUGUSTA

Oh, think of it!

MIRANDA

Love is death, and death is maidenly.
It wrestles in the brasses and the rods
Of whatsoever trestle love lies on.
What else but murder with the mackerel eye
Couples with the tenants of that bed?
Crying 'I love, I hunger and I fear!'
With arms and legs stuck forthright as the slain
Under the bloody linen of the butcher's cart.
So I say with Pericles
'Murder's as near to lust as flame to smoke.'

AUGUSTA

[*Leaning toward* MIRANDA]
Could I love again?

MIRANDA

Does the fallen drummer-boy, his heel
In muscular contraction, kick his drum?

AUGUSTA

You are too old for me, and merciless.
You who never were revengeful are become so.

MIRANDA

Not revengeful, but much another thing.

AUGUSTA

Let's jump the Day of Wrath. Let us pretend.
The play is over and the boys are put to bed.
Let's play at being Miranda and Augusta.
Say we're at some hunting-box with lords—
Say duck sniping—on a lake, or snaring
Woodcock in the hills—shooting and kissing—
Your father wore the trappings, but his aim—

MIRANDA

Was wild.

AUGUSTA

So let us both forget him.
I think the gryphon moved. We have a carriage!
Let's go to Ostend, Monte Carlo, Brighton;
The Lido, Palm Beach, Breisgau, Carcassonne—
And don't forget the flares and chandeliers—
The pleasure gardens, Vauxhall, Fontainbleau,
The Trianon, and fountains, and the music!

MIRANDA

[*Smiling*]
No fountains—no flambeaux, no music nor no gallants.

AUGUSTA

Then on to Longchamp, Ascot, Aintree, Epsom!
Regattas, fairs; horse racing in the Corso?

Anything. Bartholomews. Let's catch
A fairing at a stall; let's dance a jig.
Let's to Billingsgate with fife and drum!

MIRANDA

Have you forgotten Calvin?

AUGUSTA

I'll sit in a supper box with Richelieu—
But later. Now we're off for Maxime's, only
Call in the caterers, the pigeons, larks and torches;
Let us join the gentlemen!
   [*Without asking permission,* AUGUSTA *takes off* MIRANDA'S
   *shoes, puts them on her own feet, and in exchange puts hers
   on* MIRANDA]
Love puts forth her foot; let's to the opera.

MIRANDA

Love puts forth her foot, and in my shoes.

AUGUSTA

   [*Holding up her hand*]
Look!
Lying fallow at death's door these many days
I have me back my pleasant foot and hand,
The hand as seemly white as any girl's,
The ankle small and fit.
So I'll to the hunting lodge of Meyerling.
I'll romp me in an hide-away in Garmisch.
Or shall I be a Tuscan with strict flanks
Stomping, to a singer from Auvergne?
Or a Turk?

MIRANDA
                              No.

AUGUSTA

No?
Then have it I am Empress Josephine,
With an hat full of Napoleon's bees;
Some chief imprudent of the *haute noblesse*—
Or no, Lily Langtry, tipping glass of sorbet,
Waiting on the inert Prince of Somewhere
To pitch it down the pathway to his seat!
And don't forget the pinwheels and the rockets!

MIRANDA

O delayed and waiting creature!

AUGUSTA

Could you say I'd seen the baths of Caracalla?
Tickled from the keel of Lost Atlantis
All her drowned crustacean lovers bobbing
That great city, that ocean-going bride?
Or have I been a Tudor crone, sea-hag, for nothing?
Have I ruffled, all in all, the golden hen
But to set sour eggs before foul gentlemen?

MIRANDA

I fear it.

AUGUSTA

What! Are you too *young* for me, indeed?
        [*Thinking herself into fairy-tales and legends*]
Was I ever princess in a legend?
        [*Whispers*]
Did I sleep a hundred years?

MIRANDA

Mother, there's no more time. All's done.

AUGUSTA

[*In a frantic whisper*]
Was I stolen?

MIRANDA

O unhappy wanderer—
I've seen you dig for Antony
With a kitchen spoon.

AUGUSTA

[*Pretending to check*]
Was I Svengali's evening thrush? Delsarte's
Best equation? Did I lean on Persian?
[*She takes on a most affected pose*]
With the first finger held up for the finches,
The left hand poised upon the right hand's back,
Gum Arabic curbing the restless laces,
[*Dropping the pose*]
Jess to the wrist? Or was I in the gallery
The day the guillotine was shucking heads?
Was it I who, dipping kerchief at Antoine,
Came up with Augusta on my napkin?
O Miranda, staunch me!

MIRANDA

Do not press so hard upon the point.

AUGUSTA

Never walked beside the Serpentine?
Never checked a victor's knobs and bosses
On any field of any Marathon?
Nor never, in great joy, kissed on the mouth
By a mouth deposed between me and the kissing?
I've too much nature in me, daughter,
And you too old.

MIRANDA

Ah, that mouth with cutlass in the gape
That cut you down from the forbidden tree.
Dearest, worst and sorriest, had been a man
You'd been the bloodiest villain of us all.

AUGUSTA

[*Grinning*]
Why then I am!
But you blow my candle out, could read
With your bare eyes a dead man back again.
Do not vote me of that dateless herd
Lowing without tongue—huge freight of silence—
On a frieze ten pastures down,
But pull me up as we had high carouse;
I'll willing be a transient to this world
And it be *now*—and jollity!
Or is gone all pride and merriment?
Shall I have no gales, nor games, nor country pleasures,
'Where'er I walk?' but 'crowd into a shade'?
Not scattered in the bloom, but as the wrack,
Sea-grape, its bladders and full bush
A bramble off the banks, and kicked by wind and rain?
Not gathered in the hunting hand, not sleeked,
Not prospered, tended; wholly desolate?
Take mercy on my prentice cries, Miranda,
Leave me not so sharp, unsung, and shrill;
With autumn's savage jet my bosom brooked,
My harvest awn all down, and leaning on my hand.
The once new-risen loaves of my brimmed breast
Kissed in the busk; now bowling low they knock
Their withered acorns on my knee:
So, the phoenix runs upon the ash,
As the Roman on his sword!

MIRANDA

O mother, mother!

AUGUSTA

You call this wisdom? Aii, I call it winter!
Where *are* the banquets and the cavaliers?
How near to my last travesty the spading foot?
How soon the cargo of that creeping thing
Whose very texture is the inside-kissing lip?
'Man owes a death to God', you say? So be it.
But if there is no God, then God forgive him!
You too are grown unkind with shivering.
Allay my sorrow then, you cruel girl;
Medicine me to some account more just;
Do not so fumble my futurity.

MIRANDA

Blow less hard about the stage. Be still.

AUGUSTA

Then absolve me of the mischief is Augusta.
Snatch me out, I come on me in vain.

MIRANDA

Stand to.

AUGUSTA

You won't even tell me how you are, or what.

MIRANDA

Trappist—sprung—and of an hard-won silence.

AUGUSTA

Nothing else about your history?

MIRANDA

Nothing.

AUGUSTA

Nothing at all?

MIRANDA

Nothing at all.

AUGUSTA

[*Taking up* MIRANDA's *hat*]
So then, like a Norman widow, having hung—
Speaking in metaphor—your father's hat
Upon its proper post, may I have yours?
     [*She puts on* MIRANDA's *hat*]
My daughter is winged serpent, *and* the urn.
Some damned dark Beatitude that sits
In her heart's core, mewling like an idiot,
Cribs her out of eminence and profit;
Sweeps her from the kingdom and the general world—
And she sits by, and strokes its bloody head.

MIRANDA

Observant. . . .

AUGUSTA

I'm swan-sick, girl, and more than tired of roses.
Give me then my thistles and my thorn;
The un-may'd daisies' harsh and scentless spring,
And all the weeds that of no summer wane.
The castor, spurge, the bitter root and hazel;
My short hand-bloom, my borage and my stock.
You gave me myrtles yesterday, you say?
But here's nothing again—
   Give me your hand in absence: part in meeting:
You who should have been the first born of the two.

MIRANDA

There's a cry of women!

AUGUSTA

[*Leaning forward, in an urgent whisper*]
Is it true that you had forty lovers?

MIRANDA

Bridge of asses! Would you cross on me?
So it's I was stung for winter feast!

AUGUSTA

[*Covering her face*]
Do not leave me drenching in my hands.
Do not stamp me down for tally in the earth,
The 'lo, behold!' of raveners. Be merciful.
When this body drops from off its ghost
Who'll bell that cat?

MIRANDA

[*Uncovering* AUGUSTA'S *face*]
What! not weeping after all! I had suspected it.
There are, they say, strange cattle in a tear
Go on another business than our own;
And grazing, pull our sorrow up.

AUGUSTA

It's not I wouldn't, it is that I cannot.
My natural showers have wept unnatural moons:
I'm grinned away, to catch my sons' attention.

MIRANDA

I sorrow you have been too blamed for praise.
Yet who knows, when Oedipus grubbed out
The luggage of his sight upon a pin,

For what in-caverned vision then he mined?
They say that he who digs far down for love
Brings up the brightest burning coal.
Be not your own pathetic fallacy, but be
Your own dark measure in the vein,
For we're about a tragic business, mother.

AUGUSTA

Who *are your* people?

MIRANDA

By the unrecording axis of my eye
It should be observed I have no people:
But on the dark side, there I entertain.

AUGUSTA

The bowels?

MIRANDA

It has been remarked from advent to the terror
Woman is most beast familiar—
What stroke was that?

AUGUSTA

Keeping related.
What's never been remarked is that the mother,
Fearing what it is a spirit eats,
Goes headlong through her children's guts,
Looking for bread.
But never mind
Give me news of something fabulous—
Of you? No news of that?

MIRANDA
No news of that.

AUGUSTA

No man died for you?
Nothing? No news of famous people?

MIRANDA

No famous people, and no man died.

AUGUSTA

Willow, willow, willow!
If you won't make the either of us notable,
Or put us on the index of The Book,
Or tell me anything of life at all,
Then put us near to someone who's been near it.
There was Fenimore Cooper's house, and Poe's.
I myself was once asked to a garden party—
Archbishop Benson's. Just behind the close
They saw me sitting up. Say 'Who *is* Sylvia
That all the swains adored her?'

MIRANDA

                    Indeed, who.

AUGUSTA

I've not been loved enough to be forgotten!
I am too old to be so frightened, daughter,
And unreliable with sorrow. Tell me—
You who are forever somewhat blunt,
And I where now no salt can catch me—
Tell me, was there a woman, once *so* well beloved
She yet lies still beneath a ton in India,
With reasonable hands?

MIRANDA

                    She does.

AUGUSTA

And did a legend, undersea, break water
To leap into a lover's lap?

MIRANDA

She did.

AUGUSTA

See? I remember who I am tomorrow;
Fie this striving, fancying, believing!
I have, I say, small patience with the mind
That dares oblivion, yet peoples it
With turn about of heart. I would be Helen
Forgotten, day by day, for ever and for ever!
Fie upon the whole of love's debris,
That horrid holocaust that is the price
Of passion's seizure! Why, I've even heard
That insects shed, and birds in copulation
Moult; and in some kinds the very beaks are wrung
And scattered all about the forest floor!
I've been told of boys, come to majority,
With baby mittens yet fast hot upon them,
That later, in the doff of rite, were found
Wrestling on a bed!

MIRANDA

I wonder, is there any instrument
Beside harmonica, a man, or comb
Plays full gamut to the indrawn breath?

AUGUSTA

There's a choir of howlers in the air
That only others hear. Your father's hounds
The smallest basset, loosed on Exeter
High on the leads, flushed out a vicar
Not at that point assembled in the womb.

MIRANDA

I wonder what it is that madmen hear
That calls them on a crusade that's a cheat?

AUGUSTA

If you are speaking of your father, I forgive him;
I've younger men are running 'round my mind.

MIRANDA
[*More to herself than to* AUGUSTA]
Titus, self-appointed bray of heaven;
Wived in righteous plenty; populated.
Thought himself as dedicate as Stephen,
That crusading infant long before him.
No sooner got a following, than impudence,
And hoist upon the engine of his children
Shook his rattle over Pendry, crying:
'Down with church, with schoolroom, and with king!'
And had himself precisely where he quailed.

AUGUSTA

The law! The fright! The recantation!

MIRANDA

And all his sons rolled in the marketplace—
But hands up, bidding on destruction!

AUGUSTA

Your father was a self-molested man!

MIRANDA

Where a man so lauds himself, and blows
So full a gale of women all before him,
Then defaults, what then?
He, who for fear, denies the called response,

Denies the singing, and damns the congregation!
I've often wondered how so many women
Managed so many children on one bed!

AUGUSTA

I said, you are a wicked woman!

MIRANDA

I know. The last time was the last time that you saw me.
That was another war. When I'd drawn in
My last of anything, except my book,
You took it in the dark, and gave it to my brother,
Who grinned as I'd been caught.

AUGUSTA

May God protect us! I wonder what you'll write
When I am dead and gone!

MIRANDA

My brothers say, 'Let's break Miranda!' You?
Why mother, they'd have thrown you in the pit—
The last salt-lick before oblivion,
Where the gammers of the world come down to feed—
Except I put my foot against that door.

AUGUSTA

[*With admiration*]
You almost amounted—once. I've said it.

MIRANDA

[*With bitterness*]
But, by my heaven, not the money-wink?
That drawbridge to a safe economy,
That hooded glare the condor turns on quarry,
The eyelid that absolves him of the kill?

AUGUSTA

Who are you become?

MIRANDA

[*Enigmatically*]
Have I not said it?
One of a strolling company of players?
Wardrobe mistress, tiring many parts?
You see yourself, you have my rings and boots,
My cloak and hat.

AUGUSTA

[*Back to pleasant thoughts*]
So I have!
Buckled shoes and rings, and feathered hat!
Do let's pretend we're girls again; let's play.
If dull at home, one may be skilled abroad;
There must be ways to catch a world.

MIRANDA

Ah, yes.
Every mother, in extortion for her milk—
With the keyhole iris of the cat—draws blood.
Teasing the terror for the teasing story,
And what it's worth, in foreign places, temporal,
Applauding with kill-kindly tongue of charity
As benchers in the last dispensary:
[*With the tongue*]
'Tick, tick, mercy that one took her life
In satin slippers! Only fancy!'

AUGUSTA

Minor wind, blow less major daughter!
I'd have you smaller—though cast up for glory—
Somewhat lower down, where I can catch you!

MIRANDA

So that is it! Then let us speak of men
And the quantity that I'm recalled by.
Say a burgomaster up in Uffing
Unnests me both at wedding and at funeral:
When bowing low and raising his top-hat,
I tumble from the lining of the gibus,
In the shape of one small rabbit toque.

AUGUSTA

I like that! I like to think you're honoured
Even at the bottom of a hat.

MIRANDA

If splendid folly is your appetite,
And sly Islamic humour to your taste,
Then say a Berber of the Atlas left me
One hundred horses.

AUGUSTA

                              Because you had no seat?

MIRANDA

Because I had no stable.

AUGUSTA

[*Rising*]
Daughter,
There's a battlement in every woman's heart
Whereon she keeps perpetual patrol
To dodge the man she married, for a man
Scratching in the wall.

MIRANDA

Till through some aperture in desolation
A lover creeps?

AUGUSTA

Think of it!
All through by beauty he enjoyed an ugly woman!
That man your father. I said his acts to me
Were never gentle, fond nor kind;
Nor he never held nor stroked me anywhere;
And you stood up, as in a lost equation,
As you had mended such economy.

MIRANDA

And so I should indeed, had I been able,
But metempsychosis not for asking:
And between us stands the argument.

AUGUSTA

I knew that you'd say nothing comforting.
Yet I swear the Virgin did not love
Her chirrup more than I my children.
Make me something!

MIRANDA

[*The two women are circling each other*]
Largo, largo! Hold your rate in ordinary!
Do not confuse the advent with assumption.
Nor at this starve, go throw me up for target.
The wind that knocked our generation down
Was not an harvest.
The Queen of Heaven, holding trust ajar
For the entrance and the exit of Good News
Was nothing similar.

AUGUSTA

Of course you always have it your own way;
You're the terrier runs back without the bone.

MIRANDA

How is it that women who love children
So often damn the children that they have?
Would you propose a beggared silk-worm draw
From out her haggard poke so brave a silk
Could card a paragon?

AUGUSTA

Ah, failed!

MIRANDA

Rebuke me less, for we are face to face
With this the fadged up ends of discontent:
But tie and hold us in that dear estrangement
That we may like before we too much lose us.
As the blacksmith hammers out his savage metal,
So is the infant hammered to the dance.
But if not wrapped in metric, hugged in discipline,
Rehearsed in familiarity reproved;
Grappled in the mortise of the ritual,
And turning in the spirit of the play.
Then equilibrium will be the fall;
Abide it.

AUGUSTA

Magpie!
In what pocket have you my identity?
I so disoccur in every quarter of myself
I cannot find me;
Suttee to an ember burning cold.
In your valid and unshaken company
I still dangle for the cockatrice
My unsucked eggs.

MIRANDA

Where the martyr'd wild fowl fly the portal
High in the honey of cathedral walls,
There is the purchase, governance and mercy.
Where careful sorrow and observed compline
Sweat their gums and mastics to the hive
Of whatsoever stall the head's heaved in—
There is the amber. As the high plucked banks
Of the viola rend out the unplucked strings below—
There is the antiphon.
I've seen loves so eat each other's mouth
Till that the common clamour, co-intwined,
Wrung out the hidden singing in the tongue
Its chaste economy—there is the adoration.
So the day, day fit for dying in
Is the plucked accord.

AUGUSTA

And how am I, in this kingfisher night,
To brim me to the brim and stay uncaught?
My calendar is hulled, my lands in plague;
The locust, jacket-jumped, claws to my stile
So we stare on each the other with unbuttoned eyes
In such abandoned case as kills the heart.
Would you call a plague of absence, company?

MIRANDA

Yes.

AUGUSTA

So the haggard cries in vain. 'Alas!'
We admire each other in our cruel way.
Unpack your purse—afford me. But no matter;
What have you, after all.

MIRANDA

The loss.

AUGUSTA

What does that mean? Never mind that either.
When I'm dead and gone, put me to a tree.

MIRANDA

Presently.

AUGUSTA

Why don't you love us any more?
That is the question—
Where *is* Miranda?

MIRANDA

The question is, why do I? Where's Miranda?
Thugged to death, not slain upon the altar
Where's that coign and cupboard of the heart
That mothers used to keep their warbler in?
The gate's been jimmied and the imp has flown,
Scotched by the sword her people snatched
From the gate of Eden, for a whip
To beat her, reeling like an headless cock,
Ramshackle, aghast, and staring all abroad—
A gaze contained in nothing.
What echoes, think you, swarmed that bloody head?
Bushelled in the mind's confessional,
Foxed down its gullet to the rump,
Quaking with unhouselled mouth agape,
Lashing at the lattice with her paws.—
What say of that?

AUGUSTA

[*Sadly*]
Women were not saved, then, after all.

MIRANDA

Saved!
I've seen my people set the canine tooth
Into the Host;
I've heard them lapping at the wound.
What think you?

AUGUSTA

God have mercy on me!

MIRANDA

God have mercy on us all; and may He
Forgive me my abominable innocence
That I can't think what it is I've done,
Who have not seen my people many years,
To so estrange us.

AUGUSTA

I want Jeremy; where is Jeremy?
God is so slow with me; where is my son?

MIRANDA

Where, indeed.

AUGUSTA

He would have stayed with me, if you had stayed.
He'd have wanted to, if you had wanted it;
You were both so fond of each the other;
He turned to you, but he couldn't stand it.

MIRANDA

What!
Would you I'd kept his mother's stalk upon him?
Dealt him a pack of tricks, cut by a sister,
In a deal that had not shuffled him?

Neither juried, judged, committed nor dismissed,
But in stound, with mouth too tender for the hook?
Why, what a thing!

AUGUSTA

Gone, gone! cast out and waning
Like a circle running from a stone
Pitched upon a frightful deed; forgotten.
I leave the whole catch to the resurrection!

MIRANDA

Do you?
Do you think there'll be no tussle in that trench?
And would you set this 'monster' up again?
You who would un-breath my dying breath
From off the tell-tale mirror plate, to blow
Into the famine of my brother's mouth,
Haggling in a market place?
Why, at the first trump of impending Doom
You'll come roaring up the galleys of the dead,–
The oar-arms banked and trussed upon the bone,–
Crying '*J'accuse!*' and hale me by the browse
And in alarm bark out 'Not this arouse!
Guilt has her, let guilt haul her house!'
Beating your belly's cage where I took stroke;
Running halt, distracted, and about;
Counting which of my hairs be summoned at the root.

AUGUSTA

Mother of Heaven!

MIRANDA

Precisely not.

[*Both women are now at the foot of the stairs.* MIRANDA *fending, with her skirts fanned wide,* AUGUSTA *following.*]

AUGUSTA

Something's wrong. Where is my Jeremy?
I *will* catch my son!
[*They begin to mount*]

MIRANDA

Key-gone generation. The figured base
So many scattered minims on the wind,
All to amuse a frightened man, his generation;
And astound one woman of great folly.

AUGUSTA

[*Savagely*]
Don't tell me there's nothing left at all!
You, who've always been too fond of death,
Will soon be as nothing as your mother!

MIRANDA

Ah, the gauntlet in the gift!
I've always been obliged to death, indeed.
It is the rate in everything I do.
It is the matter that I turn upon.
It is the hub that holds the staggered spindle;
Plumb-bob, sextant, gravity
Of the Surveyor with the cautious hand:
A portion of man's dignity, he dies.

AUGUSTA

Don't tell me anything!
I've heard the hunter crying 'Gone away!';
The howl of 'Wolf!', and weeping man also.
I tire of all the downward obsequies,
Lauds, canticles, requiems and masses;
The upraised finger pointing zero—

MIRANDA

The frantic sloth of grieving, the hidden head
By its waters eaten. The high crossed sleeves;
The muffled drum, the creeping catafalque
Toiling backward to the cot; the great stone fly
Sarcophagus, at flemish in the ways—

AUGUSTA

The excellent arrangement of catastrophe;
The nice matter of the closed account!

MIRANDA

Perambulator rolling to the tomb;
Death with a baby in its mouth. Procession
Turning arc-wise to the turning cradle:
High plumed mares, with sea-salt heavy tassels—

AUGUSTA

Pomp and circumstance of childhood, driven
By an headless coachman, whistling—

MIRANDA

                                    'Who passes by this road so late?'

AUGUSTA

What's that?
Are you trying to frighten me?

MIRANDA

No, trying to make us fit to be forgotten.

AUGUSTA

You are frightening me. Where is my youth?

MIRANDA

At this moment, bent down to greet your shadow,
Running on all fours to keep you company.

AUGUSTA

[*Pushing at* MIRANDA]
Let me go; I know your citizens of silence—
[*Hearing* DUDLEY *and* ELISHA *making their escape*]
Out of my way, you tool of earth!
Should I cry now, whose cries were *always* swindled?
Let me go, I say!

MIRANDA

[*Trying to prevent* AUGUSTA *from reaching the top landing*]
Be not so swift to see and know.

AUGUSTA

[*Stopping short*]
Are you staying?

MIRANDA

I am staying.

AUGUSTA

Why?

MIRANDA

Is it really possible that you don't know
That your sons have come to hunt you down?
I was in the panel once before
When you were all but small bread in the basket
Undertakers rock before the quand'ry.
I heard my brothers move through price of pine
To a bargain—burning on a shovel.
Even then, reverberation of a coin

Spent in sorrow's haste so shook their being
That coursing the journey of that dole
They trembled half a day. You have such sons
Would mate the pennies on a dead man's eyes
To breed the sexton's fee.

> [*At this point the departure of* DUDLEY *and* ELISHA *is only too
> clearly audible.* MIRANDA *and* AUGUSTA *having reached the
> other side of the landing, now descend in the order in which
> they mounted.*]

AUGUSTA

Out of my way! I think my sons have left me!

MIRANDA

Stay with me. They left you long ago.

AUGUSTA

Stay? What, in this place, and uninhabited?
No!

MIRANDA

Yes.
They chased you home to lose you.
This is your habit, they the lost account,
They ride the whirlwind on an empty saddle;
Your grave is also on a journey, join it:
Save your death.

AUGUSTA

No! Yes. They call me hermit-crab, and shut
The orifices of the heart, lest I crawl in.
    [*Given pause*]
Man, by its titter underground, finds gold,
And with what passion does he dig it up!

But let it be the heavy mother lode,
With what passion will he dig her in!

MIRANDA

Then stay with me and uncle Jonathan
And do as I.
Caught in the utmost meridian and parallel—
As of a moor-hen, watching a hawk heel in,—
Draw 'round in dust the broken wing
Its last veronica.

> [MIRANDA *and* AUGUSTA *are now at the foot of the stairs. A sudden derisive blast of the car-horn announces the departure of* DUDLEY *and* ELISHA. *Hearing it,* AUGUSTA *seizes the curfew-bell, beating about* MIRANDA *its loud toll.*]

AUGUSTA

Stop them! Stop them! *You* let them get away!
It's your fault! You—you—you!

MIRANDA

[*Fending*] Wait. I'll be kinder later.

AUGUSTA

I know you. You are the one would lay
Me ticking down, ten cities deep!

MIRANDA

Nay, sparrow.
I'd lay you in the journey of your bed,
And un-bed you, and I could, in paradise.

AUGUSTA

Then why did you let me grow so old?
And let them get away—and Jeremy?

You are to blame, to blame, you are to blame—
Lost—lost—lost, lost—

> [AUGUSTA *brings the bell down on* MIRANDA. *Both fall across
> the gryphon, pulling down the curtains, gilt crown and all.
> The ringing has ceased.* BURLEY *appears on the balcony, carry-
> ing a lamp.* JACK *turns in from the fallen portion of the wall.*]

BURLEY

What's done, Jeremy?

JACK

Ah, then Miranda knew. What's done?
Why, everything's done, uncle.

BURLEY

Both?

JACK

Both.
I might have known, being weary of the world,
And all the bootless roar of vindication,
She'd not defend herself. But could I know
Which would be brought to child-bed of the other?

BURLEY

Why did you do it?

JACK

Why?
Do I carry the ensign of the Medici?
Am I my father
That I should know what price the token price
That cashing in the utmost treasure would exact?
This is the hour of the uncreate;
The season of the sorrowless lamenting:

Say then,
'Jeremy, thou fool—thou soul of no abiding!'
As the slayer snuffling 'round the kill,
Breathing his contagion out before him,
Draws up the victim with his steaming nose—
So I, who thought to medicine contumely
With a doll's hutch—that catches villains!—
Find I've breathed up disaster and myself.
Say I was of home so utterly bereft,
I dug me one, and pushed my terror in.
Stand back, uncle.

[BURLEY *watches in silence as* JACK, *with what appears to be indifference, leaves the stage.*]

CURTAIN

Nightwood

TO PEGGY GUGGENHEIM AND JOHN FERRAR HOLMS

Introduction

When the question is raised, of writing an introduction to a book of a creative order, I always feel that the few books worth introducing are exactly those which it is an impertinence to introduce. I have already committed two such impertinences; this is the third, and if it is not the last no one will be more surprised than myself. I can justify this preface only in the following way. One is liable to expect other people to see, on their first reading of a book, all that one has come to perceive in the course of a developing intimacy with it. I have read *Nightwood* a number of times, in manuscript, in proof, and after publication. What one can do for other readers —assuming that if you read this preface at all you will read it first—is to trace the more significant phases of one's own appreciation of it. For it took me, with this book, some time to come to an appreciation of its meaning as a whole.

In describing *Nightwood* for the purpose of attracting readers to the English edition, I said that it would "appeal primarily to readers of poetry." This is well enough for the brevity of advertisement, but I am glad to take this opportunity to amplify it a little. I do not want to suggest that the distinction of the book is primarily verbal, and still less that the astonishing language covers a vacuity of content. Unless the term "novel" has become too debased to apply, and if it means a book in which living characters are created and shown in significant relationship, this book is a novel. And I do not mean that Miss Barnes's style is "poetic prose." But I do mean that most contemporary novels are not really "written." They obtain what reality they have largely from an accurate rendering of the noises that human beings currently make in their daily simple needs of communication; and what part of a novel is not composed of these noises consists of a prose which is no more alive than that of a competent newspaper writer or government official. A prose that is altogether alive demands something of the reader that the ordinary novel-reader is not prepared to give. To say that *Nightwood* will appeal primarily to readers of poetry does not mean that it is not a novel, but that it is so good a novel that only sensibilities trained on poetry can wholly appreciate it. Miss Barnes's prose has the prose rhythm that is prose style, and the musical pattern which is not that of verse. This prose rhythm may be more or less complex or elaborate, according to the purposes of the writer; but whether simple or complex, it is what raises the matter to be communicated, to the first intensity.

When I first read the book I found the opening movement rather slow and dragging, until the appearance of the doctor. And throughout the first reading, I was under the impression that it was the doctor alone who gave the book its vitality; and I believed the final chapter to be superfluous. I am now convinced that the final chapter is essential, both dramatically and musically. It was notable, however, that as the other characters, on repeated reading, became alive for me, and while the focus shifted, the figure of the doctor was by no means diminished. On the contrary, he came to take on a different and more profound importance when seen as a constituent of a whole pattern. He ceased to be like the brilliant actor in an otherwise unpersuasively performed play for whose re-entrance one impatiently awaits. However in actual life such a character might seem to engross conversation, quench reciprocity, and blanket less voluble people; in the book his role is nothing of the kind. At first we only hear the doctor talking; we do not understand why he talks. Gradually one comes to see that together with his egotism and swagger—Dr. Matthew-Mighty-grain-of-salt-Dante-O'Connor—he has also a desperate disinterestedness and a deep humility. His humility does not often appear so centrally as in the prodigious scene in the empty church, but it is what throughout gives him his helpless power among the helpless. His monologues, brilliant and witty in themselves as they are, are not dictated by an indifference to other human beings, but on the contrary by a hypersensitive awareness of them. When Nora comes to visit him in the night (*Watchman, What of the Night?*) he perceives at once that the only thing he can do for her ("he was extremely put out, having expected someone else")— the only way to "save the situation"—is to talk torrentially, even though she hardly takes in anything he says, but reverts again and again to her obsession. It is his revulsion against the strain of squeezing himself dry for other people, and getting no sustenance in return, that sends him raving at the end. *The people in my life who have made my life miserable, coming to me to learn of degradation and the night.* But most of the time he is talking to drown the still small wailing and whining of humanity, to make more supportable its shame and less ignoble its misery.

Indeed, such a character as Doctor O'Connor could not be real alone in a gallery of dummies: such a character needs other real, if less conscious, people in order to realize his own reality. I cannot think of any character in the book who has not gone on living in my mind. Felix and his child are oppressively real. Sometimes in a phrase the characters spring to life so suddenly that one is taken aback, as if one had touched a wax-work figure and discovered that it was a live policeman. The doctor says to Nora, *I was doing well enough until you kicked my stone over, and out I come, all moss and eyes.* Robin Vote (the most puzzling of all, because we find her quite real without quite understanding the means by which the author has made her so) *is the vision of an eland coming down an aisle of trees, chapleted with orange blossoms and bridal veil, a hoof raised in the economy of fear;* and later she has *temples like those of young beasts cutting horns, as if they were sleeping eyes.* Sometimes also a situation, which we had already comprehended loosely, is concentrated into a horror of intensity by a phrase, as when Nora suddenly thinks on seeing the doctor in bed, *"God, children know something they can't tell; they like Red Riding Hood and the wolf in bed!"*

The book is not simply a collection of individual portraits; the characters are all knotted together, as people are in real life, by what we may call chance or destiny, rather than by deliberate choice of each other's company: it is the whole pattern that they form, rather than any individual constituent, that is the focus of interest. We come to know them through their effect on each other, and by what they say to each other about the others. And finally, it ought to be superfluous to observe—but perhaps to anyone reading the book for the first time, it is not superfluous—that the book is not a psychopathic study. The miseries that people suffer through their particular abnormalities of temperament are visible on the surface: the deeper design is that of the human misery and bondage which is universal. In normal lives this misery is mostly concealed; often, what is most wretched of all, concealed from the sufferer more effectively than from the observer. The sick man does not know what is wrong with him; he partly wants to know, and mostly wants to conceal the knowledge from himself. In the Puritan morality that I remember, it was tacitly assumed that if one was thrifty, enterprising, intelligent, practical and prudent in not violating social conventions, one ought to have a happy and "successful" life. Failure was due to some weakness or perversity peculiar to the individual; but the decent man need have no nightmares. It is now rather more common to assume that all individual misery is the fault of "society," and is remediable by alterations from without. Fundamentally the two philosophies, however different they may appear in operation, are the same. It seems to me that all of us, so far as we attach ourselves to created objects and surrender our wills to temporal ends, are eaten by the same worm. Taken in this way, *Nightwood* appears with profounder significance. To regard this group of people as a horrid sideshow of freaks is not only to miss the point, but to confirm our wills and harden our hearts in an inveterate sin of pride.

I should have considered the foregoing paragraph impertinent, and perhaps too pretentious for a preface meant to be a simple recommendation of a book I greatly admire, were it not that one review (at least), intended in praise of the book, has already appeared which would in effect induce the reader to begin with this mistaken attitude. Otherwise, generally, in trying to anticipate a reader's misdirections, one is in danger of provoking him to some other misunderstanding unforeseen. This is a work of creative imagination, not a philosophical treatise. As I said at the beginning, I am conscious of impertinence in introducing the book at all; and to have read a book a good many times does not necessarily put one in the right knowledge of what to say to those who have not yet read it. What I would leave the reader prepared to find is the great achievement of a style, the beauty of phrasing, the brilliance of wit and characterisation, and a quality of horror and doom very nearly related to that of Elizabethan tragedy.

T. S. Eliot

1937

Note to Second Edition

The foregoing preface, as the reader will have just observed, was written twelve years ago. As my admiration for the book has not diminished, and my only motive for revision would be to remove or conceal evidences of my own immaturity at the time of writing

—a temptation which may present itself to any critic reviewing his own words at twelve years' distance—I have thought best to leave unaltered a preface which may still, I hope, serve its original purpose of indicating an approach which seems to me helpful for the new reader.

T.S.E.

1949

Bow Down

Early in 1880, in spite of a well-founded suspicion as to the advis-
ability of perpetuating that race which has the sanction of the
Lord and the disapproval of the people, Hedvig Volkbein—a
Viennese woman of great strength and military beauty, lying upon
a canopied bed of a rich spectacular crimson, the valance stamped
with the bifurcated wings of the House of Hapsburg, the feather
coverlet an envelope of satin on which, in massive and tarnished
gold threads, stood the Volkbein arms—gave birth, at the age of
forty-five, to an only child, a son, seven days after her physician
predicted that she would be taken.

Turning upon this field, which shook to the clatter of morning
horses in the street beyond, with the gross splendour of a general
saluting the flag, she named him Felix, thrust him from her, and
died. The child's father had gone six months previously, a victim
of fever. Guido Volkbein, a Jew of Italian descent, had been both
a gourmet and a dandy, never appearing in public without the
ribbon of some quite unknown distinction tinging his buttonhole

with a faint thread. He had been small, rotund, and haughtily timid, his stomach protruding slightly in an upward jutting slope that brought into prominence the buttons of his waistcoat and trousers, marking the exact centre of his body with the obstetric line seen on fruits—the inevitable arc produced by heavy rounds of burgundy, schlagsahne, and beer.

The autumn, binding him about, as no other season, with racial memories, a season of longing and of horror, he had called his weather. Then walking in the Prater he had been seen carrying in a conspicuously clenched fist the exquisite handkerchief of yellow and black linen that cried aloud of the ordinance of 1468, issued by one Pietro Barbo, demanding that, with a rope about its neck, Guido's race should run in the Corso for the amusement of the Christian populace, while ladies of noble birth, sitting upon spines too refined for rest, arose from their seats, and, with the red-gowned cardinals and the *Monsignori*, applauded with that cold yet hysterical abandon of a people that is at once unjust and happy; the very Pope himself shaken down from his hold on heaven with the laughter of a man who forgoes his angels that he may recapture the beast. This memory and the handkerchief that accompanied it had wrought in Guido (as certain flowers brought to a pitch of florid ecstasy no sooner attain their specific type than they fall into its decay) the sum total of what is the Jew. He had walked, hot, incautious and damned, his eyelids quivering over the thick eyeballs, black with the pain of a participation that, four centuries later, made him a victim, as he felt the echo in his own throat of that cry running the Piazza Montanara long ago, "*Roba vecchia!*"—the degradation by which his people had survived.

Childless at fifty-nine, Guido had prepared out of his own heart for his coming child a heart, fashioned on his own preoccupation, the remorseless homage to nobility, the genuflexion the hunted body makes from muscular contraction, going down before the impending and inaccessible, as before a great heat. It had made Guido, as it was to make his son, heavy with impermissible blood.

And childless he had died, save for the promise that hung at the

Christian belt of Hedvig. Guido had lived as all Jews do, who, cut off from their people by accident or choice, find that they must inhabit a world whose constituents, being alien, force the mind to succumb to an imaginary populace. When a Jew dies on a Christian bosom he dies impaled. Hedvig, in spite of her agony, wept upon an outcast. Her body at that moment became the barrier and Guido died against that wall, troubled and alone. In life he had done everything to span the impossible gap; the saddest and most futile gesture of all had been his pretence to a barony. He had adopted the sign of the cross; he had said that he was an Austrian of an old, almost extinct line, producing, to uphold his story, the most amazing and inaccurate proofs: a coat of arms that he had no right to and a list of progenitors (including their Christian names) who had never existed. When Hedvig came upon his black and yellow handkerchiefs he had said that they were to remind him that one branch of his family had bloomed in Rome.

He had tried to be one with her by adoring her, by imitating her goose-step of a stride, a step that by him adopted became dislocated and comic. She would have done as much, but sensing something in him blasphemed and lonely, she had taken the blow as a Gentile must—by moving toward him in recoil. She had believed whatever he had told her, but often enough she had asked: "What is the matter?"—that continual reproach which was meant as a continual reminder of her love. It ran through his life like an accusing voice. He had been tormented into speaking highly of royalty, flinging out encomiums with the force of small water made great by the pressure of a thumb. He had laughed too heartily when in the presence of the lower order of title, as if, by his good nature, he could advance them to some distinction of which they dreamed. Confronted with nothing worse than a general in creaking leather and with the slight repercussion of movement common to military men, who seem to breathe from the inside out, smelling of gunpowder and horse flesh, lethargic yet prepared for participation in a war not yet scheduled (a type of which Hedvig had been very fond), Guido had shaken with an unseen trembling. He

saw that Hedvig had the same bearing, the same though more con-
densed power of the hand, patterned on seizure in a smaller mould,
as sinister in its reduction as a doll's house. The feather in her hat
had been knife-clean and quivering as if in an heraldic wind; she
had been a woman held up to nature, precise, deep-bosomed and
gay. Looking at the two he had become confused as if he were
about to receive a reprimand, not the officer's, but his wife's.

When she had danced, a little heady with wine, the dance floor
had become a tactical manoeuvre; her heels had come down staccato
and trained, her shoulders as conscious at the tips as those which
carry the braid and tassels of promotion; the turn of her head had
held the cold vigilance of a sentry whose rounds are not without
apprehension. Yet Hedvig had done what she could. If ever there
was a massive *chic* she had personified it—yet somewhere there had
been anxiety. The thing that she had stalked, though she herself
had not been conscious of it, was Guido's assurance that he was a
Baron. She had believed it as a soldier "believes" a command.
Something in her sensitory predicament—upon which she herself
would have placed no value—had told her much better. Hedvig
had become a Baroness without question.

In the Vienna of Volkbein's day there were few trades that wel-
comed Jews, yet somehow he had managed, by various deals in
household goods, by discreet buying of old masters and first edi-
tions and by money changing, to secure for Hedvig a house in the
Inner City, to the north overlooking the Prater, a house that, large,
dark and imposing, became a fantastic museum of their encounter.

The long rococo halls, giddy with plush and whorled designs in
gold, were peopled with Roman fragments, white and disassociated;
a runner's leg, the chilly half-turned head of a matron stricken at
the bosom, the blind bold sockets of the eyes given a pupil by
every shifting shadow so that what they looked upon was an act
of the sun. The great salon was of walnut. Over the fireplace hung
impressive copies of the Medici shield and, beside them, the
Austrian bird.

Three massive pianos (Hedvig had played the waltzes of her

time with the masterly stroke of a man, in the tempo of her blood, rapid and rising—that quick mannerliness of touch associated with the playing of the Viennese, who, though pricked with the love of rhythm, execute its demands in the duelling manner) sprawled over the thick dragon's-blood pile of rugs from Madrid. The study harboured two rambling desks in rich and bloody wood. Hedvig had liked things in twos and threes. Into the middle arch of each desk silver-headed brads had been hammered to form a lion, a bear, a ram, a dove, and in their midst a flaming torch. The design was executed under the supervision of Guido who, thinking on the instant, claimed it as the Volkbein field, though it turned out to be a bit of heraldry long since in decline beneath the papal frown. The full length windows (a French touch that Guido thought handsome) overlooking the park were curtained in native velvets and stuffs from Tunis, and the Venetian blinds were of that peculiarly sombre shade of red so loved by the Austrians. Against the panels of oak that reared themselves above the long table and up to the curving ceiling hung life-sized portraits of Guido's claim to father and mother. The lady was a sumptuous Florentine with bright sly eyes and overt mouth. Great puffed and pearled sleeves rose to the pricked-eared pointings of the stiff lace about the head, conical and braided. The deep accumulation of dress fell about her in groined shadows; the train, rambling through a vista of primitive trees, was carpet-thick. She seemed to be expecting a bird. The gentleman was seated precariously on a charger. He seemed not so much to have mounted the animal as to be about to descend upon him. The blue of an Italian sky lay between the saddle and the buff of the tightened rump of the rider. The charger had been caught by the painter in the execution of a falling arc, the mane lifted away in a dying swell, the tail forward and in between thin bevelled legs. The gentleman's dress was a baffling mixture of the Romantic and the Religious, and in the cradling crook of his left arm he carried a plumed hat, crown out. The whole conception might have been a Mardi Gras whim. The gentleman's head, stuck on at a three-quarter angle, had a remarkable resemblance to Guido Volkbein, the same sweeping Cabalistic line of nose, the features seasoned and warm save where the virgin blue of the eyeballs curved out the lids as if another medium than that of sight had taken its stand beneath that flesh. There was no interval in the speed of that stare, endless and objective. The likeness was accidental. Had anyone cared to look into the matter they would have discovered these canvases to be reproductions of two intrepid and ancient actors. Guido had found them in some forgotten and dusty corner and had purchased them when he had been sure that he would need an alibi for the blood.

At this point exact history stopped for Felix who, thirty years later, turned up in the world with these facts, the two portraits and nothing more. His aunt, combing her long braids with an amber comb, told him what she knew, and this had been her only knowledge of his past. What had formed Felix from the date of his birth to his coming to thirty was unknown to the world, for the step of the wandering Jew is in every son. No matter where and when you meet him you feel that he has come from some place— no matter from what place he has come—some country that he has devoured rather than resided in, some secret land that he has been nourished on but cannot inherit, for the Jew seems to be everywhere from nowhere. When Felix's name was mentioned, three or more persons would swear to having seem him the week before in three different countries simultaneously.

Felix called himself Baron Volkbein, as his father had done before him. How Felix lived, how he came by his money—he knew figures as a dog knows the covey and as indefatigably he pointed and ran—how he mastered seven languages and served that knowledge well, no one knew. Many people were familiar with his figure and face. He was not popular, though the posthumous acclaim meted out to his father secured from his acquaintances the peculiar semi-circular stare of those who, unwilling to greet with earthly equality, nevertheless give to the living branch (because of death and its sanction) the slight bend of the head—a reminiscent pardon for future apprehension—a bow very common to us when in the presence of this people.

Felix was heavier than his father and taller. His hair began too far back on his forehead. His face was a long stout oval, suffering a laborious melancholy. One feature alone spoke of Hedvig, the mouth, which, though sensuous from lack of desire as hers had been from denial, pressed too intimately close to the bony structure of the teeth. The other features were a little heavy, the chin, the nose, and the lids; into one was set his monocle which shone, a round blind eye in the sun.

He was usually seen walking or driving alone, dressed as if expecting to participate in some great event, though there was no function in the world for which he could be said to be properly garbed; wishing to be correct at any moment, he was tailored in part for the evening and in part for the day.

From the mingled passions that made up his past, out of a diversity of bloods, from the crux of a thousand impossible situations, Felix had become the accumulated and single—the embarrassed.

His embarrassment took the form of an obsession for what he termed "Old Europe": aristocracy, nobility, royalty. He spoke any given title with a pause before and after the name. Knowing circumlocution to be his only contact, he made it interminable and exacting. With the fury of a fanatic he hunted down his own disqualification, rearticulating the bones of the Imperial Courts long forgotten (those long remembered can alone claim to be long forgotten), listening with an unbecoming loquacity to officials and guardians for fear that his inattention might lose him some fragment of his resuscitation. He felt that the great past might mend a little if he bowed low enough, if he succumbed and gave homage.

In nineteen hundred and twenty he was in Paris (his blind eye had kept him out of the army), still spatted, still wearing his cutaway, bowing, searching, with quick pendulous movements, for the correct thing to which to pay tribute: the right street, the right café, the right building, the right vista. In restaurants he

bowed slightly to anyone who looked as if he might be "some-
one," making the bend so imperceptible that the surprised person
might think he was merely adjusting his stomach. His rooms were
taken because a Bourbon had been carried from them to death. He
kept a valet and a cook; the one because he looked like Louis the
Fourteenth, and the other because she resembled Queen Victoria,
Victoria in another cheaper material, cut to the poor man's purse.

In his search for the particular *Comédie humaine* Felix had
come upon the odd. Conversant with edicts and laws, folk story
and heresy, taster of rare wines, thumber of rarer books and old
wives' tales—tales of men who became holy and of beasts that be-
came damned—read in all plans for fortifications and bridges, given
pause by all graveyards on all roads, a pedant of many churches
and castles, his mind dimly and reverently reverberated to Madame
de Sévigné, Goethe, Loyola and Brantôme. But Loyola sounded
the deepest note; he was alone, apart and single. A race that has
fled its generations from city to city has not found the necessary
time for the accumulation of that toughness which produces
ribaldry, nor, after the crucifixion of its ideas, enough forgetfulness
in twenty centuries to create legend. It takes a Christian, standing
eternally in the Jew's salvation, to blame himself and to bring up
from that depth charming and fantastic superstitions through
which the slowly and tirelessly milling Jew once more becomes the
"collector" of his own past. His undoing is never profitable until
some *goy* has put it back into such shape that it can again be
offered as a "sign." A Jew's undoing is never his own, it is God's;
his rehabilitation is never his own, it is a Christian's. The Christian
traffic in retribution has made the Jew's history a commodity; it is
the medium through which he receives, at the necessary moment,
the serum of his own past that he may offer it again as his blood.
In this manner the Jew participates in the two conditions; and in
like manner Felix took the breast of this wet nurse whose milk was
his being but which could never be his birthright.

Early in life Felix had insinuated himself into the pageantry of
the circus and the theatre. In some way they linked his emotions

to the higher and unattainable pageantry of kings and queens. The more amiable actresses of Prague, Vienna, Hungary, Germany, France and Italy, the acrobats and sword-swallowers, had at one time or another allowed him their dressing rooms—sham salons in which he aped his heart. Here he had neither to be capable nor alien. He became for a little while a part of their splendid and reeking falsification.

The people of this world, with desires utterly divergent from his own, had also seized on titles for a purpose. There was a Princess Nadja, a Baron von Tink, a Principessa Stasera y Stasero, a King Buffo and a Duchess of Broadback: gaudy, cheap cuts from the beast life, immensely capable of that great disquiet called entertainment. They took titles merely to dazzle boys about town, to make their public life (and it was all they had) mysterious and perplexing, knowing well that skill is never so amazing as when it seems inappropriate. Felix clung to his title to dazzle his own estrangement. It brought them together.

Going among these people, the men smelling weaker and the women stronger than their beasts, Felix had that sense of peace that formerly he had experienced only in museums. He moved with a humble hysteria among the decaying brocades and laces of the *Carnavalet*; he loved that old and documented splendour with something of the love of the lion for its tamer—that sweat-tarnished spangled enigma that, in bringing the beast to heel, had somehow turned toward him a face like his own, but which though curious and weak, had yet picked the precise fury from his brain.

Nadja had sat back to Felix, as certain of the justice of his eye as she would have been of the linear justice of a Rops, knowing that Felix tabulated precisely the tense capability of her spine with its lashing curve swinging into the hard compact cleft of her rump, as angrily and as beautifully as the more obvious tail of her lion.

The emotional spiral of the circus, taking its flight from the immense disqualification of the public, rebounding from its illimitable hope, produced in Felix longing and disquiet. The circus was a loved thing that he could never touch, therefore never know.

The people of the theatre and the ring were for him as dramatic and as a monstrous as a consignment on which he could never bid. That he haunted them as persistently as he did was evidence of something in his nature that was turning Christian.

He was, in like manner, amazed to find himself drawn to the church, though this tension he could handle with greater ease; its arena, he found, was circumscribed to the individual heart.

It was to the Duchess of Broadback (Frau Mann) that Felix owed his first audience with a "gentleman of quality." Frau Mann, then in Berlin, explained that this person had been "somewhat mixed up with her in the past." It was with the utmost difficulty that he could imagine her "mixed up" with anyone, her coquetries were muscular and localized. Her trade—the trapeze—seemed to have preserved her. It gave her, in a way, a certain charm. Her legs had the specialized tension common to aerial workers; something of the bar was in her wrists, the tan bark in her walk, as if the air, by its very lightness, by its very non-resistance, were an almost insurmountable problem, making her body, though slight and compact, seem much heavier than that of women who stay upon the ground. In her face was the tense expression of an organism surviving in an alien element. She seemed to have a skin that was the pattern of her costume: a bodice of lozenges, red and yellow, low in the back and ruffled over and under the arms, faded with the reek of her three-a-day control, red tights, laced boots—one somehow felt they ran through her as the design runs through hard holiday candies, and the bulge in the groin where she took the bar, one foot caught in the flex of the calf, was as solid, specialized and as polished as oak. The stuff of the tights was no longer a covering, it was herself; the span of the tightly stitched crotch was so much her own flesh that she was as unsexed as a doll. The needle that had made one the property of the child made the other the property of no man.

"Tonight," Frau Mann said, turning to Felix, "we are going to be amused. Berlin is sometimes very nice at night, *nicht wahr?* And the Count is something that must be seen. The place is very handsome, red and blue, he's fond of blue, God knows why, and he is fond of impossible people, so we are invited—" The Baron moved his foot in. "He might even have the statues on."

"Statues?" said Felix.

"The living statues," she said. "He simply adores them." Felix dropped his hat; it rolled and stopped.

"Is he German?" he said.

"Oh, no, Italian, but it does not matter, he speaks anything, I think he comes to Germany to change money—he comes, he goes away, and everything goes on the same, except that people have something to talk about."

"What did you say his name was?"

"I didn't, but he calls himself Count Onatorio Altamonte. I'm sure it's quite ridiculous, he says he is related to every nation—that should please you. We will have dinner, we will have champagne." The way she said "dinner" and the way she said "champagne" gave meat and liquid their exact difference, as if by having surmounted two mediums, earth and air, her talent, running forward, achieved all others.

"Does one enjoy oneself?" he asked.

"Oh, absolutely."

She leaned forward; she began removing the paint with the hurried technical felicity of an artist cleaning a palette. She looked at the Baron derisively. "*Wir setzen an dieser Stelle über den Fluss—*" she said.

Standing about a table at the end of the immense room, looking as if they were deciding the fate of a nation, were grouped ten men, all in parliamentary attitudes, and one young woman. They were listening, at the moment of the entrance of Felix and the Duchess of Broadback, to a middle-aged "medical student" with shaggy eyebrows, a terrific widow's peak, over-large dark eyes, and a heavy way of standing that was also apologetic. The man was Dr. Matthew O'Connor, an Irishman from the Barbary Coast (Pacific Street, San Francisco), whose interest in gynaecology had driven him half around the world. He was taking the part of host, the Count not yet having made his appearance, and was telling of himself, for he considered himself the most amusing predicament.

"We may all be nature's noblemen," he was saying, and the mention of a nobleman made Felix feel happier the instant he caught the word, though what followed left him in some doubt, "but think of the stories that do not amount to much! That is, that are forgotten in spite of all man remembers (unless he remembers himself) merely because they befell him without distinction of office or title—that's what we call legend and it's the best a poor man may do with his fate; the other"—he waved an arm— "we call history, the best the high and mighty can do with theirs. Legend is unexpurgated, but history, because of its actors, is deflowered—every nation with a sense of humour is a lost nation, and every woman with a sense of humour is a lost woman. The Jews are the only people who have sense enough to keep humour in the family; a Christian scatters it all over the world."

"*Ja! das ist ganz richtig—*" said the Duchess in a loud voice, but the interruption was quite useless. Once the doctor had his audience—and he got his audience by the simple device of pronouncing at the top of his voice (at such moments as irritable and possessive as a maddened woman's) some of the more boggish and biting of the shorter early Saxon verbs—nothing could stop him. He merely turned his large eyes upon her and having done so noticed her and her attire for the first time, which, bringing suddenly to his mind something forgotten but comparable, sent him into a burst of laughter, exclaiming: "Well, but God works in mysterious ways to bring things up in my mind! Now I am thinking of Nikka, the nigger who used to fight the bear in the *Cirque de Paris*. There he was, crouching all over the arena without a stitch on, except an ill-concealed loin-cloth all abulge as if with a deep-sea catch, tattooed from head to heel with all the *ameublement* of depravity! Garlanded with rosebuds and hackwork of the devil— was he a sight to see! Though he couldn't have done a thing (and I know what I am talking about in spite of all that has been said

about the black boys) if you had stood him in a gig-mill for a week,
though (it's said) at a stretch it spelled Desdemona. Well then,
over his belly was an angel from Chartres; on each buttock, half
public, half private, a quotation from the book of magic, a confir-
mation of the Jansenist theory, I'm sorry to say and here to say it.
Across his knees, I give you my word, 'I' on one and on the other,
'can,' put those together! Across his chest, beneath a beautiful
caravel in full sail, two clasped hands, the wrist bones fretted with
point lace. On each bosom an arrow-speared heart, each with dif-
ferent initials but with equal drops of blood; and running into the
arm-pit, all down one side, the word said by Prince Arthur Tudor,
son of King Henry the Seventh, when on his bridal night he called
for a goblet of water (or was it water?). His Chamberlain, wonder-
ing at the cause of such drought, remarked on it and was answered
in one word so wholly epigrammatic and in no way befitting the
great and noble British Empire that he was brought up with a
start, and that is all we will ever know of it, unless," said the doc-
tor, striking his hand on his hip, "you are as good at guessing as
Tiny M'Caffery."

"And the legs?" Felix asked uncomfortably.

"The legs," said Doctor O'Connor, "were devoted entirely to
vine work, topped by the swart rambler rose copied from the cop-
ing of the Hamburg house of Rothschild. Over his *dos*, believe it
or not and I shouldn't, a terse account in early monkish script—
called by some people indecent, by others Gothic—of the really
deplorable condition of Paris before hygiene was introduced, and
nature had its way up to the knees. And just above what you
mustn't mention, a bird flew carrying a streamer on which was
incised, '*Garde tout!*' I asked him why all this barbarity; he an-
swered he loved beauty and would have it about him."

"Are you acquainted with Vienna?" Felix inquired.

"Vienna," said the doctor, "the bed into which the common
people climb, docile with toil, and out of which the nobility fling
themselves, ferocious with dignity—I do, but not so well but that
I remember some of it still. I remember young Austrian boys going

to school, flocks of quail they were, sitting out their recess in different spots in the sun, rosy-cheeked, bright-eyed, with damp rosy mouths, smelling of the herd childhood, facts of history glimmering in their minds like sunlight, soon to be lost, soon to be forgotten, degraded into proof. Youth is cause, effect is age; so with the thickening of the neck we get data."

"I was not thinking of its young boys, but of its military superiority, its great names," Felix said, feeling that the evening was already lost, seeing that as yet the host had not made his appearance and that no one seemed to know it or to care, and that the whole affair was to be given over to this volatile person who called himself a doctor.

"The army, the celibate's family!" nodded the doctor. "His one safety."

The young woman, who was in her late twenties, turned from the group, coming closer to Felix and the doctor. She rested her hands behind her against the table. She seemed embarrassed. "Are you both really saying what you mean, or are you just talking?" Having spoken, her face flushed, she added hurriedly, "I am doing advance publicity for the circus; I'm Nora Flood."

The doctor swung around, looking pleased. "Ah!" he said, "Nora suspects the cold incautious melody of time crawling, but," he added, "I've only just started." Suddenly he struck his thigh with his open hand. "Flood, Nora, why, sweet God, my girl, I helped to bring you into the world!"

Felix, as disquieted as if he were expected to "do something" to avert a catastrophe (as one is expected to do something about an overturned tumbler, the contents of which is about to drip over the edge of the table and into a lady's lap), on the phrase "time crawling" broke into uncontrollable laughter, and though this occurrence troubled him the rest of his life he was never able to explain it to himself. The company, instead of being silenced, went on as if nothing had happened, two or three of the younger men were talking about something scandalous, and the Duchess in her loud empty voice was telling a very stout man something about the living statues. This only added to the Baron's torment. He began waving his hands, saying, "Oh, please! please!" and suddenly he had a notion that he was doing something that wasn't laughing at all, but something much worse, though he kept saying to himself, "I am laughing, really laughing, nothing else whatsoever!" He kept waving his arms in distress and saying, "Please, please!" staring at the floor, deeply embarrassed to find himself doing so.

As abruptly he sat straight up, his hands on the arms of the chair, staring fixedly at the doctor who was leaning forward as he drew a chair up exactly facing him. "Yes," said the doctor, and he was smiling, "you will be disappointed! *In questa tomba oscura*— oh, unfaithful one! I am no herbalist, I am no Rutebeuf, I have no panacea, I am not a mountebank—that is, I cannot or will not stand on my head. I'm no tumbler, neither a friar, nor yet a thirteenth-century Salome dancing arse up on a pair of Toledo blades—try to get any lovesick girl, male or female, to do that to-day! If you don't believe such things happened in the long back of yesterday look up the manuscripts in the British Museum or go to the cathedral of *Clermont-Ferrand*, it's all one to me; become as the rich Mussulmans of Tunis who hire silly women to reduce the hour to its minimum of sense, still it will not be a cure, for there is none that takes place at all at once in any man. You know what man really desires?" inquired the doctor, grinning into the immobile face of the Baron. "One of two things: to find someone who is so stupid that he can lie to her, or to love someone so much that she can lie to him."

"I was not thinking of women at all," the Baron said, and he tried to stand up.

"Neither was I," said the doctor. "Sit down." He refilled his glass. "The *fine* is very good," he said.

Felix answered, "No, thank you, I never drink."

"You will," the doctor said. "Let us put it the other way; the Lutheran or Protestant church versus the Catholic. The Catholic is the girl that you love so much that she can lie to you, and the Protestant is the girl that loves you so much that you can lie to

her, and pretend a lot that you do not feel. Luther, and I hope you
don't mind my saying so, was as bawdy an old ram as ever trampled
his own straw, because the custody of the people's 'remissions' of
sins and indulgences had been snatched out of his hands, which
was in that day in the shape of half of all they had and which the
old monk of Wittenberg had intended to get off with in his own
way. So, of course, after that, he went wild and chattered like a
monkey in a tree and started something he never thought to start
(or so the writing on his side of the breakfast table would seem to
confirm), an obscene megalomania—and wild and wanton stranger
that *that* is, it must come clear and cool and long or not at all.
What do you listen to in the Protestant church? To the words of
a man who has been chosen for his eloquence—and not too elo-
quent either, mark you, or he gets the bum's rush from the pulpit,
for fear that in the end he will use his golden tongue for political
ends. For a golden tongue is never satisfied until it has wagged
itself over the destiny of a nation, and this the church is wise
enough to know.

"But turn to the Catholic church, go into mass at any moment—
what do you walk in upon? Something that's already in your blood.
You know the story that the priest is telling as he moves from one
side of the altar to the other, be he a cardinal, Leo X, or just some
poor bastard from Sicily who has discovered that *pecca fortiter*
among his goats no longer masses his soul, and has, God knows,
been God's child from the start—it makes no difference. Why?
Because you are sitting there with your own meditations *and* a
legend (which is nipping the fruit as the wren bites), and mingling
them both with the Holy Spoon, which is that story; or you can
get yourself into the confessional, where, in sonorous prose, lacking
contrition (if you must) you can speak of the condition of the
knotty, tangled soul and be answered in Gothic echoes, mutual
and instantaneous—one saying hail to your farewell. Mischief un-
ravels and the fine high hand of Heaven proffers the skein again,
combed and forgiven!

"The one House," he went on, "is hard, as hard as the gift of gab, and the other is as soft as a goat's hip, and you can blame no man for anything, and you can't like them at all."

"Wait!" said Felix.

"Yes?" said the doctor.

Felix bending forward, deprecatory and annoyed, went on: "I like the prince who was reading a book when the executioner touched him on the shoulder telling him that it was time, and he, arising, laid a papercutter between the pages to keep his place and closed the book."

"Ah," said the doctor, "that is not man living in his moment, it is man living in his miracle." He refilled his glass. *"Gesundheit,"* he said; *"Freude sei Euch von Gott beschieden, wie heut' so immerdar!"*

"You argue about sorrow and confusion too easily," Nora said.

"Wait!" the doctor answered. "A man's sorrow runs uphill; true it is difficult for him to bear, but it is also difficult for him to keep. I, as a medical man, know in what pocket a man keeps his heart and soul, and in what jostle of the liver, kidneys and genitalia these pockets are pilfered. There is no pure sorrow. Why? It is bedfellow to lungs, lights, bones, guts and gall! There are only confusions; about that you are quite right, Nora my child, confusions and defeated anxieties—there you have us, one and all. If you are a gymnosophist you *can* do without clothes, and if you are gimp-legged you will know more wind between the knees than another; still it is confusion; God's chosen walk close to the wall.

"I was in a war once myself," the doctor went on, "in a little town where the bombs began tearing the heart out of you, so that you began to think of all the majesty in the world that you would not be able to think of in a minute, if the noise came down and struck in the right place; I was scrambling for the cellar—and in it was an old Breton woman and a cow she had dragged with her, and behind that someone from Dublin saying, 'Glory be to God!' in a whisper at the far end of the animal. Thanks be to my Maker I had her head on, and the poor beast trembling on her four legs so I knew all at once that the tragedy of the beast can be two legs more awful than a man's. She was softly dropping her dung at the far end where the thin Celtic voice kept coming up saying, 'Glory be to Jesus!' and I said to myself, 'Can't the morning come now, so I can see what my face is mixed up with?' At that a flash of lightning went by and I saw the cow turning her head straight back so her horns made two moons against her shoulders, the tears soused all over her great black eyes.

"I began talking to her, cursing myself and the mick, and the old woman looking as if she were looking down her life, sighting it, the way a man looks down the barrel of a gun for an aim. I put my hand on the poor bitch of a cow and her hide was running water under my hand, like water tumbling down from Lahore, jerking against my hand as if she wanted to go, standing still in one spot; and I thought, there are directions and speeds that no one has calculated, for believe it or not that cow had gone somewhere very fast that we didn't know of, and yet was still standing there."

The doctor lifted the bottle. "Thank you," said Felix, "I never drink spirits."

"You will," said the doctor.

"There's one thing that has always troubled me," the doctor continued, "this matter of the guillotine. They say that the headsman has to supply his own knife, as a husband is supposed to supply his own razor. That's enough to rot his heart out before he has whittled one head. Wandering about the *Boul' Mich'* one night, flittering my eyes, I saw one with a red carnation in his buttonhole. I asked him what he was wearing it for, just to start up a friendly conversation; he said, 'It's the headsman's prerogative'—and I went as limp as a blotter snatched from the Senate. 'At one time,' he said, 'the executioner gripped it between his teeth.' At that my bowels turned turtle, seeing him in my mind's eye stropping the cleaver with a bloom in his mouth, like Carmen, and he the one man who is supposed to keep his gloves on in church! They often end by slicing themselves up; it's a rhythm that finally meets their own neck. He leaned forward and drew a finger across mine and said, 'As much hair as thick as that makes it a little difficult,' and at that moment I got heart failure for the rest of my life. I put down a franc and flew like the wind, the hair on my back standing as high as Queen Anne's ruff! And I didn't stop until I found myself spang in the middle of the *Musée de Cluny*, clutching the rack."

A sudden silence went over the room. The Count was standing in the doorway, rocking on his heels, either hand on the sides of the door; a torrent of Italian, which was merely the culmination of some theme he had begun in the entrance hall, was abruptly halved as he slapped his leg, standing tall and bent and peering. He moved forward into the room, holding with thumb and fore-finger the centre of a round magnifying glass which hung from a broad black ribbon. With the other hand he moved from chair to table, from guest to guest. Behind him, in a riding habit, was a young girl. Having reached the sideboard he swung around with gruesome nimbleness.

"Get out!" he said softly, laying his hand on the girl's shoulder. "Get out, get out!" It was obvious he meant it; he bowed slightly.

As they reached the street the Duchess caught a swirling hem of lace about her chilling ankles. "Well, my poor devil?" she said, turning to Felix.

"Well!" said Felix. "What was that about, and why?"

The doctor hailed a cab with the waving end of bulldog cane. "That can be repaired at any bar," he said.

"The name of that," said the Duchess, pulling on her gloves, "is a brief audience with the great, brief, but an audience!"

As they went up the darkened street Felix felt himself turning scarlet. "Is he really a Count?" he asked.

"*Herr Gott!*" said the Duchess. "Am I what I say? Are you? Is the doctor?" She put her hand on his knee. "Yes or no?"

The doctor was lighting a cigarette and in its flare the Baron saw that he was laughing silently. "He put us out for one of those hopes that is about to be defeated." He waved his gloves from the window to other guests who were standing along the curb, hailing vehicles.

"What do you mean?" the Baron said in a whisper.

"Count Onatorio Altamonte—may the name eventually roll over the Ponte Vecchio and into the Arno—suspected that he had come upon his last erection."

The doctor began to sing, "*Nur eine Nacht.*"

Frau Mann, with her face pressed against the cab window, said. "It's snowing." At her words Felix turned his coat collar up.

"Where are we going?" he asked Frau Mann. She was quite gay again.

"Let us go to Heinrich's; I always do when it's snowing. He mixes the drinks stronger then, and he's a good customer; he always takes in the show."

"Very well," said the doctor, preparing to rap on the window. "Where is thy Heinrich?"

"Go down *Unter den Linden*," Frau Mann said. "I'll tell you when."

Felix said, "If you don't mind, I'll get down here." He got down, walking against the snow.

Seated in the warmth of the favoured café, the doctor, unwinding his scarf, said: "There's something missing and whole about the Baron Felix—damned from the waist up, which reminds me of Mademoiselle Basquette, who was damned from the waist down, a girl without legs, built like a medieval abuse. She used to wheel herself through the Pyrenees on a board. What there was of her was beautiful in a cheap traditional sort of way, the face that one sees on people who come to a racial, not a personal, amazement. I wanted to give her a present for what of her was missing, and she said, 'Pearls—they go so well with everything!' Imagine, and the other half of her still in God's bag of tricks! Don't tell me that what was missing had not taught her the value of what was present. Well, in any case," the doctor went on, rolling down his gloves, "a sailor saw her one day and fell in love with her. She was going uphill and the sun was shining all over her back; it made a saddle across her bent neck and flickered along the curls of her head, gorgeous and bereft as the figurehead of a Norse vessel that the ship has abandoned. So he snatched her up, board and all, and took her away and had his will; when he got good and tired of her, just for gallantry, he put her down on her board about five miles out of town, so she had to roll herself back again, weeping something fearful to see, because one is accustomed to see tears falling down to the feet. Ah, truly, a pin board may come up to the chin of a woman and still she will find reason to weep. I tell you, Madame, if one gave birth to a heart on a plate, it would say 'Love' and twitch like the lopped leg of a frog."

"*Wunderbar!*" exclaimed Frau Mann. "*Wunderbar,* my God!"

"I'm not through," said the doctor, laying his gloves across his knees, "someday I am going to see the Baron again, and when I do I shall tell him about the mad Wittelsbach. He'll look as distressed as an owl tied up in a muffler."

"Ah," exclaimed Frau Mann, "he will enjoy it. He is so fond of titles."

"Listen," the doctor said, ordering a round, "I don't want to talk of the Wittelsbach. Oh, God, when I think back to my past, everyone in my family a beauty, my mother, with hair on her head as red as a fire kicked over in spring (and that was early in the '80's when a girl was the toast of the town, and going the limit meant lobster à la Newburg). She had a hat on her as big as the top of a table, and everything on it but running water; her bosom clinched into a corset of buckram, and my father sitting up beside her (snapped while they were riding on a roller-coaster). He had on one of those silly little yellow jackets and a tan bowler just up over his ears, and he must have been crazy, for he was sort of cross-eyed— maybe it was the wind in his face or thoughts of my mother where he couldn't do anything about it."

Frau Mann took up her glass, looking at it with one eye closed. "I've an album of my own," she said in a warm voice, "and everyone in it looks like a soldier—even though they are dead."

The doctor grinned, biting his teeth. Frau Mann tried to light a cigarette; the match wavered from side to side in her unsteady hand.

Frau Mann was slightly tipsy, and the insistent hum of the doctor's words was making her sleepy.

Seeing that Frau Mann dozed, the doctor got up lightly and tip-toed noiselessly to the entrance. He said to the waiter in bad German: "The lady will pay," opened the door, and went quietly into the night.

La Somnambule

Close to the church of *St. Sulpice*, around the corner in the *rue Servandoni*, lived the doctor. His small slouching figure was a feature of the *Place*. To the proprietor of the *Café de la Mairie du VI*[e] he was almost a son. This relatively small square, through which tram lines ran in several directions, bounded on the one side by the church and on the other by the court, was the doctor's "city." What he could not find here to answer to his needs could be found in the narrow streets that ran into it. Here he had been seen ordering details for funerals in the *parlour* with its black broadcloth curtains and mounted pictures of hearses; buying holy pictures and *petits Jésus* in the *boutique* displaying vestments and flowering candles. He had shouted down at least one judge in the *Mairie du Luxembourg* after a dozen cigars had failed to bring about his ends.

He walked, pathetic and alone, among the pasteboard booths of the *Foire St. Germain* when for a time its imitation castles squatted in the square. He was seen coming at a smart pace down the left side of the church to go into Mass, bathing in the holy water stoup as if he were its single and beholden bird, pushing aside weary French maids and local tradespeople with the impatience of a soul in physical stress.

Sometimes, late at night, before turning into the *Café de la Mairie du VIe*, he would be observed staring up at the huge towers of the church which rose into the sky, unlovely but reassuring, running a thick warm finger around his throat, where, in spite of its custom, his hair surprised him, lifting along his back and creeping up over his collar. Standing small and insubordinate, he would watch the basins of the fountain loosing their skirts of water in a ragged and flowing hem, sometimes crying to a man's departing shadow: "Aren't you the beauty!"

To the *Café de la Mairie du VIe* he brought Felix, who turned up in Paris some weeks after the encounter in Berlin. Felix thought to himself that undoubtedly the doctor was a great liar, but a valuable liar. His fabrications seemed to be the framework of a forgotten but imposing plan; some condition of life of which he was the sole surviving retainer. His manner was that of a servant of a defunct noble family, whose movements recall, though in a degraded form, those of a late master. Even the doctor's favourite gesture—plucking hairs out of his nostrils—seemed the "vulgarization" of what was once a thoughtful plucking of the beard.

As the altar of a church would present but a barren stylization but for the uncalculated offerings of the confused and humble; as the *corsage* of a woman is made suddenly martial and sorrowful by the rose thrust among the more decorous blooms by the hand of a lover suffering the violence of the overlapping of the permission to bestow a last embrace, and its withdrawal: making a vanishing and infinitesimal bull's-eye of that which had a moment before been a buoyant and showy bosom, by dragging time out of his bowels (for a lover knows two times, that which he is given, and that which he must make)—so Felix was astonished to find that the most touching flowers laid on the altar he had raised to his imagination were placed there by the people of the underworld, and that the reddest was to be the rose of the doctor.

After a long silence in which the doctor had ordered and consumed a *Chambéry fraise* and the Baron a coffee, the doctor remarked that the Jew and the Irish, the one moving upward and the other down, often meet, spade to spade in the same acre.

"The Irish may be as common as whale-shit—excuse me—on the bottom of the ocean—forgive me—but they do have imagination and," he added, "creative misery, which comes from being smacked down by the devil, and lifted up again by the angels. *Misericordioso!* Save me, Mother Mary, and never mind the other fellow! But the Jew, what is he at his best? Never anything higher than a meddler—pardon my wet glove—a supreme and marvellous meddler often, but a meddler nevertheless." He bowed slightly from the hips. "All right, Jews meddle and we lie, that's the difference, the fine difference. We say someone is pretty for instance, whereas, if the truth were known, they are probably as ugly as Smith going backward, but by our lie we have made that very party powerful, such is the power of the charlatan, the great strong! They drop on anything at any moment, and that sort of thing makes the mystic in the end, and," he added, "it makes the great doctor. The only people who really *know* anything about medical science are the nurses, and they never tell; they'd get slapped if they did. But the great doctor, he's a divine idiot and a wise man. He closes one eye, the eye that he studied with, and putting his fingers on the arteries of the body says: 'God, whose roadway this is, has given me permission to travel on it also,' which Heaven help the patient, is true; in this manner he comes on great cures, and sometimes upon that road is disconcerted by that Little Man." The doctor ordered another *Chambéry* and asked the Baron what he would have; being told that he wished nothing for the moment, the doctor added: "No man needs curing of his individual sickness; his universal malady is what he should look to."

The Baron remarked that this sounded like dogma.

The doctor looked at him. "Does it? Well, when you see that Little Man you know you will be shouldered from the path."

"I also know this," he went on: "One cup poured into another makes different waters; tears shed by one eye would blind if wept into another's eye. The breast we strike in joy is not the breast we strike in pain; any man's smile would be consternation on another's mouth. Rear up, eternal river, here comes grief! Man has no foot-hold that is not also a bargain. So be it! Laughing I came into Pacific Street, and laughing I'm going out of it; laughter is the pauper's money. I like paupers and bums," he added, "because they are impersonal with misery, but me—me, I'm taken most and chiefly for a vexatious bastard and gum on the bow, the wax that clots the gall or middle blood of man known as the heart or Bundle of Hiss. May my dilator burst and my speculum rust, may panic seize my index finger before I point out my man."

His hands (which he always carried like a dog who is walking on his hind legs) seemed to be holding his attention, then he said, raising his large melancholy eyes with the bright twinkle that often came into them: "Why is it that whenever I hear music I think I'm a bride?"

"Neurasthenia," said Felix.

He shook his head. "No, I'm not neurasthenic; I haven't that much respect for people—the basis, by the way, of all neuras-thenia."

"Impatience."

The doctor nodded. "The Irish are impatient for eternity; they lie to hurry it up, and they maintain their balance by the dexterity of God, God and the Father."

"In 1685," the Baron said with dry humour, "the Turks brought coffee into Vienna, and from that day Vienna, like a woman, had one impatience, something she liked. You know, of course, that Pitt the younger was refused alliance because he was foolish enough to proffer tea; Austria and tea could never go together. All cities have a particular and special beverage suited to them. As for God and the Father—in Austria they were the Emperor." The doctor looked up. The *chasseur* of the *Hôtel Récamier* (whom he knew far too well) was approaching them at a run.

"Eh!" said the doctor, who always expected anything at any hour. "Now what?" The boy, standing before him in a red-and-black-striped vest and flapping soiled apron, exclaimed in Midi French that a lady in twenty-nine had fainted and could not be brought out of it.

The doctor got up slowly, sighing. "Pay," he said to Felix, "and follow me." None of the doctor's methods being orthodox, Felix was not surprised at the invitation, but did as he was told.

On the second landing of the hotel (it was one of those middle-class hostelries which can be found in almost any corner of Paris, neither good nor bad, but so typical that it might have been moved every night and not have been out of place) a door was standing open, exposing a red-carpeted floor, and at the further end two narrow windows overlooking the square.

On a bed, surrounded by a confusion of potted plants, exotic palms and cut flowers, faintly over-sung by the notes of unseen birds, which seemed to have been forgotten—left without the usual silencing cover, which, like cloaks on funeral urns, are cast over their cages at night by good housewives—half flung off the support of the cushions from which, in a moment of threatened conscious-ness she had turned her head, lay the young woman, heavy and dishevelled. Her legs, in white flannel trousers, were spread as in a dance, the thick-lacquered pumps looking too lively for the arrested step. Her hands, long and beautiful, lay on either side of her face.

The perfume that her body exhaled was of the quality of that earth-flesh, fungi, which smells of captured dampness and yet is so dry, overcast with the odour of oil of amber, which is an inner malady of the sea, making her seem as if she had invaded a sleep incautious and entire. Her flesh was the texture of plant life, and beneath it one sensed a frame, broad, porous and sleep-worn, as if sleep were a decay fishing her beneath the visible surface. About her head there was an effulgence as of phosphorus glowing about the circumference of a body of water—as if her life lay through her in ungainly luminous deteriorations—the troubling structure of the born somnambule, who lives in two worlds—meet of child and desperado.

Like a painting by the *douanier* Rousseau, she seemed to lie in a jungle trapped in a drawing room (in the apprehension of which the walls have made their escape), thrown in among the carnivorous flowers as their ration; the set, the property of an unseen *dompteur*, half lord, half promoter, over which one expects to hear the strains of an orchestra of wood-winds render a serenade which will popularize the wilderness.

Felix, out of delicacy, stepped behind the palms. The doctor with professional roughness, brought to a pitch by his eternal fear of meeting with the law (he was not a licensed practitioner), said: "Slap her wrists, for Christ's sake. Where in hell is the water pitcher!"

He found it, and with amiable heartiness flung a handful against her face.

A series of almost invisible shudders wrinkled her skin as the water dripped from her lashes, over her mouth and on to the bed. A spasm of waking moved upward from some deep-shocked realm, and she opened her eyes. Instantly she tried to get to her feet. She said, "I was all right," and fell back into the pose of her annihilation.

Experiencing a double confusion, Felix now saw the doctor, partially hidden by the screen beside the bed, make the movements common to the "dumbfounder," or man of magic; the gestures of one who, in preparing the audience for a miracle, must pretend that there is nothing to hide; the whole purpose that of making the back and elbows move in a series of "honesties," while in reality the most flagrant part of the hoax is being prepared.

Felix saw that this was for the purpose of snatching a few drops from a perfume bottle picked up from the night table; of dusting his darkly bristled chin with a puff, and drawing a line of rouge across his lips, his upper lip compressed on his lower, in order to have it seem that their sudden embellishment was a visitation of nature; still thinking himself unobserved, as if the whole fabric of magic had begun to decompose, as if the mechanics of machination were indeed out of control and were simplifying themselves back to their origin, the doctor's hand reached out and covered a loose hundred franc note lying on the table.

With a tension in his stomach, such as one suffers when watching an acrobat leaving the virtuosity of his safety in a mad unravelling whirl into probable death, Felix watched the hand descend, take up the note, and disappear into the limbo of the doctor's pocket. He knew that he would continue to like the doctor, though he was aware that it would be in spite of a long series of convulsions of the spirit, analogous to the displacement in the fluids of the oyster, that must cover its itch with a pearl; so he would have to cover the doctor. He knew at the same time that this stricture of acceptance (by which what we must love is made into what we can love) would eventually be a part of himself, though originally brought on by no will of his own.

Engrossed in the coils of this new disquiet, Felix turned about. The girl was sitting up. She recognized the doctor. She had seen him somewhere. But, as one may trade ten years at a certain shop and be unable to place the shopkeeper if he is met in the street or in the *promenoir* of a theatre, the shop being a portion of his identity, she struggled to place him now that he had moved out of his frame.

"*Café de la Mairie du VIe*," said the doctor, taking a chance in order to have a hand in her awakening.

She did not smile, though the moment he spoke she placed him. She closed her eyes, and Felix, who had been looking into them intently because of their mysterious and shocking blue, found himself seeing them still faintly clear and timeless behind the lids— the long unqualified range in the iris of wild beasts who have not tamed the focus down to meet the human eye.

The woman who presents herself to the spectator as a "picture" forever arranged is, for the contemplative mind, the chiefest danger. Sometimes one meets a woman who is beast turning human. Such a person's every movement will reduce to an image of a forgotten experience; a mirage of an eternal wedding cast on the racial memory; as insupportable a joy as would be the vision of an eland coming down an aisle of trees, chapleted with orange blossoms and bridal veil, a hoof raised in the economy of fear, stepping in the trepidation of flesh that will become myth; as the unicorn is neither man nor beast deprived, but human hunger pressing its breast to its prey.

Such a woman is the infected carrier of the past: before her the structure of our head and jaws ache—we feel that we could eat her, she who is eaten death returning, for only then do we put our face close to the blood on the lips of our forefathers.

Something of this emotion came over Felix, but being racially incapable of abandon, he felt that he was looking upon a figure-head in a museum, which though static, no longer roosting on its cutwater, seemed yet to be going against the wind; as if this girl were the converging halves of a broken fate, setting face, in sleep, toward itself in time, as an image and its reflection in a lake seem parted only by the hesitation in the hour.

In the tones of this girl's voice was the pitch of one enchanted with the gift of postponed abandon: the low drawling "aside" voice of the actor who, in the soft usury of his speech, withholds a vocabulary until the profitable moment when he shall be facing his audience—in her case a guarded extempore to the body of what would be said at some later period when she would be able to "see" them. What she now said was merely the longest way to a quick dismissal. She asked them to come to see her when she would be "able to feel better."

Pinching the *chasseur*, the doctor inquired the girl's name. "Mademoiselle Robin Vote," the *chasseur* answered.

Descending into the street, the doctor, desiring "one last before bed," directed his steps back to the café. After a short silence he asked the Baron if he had ever thought about women and marriage. He kept his eyes fixed on the marble of the table before him, knowing that Felix had experienced something unusual.

The Baron admitted that he had; he wished a son who would feel as he felt about the "great past." The doctor then inquired, with feigned indifference, of what nation he would choose the boy's mother.

"The American," the Baron answered instantly. "With an American anything can be done."

The doctor laughed. He brought his soft fist down on the table —now he was sure. "Fate and entanglement," he said, "have begun again—the dung beetle rolling his burden uphill—oh, the hard climb! Nobility, very well, but what is it?" The Baron started to answer him, but the doctor held up his hand. "Wait a minute! I know—the few that the many have lied about well and long enough to make them deathless. So you must have a son," he paused. "A king is the peasant's actor, who becomes so scandalous that he has to be bowed down to—scandalous in the higher sense naturally. And why must he be bowed down to? Because he has been set apart as the one dog who need not regard the rules of the house; they are so high that they can defame God and foul their rafters! But the people—that's different—they are church-broken, nation-broken—they drink and pray and piss in the one place. Every man has a house-broken heart except the great man. The people love their church and know it, as a dog knows where he was made to conform, and there he returns by his instinct. But to the graver permission, the king, the tsar, the emperor, who may relieve themselves on high heaven—to them they bow down—only." The Baron, who was always troubled by obscenity, could never, in the case of the doctor, resent it; he felt the seriousness, the melancholy hidden beneath every jest and malediction that the doctor uttered, therefore he answered him seriously. "To pay homage to our past is the only gesture that also includes the future."

"And so a son?"

"For that reason. The modern child has nothing left to hold to, or, to put it better, he has nothing to hold with. We are adhering to life now with our last muscle—the heart."

"The last muscle of aristocracy is madness—remember that—" the doctor leaned forward—"the last child born to aristocracy is sometimes an idiot, out of respect—we go up—but we come down."

The Baron dropped his monocle; the unarmed eye looked straight ahead. "It's not necessary," he said, then he added, "But you are American, so you don't believe."

"Ho!" hooted the doctor, "because I'm American I believe anything, so I say beware! In the king's bed is always found, just before it becomes a museum piece, the droppings of the black sheep"—he raised his glass. "To Robin Vote," he said. "She can't be more than twenty."

With a roar the steel blind came down over the window of the *Café de la Mairie du VIe*.

Felix, carrying two volumes on the life of the Bourbons, called the next day at the *Hôtel Récamier*. Miss Vote was not in. Four afternoons in succession he called, only to be told that she had just left. On the fifth, turning the corner of the *rue Bonaparte*, he ran into her.

Removed from her setting—the plants that had surrounded her, the melancholy red velvet of the chairs and the curtains, the sound, weak and nocturnal, of the birds—she yet carried the quality of the "way back" as animals do. She suggested that they should walk together in the gardens of the Luxembourg toward which her steps had been directed when he addressed her. They walked in the bare chilly gardens and Felix was happy. He felt that he could talk to her, tell her anything, though she herself was so silent. He told her he had a post in the *Crédit Lyonnais*, earning two thousand five hundred francs a week; a master of seven tongues, he was useful to the bank, and, he added, he had a trifle saved up, gained in speculations.

He walked a little short of her. Her movements were slightly headlong and sideways; slow, clumsy and yet graceful, the ample gait of the night-watch. She wore no hat, and her pale head, with its short hair growing flat on the forehead made still narrower by

the hanging curls almost on a level with the finely arched eye-
brows, gave her the look of cherubs in Renaissance theatres; the
eyeballs showing slightly rounded in profile, the temples low and
square. She was gracious and yet fading, like an old statue in a
garden, that symbolizes the weather through which it has endured,
and is not so much the work of man as the work of wind and rain
and the herd of the seasons, and though formed in man's image
is a figure of doom. Because of this, Felix found her presence pain-
ful, and yet a happiness. Thinking of her, visualizing her, was an
extreme act of the will; to recall her after she had gone, however,
was as easy as the recollection of a sensation of beauty without its
details. When she smiled the smile was only in the mouth and a
little bitter: the face of an incurable yet to be stricken with its
malady.

As the days passed they spent many hours in museums, and
while this pleased Felix immeasurably, he was surprised that often
her taste, turning from an appreciation of the excellent, would also
include the cheaper and debased, with an emotion as real. When
she touched a thing, her hands seemed to take the place of the eye.
He thought: "She has the touch of the blind who, because they
see more with their fingers, forget more in their minds." Her fingers
would go forward, hesitate, tremble, as if they had found a face
in the dark. When her hand finally came to rest, the palm closed;
it was as if she had stopped a crying mouth. Her hand lay still and
she would turn away. At such moments Felix experienced an un-
accountable apprehension. The sensuality in her hands frightened
him.

Her clothes were of a period that he could not quite place. She
wore feathers of the kind his mother had worn, flattened sharply
to the face. Her skirts were moulded to her hips and fell down-
ward and out, wider and longer than those of other women, heavy
silks that made her seem newly ancient. One day he learned the
secret. Pricing a small tapestry in an antique shop facing the Seine,
he saw Robin reflected in a door mirror of a back room, dressed
in a heavy brocaded gown which time had stained in places, in

others split, yet which was so voluminous that there were yards enough to refashion.

He found that his love for Robin was not in truth a selection; it was as if the weight of his life had amassed one precipitation. He had thought of making a destiny for himself, through laborious and untiring travail. Then with Robin it seemed to stand before him without effort. When he asked her to marry him it was with such an unplanned eagerness that he was taken aback to find himself accepted, as if Robin's life held no volition for refusal.

He took her first to Vienna. To reassure himself he showed her all the historic buildings. He kept saying to himself that sooner or later, in this garden or that palace, she would suddenly be moved as he was moved. Yet it seemed to him that he too was a sightseer. He tried to explain to her what Vienna had been before the war; what it must have been before he was born; yet his memory was confused and hazy, and he found himself repeating what he had read, for it was what he knew best. With methodical anxiety he took her over the city. He said, "You are a Baronin now." He spoke to her in German as she ate the heavy *Schnitzel* and dumplings, clasping her hand about the thick handle of the beer mug. He said: "*Das Leben ist ewig, darin liegt seine Schönheit.*"

They walked before the Imperial Palace in a fine hot sun that fell about the clipped hedges and the statues warm and clear. He went into the *Kammergarten* with her and talked, and on into the *Gloriette*, and sat on first one bench and then another. Brought up short, he realized that he had been hurrying from one to the other as if they were orchestra chairs, as if he himself were trying not to miss anything; now, at the extremity of the garden, he was aware that he had been anxious to see every tree, every statue at a different angle.

In their hotel, she went to the window and pulled aside the heavy velvet hangings, threw down the bolster that Vienna uses against the wind at the ledge, and opened the window, though the night air was cold. He began speaking of Emperor Francis Joseph and of the whereabouts of Charles the First. And as he spoke Felix laboured under the weight of his own remorseless recreation of the great, generals and statesmen and emperors. His chest was as heavy as if it were supporting the combined weight of their apparel and their destiny. Looking up after an interminable flow of fact and fancy, he saw Robin sitting with her legs thrust out, her head thrown back against the embossed cushion of the chair, sleeping, one arm fallen over the chair's side, the hand somehow older and wiser than her body; and looking at her he knew that he was not sufficient to make her what he had hoped; it would require more than his own argument. It would require contact with persons exonerated of their earthly condition by some strong spiritual bias, some one of that old régime, some old lady of the past courts, who only remembered others when trying to think of herself.

On the tenth day, therefore, Felix turned about and re-entered Paris. In the following months he put his faith in the fact that Robin had Christian proclivities, and his hope in the discovery that she was an enigma. He said to himself, that possibly she had greatness hidden in the non-committal. He felt that her attention, somehow in spite of him, had already been taken by something not yet in history. Always she seemed to be listening to the echo of some foray in the blood that had no known setting, and when he came to know her this was all he could base his intimacy upon. There was something pathetic in the spectacle: Felix reiterating the tragedy of his father. Attired like some haphazard in the mind of a tailor, again in the ambit of his father's futile attempt to encompass the rhythm of his wife's stride, Felix, with tightly held monocle, walked beside Robin, talking to her, drawing her attention to this and that, wrecking himself and his peace of mind in an effort to acquaint her with the destiny for which he had chosen her —that she might bear sons who would recognize and honour the past. For without such love, the past as he understood it, would die away from the world. She was not listening and he said in an angry mood, though he said it calmly, "I am deceiving you!" And he wondered what he meant, and why she did not hear.

"A child," he pondered. "Yes, a child!" and then he said to himself, "Why has it not come about?" The thought took him abruptly in the middle of his accounting. He hurried home in a flurry of anxiety, like a boy who has heard a regiment on parade, toward which he cannot run because he has no one from whom to seek permission, yet runs haltingly nevertheless. Coming face to face with her, all that he could stammer out was: "Why is there no child? *Wo ist das Kind? Warum? Warum?*"

Robin prepared herself for her child with her only power: a stubborn cataleptic calm, conceiving herself pregnant before she was; and, strangely aware of some lost land in herself, she took to going out; wandering the countryside; to train travel, to other cities, alone and engrossed. Once, not having returned for three days, and Felix nearly beside himself with terror, she walked in late at night and said she had been halfway to Berlin.

Suddenly she took the Catholic vow. She came into the church silently. The prayers of the suppliants had not ceased nor had anyone been broken of their meditation. Then, as if some inscrutable wish for salvation, something monstrously unfulfilled, had thrown a shadow, they regarded her, to see her going softly forward and down, a tall girl with the body of a boy.

Many churches saw her: *St. Julien le Pauvre*, the church of *St. Germain des Prés, Ste. Clothilde*. Even on the cold tiles of the Russian church, in which there is no pew, she knelt alone, lost and conspicuous, her broad shoulders above her neighbours, her feet large and as earthly as the feet of a monk.

She strayed into the *rue Picpus*, into the gardens of the convent of *L'Adoration Perpétuelle*. She talked to the nuns and they, feeling that they were looking at someone who would never be able to ask for, or receive, mercy, blessed her in their hearts and gave her a sprig of rose from the bush. They showed her where Jean Valjean had kept his rakes, and where the bright little ladies of the *pension* came to quilt their covers; and Robin smiled, taking the spray, and looked down at the tomb of Lafayette and thought her unpeopled thoughts. Kneeling in the chapel, which was never without a nun

going over her beads, Robin, trying to bring her mind to this abrupt
necessity, found herself worrying about her height. Was she still
growing?

She tried to think of the consequence to which her son was to be
born and dedicated. She thought of the Emperor Francis Joseph.
There was something commensurate in the heavy body with the
weight in her mind, where reason was inexact with lack of neces-
sity. She wandered to thoughts of women, women that she had
come to connect with women. Strangely enough these were women
in history, Louise de la Vallière, Catherine of Russia, Madame de
Maintenon, Catherine de' Medici, and two women out of litera-
ture, Anna Karenina and Catherine Heathcliff; and now there was
this woman Austria. She prayed, and her prayer was monstrous be-
cause in it there was no margin left for damnation or forgiveness,
for praise or for blame—those who cannot conceive a bargain can-
not be saved or damned. She could not offer herself up; she only
told of herself in a preoccupation that was its own predicament.

Leaning her childish face and full chin on the shelf of the *prie-
dieu,* her eyes fixed, she laughed, out of some hidden capacity,
some lost subterranean humour; as it ceased, she leaned still
further forward in a swoon, waking and yet heavy, like one in sleep.

When Felix returned that evening Robin was dozing in a chair,
one hand under her cheek and one arm fallen. A book was lying on
the floor beneath her hand. The book was the memoirs of the
Marquis de Sade; a line was underscored: *Et lui rendant sa cap-
tivité les milles services qu'un amour dévoué est seul capable de
rendre,* and suddenly into his mind came the question: "What is
wrong?"

She awoke but did not move. He came and took her by the arm
and lifted her toward him. She put her hand against his chest and
pushed him, she looked frightened, she opened her mouth but no
words came. He stepped back, he tried to speak, but they moved
aside from each other saying nothing.

That night she was taken with pains. She began to curse loudly,

a thing that Felix was totally unprepared for; with the most fool-
ish gestures he tried to make her comfortable.

"Go to hell!" she cried. She moved slowly, bent away from him,
chair by chair; she was drunk—her hair was swinging in her eyes.

Amid loud and frantic cries of affirmation and despair Robin
was delivered. Shuddering in the double pains of birth and fury,
cursing like a sailor, she rose up on her elbow in her bloody gown,
looking about her in the bed as if she had lost something. "Oh, for
Christ's sake, for Christ's sake!" she kept crying like a child who
has walked into the commencement of a horror.

A week out of bed she was lost, as if she had done something
irreparable, as if this act had caught her attention for the first time.

One night, Felix, having come in unheard, found her standing
in the centre of the floor holding the child high in her hand as if
she were about to dash it down, but she brought it down gently.

The child was small, a boy, and sad. It slept too much in a
quivering palsy of nerves; it made few voluntary movements; it
whimpered.

Robin took to wandering again, to intermittent travel from which
she came back hours, days later, disinterested. People were uneasy
when she spoke to them, confronted with a catastrophe that had
yet no beginning.

Felix had each day the sorrow born with him; for the rest, he
pretended that he noticed nothing. Robin was almost never home;
he did not know how to inquire for her. Sometimes coming into a
café he would creep out again because she stood before the bar—
sometimes laughing, but more often silent, her head bent over her
glass, her hair swinging; and about her people of every sort.

One night, coming home about three, he found her in the dark-
ness, standing, back against the window, in the pod of the curtain,
her chin so thrust forward that the muscles in her neck stood out.
As he came toward her she said in a fury, "I didn't want him!"
Raising her hand she struck him across the face.

He stepped away; he dropped his monocle and caught at it

swinging; he took his breath backward. He waited a whole second, trying to appear casual. "You didn't want him," he said. He bent down pretending to disentangle his ribbon. "It seems I could not accomplish that."

"Why not be secret about him?" she said. "Why talk?"

Felix turned his body without moving his feet. "What shall we do?"

She grinned, but it was not a smile. "I'll get out," she said. She took up her cloak; she always carried it dragging. She looked about her, about the room, as if she were seeing it for the first time.

For three or four months the people of the quarter asked for her in vain. Where she had gone no one knew. When she was seen again in the quarter, it was with Nora Flood. She did not explain where she had been; she was unable or unwilling to give an account of herself. The doctor said: "In America, that's where Nora lives. I brought her into the world and I should know."

Night Watch

The strangest "salon" in America was Nora's. Her house was couched in the centre of a mass of tangled grass and weeds. Before it fell into Nora's hands the property had been in the same family two hundred years. It had its own burial ground, and a decaying chapel in which stood in tens and tens mouldering psalm books, laid down some fifty years gone in a flurry of forgiveness and absolution.

It was the "pauper's" salon for poets, radicals, beggars, artists, and people in love; for Catholics, Protestants, Brahmins, dabblers in black magic and medicine; all these could be seen sitting about her oak table before the huge fire, Nora listening, her hand on her hound, the firelight throwing her shadow and his high against the wall. Of all that ranting, roaring crew, she alone stood out. The equilibrium of her nature, savage and refined, gave her bridled skull a look of compassion. She was broad and tall, and though her skin was the skin of a child, there could be seen coming, early in her life, the design that was to be the weather-beaten grain of her face, that wood in the work; the tree coming forward in her, an undocumented record of time.

She was known instantly as a Westerner. Looking at her, foreigners remembered stories they had heard of covered wagons; animals going down to drink; children's heads, just as far as the eyes, looking in fright out of small windows, where in the dark another race crouched in ambush; with heavy hems the women becoming large, flattening the fields where they walked; God so ponderous in their minds that they could stamp out the world with him in seven days.

At these incredible meetings one felt that early American history was being re-enacted. The Drummer Boy, Fort Sumter, Lincoln, Booth, all somehow came to mind; Whigs and Tories were in the air; bunting and its stripes and stars, the swarm increasing slowly and accurately on the hive of blue; Boston tea tragedies, carbines, and the sound of a boy's wild calling; Puritan feet, long upright in the grave, striking the earth again, walking up and out of their custom; the calk of prayers thrust in the heart. And in the midst of this, Nora.

By temperament Nora was an early Christian; she believed the word. There is a gap in "world pain" through which the singular falls continually and forever; a body falling in observable space, deprived of the privacy of disappearance; as if privacy, moving relentlessly away, by the very sustaining power of its withdrawal kept the body eternally moving downward, but in one place, and perpetually before the eye. Such a singular was Nora. There was some derangement in her equilibrium that kept her immune from her own descent.

Nora had the face of all people who love the people—a face that would be evil when she found out that to love without criticism is to be betrayed. Nora robbed herself for everyone; incapable of giving herself warning, she was continually turning about to find herself diminished. Wandering people the world over found her profitable in that she could be sold for a price forever, for she carried her betrayal money in her own pocket.

Those who love everything are despised by everything, as those who love a city, in its profoundest sense, become the shame of that city, the *détraqués*, the paupers; their good is incommunicable, out-witted, being the rudiment of a life that has developed, as in man's body are found evidences of lost needs. This condition had struck even into Nora's house; it spoke in her guests, in her ruined gardens where she had been wax in every work of nature.

Whenever she was met, at the opera, at a play, sitting alone and apart, the programme face down on her knee, one would discover in her eyes, large, protruding and clear, that mirrorless look of polished metals which report not so much the object as the move-ment of the object. As the surface of a gun's barrel, reflecting a scene, will add to the image the portent of its construction, so her eyes contracted and fortified the play before her in her own un-conscious terms. One sensed in the way she held her head that her ears were recording Wagner or Scarlatti, Chopin, Palestrina, or the lighter songs of the Viennese school, in a smaller but more intense orchestration.

And she was the only woman of the last century who could go up a hill with the Seventh Day Adventists and confound the seventh day—with a muscle in her heart so passionate that she made the seventh day immediate. Her fellow worshippers believed in that day and the end of the world out of a bewildered entangle-ment with the six days preceding it; Nora believed for the beauty of that day alone. She was by fate one of those people who are born unprovided for, except in the provision of herself.

One missed in her a sense of humour. Her smile was quick and definite, but disengaged. She chuckled now and again at a joke, but it was the amused grim chuckle of a person who looks up to discover that they have coincided with the needs of nature in a bird.

Cynicism, laughter, the second husk into which the shucked man crawls, she seemed to know little or nothing about. She was one of those deviations by which man thinks to reconstruct himself.

To "confess" to her was an act even more secret than the com-munication provided by a priest. There was no ignominy in her;

she recorded without reproach or accusation, being shorn of self-reproach or self-accusation. This drew people to her and frightened them; they could neither insult nor hold anything against her, though it embittered them to have to take back injustice that in her found no foothold. In court she would have been impossible; no one would have been hanged, reproached or forgiven because no one would have been "accused." The world and its history were to Nora like a ship in a bottle; she herself was outside and unidentified, endlesly embroiled in a preoccupation without a problem.

Then she met Robin. The Denckman circus, which she kept in touch with even when she was not working with it (some of its people were visitors to her house), came into New York in the fall of 1923. Nora went alone. She came into the circle of the ring, taking her place in the front row.

Clowns in red, white and yellow, with the traditional smears on their faces, were rolling over the sawdust, as if they were in the belly of a great mother where there was yet room to play. A black horse, standing on trembling hind legs that shook in apprehension of the raised front hooves, his beautiful ribboned head pointed down and toward the trainer's whip, pranced slowly, the foreshanks flickering to the whip. Tiny dogs ran about trying to look like horses, then in came the elephants.

A girl sitting beside Nora took out a cigarette and lit it; her hands shook and Nora turned to look at her; she looked at her suddenly because the animals, going around and around the ring, all but climbed over at that point. They did not seem to see the girl, but as their dusty eyes moved past, the orbit of their light seemed to turn on her. At that moment Nora turned.

The great cage for the lions had been set up, and the lions were walking up and out of their small strong boxes into the arena. Ponderous and furred they came, their tails laid down across the the floor, dragging and heavy, making the air seem full of withheld strength. Then as one powerful lioness came to the turn of the bars, exactly opposite the girl, she turned her furious great head with its yellow eyes afire and went down, her paws thrust through the bars

and, as she regarded the girl, as if a river were falling behind im-
passable heat, her eyes flowed in tears that never reached the
surface. At that the girl rose straight up. Nora took her hand.
"Let's get her out of here!" the girl said, and still holding her hand
Nora took her out.

In the lobby Nora said, "My name is Nora Flood," and she
waited. After a pause the girl said, "I'm Robin Vote." She looked
about her distractedly. "I don't want to be here." But it was all
she said; she did not explain where she wished to be.

She stayed with Nora until the mid-winter. Two spirits were
working in her, love and anonymity. Yet they were so "haunted"
of each other that separation was impossible.

Nora closed her house. They travelled from Munich, Vienna
and Budapest into Paris. Robin told only a little of her life, but
she kept repeating in one way or another her wish for a home, as
if she were afraid she would be lost again, as if she were aware,
without conscious knowledge, that she belonged to Nora, and that
if Nora did not make it permanent by her own strength, she would
forget.

Nora bought an apartment in the *rue du Cherche-Midi*. Robin
had chosen it. Looking from the long windows one saw a fountain
figure, a tall granite woman bending forward with lifted head; one
hand was held over the pelvic round as if to warn a child who goes
incautiously.

In the passage of their lives together every object in the garden,
every item in the house, every word they spoke, attested to their
mutual love, the combining of their humours. There were circus
chairs, wooden horses bought from a ring of an old merry-go-
round, Venetian chandeliers from the Flea Fair, stage-drops from
Munich, cherubim from Vienna, ecclesiastical hangings from
Rome, a spinet from England, and a miscellaneous collection of
music boxes from many countries; such was the museum of their
encounter, as Felix's hearsay house had been testimony of the age
when his father had lived with his mother.

When the time came that Nora was alone most of the night and part of the day, she suffered from the personality of the house, the punishment of those who collect their lives together. Unconsciously at first, she went about disturbing nothing; then she became aware that her soft and careful movements were the outcome of an un-reasoning fear—if she disarranged anything Robin might become confused—might lose the scent of home.

Love becomes the deposit of the heart, analogous in all degrees to the "findings" in a tomb. As in one will be charted the taken place of the body, the raiment, the utensils necessary to its other life, so in the heart of the lover will be traced, as an indelible shadow, that which he loves. In Nora's heart lay the fossil of Robin, intaglio of her identity, and about it for its maintenance ran Nora's blood. Thus the body of Robin could never be unloved, corrupt or put away. Robin was now beyond timely changes, except in the blood that animated her. That she could be spilled of this fixed the walking image of Robin in appalling apprehension on Nora's mind—Robin alone, crossing streets, in danger. Her mind became so transfixed that, by the agency of her fear, Robin seemed enor-mous and polarized, all catastrophes ran toward her, the magnet-ized predicament; and crying out, Nora would wake from sleep, going back through the tide of dreams into which her anxiety had thrown her, taking the body of Robin down with her into it, as the ground things take the corpse, with minute persistence, down into the earth, leaving a pattern of it on the grass, as if they stitched as they descended.

Yes now, when they were alone and happy, apart from the world in their appreciation of the world, there entered with Robin a com-pany unaware. Sometimes it rang clear in the songs she sang, some-times Italian, sometimes French or German, songs of the people, debased and haunting, songs that Nora had never heard before, or that she had never heard in company with Robin. When the cadence changed, when it was repeated on a lower key, she knew that Robin was singing of a life that she herself had no part in; snatches of harmony as tell-tale as the possessions of a traveller from a foreign land! songs like a practised whore who turns away from no one but the one who loves her. Sometimes Nora would sing them after Robin, with the trepidation of a foreigner repeating words in an unknown tongue, uncertain of what they may mean. Sometimes unable to endure the melody that told so much and so little, she would interrupt Robin with a question. Yet more distressing would be the moment when, after a pause, the song would be taken up again from an inner room where Robin, unseen, gave back an echo of her unknown life more nearly tuned to its origin. Often the song would stop altogether, until unthinking, just as she was leaving the house, Robin would break out again in anticipation, changing the sound from a reminiscence to an expectation.

Yet sometimes, going about the house, in passing each other, they would fall into an agonized embrace, looking into each other's face, their two heads in their four hands, so strained together that the space that divided them seemed to be thrusting them apart. Sometimes in these moments of insurmountable grief Robin would make some movement, use a peculiar turn of phrase not habitual to her, innocent of the betrayal, by which Nora was informed that Robin had come from a world to which she would return. To keep her (in Robin there was this tragic longing to be kept, knowing herself astray) Nora knew now that there was no way but death. In death Robin would belong to her. Death went with them, together and alone; and with the torment and catastrophe, thoughts of resurrection, the second duel.

Looking out into the fading sun of the winter sky, against which a little tower rose just outside the bedroom window, Nora would tabulate by the sounds of Robin dressing the exact progress of her toilet; chimes of cosmetic bottles and cream jars; the faint perfume of hair heated under the electric curlers; seeing in her mind the changing direction taken by the curls that hung on Robin's forehead, turning back from the low crown to fall in upward curves to the nape of the neck, the flat uncurved back head that spoke of some awful silence. Half narcoticized by the sounds and the knowledge that this was in preparation for departure, Nora spoke to herself: "In the resurrection, when we come up looking backward at each other, I shall know you only of all that company. My ear shall turn in the socket of my head; my eyeballs loosened where I am the whirlwind about that cashed expense, my foot stubborn on the cast of your grave." In the doorway Robin stood. "Don't wait for me," she said.

In the years that they lived together, the departures of Robin became a slowly increasing rhythm. At first Nora went with Robin; but as time passed, realizing that a growing tension was in Robin, unable to endure the knowledge that she was in the way or forgotten, seeing Robin go from table to table, from drink to drink, from person to person, realizing that if she herself were not there Robin might return to her as the one who, out of all the turbulent night, had not been lived through, Nora stayed at home, lying awake or sleeping. Robin's absence, as the night drew on, became a physical removal, insupportable and irreparable. As an amputated hand cannot be disowned because it is experiencing a futurity, of which the victim is its forebear, so Robin was an amputation that Nora could not renounce. As the wrist longs, so her heart longed, and dressing she would go out into the night that she might be "beside herself," skirting the café in which she could catch a glimpse of Robin.

Once out in the open Robin walked in a formless meditation, her hands thrust into the sleeves of her coat, directing her steps toward that night life that was a known measure between Nora and the cafés. Her meditations, during this walk, were a part of the pleasure she expected to find when the walk came to an end. It was this exact distance that kept the two ends of her life—Nora and the cafés—from forming a monster with two heads.

Her thoughts were in themselves a form of locomotion. She walked with raised head, seeming to look at every passer-by, yet her gaze was anchored in anticipation and regret. A look of anger, intense and hurried, shadowed her face and drew her mouth down as she neared her company; yet as her eyes moved over the façades

of the buildings, searching for the sculptured head that both she
and Nora loved (a Greek head with shocked protruding eyeballs,
for which the tragic mouth seemed to pour forth tears), a quiet
joy radiated from her own eyes; for this head was a remembrance
of Nora and her love, making the anticipation of the people she
was to meet set and melancholy. So, without knowing she would
do so, she took the turn that brought her into this particular street.
If she was diverted, as was sometimes the case, by the interposition
of a company of soldiers, a wedding or a funeral, then by her
agitation she seemed a part of the function to the persons she
stumbled against, as a moth by his very entanglement with the
heat that shall be his extinction, is associated with flame as a com-
ponent part of its activity. It was this characteristic that saved
her from being asked too sharply "where" she was going; pedes-
trians who had it on the point of their tongues, seeing her rapt and
confused, turned instead to look at each other.

The doctor, seeing Nora out walking alone, said to himself, as
the tall black-caped figure passed ahead of him under the lamps,
"There goes the dismantled—Love has fallen off her wall. A re-
ligious woman," he thought to himself, "without the joy and safety
of the Catholic faith, which at a pinch covers up the spots on the
wall when the family portraits take a slide; take that safety from
a woman," he said to himself, quickening his step to follow her,
"and love gets loose and into the rafters. She sees her everywhere,"
he added, glancing at Nora as she passed into the dark. "Out look-
ing for what she's afraid to find—Robin. There goes mother of
mischief, running about, trying to get the world home."

Looking at every couple as they passed, into every carriage and
car, up to the lighted windows of the houses, trying to discover
not Robin any longer, but traces of Robin, influences in her life
(and those which were yet to be betrayed), Nora watched every
moving figure for some gesture that might turn up in the move-
ments made by Robin; avoiding the quarter where she knew her
to be, where by her own movements the waiters, the people on
the terraces, might know that she had a part in Robin's life.

Returning home, the interminable night would begin. Listening to the faint sounds from the street, every murmur from the garden, an unevolved and tiny hum that spoke of the progressive growth of noise that would be Robin coming home, Nora lay and beat her pillow without force, unable to cry, her legs drawn up. At times she would get up and walk, to make something in her life outside more quickly over, to bring Robin back by the very velocity of the beating of her heart. And walking in vain, suddenly she would sit down on one of the circus chairs that stood by the long window overlooking the garden, bend forward, putting her hands between her legs, and begin to cry, "Oh, God! Oh, God! Oh, God!" repeated so often that it had the effect of all words spoken in vain. She nodded and awoke again and began to cry before she opened her eyes, and went back to the bed and fell into a dream which she recognized; though in the finality of this version she knew that the dream had not been "well dreamt" before. Where the dream had been incalculable, it was now completed with the entry of Robin.

Nora dreamed that she was standing at the top of a house, that is, the last floor but one—this was her grandmother's room—an expansive, decaying splendour; yet somehow, though set with all the belongings of her grandmother, was as bereft as the nest of a bird which will not return. Portraits of the great-uncle, Llewellyn, who died in the Civil War, faded pale carpets, curtains that resembled columns from their time in stillness—a plume and an ink well—the ink faded into the quill; standing, Nora looked down into the body of the house, as if from a scaffold, where now Robin had entered the dream, lying among a company below. Nora said to herself, "The dream will not be dreamed again." A disc of light, which seemed to come from someone or thing standing behind her and which was yet a shadow, shed a faintly luminous glow upon the upturned still face of Robin, who had the smile of an "only survivor," a smile which fear had married to the bone.

From round about her in anguish Nora heard her own voice saying, "Come up, this is Grandmother's room," yet knowing it was impossible because the room was taboo. The louder she cried out the farther away went the floor below, as if Robin and she, in their extremity, were a pair of opera glasses turned to the wrong end, diminishing in their painful love; a speed that ran away with the two ends of the building, stretching her apart.

This dream that now had all its parts had still the former quality of never really having been her grandmother's room. She herself did not seem to be there in person, nor able to give an invitation. She had wanted to put her hands on something in this room to prove it; the dream had never permitted her to do so. This chamber that had never been her grandmother's, which was, on the contrary, the absolute opposite of any known room her grandmother had ever moved or lived in, was nevertheless saturated with the lost presence of her grandmother, who seemed in the continual process of leaving it. The architecture of dream had rebuilt her everlasting and continuous, flowing away in a long gown of soft folds and chin laces, the pinched gatherings that composed the train taking an upward line over the back and hips in a curve that not only bent age but fear of bent age demands.

With this figure of her grandmother who was not entirely her recalled grandmother went one of her childhood, when she had run into her at the corner of the house—the grandmother who, for some unknown reason, was dressed as a man, wearing a billy-cock and a corked moustache, ridiculous and plump in tight trousers and a red waistcoat, her arms spread saying with a leer of love, "My little sweetheart!"—her grandmother "drawn upon" as a pre-historic ruin is drawn upon, symbolizing her life out of her life, and which now appeared to Nora as something being done to Robin, Robin disfigured and eternalized by the hieroglyphics of sleep and pain.

Waking, she began to walk again, and looking out into the garden in the faint light of dawn, she saw a double shadow falling from the statue, as if it were multiplying, and thinking perhaps this was Robin, she called and was not answered. Standing motionless, straining her eyes, she saw emerge from the darkness the light of Robin's eyes, the fear in them developing their luminosity until, by the intensity of their double regard, Robin's eyes and hers met. So they gazed at each other. As if that light had power to bring what was dreaded into the zone of their catastrophe, Nora saw the body of another woman swim up into the statue's obscurity, with head hung down, that the added eyes might not augment the illumination; her arms about Robin's neck, her body pressed to Robin's, her legs slackened in the hang of the embrace.

Unable to turn her eyes away, incapable of speech, experiencing a sensation of evil, complete and dismembering, Nora fell to her knees, so that her eyes were not withdrawn by her volition, but dropped from their orbit by the falling of her body. Her chin on the sill, she knelt, thinking, "Now they will not hold together," feeling that if she turned away from what Robin was doing, the design would break and melt back into Robin alone. She closed her eyes, and at that moment she knew an awful happiness. Robin, like something dormant, was protected, moved out of death's way by the successive arms of women; but as she closed her eyes, Nora said "Ah!" with the intolerable automatism of the last "Ah!" in a body struck at the moment of its final breath.

"The Squatter"

Jenny Petherbridge was a widow, a middle-aged woman who had been married four times. Each husband had wasted away and died; she had been like a squirrel racing a wheel day and night in an endeavour to make them historical; they could not survive it.

She had a beaked head and the body, small, feeble, and ferocious, that somehow made one associate her with Judy; they did not go together. Only severed could any part of her have been called "right." There was a trembling ardour in her wrists and fingers as if she were suffering from some elaborate denial. She looked old, yet expectant of age; she seemed to be steaming in the vapours of someone else about to die; still she gave off an odour to the mind (for there are purely mental smells that have no reality) of a woman about to be *accouchée*. Her body suffered from its fare, laughter and crumbs, abuse and indulgence. But put out a hand to touch her, and her head moved perceptibly with the broken arc of two instincts, recoil and advance, so that the head rocked timidly and aggressively at the same moment, giving her a slightly shuddering and expectant rhythm.

She writhed under the necessity of being unable to wear anything becoming, being one of those panicky little women who, no matter what they put on, look like a child under penance.

She had a fancy for tiny ivory or jade elephants; she said they were luck; she left a trail of tiny elephants wherever she went; and she went hurriedly and gasping.

Her walls, her cupboards, her bureaux, were teeming with second-hand dealings with life. It takes a bold and authentic robber to get first-hand plunder. Someone else's marriage ring was on her finger; the photograph taken of Robin for Nora sat upon her table. The books in her library were other people's selections. She lived among her own things like a visitor to a room kept "exactly as it was when—" She tiptoed, even when she went to draw a bath, nervous and *andante*. She stopped, fluttering and febrile, before every object in her house. She had no sense of humour or peace or rest, and her own quivering uncertainty made even the objects which she pointed out to the company, as, "My virgin from Palma," or, "The left-hand glove of La Duse," recede into a distance of uncertainty, so that it was almost impossible for the onlooker to see them at all. When anyone was witty about a contemporary event, she would look perplexed and a little dismayed, as if someone had done something that really should not have been done; therefore her attention had been narrowed down to listening for *faux pas*. She frequently talked about something being the "death of her," and certainly anything could have been had she been the first to suffer it. The words that fell from her mouth seemed to have been lent to her; had she been forced to invent a vocabulary for herself, it would have been a vocabulary of "ah" and "oh." Hovering, trembling, tiptoeing, she would unwind anecdote after anecdote in a light rapid lisping voice which one always expected to change, to drop and to become the "every day" voice; but it never did. The stories were humorous, well told. She would smile, toss her hands up, widen her eyes; immediately everyone in the room had a certain feeling of something lost, sensing that there was one person who was missing the importance of the moment, who had not heard the story; the teller herself.

She had endless cuttings and scraps from journals and old theatre programmes, haunted the *Comédie Française*, spoke of Molière, Racine and *La Dame aux Camélias*. She was generous with money. She made gifts lavishly and spontaneously. She was the worst recipient of presents in the world. She sent bushel baskets of camellias to actresses because she had a passion for the characters they portrayed. The flowers were tied with yards of satin ribbon, and a note accompanied them, effusive and gentle. To men she sent books by the dozen; the general feeling was that she was a well-read woman, though she had read perhaps ten books in her life.

She had a continual rapacity for other people's facts; absorbing time, she held herself responsible for historic characters. She was avid and disorderly in her heart. She defiled the very meaning of personality in her passion to be a person; somewhere about her **was** the tension of the accident that made the beast the human endeavour.

She was nervous about the future; it made her indelicate. She was one of the most unimportantly wicked women of her time— because she could not let her time alone, and yet could never be a part of it. She wanted to be the reason for everything and so was the cause of nothing. She had the fluency of tongue and action meted out by divine providence to those who cannot think for themselves. She was master of the over-sweet phrase, the over-tight embrace.

One inevitably thought of her in the act of love emitting florid *commedia dell' arte* ejaculations; one should not have thought of her in the act of love at all. She thought of little else, and though always submitting to the act, spoke of and desired the spirit of love; yet was unable to attain it.

No one could intrude upon her because there was no place for intrusion. This inadequacy made her insubordinate—she could not participate in a great love, she could only report it. Since her emotional reactions were without distinction, she had to fall back on the emotions of the past, great loves already lived and related, and those she seemed to suffer and grow glad.

When she fell in love it was with a perfect fury of accumulated dishonesty; she became instantly a dealer in second-hand and therefore incalculable emotions. As, from the solid archives of usage, she had stolen or appropriated the dignity of speech, so she appropriated the most passionate love that she knew. Nora's for Robin. She was a "squatter" by instinct.

Jenny knew about Nora immediately; to know Robin ten minutes was to know about Nora. Robin spoke of her in long, rambling, impassioned sentences. It had caught Jenny by the ear—she listened, and both loves seemed to be one and her own. From that moment the catastrophe was inevitable. This was in nineteen hundred and twenty-seven.

At their subsequent engagements, Jenny was always early and Robin late. Perhaps at the *Ambassadeurs* (Jenny feared meeting Nora). Perhaps dinner in the *Bois*—Jenny had the collective income four dead husbands could afford—Robin would walk in, with the aggressive slide to the foot common to tall people, slurred in its accent by the hipless smoothness of her gait—her hands in her pockets, the trench coat with the belt hanging, scowling and reluctant. Jenny leaning far over the table, Robin far back, her legs thrust under her, to balance the whole backward incline of the body, and Jenny so far forward that she had to catch her small legs in the back rung of the chair, ankle out and toe in, not to pitch forward on the table—thus they presented the two halves of a movement that had, as in sculpture, the beauty and the absurdity of a desire that is in flower but that can have no burgeoning, unable to execute its destiny; a movement that can divulge neither caution nor daring, for the fundamental condition for completion was in neither of them; they were like Greek runners, with lifted feet but without the relief of the final command that would bring the foot down—eternally angry, eternally separated, in a cataleptic frozen gesture of abandon.

The meeting at the opera had not been the first, but Jenny, seeing the doctor in the *promenoir*, aware of his passion for gossip, knew she had better make it seem so; as a matter of fact she had met Robin a year previously.

Though Jenny knew her safety lay in secrecy, she could not bear her safety; she wanted to be powerful enough to dare the world—and knowing she was not, the knowledge added to that already great burden of trembling timidity and fury.

On arriving at her house with the doctor and Robin, Jenny found several actresses awaiting her, two gentlemen, and the Marchesa de Spada, a very old rheumatic woman (with an antique spaniel, which suffered from asthma), who believed in the stars. There was talk about fate, and every hand in the room was searched and every destiny turned over and discussed. A little girl (Jenny called her niece, though she was no relation) sat at the far end of the room. She had been playing, but the moment Robin entered she ceased and sat, staring under her long-lashed eyelids at no one else, as if she had become prematurely aware. This was the child Jenny spoke of later when she called on Felix.

The Marchesa remarked that everyone in the room had been going on from interminable sources since the world began and would continue to reappear, but that there was one person who had come to the end of her existence and would return no more. As she spoke she looked slyly at Robin, who was standing by the piano speaking to the child in an undertone; and at the Marchesa's words Jenny began to tremble slightly, so that every point of her upstanding hair—it stood about her head in a bush, virile and unlovely—quivered. She began to pull herself along the enormous sofa toward the Marchesa, her legs under her, and suddenly she stood up.

"Order the carriage!" she cried. "Immediately! We will go driving; we need a little air!" She turned her back and spoke in agitation. "Yes, yes," she said, "the carriages! It is so close in here!"

"What carriages?" said the doctor, and he looked from one to the other. "What carriages?" He could hear the maid unlocking the front door, calling out to the coachmen. He could hear the clear ringing sound of wheels drawn close to the curb and the muttered cries of a foreign voice. Robin turned around and said, a malign gentle smile on her mouth, "Now she is in a panic, and we will have to do something." She put her glass down and stood, her back to the room, her broad shoulders drawn up, and though she was drunk, there was a withdrawal in her movement and a wish to be gone.

"She will dress up now," she said. She leaned back against the piano, pointing with the hand that held her glass. "Dress up; wait, you will see." Then she added, thrusting her chin forward so that the cords in her neck stood out: "Dress up in something old."

The doctor, who was more uncomfortable perhaps than anyone in the room and yet who could not forbear scandal, in order to gossip about the "manifestations of our time" at a later date, made a slight gesture and said, "Hush!" And sure enough, at that moment, Jenny appeared in the doorway to the bedroom, got up in a hoop, a bonnet and a shawl, and stood looking at Robin who was paying no attention to her, deep in conversation with the child. Jenny with the burning interest of a person who is led to believe herself a part of the harmony of a concert to which she is listening, appropriating in some measure its identity, emitted short exclamatory ejaculations.

There were, it turned out, three carriages in all, those open hacks that may still be had in Paris if they are hunted up in time. Jenny had a standing order with them, and when they were not called upon still they circled about her address, like flies about a bowl of cream. The three cabbies were hunched up on their boxes, their coats about their ears, for though it was an early autumn night, it had become very chilly by twelve o'clock. They had been ordered for eleven and had been sitting on their boxes for the past hour.

Jenny, cold with dread lest Robin should get into one of the other carriages with a tall slightly surprised English girl, seated herself in the farthest corner of the foremost *fiacre* and called,

"Here, here," leaving the rest of the guests to dispose of themselves. The child, Sylvia, sat across from her, the ragged gray rug held in two clenched hands. There was a great deal of chattering and laughter when to her horror Jenny saw that Robin was moving toward the second carriage in which the English girl had already seated herself. "Ah, no, no!" Jenny cried, and began beating the upholstery, sending up a cloud of dust. "Come here," she said in an anguished voice, as if it were the end of her life. "Come here with me, both of you," she added in a lowered and choking tone; and assisted by the doctor, Robin got in, the young Englishwoman, to Jenny's consternation, taking the seat by her side.

Doctor O'Connor now turned to the driver and called out: "*Écoute, mon gosse, va comme si trente-six diables étaient accrochés à tes fesses!*" Then waving his hand in a gesture of abandon, he added: "Where to but the woods, the sweet woods of Paris! *Fais le tour du Bois!*" he shouted, and slowly the three carriages, horse behind horse, moved out into the *Champs Elysées*.

Jenny, with nothing to protect her against the night but her long Spanish shawl, which looked ridiculous over her flimsy hoop and bodice, a rug over her knees, had sunk back with collapsed shoulders. With darting, incredible swiftness, her eyes went from one girl to the other, while the doctor, wondering how he had managed to get himself into the carriage which held three women and a child, listened to the faint laughter from the carriages behind, feeling, as he listened, a twinge of occult mystery. "Ah!" he said under his breath. "Just the girl that God forgot." Saying which, he seemed to be precipitated into the halls of justice, where he had suffered twenty-four hours. "Oh, God help us," he said, speaking aloud, at which the child turned slightly on her seat, her head, with large intelligent eyes directed toward him, which, had he noticed, would have silenced him instantly (for the doctor had a mother's reverence for childhood). "What manner of man is it that has to adopt his brother's children to make a mother of himself, and in his sleep lies with his brother's wife to get him a future— it's enough to bring down the black curse of Kerry."

"What?" said Jenny in a loud voice, hoping to effect a break in the whispered conversation between Robin and the English girl. The doctor turned up his coat collar.

"I was saying, madame, that by his own peculiar perversity God has made me a liar—"

"What, what is that you say?" demanded Jenny, her eyes still fixed on Robin so that her question seemed to be directed rather to that corner of the carriage than to the doctor.

"You see before you, madame," he said, "one who was created in anxiety. My father, Lord rest his soul, had no happiness of me from the beginning. When I joined the army he relented a little because he had a suspicion that possibly in that fracas which occasionally puts a son on the list of 'not much left since,' I might be damaged. After all, he had no desire to see my ways corrected with a round of buckshot. He came in to me early in the dawn as I lay in my bed to say that he forgave me and that indeed he hoped to be forgiven; that he had never understood, but that he had, by much thought, by heavy reading, come back with love in his hand, that he was sorry, that he came to say so, that he hoped I could conduct myself like a soldier. For a moment he seemed to realize my terrible predicament: to be shot for man's meat, but to go down like a girl, crying in the night for her mother. So I got up in bed on my knees and crawled to the foot where he stood, and cast my arms about him and said, 'No matter what you have done or thought, you were right, and there's nothing in my heart but love for you and respect.'"

Jenny had shrunk into her rug and was not listening. Her eyes followed every movement of Robin's hand, which was laid now on the child's hand, now stroking her hair, the child smiling up into the trees.

"Oh," said the doctor, "for the love of God!"

Jenny began to cry slowly, the tears wet, warm, and sudden in the odd misery of her face. It made the doctor sad, with that unhappy yet pleasantly regrettable discomfort on which he usually launched his better meditations.

He remarked, and why he did not know, that by weeping she appeared like a single personality who, by multiplying her tears, brought herself into the position of one who is seen twenty times in twenty mirrors—still only one, but many times distressed. Jenny began to weep outright. As the initial soft weeping had not caught Robin's attention, now Jenny used the increase and the catching in her throat to attract her, with the same insistent fury one feels when trying to attract a person in a crowded room. The weeping became as accurate as the monotonous underplay in a score, in spite of the incapacity of her heart. The doctor, sitting now a little slumped forward, said in an almost professional voice (they were now long past the pond and the park and were circling back again toward the lower parts of town), "Love of woman for woman, what insane passion for unmitigated anguish and motherhood brought that into the mind?"

"Oh, oh," she said, "look at her!" She abruptly made a gesture toward Robin and the girl, as if they were no longer present, as if they were a vista passing out of view with the movement of the horses. "Look, she brings love down to a level!" She hoped that Robin would hear.

"Ah!" he said. "Love, that terrible thing!"

She began to beat the cushions with her doubled fist. "What could you know about it? Men never know anything about it, why should they? But a woman should know—they are finer, more sacred; my love is sacred and my love is great!"

"Shut up," Robin said, putting her hand on her knee. "Shut up, you don't know what you are talking about. You talk all the time and you never know anything. It's such an awful weakness with you. Identifying yourself with God!" She was smiling, and the English girl, breathing very quickly, lit a cigarette. The child remained speechless, as she had been for the duration of the drive, her head turned as if fixed, looking at Robin and trying to hold her slight legs, that did not reach the floor, from shaking with the shaking of the carriage.

Then Jenny struck Robin, scratching and tearing in hysteria, striking, clutching and crying. Slowly the blood began to run down Robin's cheeks, and as Jenny struck repeatedly Robin began to go forward as if brought to the movement by the very blows themselves, as if she had no will, sinking down in the small carriage, her knees on the floor, her head forward as her arm moved upward in a gesture of defence; and as she sank, Jenny also, as if compelled to conclude the movement of the first blow, almost as something seen in retarded action, leaned forward and over, so that when the whole of the gesture was completed, Robin's hands were covered by Jenny's slight and bending breast, caught in between the bosom and the knees. And suddenly the child flung herself down on the seat, face outward, and said in a voice not suitable for a child because it was controlled with terror: "Let me go! Let me go! Let me go!"

The carriage at this moment drew smartly up into the *rue du Cherche-Midi*. Robin jumped before the carriage stopped, but Jenny was close behind her, following her as far as the garden.

It was not long after this that Nora and Robin separated; a little later Jenny and Robin sailed for America.

Watchman, What of the Night?

About three in the morning, Nora knocked at the little glass door of the *concierge's* loge, asking if the doctor was in. In the anger of broken sleep the *concierge* directed her to climb six flights, where at the top of the house, to the left, she would find him.

Nora took the stairs slowly. She had not known that the doctor was so poor. Groping her way she rapped, fumbling for the knob. Misery alone would have brought her, though she knew the late hours indulged in by her friend. Hearing his "Come in," she opened the door and for one second hesitated, so incredible was the disorder that met her eyes. The room was so small that it was just possible to walk sideways up to the bed; it was as if being condemned to the grave, the doctor had decided to occupy it with the utmost abandon.

A pile of medical books, and volumes of a miscellaneous order, reached almost to the ceiling, waterstained and covered with dust. Just above them was a very small barred window, the only ventilation. On a maple dresser, certainly not of European make, lay a rusty pair of forceps, a broken scalpel, half a dozen odd instruments that she could not place, a catheter, some twenty perfume bottles, almost empty, pomades, creams, rouges, powder boxes and puffs. From the half-open drawers of this chiffonier hung laces, ribands, stockings, ladies' underclothing and an abdominal brace, which gave the impression that the feminine finery had suffered venery. A swill-pail stood at the head of the bed, brimming with abominations. There was something appallingly degraded about the room, like the rooms in brothels, which give even the most innocent a sensation of having been accomplice; yet this room was also muscular, a cross between a *chambre à coucher* and a boxer's training camp. There is a certain belligerence in a room in which a woman has never set foot; every object seems to be battling its own compression—and there is a metallic odour, as of beaten iron in a smithy.

In the narrow iron bed, with its heavy and dirty linen sheets, lay the doctor in a woman's flannel nightgown.

The doctor's head, with its over-large black eyes, its full gunmetal cheeks and chin, was framed in the golden semi-circle of a wig with long pendent curls that touched his shoulders, and falling back against the pillow, turned up the shadowy interior of their cylinders. He was heavily rouged and his lashes painted. It flashed into Nora's head: "God, children know something they can't tell; they like Red Riding Hood and the wolf in bed!" But this thought, which was only the sensation of a thought, was of but a second's duration as she opened the door; in the next, the doctor had snatched the wig from his head, and sinking down in the bed drew the sheets up over his breast. Nora said, as quickly as she could recover herself: "Doctor, I have come to ask you to tell me everything you know about the night." As she spoke, she wondered why she was so dismayed to have come upon the doctor at the hour when he had evacuated custom and gone back into his dress.

The doctor said, "You see that you can ask me anything," thus laying aside both their embarrassments.

She said to herself: "Is not the gown the natural raiment of extremity? What nation, what religion, what ghost, what dream, has not worn it—infants, angels, priests, the dead; why should not the doctor, in the grave dilemma of his alchemy, wear his dress?" She thought: "He dresses to lie beside himself, who is so constructed that love, for him, can be only something special; in a room that giving back evidence of his occupancy, is as mauled as the last agony."

"Have you ever thought of the night?" the doctor inquired with a little irony; he was extremely put out, having expected someone else, though his favourite topic, and one which he talked on whenever he had a chance, was the night.

"Yes," said Nora, and sat down on the only chair. "I've thought of it, but thinking about something you know nothing about does not help."

"Have you," said the doctor, "ever thought of the peculiar polarity of times and times; and of sleep? Sleep the slain white bull? Well, I, Dr. Matthew-Mighty-grain-of-salt-Dante-O'Connor, will tell you how the day and the night are related by their division. The very constitution of twilight is a fabulous reconstruction of fear, fear bottom-out and wrong side up. Every day is thought upon and calculated, but the night is not premeditated. The Bible lies the one way, but the night-gown the other. The night, 'Beware of that dark door!'"

"I used to think," Nora said, "that people just went to sleep, or if they did not go to sleep that they were themselves, but now—" she lit a cigarette and her hands trembled—"now I see that the night does something to a person's identity, even when asleep."

"Ah!" exclaimed the doctor. "Let a man lay himself down in the Great Bed and his 'identity' is no longer his own, his 'trust' is not with him, and his 'willingness' is turned over and is of another permission. His distress is wild and anonymous. He sleeps in a Town of Darkness, member of a secret brotherhood. He neither knows himself nor his outriders; he berserks a fearful dimension and dismounts, miraculously, in bed!

"His heart is tumbling in his chest, a dark place! Though some go into the night as a spoon breaks easy water, others go head foremost against a new connivance; their horns make a dry crying, like the wings of the locust, late come to their shedding.

"Have you thought of the night, now, in other times, in foreign countries—in Paris? When the streets were gall high with things you wouldn't have done for a dare's sake, and the way it was then; with the pheasants' necks and the goslings' beaks dangling against the hocks of the gallants, and not a pavement in the place, and everything gutters for miles and miles, and a stench to it that plucked you by the nostrils and you were twenty leagues out! The criers telling the price of wine to such effect that the dawn saw good clerks full of piss and vinegar, and blood-letting in side streets where some wild princess in a night-shift of velvet howled under a leech; not to mention the palaces of Nymphenburg echoing back to Vienna with the night trip of late kings letting water into plush cans and fine woodwork! No," he said, looking at her sharply, "I can see you have not! You should, for the night has been going on for a long time."

She said, "I've never known it before—I thought I did, but it was not knowing at all."

"Exactly," said the doctor. "You thought you knew, and you hadn't even shuffled the cards—now the nights of one period are not the nights of another. Neither are the nights of one city the nights of another. Let us take Paris for an instance, and France for a fact. Ah, *mon dieu! La nuit effroyable! La nuit, qui est une immense plaine, et la cœur qui est une petite extrémité!* Ah, good Mother mine, *Notre Dame-de-bonne-Garde!* Intercede for me now, while yet I explain what I'm coming to! French nights are those which all nations seek the world over—and have you noticed that? Ask Dr. Mighty O'Connor; the reason the doctor knows everything is because he's been everywhere at the wrong time and has now become anonymous."

"But," Nora said, "I never thought of the night as a life at all— I've never lived it—why did she?"

"I'm telling you of French nights at the moment," the doctor went on, "and why we all go into them. The night and the day are two travels, and the French—gut-greedy and fist-tight though they often are—alone leave testimony of the two in the dawn; we tear up one for the sake of the other; not so the French.

"Any why is that; because they think of the two as one continually and keep it before their mind as the monks who repeat, 'Lord Jesus Christ, Son of God, have mercy upon me!' some twelve thousand or more times a twenty-four hours, so that it is finally in the head, good or bad, without saying a word. Bowing down from the waist, the world over they go, that they may revolve about the Great Enigma—as a relative about a cradle—and the Great Enigma can't be thought of unless you turn the head the other way, and come upon thinking with the eye that you fear, which is called the back of the head; it's the one we use when looking at the beloved in a dark place, and she is a long time coming from a great way. We swoon with the thickness of our own tongue when we say, 'I love you,' as in the eye of a child lost a long while will be found the contraction of that distance—a child going small in the claws of a beast, coming furiously up the furlongs of the iris. We are but skin about a wind, with muscles clenched against mortality. We sleep in a long reproachful dust against ourselves. We are full to the gorge with our own names for misery. Life, the pastures in which the night feeds and prunes the cud that nourishes us to despair. Life, the permission to know death. We were created that the earth might be made sensible of her inhuman taste; and love that the body might be so dear that even the earth should roar with it. Yes, we who are full to the gorge with misery should look well around, doubting everything seen, done, spoken, precisely because we have a word for it, and not its alchemy.

"To think of the acorn it is necessary to become the tree. And the tree of night is the hardest tree to mount, the dourest tree to scale, the most difficult of branch, the most febrile to the touch, and sweats a resin and drips a pitch against the palm that computation has not gambled. Gurus, who, I trust you know, are Indian teachers, expect you to contemplate the acorn ten years at a stretch, and if, in that time, you are no wiser about the nut, you are not very bright, and that may be the only certainty with which you will come away, which is a post-graduate melancholy—for no man can find a greater truth than his kidney will allow. So I, Dr. Matthew Mighty O'Connor, ask you to think of the night the day long, and of the day the night through, or at some reprieve of the brain it will come upon you heavily—an engine stalling itself upon your chest, halting its wheels against your heart; unless you have made a roadway for it.

"The French have made a detour of filthiness—Oh, the good dirt! Whereas you are of a clean race, of a too eagerly washing people, and this leaves no road for you. The brawl of the Beast leaves a path for the Beast. You wash your brawl with every thought, with every gesture, with every conceivable emollient and *savon*, and expect to find your way again. A Frenchman makes a navigable hour with a tuft of hair, a wrenched *bretelle*, a rumpled bed. The tear of wine is still in his cup to catch back the quantity of its bereavement; his *cantiques* straddle two backs, night and day."

"But, what am I to do?" she said.

"Be as the Frenchman, who puts a *sou* in the poor-box at night that he may have a penny to spend in the morning—he can trace himself back by his sediment, vegetable and animal, and so find himself in the odour of wine in its two travels, in and out, packed down beneath an air that has not changed its position during that strategy.

"The American, what then? He separates the two for fear of indignities, so that the mystery is cut in every cord; the design wildcats down the *charter mortalis*, and you get crime. The startled bell in the stomach begins to toll, the hair moves and drags upward, and you go far away backward by the crown, your conscience belly out and shaking.

"Our bones ache only while the flesh is on them. Stretch it as thin as the temple flesh of an ailing woman and still it serves to ache the bone and to move the bone about; and in like manner the night is a skin pulled over the head of day that the day may be in a torment. We will find no comfort until the night melts away; until the fury of the night rots out its fire."

"Then," Nora said, "it means—I'll never understand her—I'll always be miserable—just like this."

"Listen! Do things look in the ten and twelve of noon as they look in the dark? Is the hand, the face, the foot, the same face and hand and foot seen by the sun? For now the hand lies in a shadow; its beauties and its deformities are in a smoke—there is a sickle of doubt across the cheek bone thrown by the hat's brim, so there is half a face to be peered back into speculation. A leaf of darkness has fallen under the chin and lies deep upon the arches of the eyes; the eyes themselves have changed their colour. The very mother's head you swore by in the dock is a heavier head, crowned with ponderable hair.

"And what of the sleep of animals? The great sleep of the elephant, and the fine thin sleep of the bird?"

Nora said: "I can't stand it, I don't know how—I am frightened. What is it? What is it in her that is doing this?"

"Oh, for God's sake!" the doctor said, "give me the smelling salts." She got up, looking among the debris on the stand. Inhaling, he pushed his head back into the pillow; then he said:

"Take history at night; have you ever thought of that, now? Was it at night that Sodom became Gomorrah? It was at night, I swear! A city given over to the shades, and that's why it has never been countenanced or understood to this day. Wait, I'll be coming to that! All through the night Rome went burning. Put that in the noontide and it loses some of its age-old significance, does it not? Why? Because it has existed to the eye of the mind all these years against a black sky. Burn Rome in a dream, and you reach and claw down the true calamity. For dreams have only the pigmentation of fact. A man who has to deal in no colour cannot find his match, or, if he does, it is for a different rage. Rome was the egg, but colour was the tread."

"Yes," said Nora.

"The dead have committed some portion of the evil of the night; sleep and love, the other. For what is not the sleeper responsible? What converse does he hold, and with whom? He lies down with his Nelly and drops off into the arms of his Gretchen. Thousands unbidden come to his bed. Yet how can one tell truth when it's never in the company? Girls that the dreamer has not fashioned himself to want scatter their legs about him to the blows of Morpheus. So used is he to sleep that the dream that eats away its boundaries finds even what is dreamed an easier custom with the years, and at that banquet the voices blend and battle without pitch. The sleeper is the proprietor of an unknown land. He goes about another business in the dark—and we, his partners, who go to the opera, who listen to gossip of café friends, who walk along the boulevards, or sew a quiet seam, cannot afford an inch of it; because, though we would purchase it with blood, it has no contour and no till. She who stands looking down upon her who lies sleeping knows the horizontal fear, the fear unbearable. For man goes only perpendicularly against his fate. He was neither formed to know that other nor compiled of its conspiracy.

"You beat the liver out of a goose to get a *pâté*; you pound the muscles of a man's *cardia* to get a philosopher."

"Is that what I am to learn?" she asked bitterly.

The doctor looked at her. "For the lover, it is the night into which his beloved goes," he said, "that destroys his heart; he wakes her suddenly, only to look the hyena in the face that is her smile, as she leaves that company.

"When she sleeps, is she not moving her leg aside for an unknown garrison? Or in a moment, that takes but a second, murdering us with an axe? Eating our ear in a pie, pushing us aside with the back of her hand, sailing to some port with a ship full of sailors and medical men? And what of our own sleep? We go to it no better—and betray her with the very virtue of our days. We are continent a long time, but no sooner has our head touched the pillow, and our eyes left the day, than a host of merrymakers take and get. We wake from our doings in a deep sweat for that they happened in a house without an address, in a street in no town, citizened with people with no names with which to deny them. Their very lack of identity makes them ourselves. For by a street number, by a house, by a name, we cease to accuse ourselves. Sleep demands of us a guilty immunity. There is not one of us who, given an eternal incognito, a thumbprint nowhere set against our souls, would not commit rape, murder and all abominations. For if pigeons flew out of his bum, or castles sprang out of his ears, man would be troubled to know which was his fate, a house, a bird or a man. Possibly that one only who shall sleep three generations will come up uninjured out of that unpeopled annihilation." The doctor turned heavily in bed.

"For the thickness of the sleep that is on the sleeper we 'forgive,' as we 'forgive' the dead for the account of the earth that lies upon them. What we do not see, we are told, we do not mourn; yet night and sleep trouble us, suspicion being the strongest dream and dread the thong. The heart of the jealous knows the best and the most satisfying love, that of the other's bed, where the rival perfects the lover's imperfections. Fancy gallops to take part in that duel, unconstrained by any certain articulation of the laws of that unseen game.

"We look to the East for a wisdom that we shall not use—and to the sleeper for the secret that we shall not find. So, I say, what of the night, the terrible night? The darkness is the closet in which your lover roosts her heart, and that night-fowl that caws against her spirit and yours, dropping between you and her the awful estrangement of his bowels. The drip of your tears is his implacable pulse. Night people do not bury their dead, but on the neck of you, their beloved and waking, sling the creature, husked of its gestures. And where you go, it goes, the two of you, your living and her dead, that will not die; to daylight, to life, to grief, until both are carrion.

"Wait! I'm coming to the night of nights—the night you want to know about the most of all—for even the greatest generality has a little particular; have you thought of that? A high price is demanded of any value, for a value is in itself a detachment! We wash away our sense of sin, and what does that bath secure us? Sin, shining bright and hard. In what does a Latin bathe? True dust. We have made the literal error. We have used water, we are thus too sharply reminded. A European gets out of bed with a disorder that holds the balance. The layers of his deed can be traced back to the last leaf and the good slug be found creeping. *L'Echo de Paris* and his bed sheets were run off the same press. One may read in both the travail life has had with him—he reeks with the essential wit necessary to the 'sale' of both editions, night edition and day.

"Each race to its wrestling! Some throw the beast on the other side, with the stench of excrement, blood and flowers, the three essential oils of their plight! Man makes his history with the one hand and 'holds it up' with the other.

"Oh, God, I'm tired of this tirade. The French are dishevelled and wise; the American tries to approximate it with drink. It is his only clue to himself. He takes it when his soap has washed him too clean for identification. The Anglo-Saxon has made the literal error; using water, he has washed away his page. Misery melts him down by day, and sleep at night. His preoccupation with his business day has made his sleep insoluble."

Nora stood up, but she sat down again. "How do you stand it, then?" she demanded. "How do you live at all if this wisdom of yours is not only the truth, but also the price?"

"Ho, nocturnal hag whimpering on the thorn, rot in the grist, mildew in the corn," said the doctor. "If you'll pardon my song and singing voice, both of which were better until I gave my kidney on the left side to France in the war—and I've drunk myself half around the world cursing her for jerking it out—if I had it to do again, grand country though it is—I'd be the girl found lurking behind the army, or up with the hill folk, all of which is to rest me a little of my knowledge, until I can get back to it. I'm coming to something. *Misericordia*, am I not the girl to know of what I speak? We go to our Houses by our nature—and our nature, no matter how it is, we all have to stand—as for me, so God has made me, my house is the pissing port. Am I to blame if I've been summoned before and this my last and oddest call? In the old days I was possibly a girl in Marseilles thumping the dock with a sailor, and perhaps it's that memory that haunts me. The wise men say that the remembrance of things past is all that we have for a future, and am I to blame if I've turned up this time as I shouldn't have been, when it was a high soprano I wanted, and deep corn curls to my bum, with a womb as big as the king's kettle, and a bosom as high as the bowsprit of a fishing schooner? And what do I get but a face on me like an old child's bottom—is that a happiness, do you think?

"Jehovah, Sabaoth, Elohim, Eloi, Helion, Jodhevah, Shaddai! May God give us to die in our own way! I haunt the *pissoirs* as naturally as Highland Mary her cows down by the Dee—and by the Hobs of Hell, I've seen the same thing work in a girl. But I'll bring that up later! I've given my destiny away by garrulity, like ninety per cent of everybody else—for, no matter what I may be doing, in my heart is the wish for children and knitting. God, I never asked better than to boil some good man's potatoes and toss up a child for him every nine months by the calendar. Is it my fault that my only fireside is the outhouse? And that I can never hang my muffler, mittens and Bannybrook umbrella on anything better than a bit of tin boarding as high as my eyes, having to be brave, no matter what, to keep the mascara from running away? And do you think that those circular cottages have not brought me to great argument? Have you ever glanced at one when the night was well down, and seen it and what it looked like and resembled most, with its one coping and a hundred legs? A centipede. And you look down and choose your feet, and, ten to one, you find a bird with a light wing, or an old duck with a wooden knee, or something that has been mournful for years. What? I've held argument with others at long tables all night through about the particular merits of one district over another for such things, of one cottage over another for such things. And do you suppose I was agreed with, and had anyone any other one's ideas? There was as much disagreement as there might have been had we all been selecting a new order of government. Jed would say North, and Jod would say South, and me sitting between them going mad because I am a doctor and a collector and a talker of Latin, and a sort of petropus of the twilight and a physiognomist that can't be flustered by the wrong feature on the right face, and I said that the best port was at the *Place de la Bastille.* Whereupon I was torn into parts by a hundred voices—each of them pitched in a different *arrondissement,* until I began clapping like the good woman in the shoe, and screaming for silence; and for witchery I banged the table with a *formidable* and yelled out loud, 'Do any of you know anything about atmosphere and sea level? Well,' I says, 'sea level and atmospheric pressure and topography make all the difference in the world!' My voice cracked on the word 'difference,' soaring up divinely, and I said: 'If you think that certain things do not show from what district they come, yea, even to an *arrondissement,* then you are not out gunning for particular game, but simply any catch, and I'll have nothing to do with you! I do not discuss weighty matters with water wits!' And at that I ordered another and sat with my chin up. 'But,' said one fellow, 'it's the face that you tell by.' 'Faces is it!' I screamed, 'the face is for fools! If you fish by the face you fish out trouble, but there's always other fish when you deal with the sea. The face is what anglers catch in the daylight, but the sea is the night!' "

Nora turned away. "What am I to do?"

"Ah, mighty uncertainty!" said the doctor. "Have you thought of all the doors that have shut at night and opened again? Of women who have looked about with lamps, like you, and who have scurried on fast feet? Like a thousand mice they go this way and that, now fast, now slow, some halting behind doors, some trying to find the stairs, all approaching or leaving their misplaced mouse-meat that lies in some cranny, on some couch, down on some floor, behind some cupboard; and all the windows, great and small, from which love and fear have peered, shining and in tears. Put those windows end to end and it would be a casement that would reach around the world; and put those thousand eyes into one eye and you would have the night combed with the great blind searchlight of the heart."

Tears began to run down Nora's face.

"And do I know my Sodomites?" the doctor said unhappily, "and what the heart goes bang up against if it loves one of them, especially if it's a woman loving one of them. What do they find then, that this lover has committed the unpardonable error of not being able to exist—and they come down with a dummy in their arms. God's last round, shadow-boxing, that the heart may be murdered and swept into that still quiet place where it can sit and say: 'Once I was, now I can rest.'

"Well, that's only part of it," he said, trying to stop her crying, "and though your normal fellow will say all are alike in the dark, Negro or white, I say you can tell them, and where they came from, and what quarter they frequent, by the size and excellence—and at the Bastille (and may I be believed) they come as handsome as *mortadellas* slung on a table.

"Your *gourmet* knows, for instance, from what water his fish was snatched, he knows from what district and to what year he blesses his wine, he knows one truffle from another and whether it be Brittany root or if it came down from the North, but you gentlemen sit here and tell me that the district makes no difference—is there no one who knows anything but myself? And must I, perchance, like careful writers, guard myself against the conclusions of my readers?

"Have I not shut my eyes with the added shutter of the night and put my hand out? And it's the same with girls," he said, "those who turn the day into night, the young, the drug addict, the profligate, the drunken and that most miserable, the lover who watches all night long in fear and anguish. These can never again live the life of the day. When one meets them at high noon they give off, as if it were a protective emanation, something dark and muted. The light does not become them any longer. They begin to have an unrecorded look. It is as if they were being tried by the continual blows of an unseen adversary. They acquire an 'unwilling' set of features: they become old without reward, the widower bird sitting sighing at the turnstile of heaven, 'Hallelujah! I am sticked! *Skoll! Skoll!* I am dying!'

"Or walks the floor, holding her hands; or lies upon the floor, face down, with that terrible longing of the body that would, in misery, be flat with the floor; lost lower than burial, utterly blotted out and erased so that no stain of her could ache upon the wood, or snatched back to nothing without aim—going backward through the target, taking with her the spot where she made one—"

"Yes!" Nora said.

"Look for the girls also in the toilets at night, and you will find them kneeling in that great secret confessional crying between tongues, the terrible excommunication:

" 'May you be damned to hell! May you die standing upright! May you be damned upward! May this be damned, terrible and damned spot! May it wither into the grin of the dead, may this draw back, low riding mouth in an empty snarl of the groin! May this be your torment, may this be your damnation! God damned me before you, and after me you shall be damned, kneeling and standing away till we vanish! For what do you know of me, man's meat? I'm an angel on all fours, with a child's feet behind me, seeking my people that have never been made, going down face foremost, drinking the waters of night at the water hole of the damned, and I go into the waters, up to my heart, the terrible waters! What do you know of me? May you pass from me, damned girl! Damned and betraying!'

"There's a curse for you," he said, "and I have heard it."

"Oh!" Nora said. "Don't—don't!"

"But," he continued, "if you think that is all of the night, you're crazy! Groom, bring the shovel! Am I the golden-mouthed St. John Chrysostom, the Greek who said it with the other cheek? No, I'm a fart in a gale of wind, an humble violet under a cow pad. But," he said with sorrow, "even the evil in us comes to an end, errors may make you immortal—one woman went down the ages for sitting through *Parsifal* up to the point where the swan got his death, whereupon she screamed out, 'Godamercy, they have shot the Holy Grail!'—but not everyone is as good as that; you lay up for yourself in your old age. Nora, my child, feebleness enough to forget the passions of your youth, which you spent your years in strengthening. Think of that also. As for me, I tuck myself in at night, well content because I am my own charlatan. Yes, I, the Lily of Killarney, am composing me a new song, with tears and with jealousy, because I have read that John was his favourite, and it should have been me, Prester Matthew! The song is entitled, 'Mother, put the wheel away, I cannot spin tonight.' Its other name, 'According to me, everyone is a kind-of-a-son-of-a-bitch,' to be sung to two ocarinas and one concertina, and, if none of the world is about, to a Jew's-harp, so help me God! I am but a little child with my eyes wide open!"

"Matthew," Nora said, "what will become of her? That's what I want to know."

"To our friends," he answered, "we die every day, but to ourselves we die only at the end. We do not know death, or how often it has essayed our most vital spirit. While we are in the parlour it is visiting in the pantry. Montaigne says: 'To kill a man there is required a bright shining and clear light,' but that was spoken of the conscience toward another man. But what of our own death—permit us to reproach the night, wherein we die manifold alone. Donne says: 'We are all conceived in close prison, in our mothers' wombs we are close prisoners all. When we are born, we are but born to the liberty of the house—all our life is but a going out to the place of execution and death. Now was there ever any man seen to sleep in the Cart, between Newgate and Tyburn? Between the prison and the place of execution, does any man sleep?' Yet he says, 'Men sleep all the way.' How much more, therefore, is there upon him a close sleep when he is mounted on darkness."

"Yes," she said, "but—"

"Now, wait a minute! It's all of a certain night that I'm coming to, that I take so long coming to it," he said, "a night in the branchy pitch of fall—the particular night you want to know about —for I'm a fisher of men and my gimp is doing a *saltarello* over every body of water to fetch up what it may. I have a narrative, but you will be put to it to find it.

"Sorrow fiddles the ribs and no man should put his hand on anything; there is no direct way. The foetus of symmetry nourishes itself on cross purposes; this is its wonderful unhappiness—and now I am come to Jenny—oh, Lord, why do women have partridge blood and set out to beat up trouble? The places Jenny moults in are her only distinction, a Christian with a wanderer's rump. She smiles, and it is the wide smile of the self-abused, radiating to the face from some localized centre disturbance, the personification of the 'thief.' She has a longing for other people's property, but the moment she possesses it the property loses some of its value, for the owner's estimate is its worth. Therefore it was she took your Robin."

"What is she like?" Nora asked.

"Well," said the doctor, "I have always thought I, myself, the funniest-looking creature on the face of the earth; then I laid my eyes on Jenny—a little, hurried decaying comedy jester, the face on the fool's-stick, and with a smell about her of mouse-nests. She is a 'looter,' and eternally nervous. Even in her sleep I'll pronounce that her feet twitch and her orifices expand and contract like the iris of a suspicious eye. She speaks of people taking away her 'faith' in them, as if faith were a transportable object—all her life she has been subject to the feeling of 'removal.' Were she a soldier she would define defeat with the sentence: 'The enemy took the war away.' Having a conviction that she is somehow reduced, she sets about collecting a destiny—and for her, the sole destiny is love, anyone's love and so her own. So only someone's love is her love. The cock crew and she was laid—her present is always someone else's past, jerked out and dangling.

"Yet what she steals she keeps, through the incomparable fascination of maturation and rot. She has the strength of an incomplete accident—one is always waiting for the rest of it, for the last impurity that will make the whole; she was born at the point of death, but, unfortunately, she will not age into youth—which is a grave mistake of nature. How more tidy had it been to have been born old and have aged into a child, brought finally to the brink, not of the grave, but of the womb; in our age bred up into infants searching for a womb to crawl into, not be made to walk loth the gingerly dust of death, but to find a moist, gillflirted way. And a funny sight it would be to see us going to our separate lairs at the end of day, women wincing with terror, not daring to set foot to the street for fear of it.

"But I'm coming by degrees to the narrative of the one particular night that makes all other nights seem like something quite decent enough—and that was the night when, dressed in openwork mittens, showing the edge of a pantaloon (and certainly they had been out of style three mothers behind her), Jenny Petherbridge— for that is her name in case you'd care to know it," he said with a grin, "wrapped in a shawl of Spanish insight and Madrid fancy (as a matter of fact, the costume came later, but what do I care?) —stepped out in the early fall of the year to the Opera—I think, and I am not mistaken, it was nothing better than *Rigoletto*— walking in the galleries and whisking her eyes about for trouble —that she swore, even after, she had really never wanted to know anything about—and there laid her eyes on Robin, who was leaning forward in a box, and me pacing up and down, talking to myself in the best *Comédie Française* French, trying to keep off what I knew was going to be trouble for a generation, and wishing I was hearing the Schumann cycle—when in swishes the old sow of a Danish count. My heart aches for all poor creatures putting on dog and not a pot to piss in or a window to throw it from. And I began to think, and I don't know why, of the closed gardens of the world where all people can make their thoughts go up high because of the narrowness and beauty, or of the wide fields where the heart can spread out and thin its vulgarity (it's why I eat salad), and I thought we should all have a place to throw our flowers in, like me who, once in my youth, rated a *corbeille* of moth-orchids—and did I keep them? Don't get restless—I'm coming back to the point. No, I sat beside them a little while having my tea, and saying to myself, 'You're a pretty lot, and you do my cupboard honour, but there's a better place awaiting you—' and with that I took them by the hand around to the Catholic church, and I said, 'God is what we make Him, and life doesn't seem to be getting any better,' and tiptoed out.

"So I went around the gallery a third time, and I knew that, Hindu or no Hindu, I was in on what was wrong with the world—and I said the world's like that poor distressed moll of a Jenny, never knowing which end to put its mittens on, and pecking about like a mystified rook until this particular night gave her a hoist and set her up at the banquet (where she has been sitting dumbfounded ever since), and Robin the sleeping and troubled, looking amazed. It was more than a boy like me (who am the last woman left in this world, though I am the bearded lady) could bear, and I went into a lather of misery watching them, and thinking of you, and how in the end you'll all be locked together, like the poor beasts that get their antlers mixed and are found dead that way, their heads fattened with a knowledge of each other they never wanted, having had to contemplate each other, head-on and eye to eye, until death; well, that will be you and Jenny and Robin. You, who should have had a thousand children and Robin, who should have been all of them; and Jenny the bird, snatching the oats out of love's droppings—and I went mad, I'm like that. What an autopsy I'll make, with everything all which ways in my bowels! A kidney and a shoe cast of the Roman races; a liver and a long-spent whisper, a gall and a wrack of scolds from Milano, and my heart that will be weeping still when they find my eyes cold, not to mention a thought of Cellini in my crib of bones, thinking how he must have suffered when he knew he could not tell it for ever—(beauty's name spreads too thick). And the lining of my belly, flocked with the locks cut off in odd places that I've come on, a bird's nest to lay my lost eggs in, and my people as good as they come, as long as they have been coming, down the grim path of 'We know not' to 'We can't guess why.'

"Well, I was thinking of you, a woman at best, and you know what that means? Not much in the morning—all trussed up with pain's bridle. Then I turned my eyes on Jenny, who was turning her eyes looking for trouble, for she was then at that pitch of life that she knew to be her last moment. And do you need the doctor to tell you that that is a bad strange hour for a woman? If all women could have it all at once, you could beat them in flocks like a school of scorpions; but they come eternally, one after the other, and go head foremost into it alone. For men of my kind it isn't so bad; I've never asked better than to see the two ends of my man no matter how I might be dwindling. But for one like Jenny, the poor ruffled bitch, why, God knows, I bled for her because I knew in an instant the kind of a woman she was, one who had spent all her life rummaging through photographs of the past, searching for the one who would be found leaning sideways with a look as if angels were sliding down her hip—a great love who had been spared a face but who'd been saddled with loins, leaning against a drape of Scotch velvet with a pedestal and at the left twined with ivy, a knife in her boot and her groin pouting as if she kept her heart in it. Or searching among old books for the passion that was all renunciation and lung trouble, with flowers at the bosom—that was Jenny—so you can imagine how she trembled when she saw herself going toward fifty without a thing done to make her a tomb-piece, or anything in her past that would get a flower named for her. So I saw her coming forward, stepping lightly and trembling and looking at Robin, saying to me (I'd met her, if you call it meeting a woman when you pound her kidney), 'Won't you introduce me?' and my knees knocking together; and my heart as heavy as Adam's off ox, because you are a friend of mine and a good poor thing, God knows, who will never put a stop to anything; you may be knocked down, but you'll crawl on for ever, while there's any use to it, so I said, 'Certainly, damn it!' and brought them together. As if Robin hadn't met enough people without me making it worse."

"Yes," she said, "she met everyone."

"Well," he went on, "the house was beginning to empty, all the common clay was pouring down the steps talking of the Diva (there's something wrong with any art that makes a woman all bust!) and how she had taken her high L, and all the people looking out of the corners of their eyes to see how their neighbours were dressed, and some of them dropping their cloaks rather low to see the beast in a man snarling up in his neck—and they never guessed that it was me, with both shoulders under cover, that brought the veins to their escorts' temples—and walking high and stately—the pit of my stomach gone black in the darkness that was eating it away for thinking of you, and Robin smiling sideways like a cat with canary feathers to account for, and Jenny tripping beside her so fast that she would get ahead and have to run back with small cries of ambition, saying wistfully, 'You must come to my house for late supper.'

"God help me, I went! For who will not betray a friend, or, for that matter, himself for a whisky and soda, caviare and a warm fire—and that brings me to the ride that we took later. As Don Antonio said long ago, 'Didst thou make a night of it?' And was answered (by Claudio), 'Yes. Egad! And morning too; for about eight o'clock the next day, slap! They all soused upon their knees, kissed around, burned their commodes, drank my health, broke their glasses and so parted.' So Cibber put it, and I put it in Taylor's words: 'Did not *Periander* think fit to lie with his wife *Melissa* after she had already gone hent to heaven?' Is this not night work of another order also, but night work still? And in another place, as Montaigne says: 'Seems it not to be a lunatic humour of the moon that *Endymion* was by the lady moon lulled to sleep for many months together that she might have her joy of him who stirred not at all except in sleep.'

"Well, having picked up a child in transit, a niece of someone Jenny knew, we all went riding down the *Champs Elysées*. We went straight as a die over the *Pont Neuf* and whirled around into the *rue du Cherche-Midi*, God forgive us! Where you, weak vessel of love, were lying awake and wondering where, and all the time Jenny doing the deed that was as bad and out of place as that done by Catherine of Russia, and don't deny it, who took old Poniatovsky's throne for a water-closet. And suddenly I was glad I was simple and didn't want a thing in the world but what could be had for five francs. And I envied Jenny nothing she had in her house, though I admit I had been sort of casting my eye over a couple of books, which I would have spirited away if they hadn't been bound in calf—for I might steal the mind of Petronius, as well I knew, but never the skin of a calf—for the rest, the place was as full of the wrong thing as you would care to spend your inheritance on—well, I furnished my closet with phenomenal luck at the fair, what with shooting a row of chamber-pots and whirling a dozen wheels to the good, and everyone about me getting nothing for a thousand francs but a couple of velvet dogs, or dolls that looked as if they had been up all night. And what did I walk home with for less than five francs? A fine frying-pan that could coddle six eggs, and a raft of minor objects that one needs in the kitchen —so I looked at Jenny's possessions with scorn in my eye. It may have been all most 'unusual,' but who wants a toe-nail that is thicker than common? And that thought came to me out of the contemplation of the mad strip of the inappropriate that runs through creation, like my girl friend who married some sort of Adriatic bird who had such thick ones that he had to trim them with a horse-file—my mind is so rich that it is always wandering! Now I am back to the time when that groom walked into my life wearing a priest's collar that he had no more right to than I have to a crupper. Well, then the carriages came up with their sweet wilted horses, and Robin went down the steps first, and Jenny tearing after her saying, 'Wait! Wait!' as if she were talking to an express on its way into Boston, and dragging her shawl and running, and we all got in—she'd collected some guests who were waiting for her in the house."

The doctor was embarrassed by Nora's rigid silence; he went on. "I was leaning forward on my cane as we went down under the trees, holding it with both hands, and the black wagon I was in was being followed by a black wagon, and that by another, and the wheels were turning, and I began saying to myself: The trees are better, and grass is better, and animals are all right and the birds in the air are fine. And everything we do is decent when the mind begins to forget—the design of life; and good when we have forgotten—the design of death. I began to mourn for my spirit, and the spirits of all people who cast a shadow a long way beyond what they are, and for the beasts that walk out of the darkness alone; I began to wail for all the little beasts in their mothers, who would have to step down and begin going decent in the one fur that would last them their time. And I said to myself: For these I would go bang on my knees, but not for her—I wouldn't piss on her if she were on fire! I said, Jenny is so greedy that she wouldn't give her shit to the crows. And then I thought: Oh, the poor bitch, if she were dying, face down in a long pair of black gloves, would I forgive her? And I knew I would forgive her, or anyone making a picture. And then I began looking at the people in that carriage, very carefully raising my eyes so they would not notice anything unusual, and I saw the English girl sitting up there pleased and frightened.

"And then at the child—there was terror in it and it was running away from something grown up; I saw that she was sitting still and she was running; it was in her eyes and in her chin, drawn down, and her eyes wide open. And then I saw Jenny sitting there shaking, and I said: 'God, you are no picture!' And then Robin was going forward, and the blood running red, where Jenny had scratched her, and I screamed and thought: 'Nora will leave that girl some day; but though those two are buried at opposite ends of the earth, one dog will find them both.'"

Where the Tree Falls

Baron Felix, who had given up his place in the bank, though not his connections with it, had been seen in many countries standing before that country's palace gate, holding his gloved hands before him in the first unconcluded motion of submission; contemplating relics and parts, with a tension in his leg that took the step forward or back a little quicker than his fellow sightseer.

As at one time he had written to the press about this noble or that (and had never seen it in print), as he had sent letters to declining houses and never received an answer, he was now amassing a set of religious speculations that he eventually intended sending to the Pope. The reason for this was that as time passed it became increasingly evident that his child, if born to anything, had been born to holy decay. Mentally deficient and emotionally excessive, an addict to death; at ten, barely as tall as a child of six, wearing spectacles, stumbling when he tried to run, with cold hands and anxious face, he followed his father, trembling with an excitement that was a precocious ecstasy. Holding his father's hand, he climbed palace and church steps with the tearing swing of the leg necessitated by a measure that had not taken a child into account; staring at paintings and wax reproductions of saints, watching the priests with the quickening of the breath of those in whom concentration must take the place of participation, as in the scar of a wounded animal will be seen the shudder of its recovery.

When Guido had first spoken of wishing to enter the church, Felix had been startled out of himself. He knew that Guido was not like other children, that he would always be too estranged to be argued with; in accepting his son the Baron saw that he must accept a demolition of his own life. The child would obviously never be able to cope with it. The Baron bought his boy a Virgin in metal, hanging from a red ribbon, and placed it about his neck, and in doing so, the slight neck, bent to take the ribbon, recalled to him Robin's, as she stood back to him in the antique shop on the Seine.

So Felix began to look into the matter of the church. He searched the face of every priest he saw in the streets; he read litanies and examined chasubles and read the Credo; he inquired into the state of monasteries. He wrote, after much thought, to the Pope, a long disquisition on the state of the cloth. He touched on Franciscan monks and French priests, pointing out that any faith that could, in its profoundest unity, compose two such dissimilar types—one the Roman, shaved and expectant of what seemed, when one looked into his vacantly absorbed face, nothing more glorious than a muscular resurrection; and the other, the French priest, who seemed to be composite of husband and wife in conjunction with original sin, carrying with them good and evil in constantly quantitative ascent and descent, the unhappy spectacle of a single ego come to a several public dissolution—must be profoundly elastic.

He inquired if this might not be the outcome of the very different confessional states of the two countries. Was it not, he asked, to be taken for granted that the Italian ear must be less confounded because, possibly, it was harking the echo of its past, and the French that of the future? Was it conceivable that the "confessions" of the two nations could, in the one case, produce that living and expectant coma and, in the other, that worldly, incredible, indecent gluttony? He said that he himself had come to the conclusion that the French, the more secular, were a very porous people. Assuming this, it was then only natural that from listening to a thousand and one lay sins, the priest, upon reaching no riper age than two score, should find it difficult to absolve, the penitent having laid himself open to a peculiar kind of forgiveness; not so much absolution as exigency, for the priest was himself a vessel already filled to overflowing, and gave pardon because he could no longer hold—he signed with the cross, hastily and in stress, being, like a full bladder, embarrassed and in need of an immediate privacy. The Franciscan, on the other hand, had still a moment to wait. There was no tangent in his iris, as one who in blessing is looking for relief.

Felix received no answer. He had expected none. He wrote to clear some doubt in his mind. He knew that in all probability the child would never be "chosen." If he were, the Baron hoped that it would be in Austria, among his own people, and to that end he finally decided to make his home in Vienna.

Before leaving, however, he sought out the doctor. He was not in his lodging. The Baron aimlessly set off toward the square. He saw the small black clad figure moving toward him. The doctor had been to a funeral and was on his way to the *Café de la Mairie du VIe* to lift his spirits. The Baron was shocked to observe, in the few seconds before the doctor saw him, that he seemed old, older than his fifty odd years would account for. He moved slowly as if he were dragging water; his knees, which one seldom noticed, because he was usually seated, sagged. His dark shaved chin was lowered as if in a melancholy that had no beginning or end. The Baron hailed him, and instantly the doctor threw off his unobserved self, as one hides, hastily, a secret life. He smiled, drew himself up, raised his hand in greeting, though, as is usual with people taken unaware, with a touch of defence.

"Where have you been?" he said as he came to a standstill in the middle of the block. "I haven't seen you for months, and," he added, "it's a pity."

The Baron smiled in return. "I've been in mental trouble," he said, walking beside the doctor. "Are you," he added, "engaged for dinner?"

"No," said the doctor, "I've just buried an excellent fellow. Don't think you ever met him, a Kabyle, better sort of Arab. They have Roman blood, and can turn pale at a great pinch, which is more than can be said for most, you know," he added, walking a little sideways, as one does when not knowing where a companion is going. "Do a bit for a Kabyle, back or front, and they back up on you with a camel or a bag of dates." He sighed and passed his hand over his chin. "He was the only one I ever knew who offered me five francs before I could reach for my own. I had it framed in orange blossoms and hung it over the whatnot."

The Baron was abstracted, but he smiled out of politeness. He suggested dining in the *Bois*. The doctor was only too willing, and at the sudden good news, he made that series of half-gestures of a person taken pleasantly unaware; he half held up his hands—no gloves—he almost touched his breast pocket—a handkerchief; he glanced at his boots, and was grateful for the funeral; he was shined, fairly neat; he touched his tie, stretching his throat muscles.

As they drove through the *Bois* the doctor went over in his mind what he would order—duck with oranges, no—having eaten on a poor man's purse for so many years, habit had brought him to simple things with garlic. He shivered. He must think of something different. All he could think of was coffee and *Grand Marnier*, the big tumbler warmed with the hands, like his people warming at the peat fire. "Yes?" he said, and realized that the Baron had been speaking. The doctor lifted his chin to the night air and listened now with an intensity with which he hoped to reconstruct the sentence.

"Strange, I had never seen the Baronin in this light before," the Baron was saying, and he crossed his knees. "If I should try to put it into words, I mean how I did see her, it would be incomprehensible, for the simple reason that I find that I never did have a really clear idea of her at any time. I had an image of her, but that is not the same thing. An image is a stop the mind makes between uncertainties. I had gathered, of course, a good deal from you, and later, after she went away, from others, but this only strengthened my confusion. The more we learn of a person, the less we know. It does not, for instance, help me to know anything of Chartres above the fact that it possesses a cathedral, unless I have lived in Chartres and so keep the relative heights of the cathedral and the lives of its population in proportion. Otherwise it would only confuse me to learn that Jean of that city stood his wife upright in a well; the moment I visualize this, the deed will measure as high as the building; just as children who have a little knowledge of life will draw a man and a barn on the same scale."

"Your devotion to the past," observed the doctor, looking at the cab meter with apprehension, "is perhaps like a child's drawing."

The Baron nodded. He was troubled. "My family is preserved because I have it only from the memory of one single woman, my aunt; therefore it is single, clear and unalterable. In this I am fortunate; through this I have a sense of immortality. Our basic idea of eternity is a condition that *cannot vary*. It is the motivation of marriage. No man really wants his freedom. He gets a habit as quickly as possible—it is a form of immortality."

"And what's more," said the doctor, "we heap reproaches on the person who breaks it, saying that in so doing he has broken the image—of our safety."

The Baron acquiesced. "This quality of one sole condition, which was so much a part of the Baronin, was what drew me to her; a condition of being that she had not, at that time, even chosen, but a fluid sort of possession which gave me a feeling that I would not only be able to achieve immortality, but be free to choose my own kind."

"She was always holding God's bag of tricks upside down," murmured the doctor.

"Yet, if I tell the whole truth," the Baron continued, "the very abundance of what then appeared to me to be security, and which was, in reality, the most formless loss, gave me the same pleasure and a sense of terrible anxiety, which proved only too legitimate."

The doctor lit a cigarette.

"I took it," the Baron went on, "for acquiescence, thus making my great mistake. She was really like those people who, coming unexpectedly into a room, silence the company because they are looking for someone who is not there." He knocked on the cab window, got down and paid. As they walked up the gravel path he went on: "What I particularly wanted to ask you was, why did she marry me? It has placed me in the dark for the rest of my life."

"Take the case of the horse who knew too much," said the doctor, "looking between the branches in the morning, cypress or hemlock. She was in mourning for something taken away from her in a bombardment in the war—by the way she stood, that something lay between her hooves—she stirred no branch, though her hide was a river of sorrow; she was damned to her hocks, where the grass came waving up softly. Her eyelashes were gray-black, like the eyelashes of a nigger, and at her buttocks' soft centre a pulse throbbed like a fiddle."

The Baron, studying the menu, said, "The Petherbridge woman called on me."

"Glittering God," exclaimed the doctor, putting the card down. "Has it gone as far as that? I shouldn't have thought it."

"For the first moment," the Baron continued, "I had no idea who she was. She had spared no pains to make her toilet rusty and grievous by an arrangement of veils and flat-toned dark material with flowers in it, cut plainly and extremely tight over a very small bust, and from the waist down gathered into bulky folds to conceal, no doubt, the widening parts of a woman well over forty. She seemed hurried. She spoke of you."

The doctor put the menu on his knee. He raised his dark eyes with the bushy brows erect. "What did she say?"

The Baron answered, evidently unaware of the tender spot which his words touched: "Utter nonsense to the effect that you are seen nearly every day in a certain convent, where you bow and pray and get free meals and attend cases which are, well, illegal."

The Baron looked up. To his surprise he saw that the doctor had "deteriorated" into that condition in which he had seen him in the street, when he thought himself unobserved.

In a loud voice the doctor said to the waiter, who was within an inch of his mouth: "Yes, and with oranges, *oranges!*"

The Baron continued hastily: "She gave me uneasiness because Guido was in the room at the time. She said that she had come to buy a painting—indeed, she offered me a very good price, which I was tempted to take (I've been doing a little dealing in old masters lately) for my stay in Vienna—but, as it turned out, she wanted the portrait of my grandmother, which on no account could I bring myself to part with. She had not been in the room five minutes before I sensed that the picture was an excuse, and that what she really wanted was something else. She began talking about the Baronin almost at once, though she mentioned no name at first, and I did not connect the story with my wife until the end. She said, 'She is really quite extraordinary. I don't understand her at all, though I must say I understand her better than other people.' She added this with a sort of false eagerness. She went on: 'She always lets her pets die. She is so fond of them, and then she neglects them, the way that animals neglect themselves.'

"I did not like her to talk about this subject, as Guido is very sensitive to animals, and I could fancy what was going on in his mind; he is not like other children, not cruel, or savage. For this very reason he is called 'strange.' A child who is mature, in the sense that the heart is mature, is always, I have observed, called deficient." He gave his order and went on: "She then changed the subject—"

"Tacking into the wind like a barge."

"Well, yes, to a story about a little girl she had staying with her (she called her Sylvia); the Baronin was also staying with her at the time, though I did not know that the young woman in question was the Baronin until later—well, anyway, it appears that this little girl Sylvia had 'fallen in love' with the Baronin and that she, the Baronin, kept waking her up all through the night to ask her if she 'loved her.'

"During the holidays, while the child was away, Petherbridge became 'anxious'—that is the way she put it—as to whether or not the 'young lady had a heart.'"

"And brought the child back to prove it?" interpolated the doctor, casting an eye over the fashionable crowd beginning to fill the room.

"Exactly," said the Baron, ordering wine. "I made an exclamation, and she said quickly, 'You can't blame me; you can't accuse me of using a child for my own ends!' Well, what else does it come to?"

"That woman," the doctor said, settling himself more comfortably in his chair, "would use the third-rising of a corpse for her ends. Though," he added, "I must admit she is very generous with money."

The Baron winced. "So I gathered from her overlarge bid for the portrait. Well, she went on to say that when they met the Baronin had so obviously forgotten all about her that the child was 'ashamed.' She said 'shame went all over her.' She was already at the door when she spoke the last sentence. In fact, she conducted the whole scene as though my room were a stage that had been marked out, and at this point she must read her final lines.

"'Robin,' she said, 'Baronin Robin Volkbein; I wonder if she could be a relative.'

"For a whole minute I couldn't move. When I turned around I saw that Guido was ill. I took him in my arms and spoke to him in German. He had often put questions to me about his mother and I had managed always to direct his mind to expect her."

The doctor turned to the Baron with one of his sudden illuminations. "Exactly right. With Guido, you are in the presence of the 'maladjusted.' Wait! I am not using that word in the derogatory sense at all; in fact my great virtue is that I never use the derogatory in the usual sense. Pity is an intrusion when in the presence of a person who is a new position in an old account—which is your son. You can only pity those limited to their generation. Pity is timely and dies with the person; a pitiable man is his own last tie. You have treated Guido well."

The Baron paused, his knife bent down. He looked up. "Do you know, Doctor, I find the thought of my son's possible death at an early age a sort of dire happiness because his death is the most awful, the most fearful thing that could befall me. The unendurable is the beginning of the curve of joy. I have become entangled in the shadow of a vast apprehension which is my son; he is the central point toward which life and death are spinning, the meeting of which my final design will be composed."

"And Robin?" the doctor asked.

"She is with me in Guido; they are inseparable, and this time," the Baron said, catching his monocle, "with her full consent." He leaned down and picked up his napkin. "The Baronin," he continued, "always seemed to be looking for someone to tell her that she was innocent. Guido is very like her, except that he has his innocence. The Baronin was always searching in the wrong direction until she met Nora Flood, who seemed, from what little I knew of her, to be a very honest woman, at least by intention."

"There are some people," he went on, "who must get permission to live, and if the Baronin finds no one to give her that permission, she will make an innocence for herself; a fearful sort of primitive innocence. It may be considered 'depraved' by our generation, but our generation does not know everything." He smiled. "For instance, Guido; how many will realize his value? One's life is peculiarly one's own when one has invented it."

The doctor wiped his mouth. "In the acceptance of depravity the sense of the past is most fully captured. What is a ruin but Time easing itself of endurance? Corruption is the Age of Time. It is the body and the blood of ecstasy, religion and love. Ah, yes," the doctor added, "we do not 'climb' to heights, we are eaten away to them, and then conformity, neatness, ceases to entertain us. Man

is born as he dies, rebuking cleanliness; and there is its middle con-
dition, the slovenliness that is usually an accompaniment of the
'attractive' body, a sort of earth on which love feeds."

"That is true," Felix said with eagerness. "The Baronin had an
undefinable disorder, a sort of 'odour of memory,' like a person
who has come from some place that we have forgotten and would
give our life to recall."

The doctor reached out for the bread. "So the reason for our
cleanliness becomes apparent; cleanliness is a form of apprehen-
sion; our faulty racial memory is fathered by fear. Destiny and
history are untidy; we fear memory of that disorder. Robin did
not."

"No," Felix said in a low voice. "She did not."

"The almost fossilized state of our recollection is attested to by
our murderers and those who read every detail of crime with a pas-
sionate and hot interest," the doctor continued. "It is only by such
extreme measures that the average man can remember something
long ago; truly, not that he remembers, but that crime itself is the
door to an accumulation, a way to lay hands on the shudder of a
past that is still vibrating."

The Baron was silent a moment. Then he said: "Yes, something
of this rigour was in the Baronin, in its first faint degree; it was in
her walk, in the way she wore her clothes, in her silence, as if
speech were heavy and unclarified. There was in her every move-
ment a slight drag, as if the past were a web about her, as there is
a web of time about a very old building. There is a sensible weight
in the air around a thirteenth-century edifice," he said with a touch
of pomposity, "that is unlike the light air about a new structure;
the new building seems to repulse it, the old to gather it. So about
the Baronin there was a density, not of age, but of youth. It per-
haps accounts for my attraction to her."

"Animals find their way about largely by the keenness of their
nose," said the doctor. "We have lost ours in order not to be one
of them, and what have we in its place? A tension in the spirit

which is the contraction of freedom. But," he ended, "all dreadful events are of profit."

Felix ate in silence for a moment, then point-blank he turned to the doctor with a question. "You know my preoccupation; is my son's better?"

The doctor, as he grew older, in answering a question seemed, as old people do, to be speaking more and more to himself, and, when troubled, he seemed to grow smaller. He said: "Seek no further for calamity; you have it in your son. After all, calamity is what we are all seeking. You have found it. A man is whole only when he takes into account his shadow as well as himself—and what is a man's shadow but his prostrate astonishment? Guido is the shadow of your anxiety, and Guido's shadow is God's."

Felix said: "Guido also loves women of history."

"Mary's shadow!" said the doctor.

Felix turned. His monocle shone sharp and bright along its edge. "People say that he is not sound of mind. What do you say?"

"I say that a mind like his may be more apt than yours and mine—he is not made secure by habit—in that there is always hope."

Felix said under his breath: "He does not grow up."

Matthew answered: "The excess of his sensibilities may preclude his mind. His sanity is an unknown room: a known room is always smaller than an unknown. If I were you," the doctor continued, "I would carry that boy's mind like a bowl picked up in the dark; you do not know what's in it. He feeds on odd remnants that we have not priced; he eats a sleep that is not our sleep. There is more in sickness than the name of that sickness. In the average person is the peculiar that has been scuttled, and in the peculiar the ordinary that has been sunk; people always fear what requires watching."

Felix ordered a *fine*. The doctor smiled. "I said you would come to it," he said, and emptied his own glass at a gulp.

"I know," Felix answered, "but I did not understand. I thought you meant something else."

"What?"

Felix paused, turning the small glass around in his trembling hand. "I thought," he said, "that you meant that I would give up."

The doctor lowered his eyes. "Perhaps that is what I meant—but sometimes I am mistaken." He looked at Felix from under his heavy brows. "Man was born damned and innocent from the start, and wretchedly—as he must—on those two themes—whistles his tune."

The Baron leaned forward. He said in a low voice, "Was the Baronin damned?"

The doctor deliberated for a second, knowing what Felix had hidden in his question. "Guido is not damned," he said, and the Baron turned away quickly. "Guido," the doctor went on, "is blessed—he is peace of mind—he is what you have always been looking for. Aristocracy," he said, smiling, "is a condition in the mind of the people when they try to think of something else and better—funny," he added sharply, "that a man never knows when he has found what he has always been looking for."

"And the Baronin," Felix said, "do you ever hear from her?"

"She is in America now, but of course you know that. Yes, she writes, now and again, not to me—God forbid—to others."

"What does she say?" the Baron said, trying not to show his emotion.

"She says," the doctor answered, "'Remember me.' Probably because she has difficulty in remembering herself."

The Baron caught his monocle. "Altamonte, who has been in America, tells me that she seemed 'estranged.' Once," he said, pinching his monocle into place, "I wanted, as you, who are aware of everything, know, to go behind the scenes, back-stage as it were, to our present condition, to find, if I could, the secret of time; good, perhaps, that that is an impossible ambition for the sane mind. One has, I am now certain, to be a little mad to see into the past or the future, to be a little abridged of life to know life, the obscure life—darkly seen, the condition my son lives in; it may also be the errand on which the Baronin is going."

Taking out his handkerchief, the Baron removed his monocle, wiping it carefully.

Carrying a pocket full of medicines, and a little flask of oil for the chapping hands of his son, Felix rode into Vienna, the child beside him; Frau Mann, opulent and gay, opposite, holding a rug for the boy's feet. Felix drank heavily now, and to hide the red that flushed his cheeks he had grown a beard ending in two forked points on his chin. In the matter of drink, Frau Mann was now no bad second. Many cafés saw this odd trio, the child in the midst wearing heavy lenses that made his eyes drift forward, sitting erect, his neck holding his head at attention, watching his father's coins roll, as the night drew out, farther and farther across the floor and under the feet of the musicians as Felix called for military music, for *Wacht am Rhein*, for *Morgenrot*, for Wagner; his monocle dimmed by the heat of the room, perfectly correct and drunk, trying not to look for what he had always sought, the son of a once great house; his eyes either gazing at the ceiling or lowered where his hand, on the table, struck thumb and little finger against the wood in rhythm with the music, as if he were playing only the two important notes of an octave, the low and the high; or nodding his head and smiling at his child, as mechanical toys nod to the touch of an infant's hand, Guido pressing his own hand against his stomach where, beneath his shirt, he could feel the medallion against his flesh, Frau Mann gripping her beer mug firmly, laughing and talking loudly.

One evening, seated in his favourite café on the Ring, Felix on entering had seen instantly, but refused to admit it to himself, a tall man in the corner who, he was sure, was the Grand Duke Alexander of Russia, cousin and brother-in-law of the late Czar Nicholas—and toward whom in the early part of the evening he steadfastly refused to look. But as the clock hands pointed twelve, Felix (with the abandon of what a mad man knows to be his one hope of escape, disproof of his own madness) could not keep his eyes away, and as they arose to go, his cheeks now drained of colour, the points of his beard bent sharply down with the stiffening of his chin, he turned and made a slight bow, his head in his confusion making a complete half-swing, as an animal will turn its head away from a human, as if in mortal shame.

He stumbled as he got into his carriage. "Come," he said, taking the child's fingers in his own. "You are cold." He poured a few drops of oil and began rubbing Guido's hands.

Go Down, Matthew

"Can't you be quiet now?" the doctor said. He had come in late
one afternoon to find Nora writing a letter. "Can't you be done
now, can't you give up? Now be still, now that you know what the
world is about, knowing it's about nothing?" He took his hat and
coat off without being asked, placing his umbrella in a corner. He
came forward into the room. "And me who seems curious because
no one has seen me for a million years, and now I'm seen! Is there
such extraordinary need of misery to make beauty? Let go Hell;
and your fall will be broken by the roof of Heaven." He eyed the
tea-tray and, seeing that the tea-pot had long since become cold,
poured himself a generous port. He threw himself into a chair and
added more softly as Nora turned away from her letter, "In the
far reaches of India there is a man being still beneath a tree. Why
not rest? Why not put the pen away? Isn't it bitter enough for
Robin that she is lost somewhere without receiving mail? And
Jenny, what of her now? Taken to drink and appropriating Robin's
mind with vulgar inaccuracy, like those eighty-two plaster virgins

she bought because Robin had one good one; when you laugh at
the eighty-two standing in a row, Jenny runs to the wall, back
to the picture of her mother, and stands there between two tortures
—the past that she can't share, and the present that she can't copy.
What of her now? Looking at her quarters with harrowing, in-
delicate cries; burying her middle at both ends, searching the world
for the path back to what she wanted once and long ago! The
memory past, and only by a coincidence, a wind, the flutter of a
leaf, a surge of tremendous recollection goes through her, and
swooning she knows it gone. Cannot a beastly thing be analogous
to a fine thing if both are apprehensions? Love of two things often
makes one thing right. Think of the fish racing the sea, their love
of air and water turning them like wheels, their tails and teeth
biting the water, their spines curved round the air. Is that not
Jenny? She who could not encompass anything whole, but only
with her teeth and tail, and the spine on her sprung up. Oh, for
God's sake! Can't you rest now?"

"If I don't write to her, what am I to do? I can't sit here for
ever—thinking!"

"*Terra damnata et maledicta!*" exclaimed the doctor, banging
his fist down. "My uncle Octavius, the trout-tickler of Itchen, was
better; he ate his fish when he caught it! But you, you must unspin
fate, go back to find Robin! That's what you are going to do. In
your chair should have been set the Holy Stone, to say yes to your
yes, no to your no; instead it's lost in Westminster Abbey, and if
I could have stopped Brec on his way with it into Ireland and have
whispered in his ear I would have said, 'Wait' (though it was seven
hundred years B.C.); it might have been passed around. It might
have stopped you, but no, you are always writing to Robin. Noth-
ing will curb it. You've made her a legend and set before her head
the Eternal Light, and you'll keep to it even if it does cost her the
tearing open of a million envelopes to her end. How do you know
what sleep you raise her from? What words she must say to annul
the postman's whistle to another girl rising up on a wild elbow?
Can't you let any of us loose? Don't you know your holding on is

her only happiness and so her sole misery. You write and weep and think and plot, and all the time what is Robin doing? Chucking jackstraws, or sitting on the floor playing soldiers; so don't cry to me, who have no one to write to, and only taking in a little light laundry known as the Wash of the World. Dig a hole, drop me in! Not at all. St. Matthew's Passion by Bach I'll be. Everything can be used in a lifetime; I've discovered that."

"I've got to write to her," Nora said. "I've got to."

"No man knows it as I know it, I who am the god of darkness. Very well, but know the worst, then. What of Felix and his son Guido, that sick lamenting, fevered child? Death in the weather is a tonic to him. Like all the new young his sole provision for old age is hope of an early death. What spirits answer him who will never come to man's estate? The poor shattered eagerness. So, I say, was Robin purposely unspun? Was Jenny a sitting bitch for fun? Who knows what knives hash her apart? Can't you rest now, lay down the pen? Oh, *papelero*, have I not summed up my time! I shall rest myself some day by the brim of Saxon-les-Bains and drink it dry, or go to pieces in Hamburg at the gambling table, or end up like Madame de Staël—with an affinity for Germany. To all kinds of ends I'll come. Ah, yes, with a crupper of maiden's hair to keep my soul in place, and in my vanguard a dove especially feathered to keep to my wind, as I ride that grim horse with ample glue in every hoof to post up my deeds when I'm dropped in and sealed with earth. In time everything is possible and in space everything forgivable; life is but the intermediary vice. There is eternity to blush in. Life laid end to end is what brings on flux in the clergy—can't you rest now, put down the pen? Oh, the poor worms that never arrive! Some strangely connived angel pray for us! We shall not encompass it—the defunctive murmur in the cardiac nerve has given us all our gait. And Robin? I know where your mind is! She, the eternal momentary—Robin who was always the second person singular. Well," he said with violence, "lie weeping with a sword in your hand! Haven't I eaten a book too? Like the angels and prophets? And wasn't it a bitter book to eat? The archives of my case against the law, snatched up and out of the tale-telling files by my high important friend. And didn't I eat a page and tear a page and stamp on others and flay some and toss some into the toilet for relief's sake—then think of Jenny without a comma to eat, and Robin with nothing but a pet name—your pet name to sustain her; for pet names are a guard against loss, like primitive music. But does that sum her up? Is even the end of us an account? No, don't answer, I know that even the memory has weight. Once in the war I saw a dead horse that had been lying long against the ground. Time and the birds and its own last concentration had removed the body a great way from the head. As I looked upon that head, my memory weighed for the lost body; and because of that missing quantity even heavier hung that head along the ground. So love, when it has gone, taking time with it, leaves a memory of its weight."

She said: "She is myself. What am I to do?"

"Make birds' nests with your teeth; that would be better," he said angrily, "like my English girl friend. The birds liked them so well that they stopped making their own (does that sound like any nest you have made for any bird, and so broken it of its fate?). In the spring they form a queue by her bedroom window and stand waiting their turn, holding on to their eggs as hard as they can until she gets around to them, strutting up and down on the ledge, the eyes in their feathers a quick shine and sting, whipped with impatience, like a man waiting at a toilet door for someone inside who had decided to read the *Decline and Fall of the Roman Empire*. And then think of Robin who never could provide for her life except in you. Oh, well," he said under his breath, " 'happy are they whom privacy makes innocent.' "

Nora turned around, and speaking in a voice that she tried to make steady said: "Once, when she was sleeping, I wanted her to die. Now, that would stop nothing."

The doctor, nodding, straightened his tie with two fingers. "The number of our days is not check-rein enough to look upon the death of our love. While living we knew her too well, and never understood, for then our next gesture permitted our next mis-understanding. But death is intimacy walking backward. We are crazed with grief when she, who once permitted us, leaves to us the only recollection. We shed tears of bankruptcy then. So it's well she didn't." He sighed. "You are still in trouble—I thought you had put yourself outside of it. I might have known better, nothing is what everybody wants, the world runs on that law. Personally, if I could, I would instigate Meat-Axe Day, and out of the good-ness of my heart I would whack your head off along with a couple of others. Every man should be allowed one day and a hatchet just to ease his heart."

She said: "What will happen now, to me and to her?"

"Nothing," the doctor answered, "as always. We all go down in battle, but we all come home."

She said: "I can only find her again in my sleep or in her death; in both she has forgotten me."

"Listen," the doctor said, putting down his glass. "My war brought me many things; let yours bring you as much. Life is not to be told, call it as loud as you like, it will not tell itself. No one will be much or little except in someone else's mind, so be careful of the minds you get into, and remember Lady Macbeth, who had her mind in her hand. We can't all be as safe as that."

Nora got up nervously and began walking. "I'm so miserable, Matthew, I don't know how to talk, and I've got to. I've got to talk to somebody. I can't live this way." She pressed her hands together and, without looking at the doctor, went on walking.

"Have you got any more port?" he inquired, putting the empty bottle down. Mechanically, Nora brought him a second decanter. He took the stopper out, held it to his nose a moment, then poured himself a glass.

"You are," he said, testing the wine between his lower lip and teeth, "experiencing the inbreeding of pain. Most of us do not dare it. We wed a stranger, and so 'solve' our problem. But when you inbreed with suffering (which is merely to say that you have caught every disease and so pardoned your flesh) you are destroyed back to your structure as an old master disappears beneath the knife of the scientist who would know how it was painted. Death I imagine will be pardoned by the same identification; we all carry about with us the house of death, the skeleton, but unlike the turtle our safety is inside, our danger out. Time is a great conference planning our end, and youth is only the past putting a leg forward. Ah, to be able to hold on to suffering, but to let the spirit loose! And speaking of being destroyed, allow me to illustrate by telling you of one dark night in London when I was hurrying along, my hands before me, praying I'd get home and into bed and wake up in the morning without finding my hands on my hips. So I started for London Bridge—all this was a long time ago, and I'd better be careful or one of these days I'll tell a story that will give up my age.

"Well, I went off under London Bridge, and what should I see? A Tuppeny Upright! And do you know what a Tuppeny Upright might be? A Tuppeny is an old-time girl, and London Bridge is her last stand, as the last stand for a *grue* is Marseille if she doesn't happen to have enough pocket money to get to Singapore. For tuppence, an Upright is all anyone can expect. They used to walk along slowly, all ruffles and rags, with big terror hats on them, a pin stuck over the eye and slap up through the crown, half their shadows on the ground and the other half crawling along the wall beside them; ladies of the *haute* taking their last stroll, sauntering on their last Rotten Row, going slowly along in the dark, holding up their badgered flounces, or standing still, letting you do it, silent and as indifferent as the dead, as if they were thinking of better days, or waiting for something that they had been promised when they were little girls; their poor damned dresses hiked up and falling away over the rump, all gathers and braid, like a Crusader's mount, with all the trappings gone sideways with misery."

While the doctor had been speaking Nora had stopped, as if he had got her attention for the first time.

"And once Father Lucas said to me, 'Be simple, Matthew, life is a simple book, and an open book, read and be simple as the beasts in the field; just being miserable isn't enough—you have got to know how.' So I got to thinking and I said to myself, 'This is a terrible thing that Father Lucas has put on me—be simple like the beasts and yet think and harm nobody.' I began walking then. It had begun to snow and the night was down. I went toward the *Ile* because I could see the lights in the show-windows of Our Lady and all the children in the dark with the tapers twinkling, saying their prayers softly with that small breath that comes off little lungs, whispering fatally about nothing, which is the way children say their prayers. Then I said, 'Matthew, tonight you must find a small church where there are no people, where you can be alone like an animal, and yet think.' So I turned off and went down until I came to *St. Merri* and I went forward and there I was. All the candles were burning steadily for the troubles that people had entrusted to them and I was almost alone, only in a far corner an old peasant woman saying her beads.

"So I walked straight up to the box for the souls in Purgatory, just to show that I was a true sinner, in case there happened to be a Protestant about. I was trying to think which of my hands was the more blessed because there's a box in the *Raspail* that says the hand you give with to the Little Sisters of the Poor, that will be blessed all day. I gave it up, hoping it was my right hand. Kneeling in a dark corner, bending my head over and down, I spoke to Tiny O'Toole because it was his turn; I had tried everything else. There was nothing for it this time but to make him face the mystery so it could see him clear as it saw me. So then I whispered, 'What is this thing, Lord?' And I began to cry; the tears went like rain goes down on the world without touching the face of Heaven. Suddenly I realized that it was the first time in my life my tears were strange to me because they just went straight forward out of my eyes; I was crying because I had to embarrass Tiny like that for the good it might do him.

"I was crying and striking my left hand against the *prie-dieu*, and all the while Tiny O'Toole was lying in a swoon. I said, 'I have tried to seek, and I only find.' I said, 'It is I, my Lord, who knows there's beauty in any permanent mistake like me. Haven't I said it so? But,' I says, 'I'm not able to stay permanent unless you help me, O Book of Concealment! *C'est le plaisir qui me boule-verse!* The roaring lion goes forth, seeking his own fury! So tell me, what is permanent of me, me or him?' And there I was in the empty, almost empty church, all the people's troubles flickering in little lights all over the place. And I said, 'This would be a fine world, Lord, if you could get everybody out of it.' And there I was holding Tiny, bending over and crying, asking the question until I forgot and went on crying, and I put Tiny away then, like a ruined bird, and went out of the place and walked looking at the stars that were twinkling, and I said, 'Have I been simple like an animal, God, or have I been thinking?' "

She smiled. "Sometimes I don't know why I talk to you. You're so like a child; then again I know well enough."

"Speaking of children—and thanks for the compliment—take, for instance, the case of Don Anticolo, the young tenor from Beirut —he dipped down into his pelvis for his Wagner and plunged to his breast pit for his Verdi—he'd sung himself once and a half round the world, a widower with a small son, scarcely ten by the clock when, presto—the boy was bitten by a rat while swimming in Venezia and this brought on a fever. His father would come in and take hold of him every ten minutes (or was it every half-hour?) to see if he was less hot or hotter. His daddy was demented with grief and fear, but did he leave his bedside for a moment? He did be-cause, though the son was sick, the fleet was in. But being a father, he prayed as he drank the champagne; and he wished his son alive as he chucked over the compass and invited the crew home, bow and sprit. But when he got home the little son lay dead. The young tenor burst into tears and burned him and had the ashes put into a zinc box no bigger than a doll's crate and held ceremony over him, twelve sailors all in blue standing about the deal table, a glass in their hands, sorrow in their sea-turned eye slanting under lids thinned by the horizon, as the distracted father and singer tossed the little zinc box upon the table saying: 'This, gentlemen, is my babe, this, lads, my son, my sailors, my boy!' and at that, running to the box and catching it up and dashing it down again, repeating, and weeping, 'My son, my baby, my boy!' with trembling fingers nudging the box now here, now there, about the table until it went up and down its length a dozen times; the father behind it, following it, touching it, weeping and crying like a dog who noses a bird that has, for some strange reason, no more movement."

The doctor stood up, then sat down again. 'Yes, oh God, Robin was beautiful. I don't like her, but I have to admit that much: sort of fluid blue under her skin, as if the hide of time had been stripped from her, and with it, all transactions with knowledge. A sort of first position in attention; a face that will age only under the blows of perpetual childhood. The temples like those of young beasts cutting horns, as if they were sleeping eyes. And that look on a face we follow like a witch-fire. Sorcerers know the power of horns; meet a horn where you like and you know you have been identified. You could fall over a thousand human skulls without the same trepidation. And do old duchesses know it also! Have you ever seen them go into a large assembly of any sort, be it opera or bezique, without feathers, flowers, sprigs of oat, or some other gadget nodding above their temples!"

She had not heard him. "Every hour is my last, and," she said desperately, "one can't live one's last hour all one's life!"

He brought his hands together. "Even the contemplative life is only an effort, Nora my dear, to hide the body so the feet won't stick out. Ah," he added, "to be an animal, born at the opening of the eye, going only forward, and, at the end of day, shutting out memory with the dropping of the lid."

"Time isn't long enough," she said, striking the table. "It isn't long enough to live down her nights. God," she cried, "what is love? Man seeking his own head? The human head, so rented by misery that even the teeth weigh! She couldn't tell me the truth because she had never planned it; her life was a continual accident, and how can you be prepared for that? Everything we can't bear

in this world, some day we find in one person, and love it all at
once. A strong sense of identity gives man an idea he can do
no wrong; too little accomplishes the same. Some natures cannot
appreciate, only regret. Will Robin *only* regret?" She stopped
abruptly, gripping the back of the chair. "Perhaps not," she said,
"for even her memory wearied her." Then she said with the vio-
lence of misery. "There's something evil in me that loves evil and
degradation—purity's black backside! That loves honesty with a
horrid love; or why have I always gone seeking it at the liar's door?"

"Look here," said the doctor. "Do you know what has made
me the greatest liar this side of the moon? Telling my stories to
people like you, to take the mortal agony out of their guts, and to
stop them from rolling about, and drawing up their feet, and
screaming, with their eyes staring over their knuckles with misery
which they are trying to keep off, saying, 'Say something, Doctor,
for the love of God!' And me talking away like mad. Well, that,
and nothing else, has made me the liar I am.

"Suppose your heart were five feet across in my place, would you
break it for a heart no bigger than a mouse's mute? Would you
hurl yourself into any body of water, in the size you now are, for
any woman that you had to look for with a magnifying glass, or
any boy if he was as high as the Eiffel Tower or did droppings like
a fly? No, we all love in sizes, yet we all cry out in tiny voices to
the great booming God, the older we get. Growing old is just a
matter of throwing life away back; so you finally forgive even those
that you have not begun to forget. It is that indifference which
gives you your courage, which to tell the truth is no courage at all.
There is no truth, and you have set it between you; you have been
unwise enough to make a formula; you have dressed the unknow-
able in the garments of the known."

"Man," she said, her eyelids quivering, "conditioning himself to
fear, made God; as the prehistoric, conditioning itself to hope,
made man—the cooling of the earth, the receding of the sea. And
I, who want power, chose a girl who resembles a boy."

"Exactly," said the doctor. "You never loved anyone before, and

you'll never love anyone again, as you love Robin. Very well—
what is this love we have for the invert, boy or girl? It was they who
were spoken of in every romance that we ever read. The girl lost,
what is she but the Prince found? The Prince on the white horse
that we have always been seeking. And the pretty lad who is a girl,
what but the prince-princess in point lace—neither one and half
the other, the painting on the fan! We love them for that reason.
We were impaled in our childhood upon them as they rode through
our primers, the sweetest lie of all, now come to be in boy or girl,
for in the girl it is the prince, and in the boy it is the girl that
makes a prince a prince—and not a man. They go far back in our
lost distance where what we never had stands waiting; it was in-
evitable that we should come upon them, for our miscalculated
longing has created them. They are our answer to what our grand-
mothers were told love was, and what it never came to be; they,
the living lie of our centuries. When a long lie comes up, some-
times it is a beauty; when it drops into dissolution, into drugs and
drink, into disease and death, it has at once a singular and terrible
attraction. A man can resent and avoid evil on his own plane, but
when it is the thin blown edge of his reverie, he takes it to his
heart, as one takes to one's heart the dark misery of the close night-
mare, born and slain of the particular mind; so that if one of them
were dying of the pox, one would will to die of it too, with two
feelings, terror and joy, wedded somewhere back again into a form-
less sea where a swan (would it be ourselves, or her or him, or a
mystery of all) sinks crying."

"Love is death, come upon with passion; I know, that is why
love is wisdom. I love her as one condemned to it."

"O Widow Lazarus! Arisen from your dead! O lunatic humour
of the moon! Behold this fearful tree on which sits singing the
drearful bird—*Turdas musicus*, or European singing thrush; sitting
and singing the refrain—all in the tear-wet night—and it starts out
largo, but it ends like *I Hear You Calling Me*, or *Kiss Me Again*,
gone wild. And Diane, where is she? Diane of Ephesus in the Greek
Gardens, singing and shaken in every bosom; and Rack and Ruin,

the dogs of the Vatican, running up and down the papal esplanade and out into the Ramblar with roses in their tails to keep off care. Don't I know it all! Do you think that I, the Old Woman who lives in the closet, do not know that every child, no matter what its day, is born prehistorically and that even the wrong thought has caused the human mind incredible effort? Bend down the tree of knowledge and you'll unroost a strange bird. Suffering may be composed wickedly and of an inferior writhing. Rage and inaccuracy howl and blow the bone, for, contrary to all opinion, all suffering does *not* purify—begging everybody's pardon, which is called everybody's know. It moils and blathers some to perjury; the peritoneum boils and brings on common and cheap praying a great way sunk in pointless agony."

"Jenny," she said.

"It rots her sleep—Jenny is one of those who nip like a bird and void like an ox—the poor and lightly damned! That can be a torture also. None of us suffers as much as we should, or loves as much as we say. Love is the first lie; wisdom the last. Don't I know that the only way to know evil is through truth? The evil and the good know themselves only by giving up their secret face to face. The true good who meets the true evil (Holy Mother of Mercy! are there any such?) learns for the first time how to accept neither; the face of the one tells the face of the other the half of the story that both forgot.

"To be utterly innocent," he went on, "would be to be utterly unknown, particularly to oneself!"

"Sometimes Robin seemed to return to me," Nora said, unheeding, "for sleep and safety, but," she added bitterly, "she always went out again."

The doctor lit a cigarette; lifting his chin he blew the smoke high. "To treat her lovers to the great passionate indifference. Say!" he exclaimed, bringing his chin down. "Dawn, of course, dawn! That's when she came back frightened. At that hour the citizen of the night balances on a thread that is running thin."

"Only the impossible lasts forever; with time, it is made accessible. Robin's love and mine was always impossible, and loving each other, we no longer love. Yet we love each other like death."

"Um," murmured the doctor, "beat life like a dinner bell, yet there is one hour that won't ring—the hour of disentanglement. Oh, well," he sighed, "every man dies finally of that poison known as the-heart-in-the-mouth. Yours is in your hand. Put it back. The eater of it will get a taste for you; in the end his muzzle will be heard barking among your ribs. I'm no exception, God knows; I'm the last of my line, the fine hairline of least resistance. It's a gruesome thing that man learns only by what he has between the one leg and the other! Oh, that short dangle! We corrupt mortality by its industry. You never know which one of your ends it is that is going to be the part you can't take your mind off."

"If only you could take my mind off, Matthew—now, in this house that I took that Robin's mind and mine might go together. Surprising, isn't it, I'm happier when I'm alone now, without her, because when she was here with me, in this house, I had to watch her wanting to go and yet to stay. How much of our life do we put into a life that we may be damned? Then she was back stumbling through the house again, listening for a footstep in the court, for a way to leave and not to go, trying to absorb, with the intensity of her ear, any sound that would have made me suspicious, yet hoping I would break my heart in safety; she needed that assurance. Matthew, was it a sin that I believed her?"

"Of course, it made her life wrong."

"But when I didn't believe her any more, after the night I came to see you; that I have to think of all the time; I don't dare to stop, for fear of the moment it will come back again."

"Remorse," said the doctor, "sitting heavy, like the arse of a bull—you had the conceit of 'honesty' to keep that arse from cracking your heart; but what did she have? Only your faith in her— then you took that faith away! You should have kept it always, seeing that it was a myth; no myth is safely broken. Ah, the weakness of the strong! The trouble with you is you are not just a myth-maker, you are also a destroyer, you made a beautiful fable, then put Voltaire to bed with it; ah, the *Dead March* in 'Saul'!"

Nora said, as if she had not been interrupted, "Because after that night, I went to see Jenny. I remember the stairs. They were of brown wood, and the hall was ugly and dark, and her apartment depressing. No one would have known that she had money. The walls had mustard-coloured paper on them as far as the salon, and something hideous in red and green and black in the hall, and away at the end, a bedroom facing the hall-door, with a double-bed. Sitting up against the pillow was a doll. Robin had given me a doll. I knew then, before I asked, that this was the right house, before I said, 'You are Robin's mistress, aren't you?' That poor shuddering creature had pelvic bones I could see flying through her dress. I wanted to lean forward and laugh with terror. She was sitting there doubled up with surprise, her raven's bill coming up saying, 'Yes.' Then I looked up and there on the wall was the photograph of Robin when she was a baby (the one that she had told me was lost).

"She went to pieces; she fell forward on my lap. At her next words I saw that I was not a danger to her, but someone who might understand her torture. In great agitation she said, 'I went out this afternoon, I didn't think she could call me because you had been away to the country, Robin said, and would be back this evening and so she would have to stay home with you because you had been so good to her always; though God knows I understand there is nothing between you any longer, that you are "just good friends"; she has explained that—still, I nearly went mad when I found that she had been here and I was out. She has told me often enough, "Don't leave the house because I don't know exactly when I am going to be able to get away, because I can't hurt Nora." ' " Nora's voice broke. She went on.

"Then Jenny said, 'What are you going to do? What do you want me to do?' I knew all the time that she could do nothing but what she wanted to do, and that whatever it was, she was a liar, no matter what truth she was telling. I was dead. I felt stronger then, and I said, yes, I would have a drink. She poured out two, knocking the bottle against the glass and spilling the liquor on the dark ugly carpet. I kept thinking, what else is it that is hurting me; then I knew—the doll; the doll in there on the bed." Nora sat down, facing the doctor. "We give death to a child when we give it a doll—it's the effigy and the shroud; when a woman gives it to a woman, it is the life they cannot have, it is their child, sacred and profane; so when I saw that other doll—" Nora could not go on. She began to cry. "What part of monstrosity am I that I am always crying at its side!

"When I got home Robin had been waiting, knowing, because I was late, that something was wrong. I said, 'It is over—I can't go on. You have always lied to me, and you have denied me to her. I can't stand it any more.'

"She stood up then and went into the hall. She jerked her coat off the hook and I said, 'Have you nothing to say to me?' She turned her face to me. It was like something once beautiful found in a river—and flung herself out of the door."

"And you were crying," the doctor said, nodding. "You went about the house like someone sunken under lightness. You were ruined and you kept striking your hands together, laughing crazily and singing a little and putting your hands over your face. Stage-tricks have been taken from life, so finding yourself employing them you were confused with a sense of shame. When you went out looking for someone to go mad with, they said, 'For God's sake, look at Nora!' For the demolishing of a great ruin is always a fine and terrifying spectacle. Why is it that you want to talk to me? Because I'm the other woman that God forgot."

"There's nothing to go by, Matthew," she said. "You do not know which way to go. A man is another person—a woman is yourself, caught as you turn in panic; on her mouth you kiss your own. If she is taken you cry that you have been robbed of yourself. God laughs at me, but his laughter is my love."

"You have died and arisen for love," said Matthew. "But unlike the ass returning from the market you are always carrying the same

load. Oh, for God's sweet sake, didn't she ever disgust you! Weren't
you sometimes pleased that you had the night to yourself, wishing,
when she did come home, that it was never?"

"Never, and always; I was frightened she would be gentle again.
That," she said, "that's an awful fear. Fear of the moment when
she would turn her words, making them something between us
that nobody else could possibly share—and she would say, 'You
have got to stay with me or I can't live.' Yet one night she ran
behind me in the Montparnasse quarter, where I had gone look-
ing for her because someone had called me saying she was sick
and couldn't get home (I had stopped going out with her because
I couldn't bear to see the 'evidence of my eyes'); running behind
me for blocks saying, with a furious panting breath, 'You are a
devil! You make everything dirty!' (I had tried to take someone's
hands off her. They always put hands on her when she was drunk.)
'You make me feel dirty and tired and old!'

"I turned against the wall. The policemen and the people in the
street collected. I was cold and terribly ashamed. I said, 'Do you
mean that?' And she said she meant it. She put her head down
on one of the officers' shoulders. She was drunk. He had
her by the wrist, one hand on her behind. She did not say any-
thing about that because she did not notice and kept spitting
horrible things at me. Then I walked away very fast. My head
seemed to be in a large place. She began running after me. I kept
on walking. I was cold, and I was not miserable any more. She
caught me by the shoulder and went against me, grinning. She
stumbled and I held her, and she said, seeing a poor wretched
beggar of a whore, 'Give her some money, all of it!' She threw the
francs into the street and bent down over the filthy baggage and
began stroking her hair, gray with the dust of years, saying, 'They
are all God-forsaken, and you most of all, because they don't want
you to have your happiness. They don't want you to drink. Well,
here, drink! I give you money and permission! These women—
they are all like her,' she said with fury. 'They are all good—they
want to save us!' She sat down beside her.

"It took me and the *garçon* half an hour to get her up and into the lobby, and when I got her that far she began fighting, so that suddenly, without thinking, but out of weariness and misery, I struck her; and at that she started, and smiled, and went up the stairs with me without complaint. She sat up in bed and ate eggs and called me, 'Angel! Angel!' and ate my eggs too, turned over and went to sleep. Then I kissed her, holding her hands and feet, and I said: 'Die now, so you will be quiet, so you will not be touched again by dirty hands, so you will not take my heart and your body and let them be nosed by dogs—die now, then you will be mine forever.' (What right has anyone to that?)." She stopped. "She was mine only when she was drunk, Matthew, and had passed out. That's the terrible thing, that finally she was mine only when she was dead drunk. All the time I didn't believe her life was as it was, and yet the fact that I didn't proves something is wrong with me. I saw her always like a tall child who had grown up the length of the infant's gown, walking and needing help and safety; because she was in her own nightmare. I tried to come between and save her, but I was like a shadow in her dream that could never reach her in time, as the cry of the sleeper has no echo, myself echo struggling to answer; she was like a new shadow walking perilously close to the outer curtain, and I was going mad because I was awake and, seeing it, unable to reach it, unable to strike people down from it; and it moving, almost unwalking, with the face saintly and idiotic.

"And then that day I'll remember all my life, when I said: 'It is over now'; she was asleep and I struck her awake. I saw her come awake and turn befouled before me, she who had managed in that sleep to keep whole. Matthew, for God's sake, say something, you are awful enough to say it, say something! I didn't know, I didn't know that it was to be me who was to do the terrible thing! No rot had touched her until then, and there before my eyes I saw her corrupt all at once and withering because I had struck her sleep away, and I went mad and I've been mad ever since; and there's nothing to do; nothing! You must say something, oh, God, say something!"

"Stop it! Stop it!" he cried. "Stop screaming! Put your hands down! Stop it! You were a 'good woman,' and so a bitch on a high plane, the only one able to kill yourself and Robin! Robin was outside the 'human type'—a wild thing caught in a woman's skin, monstrously alone, monstrously vain; like the paralysed man in Coney Island (take away a man's conformity and you take away his remedy) who had to lie on his back in a box, but the box was lined with velvet, his fingers jewelled with stones, and suspended over him where he could never take his eyes off, a sky-blue mounted mirror, for he wanted to enjoy his own 'difference.' Robin is not in your life, you are in her dream, you'll never get out of it. And why does Robin feel innocent? Every bed she leaves, without caring, fills her heart with peace and happiness. She has made her 'escape' again. That's why she can't 'put herself in another's place,' she herself is the only 'position'; so she resents it when you reproach her with what she had done. She knows she is innocent because she can't do anything in relation to anyone but herself. You almost caught hold of her, but she put you cleverly away by making you the Madonna. What was your patience and terror worth all these years if you couldn't keep them for her sake? Did you have to learn wisdom on her knees?

"Oh, for God's sweet sake, couldn't you stand not learning your lesson? Because the lesson we learn is always by giving death and a sword to our lover. You are full to the brim with pride, but I am an empty pot going forward, saying my prayers in a dark place; because I know no one loves, I, least of all, and that no one loves me, that's what makes most people so passionate and bright, because they want to love and be loved, when there is only a bit of lying in the ear to make the ear forget what time is compiling. So I, Doctor O'Connor, say, creep by, softly, softly, and don't learn anything because it's always learned of another person's body; take action in your heart and be careful whom you love—for a lover who dies, no matter how forgotten, will take somewhat of you to the grave. Be humble like the dust, as God intended, and crawl, and finally you'll crawl to the end of the gutter and not be missed and not much remembered."

"Sometimes," Nora said, "she would sit at home all day, looking out of the window, playing with her toys, trains, and animals and cars to wind up, and dolls and marbles and soldiers. But all the time she was watching me to see that no one called, that the bell did not ring, that I got no mail, nor anyone hallooing in the court, though she knew that none of these things could happen. My life was hers.

"Sometimes, if she got tight by evening, I would find her standing in the middle of the room in boy's clothes, rocking from foot to foot, holding the doll she had given us—'our child'—high above her head, as if she would cast it down, a look of fury on her face. And one time, about three in the morning when she came in, she was angry because for once I had not been there all the time, waiting. She picked up the doll and hurled it to the floor and put her foot on it, crushing her heel into it; and then, as I came crying behind her, she kicked it, its china head all in dust, its skirt shivering and stiff, whirling over and over across the floor."

The doctor brought his palms together. "If you, who are blood-thirsty with love, had left her alone, what? Would a lost girl in Dante's time have been a lost girl still, and he had turned his eyes on her? She would have been remembered, and the remembered put on the dress of immunity. Do you think that Robin had no right to fight you with her only weapon? She saw in you that fearful eye that would make her a target forever. Have not girls done as much for the doll? The doll—yes, target of things past and to come. The last doll, given to age, is the girl who should have been a boy, and the boy who should have been a girl! The love of that last doll was foreshadowed in that love of the first. The doll and the immature have something right about them, the doll because it resembles but does not contain life, and the third sex because it contains life but resembles the doll. The blessed face! It should be seen only in profile, otherwise it is observed to be the conjunction of the identical cleaved halves of sexless misgiving! Their kingdom is without precedent. Why do you think I have spent near fifty years weeping over bars but because I am one of them! The uninhabited angel! That is what you have always been hunting!"

"Perhaps, Matthew, there are devils? Who knows if there are devils? Perhaps they have set foot in the uninhabited. Was I her devil trying to bring her comfort? I enter my dead and bring no comfort, not even in my dreams. There in my sleep was my grandmother, whom I loved more than anyone, tangled in the grave grass, and flowers blowing about and between her; lying there in the grave, in the forest, in a coffin of glass, and flying low, my father who is still living, low going and into the grave beside her, his head thrown back and his curls lying out, struggling with her death terribly, and me, stepping about its edges, walking and wailing without a sound; round and round, seeing them struggling with that death as if they were struggling with the sea and my life; I was weeping and unable to do anything or take myself out of it. There they were in the grave glass, and the grave water and the grave flowers and the grave time, one living and one dead and one asleep. It went on forever, though it had stopped, my father stopped beating and just lay there floating beside her, immovable, yet drifting in a tight place. And I woke up and still it was going on; it went down into the dark earth of my waking as if I were burying them with the earth of my lost sleep. This I have done to my father's mother, dreaming through my father, and have tormented them with my tears and with my dreams: for all of us die over again in somebody's sleep. And this, I have done to Robin: it is only through me that she will die over and over, and it is only through me, of all my family, that my grandfather dies, over and over. I woke and got up out of bed and putting my hands between my knees I said, 'What was that dream saying, for God's sake, what was that dream?' For it was for me also."

Suddenly Dr. Matthew O'Connor said: "It's my mother without argument I want!" And then in his loudest voice he roared:

"Mother of God! I wanted to be your son—the unknown beloved second would have done!"

"Oh, Matthew. I don't know how to go. I don't know which way to turn! Tell her, if you ever see her, that it is always with her in my arms—forever it will be that way until we die. Tell her to do what she must, but not to forget."

"Tell her yourself," said the doctor, "or sit in your own trouble silently if you like; it's the same with ermines—those fine yellow ermines that women pay such a great price for— how did they get that valuable colour? By sitting in bed all their lives and pissing the sheets, or weeping in their own way. It's the same with persons; they are only of value when they have laid themselves open to 'nuisance'—their own and the world's. Ritual itself constitutes an instruction. So we come back to the place from which I set out; pray to the good God; she will keep you. Person- ally I call her 'she' because of the way she made me; it somehow balances the mistake." He got up and crossed to the window. "That priceless galaxy of misinformation called the mind, har- nessed to that stupendous and threadbare glomerate compulsion called the soul, ambling down the almost obliterated bridle path of Well and Ill, fortuitously planned—is the holy Habeas Corpus, the manner in which the body is brought before the judge—still— in the end Robin will wish you in a nunnery where what she loved is, by surroundings, made safe, because as you are you keep 'bring- ing her up,' as cannons bring up the dead from deep water."

"In the end," Nora said, "they came to me, the girls Robin had driven frantic—to me, for comfort!" She began to laugh. "My God," she said, "the women I've held upon my knees!"

"Women,' the doctor said, "were born on the knees; that's why I've never been able to do anything about them; I'm on my own so much of the time."

"Suddenly, I knew what all my life had been, Matthew, what I hoped Robin was—the secure torment. We can hope for nothing greater, except hope. If I asked her, crying, not to go out, she would go just the same, richer in her heart because I had touched it, as she was going down the stairs."

"Lions grow their manes and foxes their teeth on that bread," interpolated the doctor.

"In the beginning, when I tried to stop her from drinking and staying out all night, and from being defiled, she would say, 'Ah, I feel so pure and gay!' as if the ceasing of that abuse was her only happiness and peace of mind; and so I struggled with her as with the coils of my own most obvious heart, holding her by the hair, striking her against my knees, as some people in trouble strike their hands too softly; and as if it were a game, she raised and dropped her head against my lap, as a child bounces in a crib to enter excitement, even if it were someone gutted on a dagger. I thought I loved her for her sake, and I found it was for my own."

"I know," said the doctor; "there you were sitting up high and fine, with a rose-bush up your arse."

She looked at him, then she smiled. "How should you know?"

"I'm a lady in no need of insults," said the doctor. "I know."

"Yes," she said. "You know what none of us know until we have died. You were dead in the beginning."

The twilight was falling. About the street lamps there was a heavy mist. "Why don't you rest now?" asked the doctor. "Your body is coming to it, you are forty and the body has a politic too, and a life of its own that you like to think is yours. I heard a spirit new once, but I knew it was a mystery eternally moving outward and on, and not my own."

"I know," she said, "*now*." Suddenly, she began to cry, holding her hands. "Matthew," she said, "have you ever loved someone and it became yourself?"

For a moment he did not answer. Taking up the decanter, he held it to the light.

"Robin can go anywhere, do anything," Nora continued, "because she forgets, and I nowhere because I remember." She came toward him. "Matthew," she said, "you think I have always been like this. Once I was remorseless, but this is another love—it goes everywhere; there is no place for it to stop—it rots me away. How could she tell me when she had nothing to tell that wasn't evidence against herself?"

The doctor said, "You know as well as I do that we were born twelve, and brought up thirteen, and that some of us lived. My brother, whom I had not seen in four years, and loved the most of all, died, and who was it but me my mother wanted to talk to? Not those who had seen him last, but me who had seen him best, as if my memory of him were himself; and because you forget Robin the best, it's to you she turns. She comes trembling, and defiant, and belligerent, all right—that you may give her back to herself again as you have forgotten her—you are the only one strong enough to have listened to the prosecution, your life; and to have built back the amazing defence, your heart!

"The scalpel and the Scriptures have taught me that little I did not already know. And I was doing well enough," he snapped, "until you kicked my stone over, and out I came, all moss and eyes; and here I sit, as naked as only those things can be, whose houses have been torn away from them to make a holiday, and it my only skin—labouring to comfort you. Am I supposed to render up my paradise—that splendid acclimation—for the comfort of weeping women and howling boys? Look at Felix now; what kind of a Jew is that? Screaming up against tradition like a bat against a window-pane, high-up over the town, his child a boy weeping 'o'er graves of hope and pleasure gone.'

"As, yes— I love my neighbour. Like a rotten apple to a rotten apple's breast affixed we go down together, nor is there a hesitation in that decay, for when I sense such, there I apply the breast the firmer, that he may rot as quickly as I, in which he stands in dire need or I miscalculate the cry. I, who am done sooner than any fruit! The heat of his suppuration has mingled his core with mine, and wrought my own to the zenith before its time. The encumbrance of myself I threw away long ago, that breast to breast I might go with my failing friends. And do they love me for it? They do not. So have I divorced myself, not only because I was born as ugly as God dared premeditate, but because with propinquity and knowledge of trouble I have damaged my own value. And death—have you thought of death? What risk do you take? Do you know which dies first, you or she? And which is the sorrier part, head or feet? I say, with that good Sir Don, the feet. Any man can look upon the head in death, but no man can look upon the feet. They are most awfully tipped up from the earth. I've thought of that also. Do you think, for Christ's sweet sake," he shouted suddenly, "that I am so happy that you should cry down my neck? Do you think there is no lament in this world, but your own? Is there not a forbearing saint somewhere? Is there no bread that does not come proffered with bitter butter? I, as good a Catholic as they make, have embraced every confection of hope, and yet I know well, for all our outcry and struggle, we shall be for the next generation not the massive dung fallen from the dinosaur, but the little speck left of a humming-bird; so as well sing our *Chi vuol la Zingarella* (how women love it!) while I warble my *Sonate au Crépuscle*, throwing in *der Erlkönig* for good measure, not to mention *Who Is Sylvia?* Who is anybody?

"Oh," he cried. "A broken heart have you! I have falling arches, flying dandruff, a floating kidney, shattered nerves *and* a broken heart! But do I scream that an eagle has me by the balls or has dropped his oyster on my head? Am I going forward screaming that it hurts, that my mind goes back, or holding my guts as if they were a coil of knives? Yet you are screaming and drawing your lip and putting your hand out and turning round and round! Do I wail to the mountains of the trouble I have had in the valley, or to every stone of the way it broke my bones, or of every lie, how it went down into my belly and built a nest to hatch me to my death there? Isn't everyone in the world peculiarly swung and me the craziest of the lot?—so that I come dragging and squealing, like a heifer on the way to slaughter, knowing his cries have only half a rod to go, protesting his death—as his death has only a rod to go to protest his screaming? Do you walk high Heaven without shoes? Are you the only person with a bare foot pressed down on a rake? Oh, you poor blind cow! Keep out of my feathers; you ruffle me the wrong way and flit about, stirring my misery! What end is sweet? Are the ends of the hair sweet when you come to number them?"

"Listen," Nora said. "You've got to listen! She would come back to me after a night all over the city and lie down beside me and she would say, 'I want to make everyone happy,' and her mouth was drawn down. 'I want everyone to be gay, gay. Only you,' she said, holding me, 'only you, you mustn't be gay or happy, not like that, it's not for you, only for everyone else in the world.' She knew she was driving me insane with misery and fright; only," she went on, "she couldn't do anything because she was a long way off and waiting to begin. It's for that reason she hates everyone near her. It's why she falls into everything, like someone in a dream. It's why she wants to be loved and left alone, all at the same time. She would kill the world to get at herself if the world were in the way, and it *is* in the way. A shadow was falling on her —mine—and it was driving her out of her wits."

She began to walk again. "I have been loved," she said, "by something strange, and it has forgotten me." Her eyes were fixed and she seemed to be talking to herself. "It was *me* made her hair stand on end because I loved her. She turned bitter because I made her fate colossal. She wanted darkness in her mind—to throw a shadow over what she was powerless to alter—her dissolute life, her life at night; and I, I dashed it down. We will never have it out now," Nora said. "It's too late. There is no last reckoning for those who have loved too long, so for me there is no end. Only I can't, I can't wait for ever!" she said frantically. "I can't live without my heart!

"In the beginning, after Robin went away with Jenny to America, I searched for her in the ports. Not literally; in another way. Suffering is the decay of the heart; all that we have loved becomes the 'forbidden' when we have not understood it all, as the pauper is the rudiment of a city, knowing something of the city, which the city, for its own destiny, wants to forget. So the lover must go against nature to find love. I sought Robin in Marseilles, in Tangier, in Naples, to understand her, to do away with my terror. I said to myself, I will do what she has done, I will love what she has loved, then I will find her again. At first it seemed that all I should have to do would be to become 'debauched,' to find the girls that she had loved; but I found that they were only little girls that she had forgotten. I haunted the cafés where Robin had lived her night-life; I drank with the men, I danced with the women, but all I knew was that others had slept with my lover and my child. For Robin is incest too; that is one of her powers. In her, past-time records, and past time is relative to us all. Yet not being the family she is more present than the family. A relative is in the foreground only when it is born, when it suffers and when it dies, unless it becomes one's lover, then it must be everything, as Robin was; yet not as much as she, for she was like a relative found in another generation. I thought, 'I will do something that she will never be able to forgive, then we can begin again as strangers.' But the sailor got no further than the hall. He said: '*Mon Dieu, il y a deux chevaux de bois dans la chambre à coucher.*' "

"Christ!" muttered the doctor.

"So," Nora continued, "I left Paris. I went through the streets of Marseilles, the waterfront of Tangier, the *basso porto* of Naples. In the narrow streets of Naples, ivies and flowers were growing over the broken-down walls. Under enormous staircases, rising open to the streets, beggars lay sleeping beside images of St. Gennaro; girls going into the churches to pray were calling out to boys in the squares. In open doorways night-lights were burning all day before gaudy prints of the Virgin. In one room that lay open to the alley, before a bed covered with a cheap heavy satin comforter, in the semi-darkness, a young girl sat on a chair, leaning over its back, one arm across it, the other hanging at her side, as if half of her slept, and half of her suffered. When she saw me she laughed, as children do, in embarrassment. Looking from her to the Madonna behind the candles, I knew that the image, to her, was what I had been to Robin, not a saint at all, but a fixed dismay, the space between the human and the holy head, the arena of the 'indecent' eternal. At that moment I stood in the centre of eroticism and death, death that makes the dead smaller, as a lover we are beginning to forget dwindles and wastes; for love and life are a bulk of which the body and heart can be drained, and I knew in that bed Robin should have put me down. In that bed we would have forgotten our lives in the extremity of memory, moulted our parts, as figures in the waxworks are moulted down to their story, so we would have broken down to our love."

The doctor staggered as he reached for his hat and coat. He stood in confused and unhappy silence—he moved toward the door. Holding the knob in his hand he turned toward her. Then he went out.

The doctor, walking with his coat-collar up, entered the *Café de la Mairie du VI*ᵉ. He stood at the bar and ordered a drink; looking at the people in the close, smoke-blue room, he said to himself, "Listen!" Nora troubled him, the life of Nora and the lives of the people in his life. "The way of a man in a fog!" he said. He hung his umbrella on the bar ledge. "To think is to be sick," he said to the barman. The barman nodded.

The people in the café waited for what the doctor would say, knowing that he was drunk and that he would talk; in great defaming sentences his betrayals came up; no one ever knew what was truth and what was not. "If you really want to know how hard a prizefighter hits," he said, looking around, "you have got to walk into the circle of his fury and be carried out by the heels, not by the count."

Someone laughed. The doctor turned slowly. "So safe as all that?" he asked sarcastically; "so damned safe? Well, wait until you get in gaol and find yourself slapping the bottoms of your feet for misery."

He put his hand out for his drink—muttering to himself: "Matthew, you have never been in time with any man's life and you'll never be remembered at all, God save the vacancy! The finest instrument goes wrong in time—that's all, the instrument gets broken, and I must remember that when everyone is strange; it's the instrument gone flat. Lapidary, engrave that on my stone when Matthew is all over and lost in a field." He looked around. "It's the instrument, gentlemen, that has lost its G string; otherwise he'd be playing a fine tune; otherwise he'd still be passing his wind with the wind of the north—otherwise touching his billycock!

"Only the scorned and the ridiculous make good stories," he added angrily, seeing the *habitués* smiling, "so you can imagine when you'll get told! Life is only long enough for one trade; try that one!"

An unfrocked priest, a stout pale man with woman's hands, on which were many rings, a friend of the doctor's, called him and asked him to have a drink. The doctor came, carefully bringing his umbrella and hat. The priest said: "I've always wanted to know whether you were ever *really* married or not."

"Should I know that?" inquired the doctor. "I've *said* I was married and I gave the girl a name and had children by her, then, presto! I killed her off as lightly as the death of swans. And was I reproached for that story! I was. Because even your friends regret weeping for a myth, as if that were not practically the fate of all the tears in the world! What if the girl *was* the wife of my brother and the children my brother's children? When I laid her down her limbs were as handsome and still as two May boughs from the cutting—did he do as much for her? I imagined about her in my heart as pure as a French print, a girl all of a little bosom and a bird cage, lying back down comfortable with the sea for a background and a rope of roses to hold her. Has any man's wife been treated better than that? Who says she might not have been mine, and the children also? Who for that matter," he said with violence, "says they are not mine? Is not a brother his brother also, the one blood cut up in lengths, one called Michael and the other Matthew? Except that people get befuddled seeing them walk in different directions. Who's to say that I'm not my brother's wife's husband and that his children were not fathered in my lap? Is it not to his honour that he strikes me as myself? And when she died, did my weeping make his weeping less?"

The ex-priest said, "Well, there's something in that, still I like to know what is what."

"You do, do you?" said the doctor. "Well then, that's why you are where you are now, right down in the mud without a feather to fly with, like the ducks in Golden Gate park—the largest park in captivity—everybody with their damnable kindness having fed them all the year round to their ruin because when it comes time for their going south they are all a bitter consternation, being too fat and heavy to rise off the water, and, my God, how they flop and struggle all over the park in autumn, crying and tearing their hair out because their nature is weighted down with bread and their migration stopped by crumbs. You wring your hands to see it, and that's another illustration of love; in the end you are too heavy to move with the greediness in your stomach. And," said the doctor, "it would be the same with me if I'd let it, what with the wind at the one end and the cyclone at the other. Yet there are some that I have neglected for my spirit's sake—the old yeomen of the Guard and the beefeaters of the Tower because of their cold kidneys and gray hairs, and the kind of boy who only knows two existences—himself in a mirror—back and front." He was very drunk now. He looked about the café. He caught someone nudging someone. He looked up at the ex-priest and cursed. "What people! All queer in a terrible way. There were a couple of queer *good* people once in this world—but none of you," he said, addressing the room, "will ever know them. You think you are all studded with diamonds, don't you? Well, part the diamonds and you'll find slug's meat. My God," he said, turning around, "when I think!" He began to pound the table with his glass. "May they all be damned! The people in my life who have made my life miserable, coming to me to learn of degradation and the night. Nora, beating her head against her heart, sprung over, her mind closing her life up like a heel on a fan, rotten to the bone for love of Robin. My God, how that woman can hold on to an idea! And that old sandpiper, Jenny! Oh, it's a grand bad story, and who says I'm a betrayer? I say, tell the story of the world to the world!"

"A sad and a corrupt age," the ex-priest said.

Matthew O'Connor called for another drink. "What do they all come to me for? Why do they all tell me everything, then expect it to lie hushed in me, like a rabbit gone home to die? And that Baron Felix, hardly muttered a word in his life, and yet his silence breeds like scum on a pond; and that boy of his, Guido, by Robin, trying to see across the Danube with the tears in his eyes, Felix holding on to his hand and the boy holding on to the image of the Virgin on a darkening red ribbon, feeling its holy lift out of the metal and calling it mother; and me not even knowing which direction my end is coming from. So, when Felix said to me, 'Is the child infirm?' I said, 'Was the Mad King of Bavaria infirm?' I'm not one to cut the knot by drowning myself in any body of water, not even the print of a horse's hoof, no matter how it has been raining."

People had begun to whisper and the waiters moved closer, watching. The ex-priest was smiling to himself, but O'Connor did not seem to see or hear anything but his own heart. "Some people," he said, "take off headfirst into *any* body of water and six glasses later someone in Haarlem gets typhoid from drinking their misery. God, take my hand and get me up out of this great argument—the more you go against your nature, the more you will know of it—hear me, Heaven! I've done and been everything that I didn't want to be or do—Lord, put the light out—so I stand here, beaten up and mauled and weeping, knowing I am not what I thought I was, a good man doing wrong, but the wrong man doing nothing much, and I wouldn't be telling you about it if I weren't talking to myself. I talk too much because I have been made so miserable by what you are keeping hushed. I'm an old worn out lioness, a coward in my corner; for the sake of my bravery I've never been one thing that I am, to find out what I am! Here lies the body of Heaven. The mocking bird howls through the pillars of Paradise, O Lord! Death in Heaven lies couched on a mackerel sky, on her breast a helmet and at her feet a foal with a silent marble mane. Nocturnal sleep is heavy on her eyes."

"Funny little man," someone said. "Never stops talking—always getting everyone into trouble by excusing them because he can't excuse himself—the Squatting Beast, coming out at night—" As he broke off, the voice of the doctor was heard: "And what am I? I'm damned, and carefully public!"

He fumbled for a cigarette, found it and lit it.

"Once upon a time, I was standing listening to a quack hanky-panky of a medicine man saying: 'Now, ladies and gentlemen, before I behead the small boy, I will endeavour to entertain you with a few parlour tricks.' He had a turban cocked over his eye and a moaning in his left ventricle which was meant to be the whine of Tophet, and a loin-cloth as big as a tent and protecting about as much. Well, he began doing his tricks. He made a tree grow out of his left shoulder and dashed two rabbits out of his cuffs and balanced three eggs on his nose. A priest, standing in the crowd, began to laugh, and a priest laughing always makes me wring my hands with doubt. The other time was when Catherine the Great sent for me to bleed her. She took to the leech with rowdy Saxon abandon, saying: 'Let him drink; I've always wanted to be in two places at once!'"

"For Heaven's sake," the ex-priest said. "Remember your century at least!"

For a moment the doctor looked angry. "See here," he said, "don't interrupt me. The reason I'm so remarkable is that I remember everyone even when they are not about. It's the boys that look as innocent as the bottom of a plate that get you into trouble, not a man with a prehistoric memory."

"Women can cause trouble too," the ex-priest said lamely.

"That's another story," the doctor said. "What else has Jenny ever done, and what else has Robin ever done? And Nora, what's she done but cause it, by taking it in at night like a bird-coop? And I myself wish I'd never had a button up my middle—for what I've done and what I've not done all goes back to that—to be recognized, a gem should lie in a wide open field; but I'm all aglitter in the underbrush! If you don't want to suffer you should tear yourself apart. Were not the several parts of Caroline of Hapsburg put in three utterly obvious piles?—her heart in the Augustiner church, her intestines in St. Stefan's and what was left of the body in the vault of the Capucines? Saved by separation. But I'm all in one piece! Oh, the new moon!" he said. "When will she come riding?"

"Drunk and telling the world," someone said. The doctor heard, but he was too far gone to care, too muddled in his mind to argue, and already weeping.

"Come," the ex-priest said, "I'll take you home."

The doctor waved his arm. "Revenge is for those who have loved a little, for anything more than that justice is hardly enough. Some day I'm going to Lourdes and scramble into the front row and talk about all of you." His eyes were almost closed. He opened them and looked about him and a fury came over him. "Christ Almighty!" he said. "Why don't they let me alone, all of them?"

The ex-priest repeated, "Come, I'll take you home."

The doctor tried to rise. He was exceedingly drunk and now extremely angry all at once. His umbrella fell to the floor with the crash of a glass as he swung his arm upward against the helping hand. "Get out! Get out!" he said. "What a damnable year, what a bloody time! How did it happen, where did it come from?"

He began to scream with sobbing laughter. "Talking to me—all of them—sitting on me as heavy as a truck horse—talking! Love falling buttered side down, fate falling arse up! Why doesn't anyone know when everything is over, except me? That fool Nora, holding on by her teeth, going back to find Robin! And Felix— eternity is only just long enough for a Jew! But there's someone else—who was it, damn it all—who was it? I've known everyone," he said, "everyone!" He came down upon the table with all his weight, his arms spread, his head between them, his eyes wide open and crying, staring along the table where the ash blew and fluttered with his gasping breath. "For Christ's sweet sake!" he said, and his voice was a whisper. "Now that you have all heard what you wanted to hear, can't you let me loose now, let me go? I've not only lived my life for nothing, but I've told it for nothing —abominable among the filthy people—I know, it's all over, everything's over, and nobody knows it but me—drunk as a fiddler's bitch—lasted too long—" He tried to get to his feet, gave it up. "Now," he said, "the end—mark my words—now *nothing, but wrath and weeping!*"

The Possessed

When Robin, accompanied by Jenny Petherbridge, arrived in New York, she seemed distracted. She would not listen to Jenny's suggestion that they should make their home in the country. She said a hotel was "good enough." Jenny could do nothing with her; it was as if the motive power which had directed Robin's life, her day as well as her night, had been crippled. For the first week or two she would not go out, then, thinking herself alone, she began to haunt the terminals, taking trains into different parts of the country, wandering without design, going into many out-of-the-way churches, sitting in the darkest corner or standing against the wall, one foot turned toward the toe of the other, her hands folded at their length, her head bent. As she had taken the Catholic vow long before, now she came into church as one renouncing something; her hands before her face, she knelt, her teeth against her palm, fixed in an unthinking stop as one who hears of death suddenly; death that cannot form until the shocked tongue has given its permission. Moving like a housewife come to set straight disorder in an unknown house, she came forward with a lighted taper, and setting it up, she turned, drawing on her thick white gloves, and with her slow headlong step, left the church. A moment later Jenny, who had followed her, looking about to be sure that she was unobserved, darted up to the sconce, snatched the candle from its spike, blew it out, re-lit it and set it back.

Robin walked the open country in the same manner, pulling at the flowers, speaking in a low voice to the animals. Those that came near, she grasped, straining their fur back until their eyes were narrowed and their teeth bare, her own teeth showing as if her hand were upon her own neck.

Because Robin's engagements were with something unseen, because in her speech and in her gestures there was a desperate anonymity, Jenny became hysterical. She accused Robin of a "sensuous communion with unclean spirits." And in putting her wickedness into words she struck herself down. She did not understand anything Robin felt or did, which was more unendurable than her absence. Jenny walked up and down her darkened hotel room, crying and stumbling.

Robin now headed up into Nora's part of the country. She circled closer and closer. Sometimes she slept in the woods; the silence that she had caused by her coming was broken again by insect and bird flowing back over her intrusion, which was forgotten in her fixed stillness, obliterating her as a drop of water is made anonymous by the pond into which it has fallen. Sometimes she slept on a bench in the decaying chapel (she brought some of her things here), but she never went further. One night she woke up to the barking, far off, of Nora's dog. As she had frightened the woods into silence by her breathing, the barking of the dog brought her up, rigid and still.

Half an acre away, Nora, sitting by a kerosene lamp, raised her head. The dog was running about the house; she heard him first on one side, then the other; he whined as he ran; barking and whining she heard him farther and farther away. Nora bent forward, listening; she began to shiver. After a moment she got up, unlocking the doors and windows. Then she sat down, her hands on her knees, but she couldn't wait. She went out. The night was well advanced. She could see nothing. She began walking toward the hill. She no longer heard the dog, but she kept on. A level above her she heard things rustling in the grass, the briars made her stumble, but she did not call.

At the top of the hill she could see, rising faintly against the sky, the weather-beaten white of the chapel; a light ran the length of the door. She began to run, cursing and crying, and blindly, without warning, plunged into the jamb of the chapel door.

On a contrived altar, before a Madonna, two candles were burning. Their light fell across the floor and the dusty benches. Before the image lay flowers and toys. Standing before them in her boy's trousers was Robin. Her pose, startled and broken, was caught at the point where her hand had reached almost to the shoulder, and at the moment Nora's body struck the wood, Robin began going down, down, her hair swinging, her arms out. The dog stood rearing back, his forelegs slanting, his paws trembling under the trembling of his rump, his hackle standing, his mouth open, the tongue slung sideways over his sharp bright teeth, whining and waiting. And down she went until her head swung against his, on all fours now, dragging her knees. The veins stood out in her neck, under her ears, swelled in her arms, and wide and throbbing, rose up on her hands as she moved forward.

The dog, quivering in every muscle, sprang back, his tongue a stiff curving terror in his mouth; moved backward, back, as she came on, whimpering too, coming forward, her head turned completely sideways, grinning and whimpering. Backed into the farthest corner, the dog reared as if to avoid something that troubled him to such agony that he seemed to be rising from the floor; then he stopped, clawing sideways at the wall, his forepaws lifted and sliding. Then head down, dragging her forelocks in the dust, she struck against his side. He let loose one howl of misery and bit at her, dashing about her, barking, and as he sprang on either side of her he always kept his head toward her, dashing his rump now this side, now that, of the wall.

Then she began to bark also, crawling after him—barking in a fit of laughter, obscene and touching. Crouching, the dog began to run with her, head-on with her head, as if to circumvent her; soft and slow his feet went padding. He ran this way and that, low down in his throat crying, and she grinning and crying with him; crying in shorter and shorter spaces, moving head to head, until she gave up, lying out, her hands beside her, her face turned and weeping; and the dog too gave up then, and lay down, his eyes bloodshot, his head flat along her knees.